G000141193

Nik Morton, from V ⬚ avy
appropriately as a V ⬚ old
many short storie⬚ ⬚nd
magazines.

Now 'retired' in Spain, Nik regularly contributes book reviews, articles, artwork and 'The Adventures of Super Scoop the Penguin' comic strip to the *Portsmouth & District Post*. He also writes for several English language periodicals in Spain. Writing as Ross Morton, Nik's first western was published by Robert Hale: *Death at Bethesda Falls*.

He was the joint runner-up in the *Harry Bowling Prize 2006* with the first chapters of his crime novel *Pain Wears No Mask*, which has been published by Libros International. He was a prizewinner in the 2007 3rd International Writing Competition, *Torrevieja – Another Look*.

Nik, Chairman of the Torrevieja Writers' Circle, is married to Jennifer; they have a daughter, Hannah and a son-in-law Farhad (Harry), who have also moved to Spain.

Visit his website: **www.freewebs.com/nikmorton**

Also by Nik Morton: **PAIN WEARS NO MASK**
(published by Libros International)
and, writing as Ross Morton, **DEATH AT BETHESDA FALLS**
(published by Robert Hale Ltd.)

The Prague Manuscript

(Tana Standish in Czechoslovakia – 1975)

The first in a series

Nik Morton

Libros
INTERNATIONAL

ISBN: 978-1-905988-46-4

Cover by Julia D Higginson

Published by Libros International

www.librosinternational.com

Acknowledgements

In memory of the late John Wilson, who was a mine of information - he already knew my puns were the pits.

Thanks... to Stuart Kay, the ellipsis-killer. Publish and be doomed!

My appreciation to the readers at Libros International; also Carol, Dawn and Ken: thanks for showing faith in this series.

Thanks, Barry Hill, for being an honest reader – and I hope you enjoy getting to know Tana better this time around!

To Jennifer with love. Holey jumpers, this brings back memories of love at first sight, Rene Cutforth, Ma Vlast and all. Oh, and lots of love to my editor too.

FOREWORD: Manuscript

Portsmouth, Hampshire, England

The agent who called himself Mr Swann entered the Queen's Hotel bar at 2p.m. just as he had promised. In my business I'd met a few spies and all of them were nondescript. After all, to be a good agent, you need to blend in, be unmemorable. Swann just didn't fit that category, so I wondered if I was wasting my time on this mysterious appointment.

He was tall, dark and sanguine. In his early fifties, maybe a little older. His black hair sported a white streak on the left; a livid jagged thin scar continued from there at the hairline all the way down that side of his face to his chin. The bottle-green worsted suit was bespoke, the shoes patent leather. He wore gloves and carried a large brown leather briefcase. Removing a dark grey trilby, he nodded at me. Spots of summer rain had peppered dark blobs on his shoulders and hat.

As I stood to greet him, he gestured for me to remain seated and strode over. He limped ever so slightly, as if one leg was shorter than the other; I'm only a reporter, not a detective, and I certainly wasn't going to measure his inside leg.

He'd implied he was still in the field but I was beginning to suspect that he'd been put out to grass. A bit harsh, I thought. Because of his physical appearance maybe nowadays he was a desk man at 'Legoland', the agents' popular name for the new headquarters building at Vauxhall Cross on the Thames.

Let's be honest, he wasn't going to melt into any background.

Besides, these days he was the wrong ethnic type for infiltration. The Twin Towers atrocity changed several priorities and a few careers come to that. Why do we in the media insist on the shorthand '9/11'? Sounds more like a deodorant brand to me. What's wrong with giving that terrible act of violence against the victims of over thirty different nations its proper name? Anyway, the world has not been the same since then and now the clandestine services were mainly gunning for fanatical terrorists, not greedy traitors or misguided ideologists, though those sort probably still existed in the woodwork, awaiting their chance to emerge.

Sitting opposite me, Swann smiled as the middle-aged blonde barmaid placed a whisky and dry ginger in front of him. Clearly, he was known in this place. Not promising, I thought, though obviously being prominent could also imply that you couldn't possibly be a spy because spies are shadow creatures. Double blind, or whatever they call it.

Maybe that's how the character James Bond got away with it for so many years, traipsing round the world using his own name more than the odd pseudonym. Now Quiller, he was much more realistic. Never did get to know his real name. And of course Quiller's author, Adam Hall, was a cover-name for the late lamented Elleston Trevor. Still, those spies were fiction; Mr Swann was fact and studying me.

Swann's eyes were a cold blue; one of them, I suddenly realized, was glass. You'd have to be quick to detect the movement, but in an instant his single orb seemed to scan the entire room and its occupants. As it happened, I'd chosen a booth where we couldn't be overheard.

Despite the very visible scar, it was obvious that he had undergone some plastic surgery: the aging skin round eyes and cheek contrasted starkly with the pristine sheen of his square jaw.

He lifted the briefcase onto his lap and clicked open the metal clasp. He fished out a bundle of paper. 'Perhaps this manuscript would prove of interest, Mr. Morton?'

I liked the man at once. No skirting round the reason for our meeting, no small talk about the lousy British weather. Straight to the point.

He handed over about a ream of Courier font typewritten paper, secured by a thick elastic band. The corners were turned and the sheets had lost their whiteness. A bit like me, I suppose. It also reminded me of my rejected manuscripts – except there were no coffee-mug stains.

'Have you heard of the Dobranice Incident?'

'No,' I said.

'It was a while ago, I must admit.' He'd never make a politician, I thought; they never admitted anything.

'So when was this incident?'

'1975.'

'Good God, the Dark Ages!' If my shaky memory was to be believed I was an idealistic nineteen-year-old, reporting the *Melody Maker* pop-scene at the time. I shook my head. 'I wasn't into world events then.' I'm fifty-one now and world-weary. Early retirement would be nice, but it wasn't going to happen since the politicians had wrecked my personal pension. At least I genuinely liked writing – and getting paid for it. Though, on reflection, no matter how much I wrote, it didn't get any easier.

'The incident was trivialized,' Swann said. 'Made barely page three in the broadsheets at the time. A postscript, really.'

'And this postscript – this manuscript concerns that "incident"?'

'Dobranice. Yes.' He handed over a single sheet, a typed list.

I glanced at it. Some place names I recognised as trouble spots from recent history, others I hadn't heard of and the rest might well be places from a *Pirates and Travellers* game:

Dobranice
Tehran
Kabul
Caldera

Izmir
Hong Kong
Elba
Naples
Peking
Bulawayo
Mogadishu
Cairo

'When you said agent, you didn't mean travel agent, by any chance?' I asked.

His mouth made a grimace but his good eye shone, betraying amusement. 'Keith warned me about your – for want of a better description – sense of humour. No, that's a list of places – where certain assignments were carried out.'

'So this manuscript is about Dobranice, the top of the list?'

'Yes. Top place on the list. Top story.' He grinned lopsidedly. 'Top secret.'

I took a good gulp of my cool *San Miguel*, just to remind me of sunnier climes. This hotel was one of the few places to stock imported Spanish beer. Most of the stuff was bottled in Britain and didn't taste the same. I glanced at a window. Needless to say, it was raining again. A sultry summer, so the weathermen promised. Weathermen and politicians – don't believe a word they say.

I nodded at the bundle of typescript, itching to get my hands on it, but I held back. 'Why give this to me?'

'Times have changed.' He sipped his whisky. 'The Old Order has gone now. Even if the thirty-year-rule allows them to release anything about the incident, I doubt if you'd ever see the full story.'

'Well, thirty years have gone, haven't they? I don't recall anything being released about this Dobranice place, though.'

'And I doubt if you will, ever. Anyway, that time-release is for Prague and Dobranice. But, as that list suggests, there are other assignments still under the thirty-year embargo. Iran, Afghanistan, Argentina. They'll definitely be considered as more recent history.

And they're all about Tana. And we feel her story should be told now.' The look in his eye seemed wistful, as if there was a history between him and this Tana person.

'Tana?'

'Tana Standish.' He nodded at the pile of paper. 'Read the manuscript – she's in there.' He looked sad, almost bereaved, the way he spoke about the mysterious Tana.

Blood throbbed in my temple. Every instinct I'd developed in the news-hunting game told me this might be worth a look. 'You said "we". Who wrote this?'

'Me. And a few others. Keith and Mike. Others. A group effort. Let's just say that we downed a few drinks and got together a number of times after the Berlin Wall came crumbling down. I know, that's a long time ago as well.' His mouth curved. 'Anyway, it made a pleasant change from dry assignment reports.'

'But -?' I offered. There always has to be a *but*.

He smiled again, thinly. 'Well, it might be best to rewrite it as fiction, Mr Morton. Just to avoid the stupidity of another *Spycatcher* circus.'

'Or the boredom of Stella Rimington's *Open Secret*?'

'Not so open, was it? In fact, not much action in her prose, I'm afraid. Now, Dobranice – it has more than enough action.' His features turned rueful. 'More than enough.'

'Anyway,' I said, 'those books were about the Security Service, MI5. This isn't, is it?'

'Indeed, you're quite right. It's a rather secret part of the Firm, actually.'

'What do you want in return?'

He studied the remains of his drink and because I wasn't psychic I couldn't fathom what he was thinking, but it was more than his words: 'Just the story. The story is the thing.'

Another question had been nagging throughout our clandestine meeting. 'Why bring this to me? I'm not exactly well-known, you know.'

'Jack Higgins turned us down.'

I glared and he grinned. 'Just joking,' he said. 'You've been around the block, if you like, you've lived through these times, even if you didn't know what was going on in secret circles. Not many do, if we're honest. We've still got one of the most secret societies on earth, right here in good old Britain. Whatever happened to "Great"?'

'Sold for a peerage, perhaps?'

He shook his head and smiled. 'I don't do politics. Not a good idea in our profession. But as I was saying, actually, Keith liked your articles for the *Portsmouth and District Post*.'

I didn't for a minute believe a word of it. Yet... I fingered the manuscript in anticipation. It seemed too good to be true. I was being handed all this secret stuff on a plate.

'All right then,' I said, 'I'll give it a go.'

'Just do her justice,' he said.

Later, how I wished I'd met Tana Standish. People like me – and those accursed politicians – sit cosily at home with our petty complaints while men and women like her fight the good fight against evil. The Cold War may have ended, but we still need people like Tana Standish, Alan Swann and Keith Tyson. And they get no thanks. Mainly, their stories go unheard and unread. At the most, their achievements probably get a footnote in a newspaper.

After several months shut away from the world of today I have finished this book, which I have called *The Prague Manuscript* - the first chronicle of Tana Standish's missions which presages several calamitous adventures with significant revelations from recent history. It is dedicated to all the secret agents who fight behind the scenes and behind the news.

CZECHOSLOVAKIA, 1975

Czechoslovakia. A country formed at the end of the First World War from the Slavonic provinces of the dissolved Austro-Hungarian Empire.

This was the country about which Neville Chamberlain said, 'How horrible, fantastic, incredible, it is that we should be digging trenches and trying on gas masks here because of a quarrel in a faraway country between people of whom we know nothing' when Germany annexed Czech Sudetenland in 1938.

The Communists took control in 1948 and declared it a People's Republic.

1975 - seven years after the Prague Spring, that brief flowering of freedom under Alexander Dubcek; fourteen years before the Velvet Revolution that ousted the Communist Party and saw a playwright become President.

Eighteen years before the country split in two - to become the Independent Republic of Slovakia and the Czech Republic - in the new worrying surge of Eastern European nationalism.

And in September of that year, eighteen-year-old Czech tennis player Martina Navratilova defected to the United States. The US President was Ford, and the month before the Dobranice Incident he had escaped two assassination attempts. Carter and Reagan were waiting in the wings, as was Margaret Thatcher.

The British Prime Minister was Wilson. Brezhnev was entrenched in the so-called Evil Empire and Gorby was a nonentity to the Western world. Within days after the Dobranice

Incident, Franco would have a heart attack and Prince Juan Carlos would take over as head of state in Spain.

October, 1975. Sakharov was awarded the Nobel Peace Prize, yet this was a time when the Cold War was very much a chilling reality.

CHAPTER ONE: Prelude

Czechoslovakia, August, 1968

Six Soviet officers stood on the balcony overlooking St Wenceslas Square and the definition through the sniper-scope was so good that Tana Standish could detect the blackheads round their noses and the bloodshot eyes that testified to late-night celebrating with alcohol. She had ten 7.5mm rounds, more than enough to kill all of them.

Tana had a steady grip but there was no risk of weapon-shake anyway as the new Giat F1 rifle rested on its bipod on the window sill. She had also made sure that, as this weapon was fresh from the French production line, it could not be traced back to England. Dressed in his brown-grey greatcoat with bright red lapel flashes, General of the Army Ivan Pavlovsky cocked his head to the left while he listened attentively to his commanders. He was thickset, with small dark eyes and a pug nose whose nostrils bristled with hair.

Try as she might, she could not detect any thoughts from the officers. But she was able to lip-read. They were in a self-congratulatory mood, since the invasion had gone well, with only a few Czech and Slovak deaths. Vodka had indeed flowed last night.

As one of the main architects of the offensive, Pavlovsky would have the honour to die first. She levelled the cross-hairs on the general's forehead, just between the close-set eyes.

For God's sake, don't! Along with the words that she snatched from Laco's tumbling thoughts came a familiar dull ache at the back of her neck. Her mouth went very dry. Tana lifted her finger away from the trigger and felt cold sweat start its trail down the side of her brow.

She turned her head as, seconds later, Laco unlocked the apartment door and rushed inside, slamming the door behind him.

'Thank God I caught you in time!' he gasped, eyes staring at the rifle on its stand.

'We agreed,' Tana said evenly, 'if we got the opportunity, it was too good to pass up.' Out of the corner of her eye she watched the Soviet officers. They weren't going anywhere. Two of them were pointing down into the street, where a car was on fire.

Laco heaved a sigh of resignation. 'We intercepted a radio message.' He rested his back against the wall by the door and slowly sank down on his haunches, head in his hands. 'They said there will be reprisals if we kill any of their officers.'

'If I was one of the other ranks,' she said, 'I'd be a bit upset about that.' But it wasn't a joking matter. *Reprisal* was not a nice word in Czechoslovakia.

She stood with smooth grace and he looked up, his wrists resting on his knees, and watched her lithe body; she was dressed in black with a belt of pouches round her small waist. Her every movement seemed fluid, controlled. Cat-like, even.

She drew the lace curtain across the window, concealing the weapon.

Kneeling beside Laco, Tana gently took his hands in hers. She understood. He was only nineteen and he didn't want another Lidice on his conscience. 'One day, we'll beat them,' she said, 'I promise.'

London, October, 1975
'Laco Valchik asked for you after we got Torrence back,' Merrick, the Operations Officer, explained nasally, podgy fingers collating

the few sheets of paper in front of him. He always sounded as if he was suffering from hay fever, but he wasn't. Ops was such a cold fish, she wondered if he had ever suffered from anything. She doubted if he had a conscience; a useful deficiency, in his line of work, which entailed sending agents over the border. His pallid features were slightly flushed as he added, 'It's before my time, but I understand you both have a history.'

Tana nodded. 'Yes, I recruited him,' she said, ignoring the innuendo. 'Just before the Soviet invasion. Young and idealistic. Just what we wanted. All fired-up to gain freedom for his people.'

'Easier said than done, though, isn't it?'

'Seven years isn't a long time in the scheme of things,' she countered.

His small glasses reflected the light so that she was unable to glimpse the eyes behind them. 'I mean, we have to be patient. Theirs is an awfully big war machine. It's not as if the Iron Curtain is just going to crumble in a day, like Jericho, is it?'

'You might be mixing metaphors there, Ops.'

'Well, possibly.' He ran a finger and thumb over his prominent cheekbones in thought, as if this action would peel back some of his memory. 'But to return to your assignment. Simple regroup and rebuild is called for.' He put up a hand. 'I know you were due to work with Fisk down at Fenner House. That spooky stuff will have to wait. Valchik was adamant. He won't accept anyone else but you.'

'I'm supposed to be flattered?'

'No, of course not. But they've taken a beating out there. I thought the least we could do was to keep the lad happy.'

'Happy doesn't enter into it, Ops. It sounds as though he has become a little distrusting. What on earth did Torrence *do*?'

'I wish I knew, Standish.' He brushed imaginary fluff off his pinstripe lapel and fingered the typed sheets on the table in front of him. 'Torrence was all nerves when we got him back. Naturally, the first thing we did was to take him down to a safe house in

Cornwall for debriefing. But he ran off and now he's missing.' He shook his head, unwilling to engage her eyes while admitting the department's blunder. 'Naturally, we're trying to locate the man, but it's obvious he wasn't up to it in Prague.' He held up his hands in surrender. 'I hold myself wholly responsible. I shouldn't have let him go.'

Tana thought back to Laco's words seven years ago. 'I'm sorry we have to let Pavlovsky and the others go.'

'So am I,' she had said with feeling in reply. Would she regret not squeezing the trigger?

Now, after seven years, perhaps she would find out.

Geraghty was small-boned and wiry and she guessed that he must be approaching his retirement. He stood alongside Tana as she sat in the dentist's chair, head back and mouth open.

Even in this position, she was comfortable enough, because she had a view of the door, the room's only access. Taped music was playing in the background – Debussy's prélude *Feux d'artifice*.

'I really don't like this, you know,' Geraghty remarked and she simply nodded. He wasn't discussing the music, but what he was about to do. Without fail they went through the same ritual each time she prepared for another assignment.

At that moment the door opened and Merrick sauntered in. 'Hello, Gerry,' he said in greeting.

Geraghty eyed Ops with cold venom; Tana knew the dentist hated being called 'Gerry'. She turned her head but decided to lie where she was, now that she was comfortable.

'Sorry to interrupt, but could I have a quick word with Standish, please?'

'Of course,' agreed the dentist. 'I'll just be in the waiting room.' Not that there was anyone out there waiting. It wasn't as if there was a queue of agents preparing to go out on assignments.

'Righto!' Merrick closed the door after the dentist and said, 'As I'm going to a briefing, I won't be able to see you off, so I thought

I'd pop in now to wish you luck.'

'Thank you,' she said.

'And I stopped by to see Enid. She said the paperwork is all set and Umbra has been fixed up as well. I haven't a clue what she means - wasn't that the name of your father's submarine?'

'Yes, Ops, it was. You have a good memory.' Or he has recently been reading her file. Not unusual, since he was sending her into enemy territory. She didn't enlighten him further.

'Oh, well, then, I'll be off. Take care.'

Then Geraghty returned to fit the suicide pill into her molar.

CHAPTER TWO: Tana

Czechoslovakia

Sharp and chill, the October wind whipped across the international airport's glistening wet apron as Tana Standish joined the other passengers descending the aircraft's gangway steps. Once on firm ground she stayed with them and headed towards Ruzyne's Customs. She expected her reception to be as cold as the weather and she wasn't disappointed.

The stern-faced Slovak policeman at the counter repeatedly scanned her passport and list of valuables. Maybe he had difficulty reading, she thought, or perhaps he was simply admiring the set of her high cheekbones.

She only hoped he hadn't been alerted to her arrival. On this occasion she was travelling under her own name; Enid had argued against it, but Tana was adamant. 'Last time I was in Prague I was Tracy Casey and there's no way I'm ever going to travel with that name again!'

'Well, all right,' Enid had conceded, 'but change your hairstyle and we'll update your passport photo.'

In dull tones the policeman enquired about her purpose for the visit and she told him she was a tourist which eventually he accepted with bad grace. His inscrutable dark eyes flickered, suggesting there was some intelligence behind them. Perhaps he wondered why on earth a tourist wanted to stay in Prague, of all places. He sighed, boredom only slightly alleviated, stamped her documents and passed her through.

Bureaucratic time-wasting never seemed to change this side of the ideological divide, she reflected.

Tana wasn't unduly surprised. Even now, so long after the Soviet force-of-arms, she'd expected the usual Iron Curtain delays, suspicions, and searching pointless questions. The Soviet invasion of Czechoslovakia that brutally ended the 'Prague Spring' may have been seven years ago - years of careful silence - but distrust and suspicion can last a lifetime when freedom is stifled.

Pure instinct made her cautious. She'd been vigilant since childhood and, given that such watchfulness had saved her life more times than she cared to count, she wasn't about to change now.

Security police were still in evidence, with ready weapons and grim faces. But her passport and visa were quite in order. The documentation said she was simply a tourist, like her fifty-odd fellow travellers. International Enterprises ('Interprises' was an adjunct of the British Secret Intelligence Service) had even booked her flight through Cedok, the Czech Tourist Office.

Most Interprises agents entered target countries openly to liaise with the British Embassies in furthering trade with Great Britain. The Soviets had been doing it for years with their trade delegations. This time, though, the Ops Officer hadn't deemed it necessary, so Tana was travelling as a tourist.

Her two lightweight cases had already been sent on to the Hotel Alcron on Stepanska, so, carrying only her small travelling case, she waded unhurriedly past the dour and earthy airport staff and the diverse groups of tourists whose previously carefree attitudes now suddenly appeared affected by the singular constraints of the Communist Bloc.

Perversely, it was good to be back after seven eventful years – dangerous and secret years in far-flung places like Karachi, Iran, Elba, Gibraltar, Hong Kong and Mombasa. Caution and deceit were second nature to her, she reminded herself and grinned. Yes, I feel quite at home again.

The sound of the heels of her calf-hugging black boots added to the general hubbub in the echoing terminal. Tana moved through the wide glass-partitioned entrance and lowered her travelling case onto the steps and checked her watch.

The British Airways flight had been a couple of minutes early - a favourable tailwind. She'd allowed for a much longer delay in Customs, so now she had at least ten minutes to wait before Laco would arrive with transport to take her the seventeen kilometres into the city.

The very air seemed grossly oppressive - and it wasn't the weather.

At least the rain had stopped. But the grey heavens stayed overcast. From the aircraft she'd seen the lights that shone between the rows of Charles Bridge's Baroque statues, while the Vltava, edged with rain-sodden trees, reflected the city's winking night lights and numerous turreted spires and domes. A beautiful city that seemed to benefit from Communist neglect; it lacked modern hoardings, neon advertisements and garish shops and she felt it was probably better for it.

After all these years it was easy enough for her to keep in check her distaste for the Soviets and their system, which had seemed to get even more corrupt. Odd, but Sir Gerald had openly regretted Kruschev being deposed the year before she joined Interprises – 'Not as shifty as Brezhnev. We thought we had a chance to work with the Russians,' he'd said. 'Now, after over a decade of Brezhnev, I'm not so sure any more.'

She really felt for the oppressed Czechs and Russians; they were regularly lied to and deprived of so much, all so that the Soviet hierarchy could live well. Where there was oppression, there was fear, betrayal and personal danger.

Still, so far she had no reason to doubt that Merrick's assessment was accurate. 'Minimal risk,' he'd said. 'A straightforward repair and rebuild assignment. I thought you'd enjoy it; a return to see old friends.' Then he'd added, with a lecherous smirk, 'Laco Valchik's still in charge, he picked up the pieces and got Torrence out. A close call, by all accounts.'

As soon as she'd heard about Torrence, Tana had contacted Enid Shorthouse, the Interprises filing clerk in the basement library. Enid had been with Sir Gerald since the beginning in 1963 and, it seemed, had a memory second only to Tana's. She knew all of the Interprises field agents and their traits. Her filing system was separate to the Ops Officer's and that's the way she liked it. Idiosyncratic. Only she could find anything. She was supposed to provide documentation and information back-up for the agents in the field. But Enid took her job too seriously to limit herself so whatever she could find out she put in her files - on paper and in her memory.

'You know, Enid,' Tana had remarked, 'all Moscow Centre has to do is to kidnap you. Interprises might as well fold up then.'

Chuckling, Enid leaned on the enquiries counter, drooping breasts encased in a *My Weekly* pattern blue-green bobbled cardigan which was well past its best. She lifted her spectacles from her pointed nose and rested them among the permed curls of her blue-rinsed hair. 'You're the only agent who knows the full extent of my knowledge, my dear.' She winked. 'The Ruskies'd have to be psychic to know, really.'

Tana grinned. 'Let's hope so. Now, what can you tell me about Reginald Torrence?'

'Torrence!' Enid's normally kindly features suddenly transformed, lines pronounced around her glaring eggshell blue eyes. 'He's a buffoon. I don't know why Sir Gerald allowed him to stay after he bungled Izmir.' She calmed down, waved a hand airily. 'Fine, he's good in the classroom, knows the theory, but his people skills are nothing to write home about, I can tell you.'

So now Tana wondered why Merrick had sent in that buffoon, as Enid called him. Apparently, he bungled the whole operation from the word go. All he had to do was consolidate the underground faction, obtain any useful information, and then return with technical requirements they might have. Instead, he blew it, the whole fabric torn at the seams, one cell disrupted, others in hiding and fearing the worst.

At least Torrence got out – thanks to Laco and his network's survivors.

Was it Torrence's fault or was there a mole in Laco's organisation?

But Tana knew that there was another quite unthinkable possibility.

She still puzzled over what happened to Toker in Istanbul last month – and Enid hadn't been any help either, save saying that Dudley Toker had been a real professional and a gentleman as far as she was concerned. 'I tell you truly, Tana, I really miss his wonderful smile and chivalrous airs. Not much gallantry about since the Sixties.'

A chilly sensation down the furry nape of her neck returned Tana abruptly to the present.

The man was obviously watching her. Hatless, close-cropped black hair, greying at the edges. Stout, short, a broken bent nose, flaring nostrils. He was so blatantly an agent of the StB, their political security police, no doubt sent from his rat-hole in Bartolemejská where they'd taken over the old convent and eighteenth century church of Saint Bartholomew. One day, maybe the church and convent would echo to hymns and psalms again instead of the plaintive cries of tormented citizens. But she wouldn't hold her breath.

All StB agents wore civilian clothes, yet they might as well have displayed placards with neon lights. It was a combination of their unrelaxed poses, their strained unawareness and something indefinable, almost as though they smelled of decay and corruption.

On the other hand, he could be KGB – they were little better, confident in their superiority and their ability to instil fear into the populace. And if so, then she was probably blown before she started.

She was aware that in the last six months Interprises had lost two other experienced agents, besides Toker. Cornelius in Helsinki and Segal in Berlin. Her thoughts naturally turned to that unthinkable possibility - the existence of a mole inside Interprises. It was unimaginable. Sir Gerald had created Interprises twelve years ago, specifically because MI6 seemed to be riddled with Soviet double agents.

Only a week earlier, James Fisk had obtained authorisation for Tana to experiment with a new probing technique on the staff of Interprises. It had risks to her mental well-being, he warned, but she had said she was willing to try. The technique used a prototype bio-feedback system combined with remote viewing. Then this mission had cropped up. Bad timing, really. Still, when she got back, they'd set it up and with any luck it just might help identify the mole, if there was one.

As the watcher's black rodent-like eyes momentarily latched onto hers, Tana's brain echoed with a loud throaty scream, a woman in extreme agony:

Completely naked, the woman was strapped to a chair, her skin blemished with electrode-burns, lathered in glistening sweat, trembling violently.

The stark moment passed. Tana didn't superficially react at all; the mental image had been too swift. But her pulse and heart rate had quickened.

The sensation was not wholly alien to her; it was akin to previous bouts of precognition. But it was also possible that it could have been a captured impression from the watcher's sewer-like mind. He looked old enough to be an apprentice during Stalin's time. Probably reliving his stimulating vile memories.

A sibilant hiss of tyres on the wet tarmac caught her attention.

The approaching dark brown Skoda's horn honked throatily and Laco's arm waved energetically from the driver's window.

Conscious of the watcher's unblinking eyes on her, Tana speedily bundled her case on the rear seat and sank in the front beside Laco.

'It's good to see you again,' Laco whispered as she clicked the door shut. For such a giant of a man, his voice then was very tender: the poet in him.

She touched his hair-covered hand on the steering wheel. 'That watcher's getting too curious.'

Laco's broad lips twisted. 'You haven't changed, I see!'

She gave him a throaty laugh. 'Nice to see you, too, Laco.'

Grinning, he engaged gear and accelerated from the kerb, leaving a spray of dirty rainwater pelting towards the suddenly aghast watcher.

Laco's prominent forehead nodded at the driving mirror. 'Got you tailed - a black Tatra, of all things!' Usually, only party officials drove in the big black Tatras. Laco grinned again.

'It seems as though they want us to know we're being watched.'

'Games, Tana. They get bored, I guess.'

She nodded, knowing he would deal with the tail in his own good time. She closed her eyes and leaned back in the old tobacco-smelling leather upholstery. She caught the odour of Laco, a mixture of dried sweat and Brut deodorant: still the same, she thought and fondly remembered their time together during the Prague Spring when he'd been a young idealist, full of fervour for the reforms of the party's 'Action Program'. She'd felt a little like a cradle-snatcher - there was an age difference of twelve years between them - but for all his youth and relative inexperience, he was a gentle and considerate lover.

In those heady days Czech hearts had filled with hope and the events even threatened to lift their normal brooding melancholy. For only a brief moment they poured out free expression in books and art and in newspapers. Until the invasion led by General Pavlovsky stamped on them.

Even now, she felt terrible about leaving Laco and her friends to face the Soviet threat. There was little she could have done, except train resistance cells. And then she had been re-assigned to Hong Kong in the following January.

Life went on and new missions took up her time and thoughts.

During one of her rest periods at Fenner House, Sir Gerald told her what happened inside Czechoslovakia as the Soviets tightened the screws. About fourteen thousand Communist Party functionaries and an astounding half a million members who refused to renounce their belief in reform were expelled from the party. At a stroke, their expulsion jeopardised their careers and future fortunes. Many educated professionals - including teachers and doctors - were forbidden to work in their profession, while dissidents were routinely imprisoned or simply vanished.

But that was seven years ago. Now, the heavy yoke of communism had settled on the backs of this country's people and their days were unremarkable and grey. Yet now, beneath the obedient surface, they were secretive again, resisting in small but heroic ways. And Laco - her protégé and ex-lover - was one of their clandestine leaders.

She was proud of what he had achieved and smiled. As they motored downhill towards Prague's centre, Tana permitted herself to relax.

Glancing at the occasional courting couple hopping around rain puddles - they could have been in any city in the West - she thought Prague seemed quite unchanged, as beautiful as ever; unrestricted even. Perhaps the Soviet iron fist hadn't crushed everything Dubcek's brief premiership had allowed. Though, naturally, the paint-daubed walls - AT ZIJE DUBCEK - 'Long Live Dubcek' - had long ago been cleansed.

Of all the tourists at the airport, she was the only one who'd drawn any interest. That definitely suggested she'd been expected. In her report back to London later, she would mention it. Just in case.

Clearly, they didn't want to arrest her, just track her. Probably hoped she'd lead them to the underground resistance. Why didn't they just track Laco? It was possible that until today, when he met her, they'd had no idea that Laco was working against the regime.

So Laco might be compromised too. Merrick's low-key mission wasn't what it seemed, she thought.

The hissing of the car lulled her brain sufficiently to snatch a surface sleep in which she could re-juggle the mission data with the latest information gleaned from Soviet defectors and come up with some ideas.

Kazakhstan

In the Kirlian Institute of Alma-Ata, the capital of Kazakhstan, Professor Bublyk paced the control room. Through the glass wall he could observe an adjoining room occupied by six men and four women, all of them sitting at desks. He smiled on them, his best students: The Group. They were all wearing headsets connected to an array of large cumbersome computers and clinical monitors. The men wore drab uniform grey coveralls while the women were dressed in clay-brown skirts and shirts.

Bublyk was tall and powerfully built, far removed from the popular image of a scientist. His hair was straw-coloured and untidy, large spectacles magnifying his penetrating grey eyes. He was fifty-six and deep crease-lines in his forehead betrayed his worry about next year's appropriations.

It was annoying but every time they sent an inspection team, he had to recount the history of mind control. As if the idiots understood even a fraction of what he told them!

'The history of mind control began with our experiments carried out by Pavlov in the Thirties to modify behaviour,' he would say. 'While the salivating dog experiments were the most well known, they were merely the precursor.'

Indeed. The precursor to more sinister work. Lenin made Pavlov a 'guest' at the Kremlin for about three months until the scientist had completed a special report, relating his research to human beings rather than dogs. Pavlov's manuscript never left the Kremlin and it laid the groundwork for NKVD brainwashing techniques such as sleep deprivation, systematic beatings and verbal indoctrination. Brain damage, Pavlovian conditioning, hypnosis, sensory stimulation, 'black psychiatry' and 'mind cleansing' were all employed to subvert the will of perceived enemies of the state.

And as Bublyk was at pains to point out, 'the ultimate brainwashing tool is the actual invasion of another person's mind with yours.' That was the motherland's version of the Holy Grail.

In the Fifties, when Bublyk first entered para-psychological research, funds were scarce, as most of the work was done without the Stalinists being aware of it. Thankfully for him, the Stalinist taboo was lifted in the early Sixties, and he finally saw funding at last become plentiful because both the KGB and the GRU leaders hoped to harness psychic energy as another weapon in their arsenal.

Bublyk explained with justified pride, 'It was Russian sleep research that detected the theta state of consciousness, which is found in dreaming sleep.' This seemed to be somehow linked to psychic awareness. If this theta state could be augmented, they would have psychic spies – or even mind-assassins. To many of his listeners it seemed far-fetched, but the potential from success, no matter how remote, meant that roubles were diverted to this new branch of research.

The Sixties were a golden time for him and those years promised much, with experiments in submarines and in space, but deliverables were scarce. It was an inexact science, prey to mood, to environment and doubtless planetary influences for all Bublyk knew.

Now, halfway through this new decade, all the pressures were building up and cracks were appearing in the structure of the State. Yuri Andropov, the head of the KGB, was asking awkward questions. He wanted results to combat the Americans. Even members of the Politburo were becoming dissatisfied, though not within the hearing of Brezhnev and his informers.

The party tricks with cards were long gone. Psychical research had come a long way, Bublyk mused, eyeing in particular Karel Yakunin, their star psychic. Yakunin's good looks and dark wavy hair transcended the drabness of his regulation clothing.

Bublyk smiled, recalling only last night when his mind roamed the dormitories and found Yakunin bedding little Raisa, the flaxen-haired Estonian psychic now sitting at the back of the room. Their coupling was against Bublyk's regulations, as he believed sexual activity drained the psychic forces - a credo shared by oriental mystics. Yet he had not reported or disciplined them as he had to admit to quite enjoying being a voyeur.

Now, The Group was capable of distance viewing, of projecting thoughts into minds in other lands or of detecting other people's thoughts in enemy countries. It was arduous work. Some of them suffered rapid weight loss and heart strain due to the exertion. Last year, two adepts died. It was no accident that the theta state was so named after the eighth letter of the Greek alphabet, suggesting a sign of doom - *thanatos*, the 'death' sign on the ballots used in voting on a sentence of life or death in ancient Greece.

And, Bublyk reflected, they still had a lot to learn. The prospects were good, but the funding committee wanted solid repeatable results, quantifiable answers. Damned bean counters! If only the measuring apparatus was up to the task!

At that moment a buzzer jerked Bublyk out of his reverie. The light was on over Yakunin's name - he'd detected someone!

Bublyk quickly scanned today's roster and noted Yakunin was covering Czechoslovakia.

He rushed over to his star psychic's desk and quickly debriefed Yakunin.

It wasn't much: a stark white background, a terrible psychic scream, and a naked woman. The identity and nationality were difficult to determine. She seemed to think in English, but there briefly impinged a jumble of several languages, some of which neither Yakunin nor Bublyk could recognize.

'She's gifted and powerful, Professor,' Yakunin observed, wiping sweat off his brow, 'whoever she is.'

Bublyk's mind detected admiration in Yakunin's thoughts and stamped severely on them, emphasizing his disapproval with a resonant scornful voice. 'She is an enemy of the State, Yakunin! To be studied, used and discarded. There is no room for approbation.'

Shaking his head after Bublyk's sudden angered invasion of his mind, Yakunin nodded, his brow creased in lines of dull pain, the colour draining from his face. 'Yes, Professor. I will try to locate her again.'

'Do that.' Bublyk turned to the intercom and instructed three more psychics to change their psychic scanning coordinates to Czechoslovakia. His pulse raced with the pleasurable anticipation of the hunt.

But although there were brief glimmerings, none of The Group could detect any further psychic emanations from Czechoslovakia today.

Czechoslovakia

Ten minutes later Tana was fully awake, slightly refreshed and with her mind open again.

Barbed wire edged the tall rounded walls of Ruzyne prison. Forbidding, dun-coloured, drab; poignantly, it reminded her of the walled-in ghettoes.

She studied Laco's face, so sombre, so old for its youthful age. Not quite the same, then - he had grown noticeably older in the intervening years. Constant stress and worry did that. 'I'm sorry, Laco.'

'About Torrence blowing my cell?' He forced a smile, similar to that used when he conceded defeat in the ice-skating championships at Bratislava. The travesty of a smile. 'He tried his best.' Laco shrugged and cornered the car. A deep puddle noisily splashed the vehicle's underbelly. 'But his best just wasn't good enough.'

Tana peered over her shoulder. 'They're still shadowing.'

'Any moment,' he soothed.

Yet another corner. Thankfully, no roadblocks. 'Haven't they heard of car radios?' she asked.

He shrugged. 'Cat and mouse. Perhaps they like to play?'

Ahead was a stationary large removals truck, its ramp down. The short street was otherwise deserted.

Laco drove straight up the wooden ramp and screeched to a halt, the front bumper nudging a device fixed to the back of the driver's cab. Heavy black tarpaulin curtains quickly lowered over the entrance.

'Quick!' Laco barked, jumping out of the Skoda. Tana was by his side seconds later, peering down a hatch in the lorry's floorboards. Below gaped a circular sewer manhole. 'It's hidden from behind by the ramp.'

Lowering himself through the hatch, Laco unsteadily balanced over the manhole. 'Close the hatch after you.'

Gripping her case, she crouched under the lorry as Laco scrambled down the metal rungs into the black fetid sewer. The stink irritated her nose.

Finally, he called up, 'Okay!'

Carefully, she climbed part way down, the rungs damp-cold, and threw Laco her case. Then she heaved the heavy grating over the manhole and blotted out what little light had filtered in.

The lapping of sewer water came nearer as she descended. She felt Laco's hand on her waist, steadying. Her calf-hugging boots hit firm paving stones: the walkway.

'I'll lead,' he said, handing her the case and flicking on a flashlight.

Tana followed.

The disgusting eye-irritating fumes, the echoes, the squeaking of rats - all brought back memories.

Poland, 1942

Tana 'celebrated' her fifth birthday stumbling through the sewers of Warsaw, her hand in her twelve-year-old brother Ishmael's. They had survived hunger and disease and managed to avoid the deportation of the children to Treblinka in July but everyone knew they would not live through the oncoming German onslaught.

Their elder brother Mordechai had told them that they must escape, promising, 'Jews will live to settle scores. Jews have lived and will endure for all eternity.' He would continue the Jewish resistance. As they slunk through the subterranean tunnels, she looked back, and Mordechai was singing a popular song of the starved ghetto: 'When we had nothing to eat, they gave us a turnip, or a beet, here, take food, take fleas, have some typhus, die of disease!'

SS Major-General Stroop reported to Himmler: 'The Warsaw Ghetto is no more' on 16th May 1942. Besides the 14,000 Jews killed in the fighting or sent to the Treblinka death camp, another 42,000 were rounded up for deportation to labour camps near Lublin. Mordechai was one of these; in his diary that survived him, he wrote, 'Though our hearts are still beating, there will never be a joy of life in them.'

Ishmael, with hollow cheeks, pallid skin and all the signs of starvation, constantly deprived himself of their meagre contraband food in order to keep Tana's strength up. Ishmael limped; he had fractured his heel escaping a German raider whilst stealing outside the wall in the Aryan section of the city.

For two days they munched sparingly on the scraps of coarse bread and stale cheese and stolen sugar.

On the third day when the food ran out, they surfaced from the rank sewers in the Christian part of the city. The outskirts of Warsaw were a great deal more repellent than below. They had long since grown accustomed to the dark and the vermin; even the smell had lost its pungency. But here, above ground, they were easy prey to demented thieves and homicidal Nazis.

Their most treasured possessions, however, were forged papers, created by a small commune of talented men and women: a travel pass each, testifying that they were young Poles of pure race.

Constantly hiding, they followed the river Wkra north for most of the way, towards the Baltic, and their forged papers helped them. When they could, they prayed. Ishmael told her about their eternal souls and how good people went to *Olam Haba*. 'People who have done good but need to be purified, they go to *Gehenom*.'

'What about the Nazis?' she asked, wide-eyed.

'Oh, they are too evil for Gehenom. They will be punished for all eternity.'

'Good,' she said.

They subsisted on vegetable refuse in farms and on the occasional rabbit.

The nights were still very cold and there were few haystacks to insulate them. The sky was filled with stars and her young mind wondered if there was any truth in the fable that when people died a star came into existence. A lot of people had died, she thought, gazing aloft, trying not to think of Mordechai.

Fortunately, Tana had remembered a map from school in Karmelicka Street; it showed the area up to the Baltic; it hadn't been up to date, but it proved invaluable. With an effort, she projected a mental image of it before her eyes and picked out salient landmarks as they travelled. All her family members had taken her memory gift for granted, hoping she would make use of it at university - but that was before the war, when hopes for a sane future had flickered briefly.

Mere scarecrows, they often robbed farms. With her feet blistered and her ribcage visible through translucent skin, Tana weakly, stubbornly clung to Ishmael's bony hand.

Their journey took almost three months and on numerous occasions it was Tana's uncanny sixth sense that saved them from capture. She seemed able to see through other people's eyes sometimes - usually at moments of heightened tension. Ishmael didn't even pretend to understand what powers she possessed, but was grateful for them.

As they approached the port of Gdynia, Ishmael explained in a faint whisper what they must do. 'We'll stow away on a ship. Wherever it docks, we can hide. It may even go across to Norway. Just think, Tana - Norway!'

Sneaking through the seaport wasn't easy. The field-grey-clad sentries, gas-mask canisters clinking, were there in force and on the alert for saboteurs. But the children's small size helped them melt into the shadows of warehouses and railway wagons. Miraculously, they avoided detection.

The dockside was swarming with threat and shadows. Tana was fearful of unfamiliar shapes and seemed to be trembling all the time. Framed in a narrow alleyway, the crosstree and derrick of a freighter's mainmast were outlined against the night skyline. Then the black hull loomed and Ishmael whispered, 'This one, we'll get aboard this one.' He had chosen well; whoever docked the ship hadn't bothered to fit rat-guards on the cables.

Weak as they were, they managed to shin painstakingly slowly up the hawser. Tana's little hands were almost raw with the roughness of the cable. Tense minutes later, they squeezed through the gap and quietly lowered themselves onto the dew-damp forecastle.

Tana cautiously followed Ishmael and scaled down a ladder onto the well deck. He partially lifted the cargo hatch tarpaulin cover and they both slid into the for'ard hold, where it was pitch-black at first. But after a while their eyes became accustomed to the darkness; it was not unlike the sewers, Tana supposed, though smelled less rank.

The hold was stacked with crates but no food. Rats scurried to the forepeak, in deep shadow, but neither Tana nor Ishmael was particularly alarmed. Even the prospect of eating these vermin as a last resort held no horrors.

Tana's stomach rumbled emptily at the memory of the last food scraps to pass her lips two days ago.

Ishmael chuckled and she imagined that he was smiling; he told her that she was to make herself comfortable, while he went 'up top' to steal some food.

Fearful for his safety, she pleaded with him not to go. He kissed her forehead and said, 'We'll starve here if I don't find something, little Tana. I promised Mordechai I'd look after you. I keep my promises.'

He was gone for ages. She had no way of knowing how long. It could have been an hour, perhaps much longer. The waiting seemed endless.

Deep in the creaking, dank-smelling hold, Tana was a little afraid. She would much rather have stayed in the sewers of Warsaw. Known terrors seemed more preferable to those unknown. Besides, she had too much imagination.

Then her heart lightened, as she recognized Ishmael's limping stride across the deck above. He sounded in a hurry. Intuitively, she knew something was wrong.

Anxiously, she scrambled up, her little knees grazing on the metal ladder. She peeked over the coaming.

Silhouetted in the searchlight beam that lanced down from the ship's bridge, Ishmael attempted to run for cover, heading towards her, dodging around winches and the cowls of ventilators. Under his arm was a brown paper parcel that was spewing apples and he left a trail of broken eggs behind him.

A German voice shrieked, 'Halt!'

Ishmael faltered. He turned to face the bridge.

Running out of the wheelhouse, a black-clad sailor leaned over the Navigation Bridge. In his arms was a sub-machine gun. Tana recognised the weapon and her heart froze.

Ishmael's face was unnaturally pale in the pinioning light. He seemed resigned. His youthful cracked mouth twisted in a breathless agonized grimace. Suddenly, he jackknifed backwards, six inches in the air to the staccato sound of the Schmeisser MP40 weapon. His outflung arms violently discarded the stolen food; most of it splashed overboard as he crumpled almost on top of Tana, inches away from her ashen face. A solitary apple rolled past his staring eyes and unthinkingly she snatched the fruit.

Ishmael's head was on one side, his right cheek squashed against the metal deck and his eyes stared at her. His lips trembled but he was unable to speak. But she caught his words, faintly echoing in her mind. '*I hope Mordechai won't be too annoyed with me when I see him...*' What little light there was went out of him and a thin gasp of air passed his lips and she felt it, like a kiss, on her cheek.

Eyes wide in shock, she slid back into the shadows under the tarpaulin.

She knelt in the dark. Her mind was completely numb. But she gripped onto the apple, her brother's last gift to her.

It seemed an age. The agony of waiting, fearing discovery, was almost too much. At one low point she even wanted to declare herself - anything to be rid of the heart-stopping suspense.

Then she heard voices talking overhead. And laughter.

Her hearing was finely tuned now. Feet trod on eggshells. But her mind was still numb so she was unable to snatch any thoughts from the nearby sailors or soldiers. Then they dragged the body of her brother away, laughing as they did so.

She heard a heavy splash and more hilarity.

But no tears came.

Very alone now, Tana hunched tighter into the hold, amidst the bulky crates, and held the apple till it was bruised: the last memento she had of Ishmael.

Even at that early age her hatred was under an iron control. She had learned quickly enough through listening to other Jews who had escaped from Treblinka that she must be circumspect when dealing with the enemy. Tana had cause to grow up quickly. Yet it was not unusual for heroes of the Warsaw uprising to be mere children of eight or nine years of age.

Finally, the sirens sounded. The freighter cast its moorings; the propellers pulsed and the ship throbbed into life.

Bow-waves caressed the hull. The lapping of water and the heaving motion signified they were finally at sea.

If only she could stay hidden until they pulled into some port.

The Baltic, 1942
Hunger drove her reluctantly to bite into the apple. It was moist and sent her pulse racing. So delicious! Thinking of Ishmael, tears at last flowed. She ate every scrap, the dry-textured bruised bits, core and all.

Like her young friends, she'd had to scavenge in Warsaw, sneaking into the Aryan quarter. The German policy had been simple and brutally logical - better to starve the inhabitants of the ghetto and save the bullets for the Front.

So, many hours after eating the apple, as the hunger pangs returned with redoubled force, twisting her stomach into knots, she decided she would have to forage onboard. At worst, if no food could be found, she would have to risk serious infection and kill and eat a rat. It presented the least physical risk, obviously - the less food-hunting trips she made, less chance of discovery. But as far as she was concerned it would have be a last resort.

The freighter was edging out of the choppy Gulf of Danzig and steaming into the Baltic when Tana emerged into the starlit night. The well deck beneath her feet vibrated to the beat of the massive engines. Her nostrils snatched the heady, salty cold air which made her want to retch.

A yellow halo surrounded the moon.

She reached the foremast.

'Halt!'

But this time no searchlight stabbed out. Allied submarines prowled out here, after all.

Praying for invisibility, Tana stood immobile, her ears attuned, detecting feet on a ladder's metal rungs. Any moment she expected the bullets to punch into her, to rip her open as they had so many of her neighbours, as they had poor Ishmael.

But in an instant she had regained control and she dived behind some winch machinery, hurting her knees and shins. Here, the smell of grease and oil mingled with the salt spray. Her senses were at fever pitch. She seemed to hear her pursuer's every step.

More shouting.

Tana heard the heavy thud of sea-boots getting closer.

The seaman was a couple of metres away. She glimpsed his black angular shape slinking between the lifeboat davits.

Frustration seethed inside her. It did not seem fair, to get so far only to fail!

A sudden deafening explosion rocked the vessel from stem to stern and the night was instantly transformed into stark red-yellow daylight. Tana felt the force of it through the deck, vibrating through her body.

Amidst a raucous hissing and dozens of men's screams, the ship canted sharply.

The drunken angle of the vessel worsened and Tana lost her footing on the slippery brine-covered deck.

She hit the metal guardrails and tried grabbing at anything she could get her hands on.

A falling lifeboat barely missed caving in her skull; it splashed, floated.

Gasping with the shock of the cold sea, Tana snatched and held onto a rope that dangled from the lifeboat.

The strength in her arms was ebbing fast when she saw a shimmering dark dreamlike shape directly ahead of her, blocking out the myriad stars. She blinked frantically, distressed at not being able to see the Ishmael and Mordechai stars.

A foreign voice called, magnified by a loudhailer. But Tana couldn't understand what he was saying. Whoever it was, he wasn't speaking in German. That was enough.

She cried out, her voice hoarse with cold and fatigue.

When the British submariners lifted her out of the Baltic - 'Bloody hell, it's a kid!' - Tana was unconscious, shivering and blue. Close to death.

Gently, they lowered her down the hollow latticework of the conning-tower hatch to waiting hands.

As a first-aid trained matelot tried reviving her with an alcoholic rub and a few sips of warm rum, Lieutenant Standish, the Commanding Officer, ordered any other survivors to be fished out. They only found two, a soldier and a sailor, both kept under armed guard in the fore-ends until they were handed over as POWs back in England.

Standing down from Action Stations on their return to less hostile waters, the crew of the submarine HMS *Umbra* made a great fuss of Tana. 'The bloody little Wonder Kid,' they called her. They began instructing her in the rudiments of English and she proved an adept pupil, though Standish admonished one matelot for teaching her a few unladylike epithets.

Later, the childless couple, Hugh and Vera Standish, adopted her, blissfully unaware of the sleepless nights she would cause.

CHAPTER THREE: Fort

Czechoslovakia 1975

'Here we are!' Laco said, disturbing Tana's memories.

He pointed up a square brick shaft at a series of step-irons. 'I'll go first. They should be expecting us.'

Oddly, she was in no hurry. She gazed narrow-eyed into the dark cavernous maze they had passed through. The ghosts from the past faded, yet it felt like she was coming home.

When they emerged, the street was empty, the flat featureless window-pocked houses black and lifeless.

Everywhere was quiet, save for the rainwater sluicing down the drains.

After replacing the manhole cover, Laco led her across to a high-gabled house in the middle of the block, up some worn stone steps, and opened the heavy door.

Tana gently touched his arm. 'Wait,' she cautioned. 'Just a moment.'

She shut down extraneous stimuli and concentrated on the building in front of her. Upstairs somewhere there were several - four or more - minds in deep anxiety, nervous fingers on weapons. And yet she couldn't detect an immediate threat to her. Turning her mind's attention to the buildings opposite, she observed that they were occupied but there was no indication of any malevolence emanating from them either.

'All right. Go on now,' she urged and they stepped through and he closed the door behind them.

In the poorly lit musty hallway they were confronted by two stocky men in their mid-twenties, one wearing rimless glasses. Both had long shoulder-length hair and ill-fitting plain clothes. They looked like time-warped students from the Sixties. Fashion, if it existed at all for the normal populace in the Eastern Bloc, was bound to be out of date. Only the party apparatchiks could afford to be contemporary with the decadent West.

'Is Jan Smidke expecting us?' Laco enquired, emptying his shoes of sewer water onto the linoleum floor. Tana's boots had remained leak-proof; if this had been a normal visit to a private home, then she would have politely removed them. But this visit wasn't normal and she had a feeling that there would be no alcohol, first toasts and clinking of glasses here tonight.

Screwing up his nose at the smell, the bespectacled man nodded. 'Yes, Laco.' He eyed Tana and said, 'I'm Janek. This is Shelepin.'

Melodious, she thought: a Slovak.

'This way,' Shelepin said, turning to climb the stairs.

The walls were papered in a bland design, its few full colours merging into an overall splodge.

Their footfalls echoed from the wooden treads.

England, 1965
'Tread carefully,' was Sir Gerald's high-pitched warning to her as she boarded the train at Waterloo ten years ago, destined for the Fort, one of MI6's training establishments, an old Napoleonic stone-walled edifice on the Gosport peninsula on the south coast of Hampshire.

Standing beside the middle-aged yet cadaverous man had been her grey-haired mother, bravely trying to fight back tears.

'Mum, I'm a big girl now, you know?' Tana said.

'Twenty-eight last May, dear, I know.' Her mother smiled back. 'But I'm worried about what Gerald's letting you get into. It's dangerous.'

'She'll be all right, Vera, my dear,' Sir Gerald piped. 'In fact, I actually pity the instructors!'

The totally inappropriate falsetto voice of Sir Gerald had taken some getting used to, as had his emaciated appearance. There seemed to be little flesh on his face. Tana had seen survivors from the concentration camps and the facial features of the majority had been drawn, almost corpse-like, the skull's bone structure clearly visible. She knew for a fact that Sir Gerald dined well and often, yet his head and, judging by how his clothes hung on his gaunt frame, his body too closely resembled some unfortunate who had endured a Nazi death-camp.

Sir Gerald had been like an uncle to her since Hugh Standish died in her childhood yet, officially, he only came into her life when she was twenty-eight, ostensibly to recruit her into his fledgling organisation, 'Interprises'.

Ten years ago. When she'd qualified for the Intelligence Officers' New Entry Course.

The day had been bleak and windswept as she hurried from the draughty Portsmouth Harbour railway station to the pontoon where she caught the little steam craft *Ferry Prince*, which seemed to be overloaded with commuters, among them Royal Navy sailors in square rig hanging onto their white hats. Halfway across the harbour, she saw one sailor lose his hat overboard and the young man swore, no doubt fearing that he'd be on a charge when he turned up at his base, HMS *Dolphin*. Away on their left she noticed the distinctive ten-storey tall tower, rumoured to have been built by German prisoners of war. Below it were the motley brick buildings of Fort Blockhouse, the submarine base, with two menacing black boats moored alongside.

On the Gosport side she had been met by a Ministry of Defence driver in dark serge who had commented disparagingly on the weather then bundled her suitcase into the back of the highly-polished Rover.

The journey seemed circuitous – the driver explained that there was a crossing called Pneumonia Bridge over the creek but it was only capable of taking pedestrians and cyclists, not cars. 'One day they might get round to building a proper road, I suppose,' he moaned, 'but it'll be after I'm drawing my pension, I shouldn't wonder!'

Eventually, they turned onto Anglesey Road, part of the district of Alverstoke where many retired admirals were supposed to live, and this led down to the coast road and Stokes Bay, which offered a sweeping panoramic view of the Solent and the Isle of Wight.

Turning left, they passed several fenced-off military establishments.

Further along still, beyond the narrow hedge-bordered coast road, she knew, were the high brick walls of the submarine base HMS *Dolphin* and the Royal Navy's Hospital *Haslar*. However, after a short drive they turned off to the right onto what appeared to be an unadopted road with a sign on their left indicating,

GOVERNMENT PROPERTY.
FORT MONCKTON ONLY.
NO UNAUTHORISED VEHICLE
BEYOND THIS POINT.

They passed this and the 15 miles per hour sign and headed towards an unprepossessing collection of brick buildings partially concealed by an overgrowth of brambles and weeds, all behind barbed wire.

Their car crossed over a drawbridge and it seemed they were expected as Fort Monckton's ponderous studded steel doors swung wide on well-oiled rails and hinges.

Passing beneath a portcullis and through a gatehouse, the vehicle stopped on the left-hand side of a courtyard.

There were buildings all round the courtyard which she learned later housed the establishment's personnel, kitchens, dining room and bar.

'Your apartment's up there, ma'am,' said the driver, nodding at the gatehouse doorway while he lifted out her suitcase.

She was shown up a narrow creaking staircase in the gatehouse to a room designated *006 - T. Standish.* Sense of humour or what? she wondered, glancing at the door next to hers: *007 - K. Tyson.* Poor sod, he or she had a lot to live up to!

'Wasn't 006 a *man* in *On Her Majesty's Secret Service*?' enquired a deep cultured voice.

Standing on the landing was a tall powerfully built man, his grey eyes shining with humour.

'It's only an apartment number,' Tana riposted.

He thrust out a huge hand. 'Keith Tyson. Apartment *007*. You must be Tana Standish?'

'You're well informed, Keith.'

He grinned and tapped a finger against the side of his nose. 'I have my spies.'

'Well, you're in the right place, then, aren't you?'

Keith Tyson was definitely in the right place and managed to live up to his instructors' expectations, it seemed, and soon became a good friend. Tana never mentioned her past and neither did Keith touch on his. The future beckoned after all.

Training had been intense and unremitting as the various NCOs were keen to whittle out the faint-hearted, the glory-seekers and the 'arrogant rich bastards', as Chief Petty Officer Hooks called those who thought they could buy their way into the Secret Intelligence Service.

She never knew whether Hooks was against the fact that they were rich or they were arrogant. But she tended to agree that, usually, they were bastards, even if born on the right side of the blanket. Perhaps they wanted to maintain the status quo where they were comfortably on top.

Yet they had no comprehension about the ruthless enemy they were training clandestinely to combat. They still believed in the Geneva Convention and gentlemen's rules. Some were straight out of PG Wodehouse, devoid of chin and common sense.

Others, she found, were more dangerous. They were scheming,

conniving bastards, ideal material for the House of Commons but totally inadequate at coping with the boredom and physical rigours of an agent.

Thankfully, during the time that Tana was on her various courses, she saw the ex-Armed Forces instructors give the thumbs down to all those suspect individuals.

Of course Sir Gerald's injunction to 'tread carefully' had also meant to be aware that any of her fellow trainees might be a potential mole. So those who were left were secretly observed by Tana, but none gave the slightest hint that they were anything other than genuine.

Thanks to her photographic memory and her emerging psychic talents, she could out-think the instructors and even anticipate the psychological traps they set to trip up her and the rest of the intake. Inevitably, she had to put up with a lot of male chauvinism, but her talents helped her in that too.

Whether in the Fort's gymnasium, the indoor pistol range or the lecture rooms, she acquitted herself well. She was driven to the neighbouring HMS *Dolphin* where she mastered the submarine escape technique in the Tank, as the Submarine Escape Training Tower was called.

And for two weeks she trained intensively as a diver in HMS *Vernon* which was on the other side of the harbour, opposite the submarine base.

Visiting lecturers trained them in demolitions and the handling of explosives, lock picking, surveillance and disguise, the latter given by Mike Clayton, a thirty-two-year-old Arabic scholar and archaeologist on leave from his secret service bailiwick in, of all places, Afghanistan.

She passed the course and went on with Keith Tyson to Bradbury Lines, Hereford, which was an old Artillery barracks taken over by 'The Regiment', 22 SAS, in 1960. The buildings, made of wood in the Second World War, were in need of repair and had been given the name 'spiders' and at first she thought it was probably due to the profusion of cobwebs, since it was such an old place, until she saw an aerial photograph depicting the eight dormitories leading off from the central hub of the barracks - just like a web. It would serve 'The Regiment' until such time as new barracks could be provided, which seemed to be on the cards.

Following their additional weapons training and escape and evasion techniques, they were posted to Hanslope Park, the Government Communications Centre just near M1 Junction 14 on the outskirts of Milton Keynes. This building, owned by the Foreign Office, was the Technical Security Department of MI6 and here Tana was instructed in the handling of cryptographic equipment and listening devices.

Finally, she was sent to Fenner House, a mansion outside Abingdon. Here she was deposited by a taxi at the double entrance gates. As the taxi pulled away and she was left alone, Tana relaxed. This was the end of the road. After a while, living out of suitcases and attending courses palled; there must be a syndrome name for it. *Coursitis*, probably.

Her auburn hair long and flowing to shoulder-length, she stood with her suitcase and read the plaque above the speaker-buzzer:

Fenner House
Psychic Phenomena Institute

Tana pressed the intercom button.

'Good morning,' squawked a metallic voice which she recognised. 'Please state your business.'

'Tana Standish to see Sir Gerald Hazzard.'

'You're early, Miss Standish. Congratulations on getting top marks.'

'Thank you. Frank, isn't it?' Frank Bennett was Sir Gerald's chauffeur and protector.

'Yes, ma'am. I'll send a buggy to pick you up. It will take about ten minutes.'

'Thank you. I can wait,' she said and sat on her suitcase.

Moments later, another taxi pulled up alongside her, its tyres missing her feet by about six inches. She didn't move at all.

The rear passenger door opened and Keith Tyson stepped out carrying a bulging green holdall. He glanced at the plaque, a frown on his face.

As the taxi pulled away Tyson turned to study her. Lowering his bag, he just stared until a grin slowly formed. 'You've changed your hair. I didn't recognise you for a moment.'

'Hello, Keith,' she said, smiling mischievously. '*Basic disguise principles* by Mike Clayton, if you recall. So you've qualified for Interprises as well?' She was pleased to see him though puzzled that while they'd trained together her psychic talent hadn't detected the slightest clue that he had been recruited by Sir Gerald.

'I guess so,' Tyson said, his surprise quite genuine. 'You must be psychic!' He laughed, nodding at the plaque and she joined in warily. Was he? Surely not! But why was he here otherwise? Unless the plaque was pure cover.

And then the gate opened electronically and a golf buggy pulled up inside. The short powerfully built driver got out and said, 'I'm Bradley. I'll take your bags. Just get in the back please.' They clambered into the back while Bradley stowed their bags on a rack.

'Well, this is all damned intriguing!' Tyson had said, shaking his head, as they drove along the tree-lined drive.

Czechoslovakia, 1975
'Damn!' Major Vassily Kasayiev shouted, his gravelly voice hardly concealing the raw murderous anger beneath the surface. A cigarette dangled from the corner of his mouth.

Grishin, the Tatra's driver, stood by the door, his cap in hand, quivering in fear. He'd whined his excuses after reporting that he'd lost Valchik and the Interprises woman. The incompetent wretch! In Stalin's day, he'd have been sent off to the salt mines. Kasayiev scowled and turned away.

Ignoring Grishin now, Kasayiev struggled out of his drenched clothes and threw them on the parquet floor. He heard Grishin scurry to pick them up as he sank his stout frame onto the unyielding chintz sofa, hairy pot belly folding over his grey woollen underpants. His wide flared nostrils twitched as the hashish cigarette began to have a calming effect.

Kasayiev released a great sigh and scratched his belly hair. So, they were planning something, otherwise there was little point to their swift evasive action. He chuckled, scarred lip curving. He glared at the soaked clothing that dripped in Grishin's arms and made a mental note to repay the Valchik pig tenfold.

Idly, he rose and looked through the grimy window down onto the wide street of Na Prikope. Here, at Number 33, was housed the Central Committee of the Communist Party of Czechoslovakia. Formerly a bank, it had been taken over after the nationalization of all the banks. Its central location made it ideal for the Committee's purposes. The underground vaults were the strongest in Prague - and soundproof. On the night of 20th/21st August 1968 the Security Service broke in here and put guns to the heads of First Secretary Dubcek and his members of the Presidium, just to ensure their obedience.

Sent to Krasnany, a village close to Bratislava, Dubcek was now working as a mechanic, his every movement monitored.

Kasayiev shook his head in bewilderment. What a fool Dubcek had been! To think he could flaunt his liberal capitalist policies under Mother Russia's nose! Yet, it still amazed him to think that Dubcek and his cronies got away with it for so long, without Brezhnev intervening.

Of course the status quo had returned to normal. And so it would stay well into the next century, he mused.

He walked over to the wardrobe against the far wall; it was made with specially imported wood from Norway. Shrugging into a red terry towel housecoat, he walked across to his desk and his big calloused hand covered the desk's buzzer.

A moment later, a Ukrainian MVD trooper stepped in and removed his distinctive blue cap. 'Sir!'

'Inform comrade Grishin that I want the English woman's hotel watched. If she returns, he is to let me know. On no account is he to apprehend her. He may follow her - *if* he's careful.'

'Very well, sir!' The specially recruited soldier of the Ministry of the Interior saluted the KGB Major seconded to the StB and shepherded the shamefaced Grishin out, then closed the door after them.

Kasayiev put out his cigarette and sat on the corner of his desk. He picked up a stiff-backed folder marked: SECRET REPORT - TANA STANDISH. Kasayiev smiled with approval. He hadn't met her but his agents had reported on her activities in Elba and Mombasa. By all accounts, she was a worthy opponent. He opened the folder, pleased to see the densely typed pages. Splendid! The interrogation of Segal had borne fruit. The fool hadn't wanted to divulge anything, of course, but there were ways to extract the truth, and nothing but the truth.

You're playing with fire, his conscience warned. Just pick her up. Interrogate her. She's a gift. With her knowledge, she could do untold damage to Interprises and even MI6. That should be enough.

But it wouldn't be, he knew. Because she was a gift, he wouldn't get most of the praise. No, agent Trumpet would get the honours. Stupid code name! Supposed to bring down the walls of MI6, is that it? If I capture her, I'll only be acting as a policeman, nothing more.

I want to roll up the underground network here, for good and all. Be finished with it. Trample on any thought of freedom in Czechoslovakia. And with such a coup behind me, I could probably ask for anything. Even retirement to a nice little dacha on the Black Sea.

Retirement. His fogged mind dwelled on the dacha and the doorway to a new life of peace and pleasure.

The door on the landing swung open as Tana, Laco and the

others reached it: they were expected.

A smell hovered, of badly imitated Turkish coffee. A solitary naked lamp illuminated the boxlike room; the only window was boarded-up, to the left. Four shabbily dressed men sat on tubular chairs facing the door, their faces impassive. Each held an American Ruger Mini-14 rifle – so, Tana thought, they're well supplied, since these weapons only went into production two years ago.

Instinctively, even though Laco's presence confirmed they were friends, Tana weighed her chances the instant the numbers and guns registered: nil. Instinct and being prepared kept her alive, after all. If there was a need, she could probably take the two leaders before she died: those on the left and right sides, as nobody important would hazard himself as the centre of attention.

'Welcome,' said the bearded Slovak on the left of his three companions, though his eyes and tone were far from welcoming. Above his unruly mop of red hair was a framed print of the National Anthem, the only anthem in the world to begin with a question: *kde domov muj* - Where is my home? A rather apt title, Tana mused, considering the country's history of turmoil. She recognised him from the files Enid supplied.

'It's an honour to meet you, Smidke,' she said. 'London is greatly in your debt.'

Smidke smiled, baring yellow teeth. He was short, stocky, his forebears probably of peasant stock: sturdy and real. He gestured theatrically and the rifles lowered and she noted now that they weren't the folding stock version, which made them harder to conceal.

Janek removed his spectacles and folded them into his breast pocket as he shut the door. It clicked as he turned the key.

Tana felt trapped. She'd have to trust their lookouts – she'd detected one across the road as they climbed the stairs.

For a few interminable seconds the house creaked around them.

Then Smidke jumped up and lumbered forward, a broad grin on

his face. 'Welcome, my friend!' He embraced Laco, almost crushing the bulky ice skater against his barrel of a chest.

Laco returned his friend's warmth then prised himself loose and nodded at Tana. 'This is Tana, an old friend. We met during the troubles of '68. She's very reliable.'

Smidke's squinting eyes studied her dubiously. His mouth soured. 'So was Torrence. Reliable, London said!' he snapped, spittle flecking his ginger goatee beard.

His three confederates shuffled uncomfortably in their chairs, nervous hands tightening on their weapons. At least no fingers were on triggers.

Janek stepped forward a pace, putting on his spectacles again. Shelepin, the quiet student, stood by the door, sallow face grim and uncompromising.

Tana broke the fragile silence. 'That's why I'm here, to find out what happened,' she said. 'I know Laco's cell was overrun, and he only got out by chance; but what did Torrence do?' She had to split open their distrust, no matter how justified it seemed to them at present.

Stony glares met her.

Laco loosened his collar and his Adam's apple bobbed.

'Torrence's report wasn't very helpful,' Tana added. He had filed an initial report before being taken down to Cornwall for intensive debriefing. 'He said that he thought he was betrayed.'

With a mellow, ironic laugh, Janek slumped down in Smidke's vacated chair, face barren but for a nervous tic under his left eye. He fumbled with his glasses, took them off and shook his head in disbelief.

Laco said, 'Janek here was the only one to get out with Torrence. Then he warned us to go to earth.'

'I see.' She moved forward and knelt on one knee by Janek and placed a hand on his shoulder. 'So, what happened?'

Janek returned her look sharply, eyes seeming to dim, as though surveying the past. Anguish was there, too. 'The bastard broke into a run as the StB approached the four of us in Wenceslas Square, outside the metro entrance. No reason. Just shit scared, I think.'

He was reliving the moment now.

Tana seized images, brief visual impressions from him:

Torrence swivelled round and darted for the new underground's entrance steps, glancing guiltily over his shoulder as he ran.

Janek yelled, 'Don't run, we'll bluff, they can't know anything!'

But Torrence wasn't listening.

Janek chased after him, calling back to the young girl and the student with her. 'Come on, they'll know something's wrong now!'

Reaching a junction, Janek stopped.

Torrence panting, resting against the tiled wall further up.

Janek looked back. The girl, Marta, was lying on the stone flags; the student, Antonin, struggled to lift her up. She must have twisted her ankle, of all bloody things! Why are women's ankles so bloody fragile?

Antonin and Marta hobbled towards Janek but suddenly, like a pack of wolves, the StB were on them. Shoes scuffled and the girl screamed and fell; a gleam of blood on her temple.

Torrence began running again; Janek heard his hurried steps, echoing.

Antonin was manacled now, and two of the three secret police were running towards Janek.

He must get Torrence out of Prague - and fast.

Janek sped after Torrence, cursing London as he ran.

'And now London sends you in - *a woman!*' He hissed a swearword, almost in tears. 'Don't they take us seriously here, for God's sake?'

Laco pressed close and leaned down, whispered in Tana's ear: 'They've got Marta and Antonin in Ruzyne jail. They'll be made to talk, but they don't really know anything worthwhile. Marta was Janek's younger sister. Naturally he's upset.'

Upset! she thought, amazed at the understatement. No amount

of sympathising would assuage the continuous rending ache Janek now experienced - as Tana had felt it too, gnawing at her, rekindling old memories of her own flight from a different breed of oppressors.

Businesslike, she stood up and addressed Smidke. 'Laco will vouch for me. I'm not like Torrence. I'm not going to run away at the first sign of trouble. My job is to re-establish Laco's cell and ensure that all your other cells are intact and under no threat of compromise.'

'We don't know if it's a good idea to carry on,' murmured Smidke. 'We want to, but if London treats our lives in such a cavalier fashion, perhaps we should call it a day, while some of us are still alive, no?'

'No,' she said firmly. 'London cares. That's why I'm here. Not to mend fences or mince words.' She studied each face in turn. 'The safety of the rest of you is paramount as far as London is concerned. Believe me.'

Her straight talking appeared to be working. Even Janek's baleful glare had softened a little.

'Torrence might have been right about one thing, though. Is it possible his presence here was known to the StB?'

Her suggestion was received with flinty hostility.

Laco cleared his throat. 'Tana, in this city, anything's possible. But it's not likely.' He shrugged his broad shoulders. 'And remember, it looks like you were expected too. You had your own watcher at the airport, didn't you?'

Janek gasped and Smidke said, 'Is this true?'

Tana nodded. 'Yes, but Laco lost our tail.'

'But that means you're compromised already. Your handler will have to pull you out, no? Send somebody else.'

Tana smiled at Smidke's serious cast of features. 'No, because I don't have a handler. The embassy doesn't even know I'm here.'

'That means the leak can't have come from them,' said Smidke. 'That's something, I suppose.'

'If there is a leak, it's either someone here in your organisation or one of my people back in London. Neither is palatable, granted.'

'Palatable?' queried Smidke. 'We're not talking about some Western fast food here, you know, we're talking about our careers and lives!'

'You're very touchy, Smidke. You must learn to relax, otherwise you're going to be no good to me or your cause.'

Smidke glared. 'I'll bear that in mind, next time the secret police cordon off our street.'

Laco cleared his throat noisily and said, 'To get back to what we were saying, I think Torrence just ran because he was scared.'

Perhaps that was all there was to it. As Enid had said, good at the theory, hopeless at the practical stuff. Tana nodded. 'Very well, we'll reorganize your cell first. How many have you left who've gone to earth?'

'Four.' He eyed the others. 'Our remaining cells are all intact but no longer operational. We're taking this mole business seriously, you understand.'

Tana nodded. 'Yes, I can see that. I'd appreciate it if you'd recall your four people, tell them I've been sent by London and that I'm investigating the possibility of smuggling out a high-ranking defector.'

Janek gasped again - he wasn't what you'd call ideal material for poker, let alone underground work, she thought. But, by God, he had guts. They all had.

Laco's eyes narrowed. 'Are you?'

She shook her head and her lips curved. 'No.'

The others glowered, unsettled in their seats.

Smidke grated, 'Why lie to our people - what purpose does that serve?'

Tana again studied their sullen faces. 'If there is a spy in any of the cells, he'll quickly tell his paymasters of the "defection"; and I'm sure that any move on their part will get to us. Then we'll know we have a spy here in our midst. If on the other hand there's no spy, then the very fact that we're contemplating such a big operation will improve your people's morale after the Torrence fiasco. Rather than waste that edge, we'll use some of our people in a bid to break out Marta and Antonin. We'll then smuggle *them* out.'

There was an intake of breath - especially from Janek. Someone swore softly.

'But,' she went on, 'only those present - *and that is all* - will know of the latter plan for the time being. All right?'

'A breakout from Ruzyne?' Janek stared. 'It's not possible, we'd have tried it!' The doubt in his voice belied the hope burning in his eyes.

Grey-green eyes glistening, she stared at Janek. '*I* believe it can work.'

He looked away and searched the suddenly admiring faces of his associates.

Turning to Jan Smidke, she continued, 'I'll require some maps of the streets surrounding Ruzyne, and any information you can glean from your men. I think some of them have been "guests" there.'

This revelation crinkled Smidke's brow. 'You know more than you lead us to believe, Tana.'

'I do, don't I?' Tana smiled. 'That's why London sent me, Jan.'

Laco stepped forward. 'Until we regroup and organise the necessary details, I think you should lie low.'

'Fair enough,' she agreed. 'No sense in making myself a target unnecessarily. But I can't risk going to one of our safe houses, the embassy might want to use it. So where do you suggest?'

'One of our sympathizers is from the privileged class - a regime propaganda artist. He has a fine country dacha a short way outside Prague, just off the Pilsen road.'

He sought agreement from the others and quickly got it. 'You'll be safe there.'

Safe from the ever-prying eyes of informers, she thought. No such thing as absolute safety. Safe from this country's oppressors? She doubted it. Yet even the enforcers of the morally bankrupt communist system feared for their lives and informed on each other. Fear and distrust bred more fear and distrust. The scourge of communism was real and worrying. Only six months ago Cambodia and Vietnam fell to the Chinese and Korean brand of that ideology. It was of little consolation that the Sino-Soviet split was still in evidence. In fact, the Russians were incensed at the American political overtures to China. It made her blood boil to realise that there were still marches and rallies for CND.

Red anger blurred Ilyichev's vision for a moment at the sight of Tana hurrying across the broad zebra crossing. His pulse raced. There could be no mistake. The overhead dual-bulbed street lamp clearly showed up her face. She was boarding a modern streamlined tram that had just drawn up at the fare-stage in the centre of Wenceslas Square's dual carriageway.

He could hardly believe his luck. Must follow the bitch, he thought, see what she gets up to.

Ilyichev swore gratingly, feeling the metal-bolted knee joint twinge as he limped over the road. He opened the door of his car that was parked slantwise to the kerb.

Although it was his duty to report her presence to his superiors, he had decided against it. Ilyichev longed for his own very personal revenge.

Northern Ireland, 1972
It had been a dull, grey-mist day on the outskirts of Belfast, with a slight breeze hovering over the gorse. Dusk was closing in. Darts of crimson raked the hazy horizon.

Disguised as a British Army Lieutenant, Ilyichev leapt over a stone wall and dashed into the down-draught of the airborne Bell Huey helicopter, its fuselage painted with the logo of TTT - TYRONE TOP TOURS, a fake air-tour business.

The leather briefcase he carried contained stolen top-secret troop deployment plans to be used in the event of any escalation of violence in Ulster. Moscow would be only too happy to train terrorists to counter the deployment. And he also had documentary proof that the SAS were secretly deployed in the province on assassination squad work; that alone was political dynamite when handed to the stupid free press who did so much harm by shouting for 'open secrets!'

To his left, on the dusty country road skirted by hedgerows, Tana's camouflage-mottled Jeep screeched to a standstill, spraying mud in its wake.

Ilyichev glanced over his shoulder and glimpsed her silhouette standing on the Jeep's bonnet.

Time was against him; he couldn't risk stopping to shoot at her. His priority was to get away with the plans.

A rifle was raised to her shoulder, telescopic sight glinting.

He zigged and zagged beneath the deafening rotors now.

Stumbling forward, he grabbed at the snaking Jacob's ladder and glanced up at Tomich who was frantically beckoning as he leaned out of the double doors.

The rifle's single report cracked loudly, even above the distinctive rotor-chopping sound of the Huey. Ilyichev heard that sound almost every night afterwards.

He gasped, air expunged from his lungs as his leg was bowled from under him.

His stomach lurched, the sudden pain seeming to explode in his chest and groin – acute heart-pounding bladder-emptying fear - and he dropped the briefcase. His leg gave way under him and his hip painfully hit the sod and he tumbled over, grazing his face on a rock. That small scar on his cheekbone now reminded him every morning when he shaved.

Fighting off the lancing pain, he struggled to his good knee and grabbed the fallen briefcase.

Other shots alerted him. He looked up.

Tana's accurate shooting had scared the pilot. The aircraft was rising steadily, circling wider and wider, away from Tana's probing rifle.

As a parting gesture, Tomich's machine gun stuttered a short burst: soil and grass fountained harmlessly far to Tana's right.

For an interminable second, Ilyichev feared Tomich would kill him, rather than let him be taken captive. Out of range, fortunately.

Headlights glaring blinding-white, a couple of camouflaged Army personnel carriers growled to a halt beside Tana's Jeep, doubtless summoned by her walkie-talkie.

Flak-jacketed paras jumped out, Bren guns at the ready, and surrounded Ilyichev who docilely raised his arms, the dusty briefcase dangling from his right hand.

Tana shouted something. A corporal hefted his portable yet cumbersome Blowpipe.

Flares blazing red, the surface-to-air missile sped supersonically at Mach 1 towards the aircraft and Ilyichev stared down at his shoes. His shoulders hunched and his face screwed up as, abruptly, the helicopter disintegrated amid an earth-shaking display of pyrotechnics.

Ilyichev's capture was kept quiet as it would have been politically embarrassing during the Strategic Arms Limitation Talks, or so decreed the Prime Minister. Then, a few months later, with his leg expertly bolted together by Army surgeons, he was exchanged through Berlin.

He now had a permanent limp, a constant galling reminder of Tana's successful intervention.

Ilyichev had a score to settle.

Czechoslovakia, 1975
The dacha was in a slight depression just off the main dual carriageway into Prague. Encircled by grassy slopes clad in spruce and birch, the high-gabled dacha sported a loggia, a white

facade and a steep shingled roof. The front door was open but there were no lights on inside.

Through his NSPU-3 image-intensifying night-sight Ilyichev had a perfect view of the building some thousand metres away. Maximum range, he calculated. He liked a challenge.

Settling down in the deeper night-shadows of a tall larch, he expertly unpacked and assembled his Dragunov SVD rifle. Just to be sure, he loaded and reloaded the ten 7.62 rounds in the magazine.

Though similar to the Kalashnikov, this rifle differed in using a short-stroke piston to operate the bolt carrier. The AK series used a long-stroke piston, which would be quite wrong in this case, since he wanted a sniper rifle and he felt the shift of balance during a long-stroke piston's movement degraded the accuracy.

He had just double-checked the weapon - switching it for single shots - when a movement below caught his attention. The timing was ideal.

Tana Standish walked out onto the loggia dressed in an opalescent nightdress. Through the sight he watched her in the doorway, breathing in deeply, her breasts straining against the frail fabric.

Savouring the dusky air, she was staring blindly, unknowingly, in his direction.

He licked his lips, taking pleasure in the role of voyeur.

The sight moved slowly over her torso and he could see the dark areolae under the material. Steadily edging the weapon downwards, he glimpsed the dark shadowy triangle between her legs.

Ilyichev let go and briefly caressed his game leg. No, he wouldn't aim at her legs, though he dearly wanted to maim her first. A straight kill was safest. Clean. Surgical.

He gripped the rifle again and levelled the crosshairs on her gently curved throat.

Angrily, he pictured again in his mind's eye Tana thwarting him in Ireland. Steadying his breath, he froze, intent only on the kill.

He squeezed the trigger.

CHAPTER FOUR: Ilyichev

Refreshed after a shower, Tana padded barefoot onto the loggia and breathed in the pine-scented air. The night sky was star-filled and the bright moon nearly gibbous. Whenever she was out in the country - or at sea - and the sky was untainted by the polluting light from cities, she recalled that time when her father Hugh Standish had rescued her from the Baltic. She might have been fooling herself, but she still believed she could identify the two stars she'd named after Mordechai and Ishmael over three decades ago. No tears, just memories.

It was surprisingly mild for October, she thought as the cool breeze whispered against her nightdress. She hoped Laco wouldn't be long over his meetings with the remainder of his cell. Seven years since they'd been together, plenty to catch up on. And she smiled in anticipation.

Yet she couldn't help but be worried too, because there was a remarkable change in him. He was transformed from an idealistic young man into a calculating and dangerous dissident. She wondered about herself. How would she have turned out, if the Standishes hadn't adopted her? Probably bitter and twisted, seething with decades of hurt and pain.

Pain swamped her, overwhelming in its suddenness.

Her leg! Stark, rapid images swept past in the blinking of an eye, in a moment's thought:

Herself, perched on the bonnet of a Jeep, firing upwards at a Huey helicopter, rifle cracking and - now, framed in the unlit doorway, in a weapon's crosshairs.

Unadulterated hate squeezed the trigger.

Ilyichev!

Without conscious thought, Tana jerked backwards and down, thrusting herself through the doorway.

Inside. Into the dark.

With a loud thunderclap the high-velocity bullet demolished part of the door jamb where an instant ago she'd been standing.

Getting to her knees, she stayed in the shadows and steadied her breathing.

Only Ilyichev's insane anger, conjuring up after-images of his revenge motive, had alerted her. Though totally familiar with the phenomenon, she never ceased to be amazed at the intensity of some people's thought-pictures, and the thousandths of seconds that the transference took.

No more impressions reached her. He'd obviously gained control over himself again.

He would be down shortly, she knew, to check his kill or to finish her off - the professional assassin. And she had no weapon in the dacha to rely on. Bringing one in had been too risky. Laco had offered her his own automatic - an ancient CZ52 whose complicated roller-locked breech she distrusted. Besides, she said he might need it more. So much for precognition, she thought with a wry smile.

The door was still open. Faint starlight percolated through a few inches. The moon must be cloud-covered now. The rest of the room was in complete darkness.

Although she was unarmed, the darkness evened up the odds - unless he used a night-sight? He would, wouldn't he? He was a professional, after all. Tana shrugged off that thought and settled down on her haunches, relaxing muscles and mind. Within seconds she was as motionless as a rock.

Slowly, she constructed a mental picture of the room and its furniture. As well as proving of possible strategic use, the exercise steadied her pulse rate.

To be expected, the light switch was at the door. A window was recessed in the wall on the right of the door, its curtains a simple print and the curtain rail was flimsy and of no strategic use.

Directly opposite the door was a large stone fireplace stacked with logs in readiness for the imminent cold weather. Surrounding this and hanging on the brick wall were decorative ceramic bowls and plates.

On the fireplace's right was a high-winged chintz-covered armchair and behind this a wooden standing lamp - a possible if unwieldy weapon. While on the fireplace's left - a glass-fronted wall bookcase. Books by Skvorecky, Kafka, Mnacko and Hrabel.

Still on the left of the door - a table covered with a cloth of a traditional Slovak blue print design. Two bowls of fruit stood in the centre of the table, with cutlery set out for two: wurst salad, dark rye bread, pats of butter - one of Laco's favourite snacks. Like many of his countrymen, he had a preoccupation with food. 'In a land that has suffered many tragedies,' he once said, 'a man must find enjoyment somewhere.' A symptom of stress, she reckoned. She had hoped to relieve that stress later tonight. Straw-plaited place mats were spaced out along the length of the table.

She crouched on the right of the doorway, about three yards back, just in front of a low-slung sofa. To the right of the fireplace highly polished teak stairs climbed to an open-plan mezzanine bedroom. Between the sofa and staircase was a low oblong coffee table. And beneath the staircase, a doorway into the kitchen, whilst on this doorway's right, a cellar door.

There wasn't a back door. Laco had chosen badly here. Though, she conceded, if a place was blown, it would be surrounded, so a rear bolthole would serve no useful purpose.

Potential weapons within reach were scarce, as she'd found in her recollection; possibly the iron poker in the hearth and the cutlery on the table. Impaling Ilyichev on a fork didn't seem like a viable option, and the knives weren't particularly suitable for throwing. Steak knives, if they'd been out, might have worked, at a pinch. Nothing else would serve.

Just her hands, her feet and her training seemed to stand between her and oblivion. Ironic, she thought, to recall Ishmael and Mordechai earlier; she didn't plan on joining them tonight.

Ilyichev wouldn't risk silhouetting himself in the doorway by switching on the lights: he wouldn't know she was unarmed. He probably didn't know if he'd hit her - though the absence of blood on the loggia would put him on his guard.

Her senses suddenly went into overdrive. A footfall on the boards outside. Hardly discernible, muted by the cool breeze. His gammy leg, else she would not have detected it. Now she understood something of the hate that had emanated from him on the instant of trigger-squeeze. Since the spy swap, he had probably suffered in some way through that injured leg. Perhaps his career had stagnated? Maybe his sex life was affected. No matter how much he tried, he would be hampered a little, always made conscious of his new limitations. All due to her actions.

But now, even though she was straining her mental feelers to the utmost, she could detect no hate at all. No thoughts, in fact.

Not good. Ilyichev had become the cold professional again.

The dacha door swung wide.

Starlight irradiated the polished wooden boards by the door.

Following a lapse of about thirty seconds, during which time he doubtless had his eyes closed to attune to the indoor darkness, Ilyichev bowled through the doorway, diving onto the edge of the thick-piled carpet. Rolling neatly, he came to rest rather loudly against the table leg. Cups rattled in their saucers. Considering he had a bad leg, he moved remarkably fast. She'd expected it but didn't move and continued her imitation of a rock.

Silence. Save for his heavy breathing, though he kept it well under control.

And still no thoughts, no anxiety

Tana rose, unbending lithe limbs. Her nightdress brushed

imperceptibly against her skin.

She stood still. But no, his hearing wasn't pitched delicately enough yet, would in fact be recovering from that jarring knock against the table; his semi-circular canals would be sorting themselves out, adjusting to this alien environment.

If he was as good as she thought, then he would be fully aware in just about a minute.

Holding the mental picture of the room in front of her, she measured off her steps towards the fireplace.

Edging round the high-backed chintz chair, she leaned down, groping for the poker. Her visual scan of the room earlier had been too hurried; the poker was a good four inches further left than she had imagined.

And as she grabbed hold of the cold metal it knocked and rattled against the brass coal-shovel in the stone fireplace.

At the same instant she dropped onto her belly on the sheepskin rug by the hearth, partially shielded by the high-backed chair.

Ilyichev's single shot puffed through the chintz and hit the stone - not far from where the poker had been a second ago. The bullet glanced off the fireplace, shattering a ceramic bowl, then hit the wall to the left with a dull thud. Laco's friend is going to be really pissed about all this damage, she thought.

That was a rifle shot - so, two cartridges fired.

As the after-echo dissipated, Tana crouched on the balls of her feet, the poker held in front of her, listening, hoping for some emotion, some giveaway sign from Ilyichev.

Nothing!

The flash from his gun had signposted his whereabouts as halfway along the edge of the table. In the seconds of noise as the shot ricocheted and she ducked, he would have moved, simply as a precaution.

If she were him, her natural instinct would be to move nearer to the fireplace, away from the open doorway and the treacherous starlight; hoping for a silhouette of her, perhaps: or, just to play safe.

The carpet would have smothered any sound his footsteps made. But her knowledge of the furniture layout helped: he hadn't bumped into any of the dining chairs along the length of the table, nor the chintz chair. And he hadn't crossed the room - or she would have glimpsed a fleeting shadow against the doorway.

She held her breath, rising very slowly. He was obviously restricting his own breathing too. Nevertheless, Tana estimated he must be midway between the chintz chair and the table.

Describing a wide arc, she swung the poker from right to left, full force behind it.

Her guess had been close: the poker met bone and flesh resistance three quarters through its sweeping journey.

Ilyichev couldn't help releasing a squeal of agony. And her mind snatched the acute pain he felt – but no thoughts.

His reflexes were very good. While the rifle clattered distinctly to the floor, he sideswiped in her direction, the edge of his hand catching her wrist just right, inflicting numbing pain.

She backed off as the poker flew out of her hand and clattered over the table, scattering dishes. It bounced against a dining chair, then finally fell with a muted *thump* to the carpet.

Ignoring the pain signals travelling up from her wrist - doubled by the pain thoughts from Ilyichev - Tana crept round behind the chintz chair.

Click! - an automatic's safety being released. He'd moved back, wasn't going to find the rifle but instead was going to rely on a pistol. Most Russian automatics held eight rounds, she recalled. Might have to start counting all over again.

It sounded as though he was between table and bookcase.

At that instant her nightdress snagged on the chair's wing, where some of the stuffing had been shot out.

The slight ripping sound was enough for Ilyichev.

Timing was in fractions of seconds now.

Ilyichev fired.

Instead of trying to retrieve the situation and release the

garment, Tana fell to the floor the same second that she snagged it, ripping the sleeve off completely.

Ilyichev's solitary bullet burned her arm as she hit the carpet.

Slightly disoriented, she knocked her shoulder into the coffee table and he'd heard, firing again, the bullet gouging into the wood surface and zinging off somewhere.

Straining her senses to detect Ilyichev's whereabouts, a part of her mind felt a warm dampness drooling down her ribcage. The shot had been close, grazing her upper inner arm. In her present intense state, the pain was minimal.

He hadn't said a word yet - and was conserving his bullets. No mad volley in the hope that one of them would get her. Two shots down.

She must promote fear or some other strong emotion in him, anything that helped her to identify his location.

Her bare foot stubbed against the fallen rifle. She wouldn't be familiar with it and trying to use it in the dark would lose vital seconds. Of course she had trained to strip down and reassemble a rifle in the dark, but each make was different. She could use it as a club, but it was unwieldy. Go for a diversion. In one swift movement she bent down, grabbed it and hurled the weapon across the room, onto the table, roughly in Ilyichev's direction.

Some crockery smashed loudly; the rifle must have slid along its length for she heard the bookcase front shatter. What a mess! It precipitated an immediate response: two shots this time. Four down, four to go?

Briefly, she snatched his thoughts: *Damn the bitch*!

He was rattled now.

Tana picked up a heavy silver dinner fork, hurled it. Tunefully, it hit the wall. Obviously not appreciative of music, he fired again. Only once. Was that three shots left?

Keep counting the bullets.

As well as that, she had also snatched the impression of eyes straining in the dark, of a heart pumping slightly faster; of the man's annoyance over the poor control of his bodily systems.

She knew where he was now. At the head of the table, by the wall bookcase or what was left of it. Between the left-hand corner and the fireplace.

She unfastened her nightdress ribbons, silently stepped out of it and loosely bundled up the garment.

'I'm here!' she said - and wasn't when the shot came. Two left?

He fired again, fearing she would come at him in a rush. Instead, she threw the nightdress at him.

Then she detected a sharp intake of breath, the shuffle of feet and a fleeting sense of panic - his heartbeat pounding - as he struggled with the garment.

Now she rushed him.

Clamping onto his gun arm at her second attempt, she crashed a well-placed knee upwards and felt it sink into his soft vulnerable groin. She followed up by throwing her whole weight against his torso.

Ilyichev thudded against the bookcase. Glass tinkled. She was so close, she fancied she could hear his insides churning.

Surprise weakened him. But not enough.

With two lucky counter-jabs against her ribcage, he broke free, though dropping his gun in the process.

But his senses were now awry, she realised. Fear seeped into his sweating pores as he strained to stare into blackness. Breathing unsteadily, heaving on air. Hate was surfacing also and there was nothing he could do about it. The best he could hope for was to escape.

He charged like a mad bull for the starlit door.

Tana kicked a dining chair in his way. As he stumbled, she was there and landed a fist on his jaw, flooring him. His hand grasped instinctively at the tablecloth and as he fell he pulled it with him, upsetting the dinner things with a clamorous noise. Why not? Every other damned thing was broken already.

Ilyichev groaned and dazedly rolled onto his back.

Tana retrieved the fallen automatic and in the time it takes to blink she checked the weapon - there was one shell left. She levelled it on him.

'Don't make any sudden moves, Ilyichev,' she growled in Russian, 'or I'll perform my own version of a vasectomy on you!'

She righted the standing lamp and switched it on. At least that wasn't broken. Bathed in its circle of light, Ilyichev lay back and screwed up his eyes against the glare. The expletives that rushed through his mind and carried to her were varied: and one she hadn't heard before.

Had the traitor tipped him off, she wondered. 'Who sent you?'

He raised his eyes, his quick intake of breath indicating all too clearly what he thought of her naked sylph-like physique. 'That's for you to find out, if you're good enough.'

Tana shrugged. 'I asked who sent you.' She kicked his gammy leg. Ilyichev swore, livid.

'This isn't British soil we're on,' she said. 'I don't have to be reticent about my methods here.' She aimed the gun at his healthy leg. 'Make them a matching pair, should I?'

His thoughts scurried maddeningly. But nowhere could she detect someone giving him orders. Fear slunk behind his veneer of bravado; she was totally unable to produce the name or image of anyone who gave him information or orders on her whereabouts.

'Well, I'll be damned,' she said. 'You weren't sent here, were you?'

The surprised look on his face told her she was right. Another lousy poker player.

So, the hideout was still secure.

Ilyichev grinned. 'I nearly got you - if I'd gone to Kasayiev as soon as I'd seen you, we might've had the tables turned now.'

Kasayiev was here, in Prague? She knew him of old. A formidable KGB major who was now going to seed. Once he had been effective but his weakness for hashish had affected his judgement over the last couple of years. Still, she'd better not underestimate the man. It was quite possible that he was the one responsible for her tail at the airport. He was bound to have some kind of dossier on her.

Ilyichev shrugged. 'You won't get out alive. Whatever you do to me, I'll be meeting you in Hell very soon!'

The alarming aspect of his speech was that he sincerely believed it. He was convinced she would fail and die.

Precognitive images had impinged in the past, of times beyond this mission, of other missions, though all the details were of a hazy dreamlike quality.

But there were many avenues for Time to follow: this she knew from experience.

Aided by her precognitive ability, she had often altered events by recognising the incident from a second-sight viewing and breaking the spell by changing the occurrence. Second-guessing *déjà vu*, she called it. As though each time-continuum were a different corridor, and each action and reaction creating subdivisions of the corridor, each a different turning point in the fabric of Time.

So, although she had seen herself ahead of this now, it was still possible that she would die on this assignment. The precognitive images could be reflections of other time-corridors, other lives, stemming from other turning points. The thought never failed to shake her a little.

The click of a gun reached her ears.

She pivoted.

A silhouette in the doorway.

The lights flashed on, blinding.

Kazakhstan

Yakunin sat upright in bed, alarmed by the sudden pain in his inner arm and the abrupt darkness that surrounded him. He was covered in sweat, his pyjamas clinging uncomfortably to his muscular body. The red night light of the dormitory filled his eyes but the after-images remained, of a woman's life being threatened, of extreme concentration and, confusingly, a Russian man's all-consuming hate.

He shuddered with the realisation that for brief seconds he had been seeing through the woman's eyes and experiencing her feelings. And then he'd woken up.

Sitting on the edge of his bed, he towelled his neck and chest and wanted to know the woman's name. He couldn't read her mind, just capture her thoughts. And you have to listen to a lot of thoughts before the mind's owner uses his or her own name. It was clear she was strong, resourceful and intelligent. She seemed to exude confidence in her own abilities. Yet she seemed to neglect her psychic side, just took it for granted. These were the main impressions he recalled from his sleep-drenched psychotronic episode.

The woman fascinated him. If he wasn't careful, he'd become obsessed with her. And if that happened, his very important work would suffer and he could end up being shipped out of The Group, perhaps even being despatched to Angola or Cuba.

He got up and walked to the window. Snow covered the desolate land as far as he could see.

At one time the view had excited him, but now he felt oppressed, trapped and manipulated. Quickly, abruptly, he channelled such thoughts deep down into his subconscious, in case Bublyk was hovering around the dorms.

For the time being he would keep to himself this knowledge about the woman and their strange relationship. Somehow, there was a strong link between him and the woman, the psychic connection so powerful that he didn't have to be wired up to the Viewing Room's apparatus in order to share her thoughts and vision.

Yakunin suddenly felt very insecure.

Czechoslovakia

'Will he be secure enough down there?' Tana asked.

Laco sipped some coffee. 'Yes, the ropes should prevent him from moving. And, as you saw, there's only one small window. The door's sturdy enough - and locked.'

'I still don't like it. He has the kind of hate that festers. You know?'

Slowly, Laco nodded. 'Only too well, Tana.'

Her hand crossed the table; his felt stronger, more sinewy than last time. 'It's like it used to be - though we're both a little older and a little wiser.' She smiled. 'Were you able to convince your cell to re-form?'

The abrupt switch, from nostalgia to business, seemed to put Laco a little off-guard. He wiped his mouth meditatively and grinned. 'Older, maybe, Tana - but you haven't changed. Not a bit!'

'No, I have. I'm slowing down, I think. A couple of years ago I'd have overcome Ilyichev much faster - and -' she indicated the starred bookcase glass - 'with less mess. My psychic resources could be on the wane, I fear.'

His eyes widened, almost in disbelief.

'No, it's commonplace. Most psychics deteriorate in their late thirties; by the time they're in their seventies their prowess is a mere memory.' She pursed her lips, shook her head. 'Ilyichev's fear-control was so good I should've concentrated more on hearing than prescient sensing.' Tana shrugged. 'Besides, I still don't understand how I tick - nobody does. While I'm able, I should be helping our researchers. I've neglected them.' James Fisk's own words, come back to haunt her, she realised, amused.

'You've got to rest sometime, Tana.'

'How do you know I haven't been?' A mischievous smile played her lips. 'Resting. Between assignments. Like an actor.'

'Torrence was a very bad agent. Or perhaps I was over-persuasive. I asked about you.' He caught her astonished look and sighed. 'He was so anxious to make friends, he told me about your last two assignments - in Hong Kong and Mombasa - at least the little that he knew.'

Tana filed the information. If Torrence's showing hadn't already cast his career in shadow, this little snippet surely would. More than anything now she wanted to ensure that Torrence was dismissed. He was a liability, and a deadly dangerous one at that. You can't unlearn knowledge. Was he honourable enough to go into secluded early retirement? She somehow doubted it. This left the unpalatable final sanction - a convenient accident.

After locking Ilyichev in the cellar and clearing away the mess, they had reset the table with fresh crockery. Laco helped her prepare another snack in the kitchen - one of her favourites, *klobásy*, spicy fried beef sausages, flavoured with mustard on rye bread. Then she showered again. Laco had insisted on treating her superficial wound, taping the bullet burn with gentle, experienced fingers. At this time he treated her as one of his wounded recruits, nothing more.

However, when the meal was finished and they each cupped a glass of Jelinek slivovice, he viewed her as a desirable woman.

They lay on the sheepskin hearthrug, in front of the roaring log fire. The wood crackled and sparked, but they were far enough away to avoid the occasional red-hot splinter.

No longer a wounded comrade, Tana lay back on the rug alongside him.

Laco leaned over, unfastened the short terry towel housecoat she'd borrowed, gently spread it wide, baring her generous breasts that were no longer so firm. Her stomach muscles were well defined. He held the glass of plum brandy against her belly; its sudden coldness tingled, perversely pleasurable, but soon warmed to her body heat.

'You know,' she said, 'I'm thirty-eight and you're what, twenty-five?'

His free hand traced a finger down to her pubic curls. 'You didn't have any qualms seven years ago. I was a mere youth then.'

'Yes, but I was being generous with my charms. Part of your training, no?'

He dabbed a finger in his brandy and moistened her labia. 'Did I pass?'

She opened her legs slightly. 'Most certainly. I suspect you're ready for the advanced lesson now.'

'My God, you mean there's an *advanced* lesson?'

She nodded, grinning, and slowly sat up and gently removed his questing hand. 'That's very nice, but all night you've steered clear of what you did while Ilyichev came to play at broken homes.'

He mock-pouted and sucked his finger. 'I know. I've hit snags - it's difficult terrain,' he said awkwardly.

'I know they don't trust me. I'm an unknown quantity - and a woman.'

There was no rancour in her voice. She understood the feelings of his cell. They'd been betrayed once; even the persuasive tongues of Janek and the others might not sway them.

Laco swallowed his brandy. 'Yes. Mainly because you're a woman.'

Tana shrugged out of the housecoat and it fell off her shoulders. She reached for the brandy glass in his hand and sipped it. 'I must see them.' Her lips glistened in the firelight. 'That's settled, isn't it?' She placed his glass alongside hers on the hearth.

He smiled. 'They don't understand.' He sought her mouth with his. 'You're more, much more than just a woman, Tana.'

And in the exquisite throes of their lovemaking one special private part of her mind saddened, for Laco was right, so horribly right. She had known love, idealistic and physical, and she loved Laco as much as she was capable. But always her psyche must provide an impenetrable barrier between her and her lover.

Once, when she had let an older man, Paul, talk her into letting him 'go all the way', she had absently spread out her prescient awareness as the man she loved entered her. Contrasts of pain and ecstasy, not too dissimilar, threshed in her body. Then she grasped hold of Paul's thoughts, just at the pinnacle. The soaring onrush of pleasure from him accentuated her own, pushed her

70

into multiple orgasms. But his thoughts had not been of her, nor of their lovemaking: he'd been reliving some lost love of long ago, far away, long-since dead. After that disturbing experience she always shut down her mind's receptors at intimate moments.

Afterwards, Laco lifted her in his arms. 'I'd better carry you to bed now,' he chuckled. 'I doubt if I'll have the strength later!'

He slowly climbed the open-plan stairs. His gesture reminded her of their first meeting. On completion of her mission in Odessa she'd been diverted to Prague, as whispers of a Russian arms build-up were spreading like wildfire. She had passed through previously, during Dubcek's eight amazing months of the Prague Spring and had been heartened by the signs of liberalisation. For a weak moment she had even dared hope that it would work. As Dubcek said, after the invasion: 'We began to trust the people, and they began to trust us.' Then she had witnessed the Soviet invasion, masterminded by General Pavlovsky, a man she almost killed.

'Just like the first time, isn't it?' he remarked, lowering her onto the bed.

'Yes. But everything's changed since then.' She grew serious. 'When can I meet your Doubting Thomases?'

He stood by the bed, erect member pointing at her. 'After you've reacquainted yourself with my John Thomas, I think you English call it, don't you?' He grinned.

'Business first, Laco,' she said with a smile, gently squeezing his scrotum. 'Your stamina's undimmed, I see, even if you are older.'

Laco slid between the sheets, discarding the feather bolsters to the floor, and snuggled up close and she caressed him. 'Then you guessed they've already set their minds on a meeting?'

'I think your reticence is quite becoming - but I must make my decision, irrespective of how many risks you fear.'

He grimaced, half-amusedly. 'Am I that obvious?'

'Sorry. I'm psychic, remember?'

He grinned, then turned serious. 'Well, it's Demek. He says we can't trust you until you prove you're worthy of our trust.' He glanced away and shrugged apologetically. 'He's young, a bit headstrong. But he has the interests of his group at heart.'

'I understand. And he has influence over your cell members?'

He nodded reluctantly.

'I see. But you'd better chastise him - before his headstrong ideas do worse damage than any ten Torrences.'

'Soon I will face that problem. But in the meantime, we *need* Demek's men. He's making a lot of noise - and the others tend to listen.'

'And what about your authority? Don't they listen to you?'

'Just like before, I'm solely in charge - as you've already seen. But we share sectors, responsibilities. One group's presently responsible for propaganda leaflets; another for culling information from the streets; another infiltrating military establishments; and so on. So I can't influence them all so easily. The headstrong might pull in other directions, if I'm not careful. But we need to believe in you, Tana. Certainly, I could stand up and shout down Demek, and they'd listen and follow me. But that's not enough, is it?'

Yes, he had aged beyond his years. God, he'd only been nineteen when they met. She nodded. 'After this latest jolt with Torrence, they're adrift, unsure of themselves.' She smiled, guiding his hand between her legs. 'I'm willing to brazen it out with this Demek.'

Silence followed, except for the gentle caressing of skin against skin.

Then, hesitantly, Laco whispered, 'He wants you to meet him in the courtyard of Hradcany Castle.'

'In the open? He must be mad! What does *that* prove?'

'Oh, I told him he was insane to suggest such a thing. But his argument's sound. If he's bold enough to risk discovery out in the open, so should you be. I think he's testing you.'

'Immature.' She sighed, partly with frustration over histrionic youths like Demek and partly because she was enjoying Laco's gentle ministrations.

'He's definitely trouble,' she said. 'I'll go, of course. But could he be our traitor?'

Laco bit his lip. 'The thought reluctantly crossed my mind after he suggested the meeting. It's possible.' He shook his head. 'But no, it's too obvious. If you were caught, all fingers would point to him.'

'Fingers... hmm... don't stop now.'

'I have no intention of stopping just yet,' he assured her.

'So. He's taking a risk as well, isn't he? If I get caught, he knows his future in the underground is finished.'

'Yes.' Her pelvis arched and he moved deeper inside.

'It's still immature of him. And what happens afterwards - assuming we survive this farcical meeting?'

'I was saving this snippet for second-last. One of my men has been approached by a new contact in Pilsen. It sounds genuine. And yet...'

'A subtle trap?'

'Not so subtle if we can think of it, surely? Could be a trap though. They know you're here - that Tatra tail we shook off proves that.'

'So?' She moaned.

'But I'm tempted.'

'Me too, right now...'

'If you're willing...'

'Don't I sound and feel willing right now?'

He grinned. 'The contact talked of a new secret weapon.'

Tana whistled. 'Interesting.' So much for this being a routine repair-and-rebuild assignment. 'Agreed. We'll organise a meeting of cells - and see this contact at Pilsen.' She looked at him, eyelids heavy with passion. 'You said that was second-last on your agenda. What's last?'

He removed his hand and rolled on top of her. 'This.'

CHAPTER FIVE: Hradcany

Against Laco's wishes, Tana first went to Hotel Alcron to collect her suitcases. 'I need a change of clothes,' she told him, though he objected, saying that he preferred to see her naked. 'And no,' she added, 'you can't afford spending valuable dollars on me at Tuzex.'

Tuzex, where almost any delicacy can be purchased if you have the marks, dollars, sterling or francs: American and European cigarettes, Dutch and Cuban cigars, Scotch whisky, French cognac and wine, Swiss and English chocolates, American fruit juices and cornflakes and EEC fashion textiles. And you were willing to queue. Because queues were endemic in the Eastern Bloc. She felt sure that even the coffins queued to get into the cemetery.

She had another reason why she wanted to go back to the hotel - she wanted to pick up a tail. It was always better to know the opposition.

Grishin's little eyes nearly popped on seeing her enter the hotel. Giving her a few minutes, he then crossed the road and entered.

In his ill-fitting suit, Grishin leant on the reception desk counter and flashed his green ID card. 'Was that the Englishwoman - Standish?'

The receptionist agreed readily enough, sweat budding suddenly at sight of the KGB crest. He haltingly explained that she had obtained alternative accommodation and was collecting her belongings. 'She hasn't even stayed here yet so how can she not like the hotel, eh?' he asked, waving his arms, eyeing the lugubrious place.

Grishin slunk outside and entered a green telephone booth across the road. Through its red-framed windows he had an uninterrupted view of the hotel entrance steps. He shoved a 25-heller piece in and dialled Kasayiev's six-figure number.

'Major!'

'What is it, Grishin?' Kasayiev's speech was slurred; doubtless, on his fourth consecutive hashish cigarette.

Grishin would dearly love to be reassigned to a new boss; he felt it in his bones that Kasayiev was on a slippery slope on his way to Siberia. But until that happened, he'd better be obedient. 'The Standish woman, sir! She's here!'

The Major's slur vanished in a heartbeat. 'Where is *here*, you damned imbecile?'

'Oh, here - the Alcron.'

'Look, Grishin.' A pause. 'I've changed my mind. We can't afford having this woman loose - she's too valuable. We'll smash Valchik's cell another time. I'm going to send you some men - then you're to arrest her. Don't tackle her on your own. Understand?'

This was more like it, Grishin thought. 'Yes. I...' He spotted Tana descending the wide hotel steps. 'She's coming - coming out now, Major - a car - can't see the number from here - it's pulling up at the kerbside! She's... no, she's not getting in.' His voice ended in a squeak.

'Well, follow her! Wherever she goes! My men will be at that booth inside ten minutes. Make a note of the number you're calling from. Contact them there. Got it?'

'Yes, Major.' Grishin thought that the Major's thought processes were not so slow after all; that was good thinking on the spur of the moment, he conceded.

Now Tana was sauntering through the milling crowds and Grishin's heart sank. 'I'll do that.' He slammed down the phone and consigned its number to memory, bolted out of the booth and squirmed through the crowds. As he hurried, he kept repeating the phone number to himself. If she hadn't been wearing that distinctive black fox-fur hat, he'd have lost her for sure.

The street was seething: car horns honked continually, sirens blared and trams rumbled. Lunatic drivers and motorcyclists tried to mow down impetuous lunatic pedestrians.

Tana adjusted her fox-fur hat; it should provide an ideal marker for the poor bastard. As she'd stood at the base of the hotel steps and lazily eyed up and down the street, one of the noisiest arteries of downtown Prague, she hadn't missed the unkempt tail trying to look innocent in the phone booth. Poor sod.

At that moment, Janek pulled up in a little grey Fiat. He was on time, which was to his credit. Timing was everything in this business.

She bundled her two cases in the back. 'I think I'll walk to the Castle - I have ample time.'

Janek just stared, spectacles glinting in the wintry sun. 'My orders...'

'Oh, forget your orders, Janek. I want to be alone in this. Laco will understand.'

He shrugged, his look indicating that perhaps Demek and the others were right, and this business wasn't suitable for a woman - especially one who seemed so impetuous.

'Meet me at Tankistu Square in two hours. In the meantime, why don't you stroll in Letná Park and admire the statue that isn't there any more.' The thirty-metre statue of Stalin was blown up when Khrushchev took over.

He scowled, not amused. 'If I could find somewhere to park!'

'Go on, Janek,' she said soothingly. 'Enjoy the fine weather while it's still with us, all right?'

His angry slit of a mouth curved just a little. 'Take care,' he offered and drove off.

Tana sighed, feeling that perhaps she had won an ally in Janek. At least he sounded as if he was concerned for her welfare.

Right now she needed to meet an undercover agent unknown to her Czech friends - or even to Merrick.

Catching a glimpse in a *cukrârny* window, she was reassured to see her shadow had left the phone booth and had latched onto her. The worried white face looked faintly absurd, reflected above two obscenely large chocolates topped with whipped cream. 'Weight Watchers' would have their work cut out in this city, she thought, licking her lips in a Pavlovian response.

She turned onto the great sweep of Wenceslas Square, flanked by trees and quality shops, and wondered how many other Ilyichevs would spot her. At least she had now formulated a plan to make use of him.

Tana passed some drab shops. The outdoor beerstands were not unduly suffering because of the despised regime. Long queues of both sexes and all ages stood outside the meat shops, probably waiting for the next batch of *horky parky,* if they were lucky.

Halfway along the long broad avenue, she could already see the top of the hill. Looking down was the huge and forbidding National Museum of Bohemia, and, barely discernible at this angle, in the middle of the road, the imposing equestrian statue of Myslbek's Saint Vaclav backed by a brown marble fountain covered with beautiful small water jets and flanked by other patron saints of Bohemia.

Just over seven years ago she'd first met Laco here, under the horse's tail, the statue plastered with posters espousing 'the new freedoms'.

A couple of trams pulled up on either side of the Saint, like suckling babes returning to mother.

Saint Vaclav. What would good King Wenceslas have to say about recent history on that very plinth where he rode? She had actually seen an eleven-year-old boy shot dead because he pushed a Czech flag down the barrel of a Soviet tank. In those first days of the invasion, over seventy Czechs and Slovaks were killed and hundreds wounded.

And here, too, twenty-one-year-old Jan Palach set fire to himself; she shivered, wondering how he had coped with so much pain; he died in hospital two days later. She'd been working in Hong Kong at the time - January '69 - and read with some horror of the defiant gesture. Before he died, he'd said, 'My act has fulfilled its purpose, let nobody else do it.' Mourners obliterated the newly painted signs reading 'Red Army Square' with 'Jan Palach Square' while chanting 'Russians Go Home!'

Later, she learned that the Soviets moved Palach's body to a secret place to stop his grave becoming a focus for further protest. The communists knew only too well - and rightly feared - the power of the people, since their corrupt system had been spawned by the massed protest of the Revolution.

Crossing the tramlines she heard the overhead wires singing the approach of a tram. She hurried to the kerb. The low winter sun's rays reflected from the enormously tall clock tower on the southern side of St Vitus's Cathedral, way over the Vltava, dominating the lesser spires of Prague with its open belfries and onion-shaped domes.

She left the street by Tuzex's main antique shop and lost her tail with ease, by simply taking off her hat and thrusting it inside her coat. Not the old hat trick? Nothing less. Mike Clayton would have been impressed, she thought.

Walking along Perlova Street, she came to a square with a fountain in the centre - where the old charcoal market of fourteenth century had harboured smithies and the miners' quarters.

A left turn, under more arches, and she eventually came upon another Tuzex. Here, on the corner of Skorepska Street, she imagined she could hear the distant echoes of Mozart's serenade, *Eine Kleine Nachtmusik* as she approached Number 420. Above the door a plaque announced that 'Mozart played here as a guest in 1787'. Tana recalled that Prague was one of Mozart's most favoured cities; his 38th Symphony was first performed here and thus became the 'Prague Symphony'. She couldn't blame him, this city held a fascination close to her own heart too. A pity it wasn't free.

Passing under an archway, she slowly whistled the Allegro from the first movement of Mozart's immortal little serenade.

And another whistler took up the melody. *Contact.*

Tana entered Parizska Street, the area of the former Ghetto. Here, in the heart of the Old Town, were the proud edifices of the Jewish faith. These synagogues told a tragic tale: the extinction of almost 90,000 Jews who lived in Czechoslovakia before the war.

Tana made a quiet little pilgrimage to the Gothic Pinkas Synagogue in Josefska Street. Painted on the walls inside were over 77,000 names of men, women and children from Bohemia and Moravia - all liquidated by the Nazis. Individuals with the promise of a future; potential architects, chemists, surgeons, artists, all slaughtered. Generations of memories and love obliterated. Innocent families wiped out, just like hers.

She had been unable to shed a tear; yet when she stopped outside and viewed the cemetery's tightly packed graves, with rooks hovering in trees and over the higgledy-piggledy tombstones, the sight moved her.

It had been a long time since she gave her heritage any thought. An overwhelming desire to 'go home' to Israel - a land she'd never visited - seeped into her, no doubt a similar experience felt by thousands of others.

But she was committed now. Her world was Interprises. And, she made a promise to James, psychic research. Next year Jerusalem, perhaps.

Here, too, she met another contact, though this one didn't whistle Mozart.

After an intriguing conversation, she left him and turned onto the cobbled pavements of the waterfront. She walked across Karluv Most, up to Hradcany Castle.

She only hoped that her tail - Grishin, her first contact called him - would stay lost while she talked with Demek.

Acacias shaded the pavement. Parked Skoda tourist coaches glistened in the wintry sunlight.

Tana walked in the wake of a tourist group, past the khaki-clad sentries on their wooden platforms, through the main entrance.

The gossiping group stopped beside some wrought-iron railings. Giant statues on pillars looked down onto them: 'The monogram here - MTI - stands for *Maria Theresa Imperatrix*,' the shapely guide explained, pointing to the railings.

Tana joined them through into the first courtyard, the Court of Honour, though she thought honour was sadly lacking in the castle's present inhabitant and his regime.

As the guide enlarged effusively on the rococo style of the surrounding buildings with their sculptured coats-of-arms and military trophies, Tana attached herself to a smaller disinterested group who were heading for the Matyas Gate at the courtyard's far side.

Once through the gate, she was in the Second Courtyard looking upon the north side's modernised ground-level stables, now a picture gallery, beneath the Spanish Hall. The presidential flag was flying - so Gustáv Husák was at home, she mused. Not a nice man, he was the great survivor who was imprisoned in the '50s by Stalinists as a 'bourgeois nationalist' yet was rehabilitated in the next decade and eventually took the reins of power from Dubcek. Once in power, he dismantled his predecessor's reforms and instituted the 'normalisation' process, invoking a police state with thousands of informers, crushing freedom and bleaching colour from the people's lives. Not a nice man, indeed. Grey people, grey buildings.

From this vantage point it was possible to see St Vitus Cathedral, Prague's Westminster, which sprouted up from and divided in half the Third Courtyard. Also, she could see the two eastern towers, Daliborka and the White Tower, both however dwarfed by the Cathedral itself.

The tourists were spreading themselves out as she crossed the courtyard. Some were looking up with hand-shaded eyes at the tall Bishop's Tower on the northern side of the square.

But Tana's attention was aimed at the centre of the courtyard. Here, a sandstone fountain stood alongside a well which was covered with a wrought-iron lid. A solitary man studied the fountain and he had his back to her.

Tana assumed it was Demek trying to look interested in the fountain's construction.

Briefly closing her eyes, she damped down the external sounds and concentrated on her immediate surroundings. It wasn't easy as there were many people in the courtyard and immediate area, all with thoughts of their own. She persisted, blanking out the mundane, and after a few moments she felt confident that Demek was alone. There were no thoughts from anyone else near him that suggested complicity or a threat. She opened her eyes to see the tourists moving ahead to view the Riding School and garden.

A second group of tourists entered the courtyard as she stood beside him and said, 'A great pity about that piece by El Grechko.'

On the second day of the Soviet invasion, a lone marksman in one of the National Museum's high windows had shot the commander of a Russian tank as the vehicle idled in the street below. Russian machine guns at once raked the whole building, stone chips flying, windows shattering. The marksman was unhurt; the C-in-C of the troops who fired back was called Marshal Grechko. The facade had since been cleaned up, primarily because people persisted in pointing to the scarred stone, saying, 'A nice bit by El Grechko.' The regime was not to be laughed at! As if.

He said, 'A shame about the facelift, yes.'

She smiled. Passwords exchanged. Quaint. Yet still effective. 'Now, Demek, let's get down to business. Where can we talk?'

'Did you bring a car?' His lips curled in a sneer. He was obviously one of the many carless citizens and took it personally.

'No - I walked.'

Blond eyebrows arched. Wearing a homburg hat, he was shabbily dressed in a threadbare brown suit. About twenty-two; more tense than Laco had been even at nineteen. A little unstable but, she felt, blatantly patriotic.

He couldn't resist looking around the courtyard. 'You were not followed, I hope?'

'I might ask you the same, Demek. But I don't want to spend the day verbally sparring with you. I want you to promise me that your men will join Laco for the breakout.'

He hunched his shoulders, noncommittally. 'I will listen; but I cannot guarantee you will have my men's support.'

Thorny little creature. She thought of what Jiri had said about Demek whilst her tail Grishin had seethed outside in Skorepksa Street.

Jiri had said, 'Demek isn't your traitor, Umbra.' She'd chosen the code name herself. It had been the name of her father's submarine when his crew pulled her out of the Baltic. 'If there's a traitor, it ain't Demek.' Jiri was most emphatic. Trained by the CIA, he was competent, reliable, a freelance.

'I'm onto something - one of the Central Committee's clerks, she's hungry for it...' He winked. 'Well, anyway, she's heard mention of the name you're interested in - in connection with another. I'm seeing her again later.'

'Is she reliable?'

'Hell, no! If she was, do you think my seduction routine would work? Nope - I'd be on my way to the salt mines by now!'

'I'm sure you enjoy playing the Don Juan, don't you?'

'It's only the sex that keeps me sane, Umbra. What's your reason?'

'Sex helps combat weight gain,' she said, 'but I can't vouch for my sanity.'

'Really?' he said, pinching his midriff. 'Clearly, I need more sex, eh?'

'I'm not offering, Jiri. Anything on my shadow?'

'Yep,' he said, turning businesslike. 'Positive ID. Name's Grishin. Works for Kasayiev. KGB Major - mysteriously seconded to the StB.'

'I've heard of Kasayiev before,' she said. 'I think he's here to get to me.'

Jiri whistled. 'Well, he's being put up at Number 33 - hence my amorous interest in sweet pimply Anna.' He sighed with mock concern. 'It's a hard life!'

Tana laughed. She knew that Jiri was probably living on his nerves, hour by hour, and only joked to ease the tension. He'd been in the field at least two years, while the most she managed at any one time was about three months. The constant threat of discovery wore you down, she knew, and she marvelled that Jiri had lasted so long. They shook hands. 'I'll be in touch,' she said.

As she left, Grishin missed her, as she had intended. Jiri got away unseen.

Now Tana said, her tone firm, 'We need your support, Demek. And two men with strong nerves.'

'Like me, my followers are sick of this "heroic silent fight" we're waging,' Demek responded. 'Instead of listening devices, tape recorders and other stuff, why can't you supply us with weapons? Can't you appreciate what it's like to live without proper freedom?'

Remembering her early childhood in Warsaw, she kept quiet.

'It's all right for you British,' he went on. 'You can always get out, go home.'

That taunt cut a nerve just a little, because that's more or less what she did in '68. Left Laco and the others to their fate. No choice. Duty called. It sounded quite hollow now though.

'But *we're* here all the time,' wailed Demek. '*We* have to face the music!'

'I've heard enough, thank you.' Her voice took on a menacing, iron force. 'I'm not interested in your childish mewling! I had heard you were reliable and brave. Brave men don't moan, they *act*! We're trying to get two innocent young people out of Ruzyne. Will you help?'

Demek paled. Tana hadn't expected her tone to affect him so strongly. Then, admittedly a bit late, her sixth sense warned her.

'*Statni Bespecnost*!' Demek hissed, staring. He seemed rooted to the spot.

Tana whirled. At the courtyard entrance she recognised Grishin advancing with two bulky StB colleagues in tow.

CHAPTER SIX: Absinthe

The crowds around them seemed to be aware that something was amiss. The nearest guide was forcefully shepherding her tourists out of the way, towards the Holy Rood Chapel in the south-east corner of the courtyard. Behind them Tana glimpsed a khaki uniform, the soldier wearing a blue hat banded with cerise: presidential guard from the main entrance, with a rifle, the only weapon in sight, which was a blessing, she supposed.

Grishin hurried ahead of the others. Doubtless the fool was anxious for the glory. His weedy face twisted into an evil grimace as he grabbed Demek's arm.

Demek swore and ineffectually tried jerking free.

Tana's swift side-kick sank into Grishin's back just over his kidneys and the force of the blow broke his grip on Demek and sent Grishin cannoning into the fountain.

One of the secret police shouted.

She grasped Grishin's arm and heaved him round in the path of his oncoming comrades. The weight of the man and the sharp quick movement tore the dressing Laco had placed over her arm's bullet-burn and she winced with the sudden pain.

'Get out!' she snarled at Demek. 'I'll hold them off. *Go on!*'

For all his rebellious nature, Demek's instinctive hesitation was only a second. He scurried across the courtyard and through into the Third, heading for the back of the Cathedral and Golden Lane, to lose himself amidst the numerous stalls along the laneway.

Grishin's flailing body bundled into the leading StB agent,

unbalancing him.

Tana sidestepped them and sank a lightning-fast instep in the other agent's solar plexus. He doubled up in time to receive the rigid knife-edge of her hand on his neck. Her bandaged arm was already throbbing as she gritted her teeth and grabbed the man and swung him at the ceremonial sentry. As the two collided the sentry dropped the rifle he'd been raising.

Grishin, half-supporting himself on the courtyard's stone flags, called to the onlookers to apprehend Tana, explaining that she had escaped from an asylum.

But she met no resistance. The bystanders, having no love for the secret police, backed off and Tana raced past them and through the courtyards and out into the square.

Shallow steps, some two hundred of them, fringed the Castle on the town side. She descended them at a jog-trot, conscious of many eyes on her.

At the foot she caught her breath and turned right by the Red Cross building and came to a small slope.

Gaining her second wind, she hurried down Kamecka Street, turned left at the end, to find herself in a square that was virtually divided in two by the imposing church of Saint Nicholas and its adjacent buildings. Franz Kafka was born near here, though the actual house was demolished. He'd have been unsurprised at the schizoid nature of the Soviet mind, she mused, stopping for a moment to ease her pulse.

Crossing in the shadows of the church's large green dome and the Town Hall's slender clock tower, she faltered a moment at the next waste-bin and dumped the fox-fur hat.

At the far end of the road she could make out the Gothic towers of Karluv Most. If driving had been permitted across there, Janek could have been waiting here instead of at Tankistu Square.

Now that she was among numerous pedestrians, she slowed her pace to attract as little attention as possible. She was definitely getting too old for this, she thought. Well, it was ten years since she performed the most intensive training at Bradbury Lines. The annual fitness test came nowhere near. Fortunately, her powers of recuperation and recovery were still strong.

Grishin might think she was intent on heading back across Karluv Most, into the Old Town. She hoped so. He'd either employed a second tail or else guessed remarkably accurately on her whereabouts. Or he was just lucky.

Unless of course someone else talked. 'Breed a little distrust and your work's virtually done for you,' said Mike Clayton in one of those moments when they'd been staking out a building and whiled away the time talking about dictatorships and oppressive regimes they'd infiltrated. Dear old Mike - was he still on his archaeological dig in Afghanistan?

Even though her photographic memory was as reliable as ever, on a couple of occasions she feared she had taken a wrong turning in the many narrow streets. At almost every corner she was confronted by statues and clocks - typical of the whole city. This was one place you could venture out without a wristwatch and never worry what the time was. She hoped that her time wasn't running out.

As she moved through the narrow streets, she put out psychic feelers, testing for any hint of threat; adrenalin was linked with telepathy and those seeking her would be pumping the stuff as if it was going out of fashion. Fear of failure did that. Her enemies would be unwittingly sending out psychic signals of their presence. She might detect them in time to save herself.

Kazakhstan
Yakunin screwed up his eyes, his mind bombarded with old buildings, clocks, statues, places he'd never seen before. It wasn't like the last time, when she'd been in the dark. He could detect no actual threat to the English woman but she was using her psychic powers forcefully in some kind of self-defence tactic.

Reluctantly, he lifted his eyes from the map and pressed the buzzer.

Bublyk was by his side in seconds. 'Have you detected her again?'

'Yes, professor, but it isn't strong. Just images of buildings, streets - as if they posed a threat to her...'

'Keep at it!' he demanded.

'A river... an island... If ... Oh, sorry, comrade professor, but I've lost the link.'

'Damn!' Bublyk said, thumping his fist into his palm. 'We need better equipment!'

As long as he doesn't want better psychics, Yakunin reflected and hastily submerged that thought.

Czechoslovakia

Tana skirted the tributary Certovka, running parallel with the Vltava. On the Kampe Island, houses reached to the water's edge, steps dipping into the water. Silhouettes of old mill wheels, rusted and idle, lent an air of mystery to the island. The rest of 'Prague's Venice' sprouted a park, a favourite haunt for lovers. It would have provided a tempting refuge - if Janek hadn't been waiting at Tankistu.

Weaving through the diplomatic section, in front of embassies and legations, the doorways to asylum were most beckoning. On some missions abroad she'd been attached to the British Embassy, actually building business links in her guise as a representative of International Enterprises. But this visit had been so low-key, Merrick hadn't even informed the ambassador of her presence in the country.

She was very aware of the infighting in London. Many in MI6 wanted Sir Gerald's outfit closed down. Fortunately, he had the ear of 'C' himself and several powerful ministers. Yet if there was a traitor in Interprises, then the main argument for the organisation was torpedoed below the waterline. Sir Gerald had created Interprises shortly after the Burgess and MacLean débâcle to provide an alternative secret service organisation that wasn't riddled with moles.

Her turning up on the embassy doorstep unexpectedly would give Sir Gerald's opponents plenty of ammunition. So she squashed such thoughts and hurried on.

Tana passed the base of a steeply terraced garden park. Wending down this fertile hill were flights of steps and pathways and a cable car. She fancied she saw a couple of figures darting along the terraces; another purposefully leapt off the cable car. Grishin's reinforcements had arrived.

The flowering gardens of Tankistu Square were dominated by a stone platform, a Soviet T34 tank perched on top, a white number '23' on its iron side. The first allied tank to enter Prague after routing the Germans. The usual Soviet propaganda, which she knew didn't quite match the truth. The Czechs granted the Germans free passage out of Prague on 8 May 1945, providing they left the city intact. In the main, that's what happened, though there were exceptions - a Gothic chapel near the Old Town Hall was destroyed by the retreating Nazis. The Soviet troops arrived the next day with nobody to fight but claimed a glorious victory nevertheless.

Janek stood to one side of this memorial to Soviet-Czechoslovak friendship.

His face lit up immediately on seeing her. 'You're late.'

She nodded, fighting down her relief, and glanced over her shoulder. They were far from safe yet.

'Trouble?' he asked anxiously.

'Yes. My tail brought friends.' She pointed up the hill. 'I shook them off, I think. But we'd better get to your car and leave the city at once.'

Janek needed no further urging.

Motoring through the suburbs, he asked, 'And Demek?'

'He should be safe. I held them off long enough at any rate.'

He sighed heavily. 'God knows how I'm going to explain all this to my wife, Janna!'

'Do you tell her everything?'

'No, of course not!'

'Then, why are you upset?' she asked.

'Well, you see, we couldn't afford an apartment. There's a terrible waiting list and I have my doubts as to the selection's fairness. So we share - like so many others - and opted for this car, our ersatz apartment if you like. But now, if they've got my registration...'

'My tail, Grishin, yes, he'll have made a note. You didn't know I was being followed?'

He shrugged. 'How was I to know? I'm not a professional spy. None of us are. I just want freedom to speak, to write, to criticise. How do you say, do our own thing.'

'Like it was seven years ago,' she said wistfully.

'Yes. Dubcek told the Soviets we had no intention of leaving the Warsaw Pact. They had no right to invade.'

'I'm sorry. I didn't realise you were using your own car. You're right. Grishin probably took the number when you dropped me at the hotel. Can you contact Janna? We'll try getting you both out as well as Marta and Antonin.'

His silence was, she guessed, many things. Thanks, naturally; embarrassment, certainly; but also unvoiced regret, for she doubted that he really wanted to run. But he'd be no use to any cause behind bars.

To the beautiful strains of Smetana's *Ma Vlast* Laco performed his speciality, a cross Mohawk turn and triple Lutz. Finally, he came to the climax. Whilst in mid-jump, he rotated his body and performed a somersault. It nearly worked. As he came crashing down, blades slashing the ice into spicules, Tana winced involuntarily, feeling the impact. But he was off his knees within seconds, to the accompaniment of rapturous applause. He completed an upright spin, then bowed as the music ended.

The Czechs idolised their ice skaters, their heroes, and Tana could sympathise easily enough. Even a small victory over your oppressors made you feel better. Whenever they were competing against the Russian teams, they had an almost insane desire to better the Soviets. The Czech ice hockey team beat Russia in an emotionally loaded final at the '69 world championships and since then they'd never let the Soviets forget their defeat - even after six years.

Being a poet of some renown made Laco quite a legend. 'Of course, I'm not in the same league as Jan Neruda and Alois Jirásek,' he once said. But Tana liked his simple verse, torn from his heart. She wondered if his popularity was perhaps to a certain extent his shield. Surely the authorities knew of Laco's clandestine alliances? Yet they were not super-efficient, though their propaganda might infer they were.

Laco clumped onto the wooden boards, cocked his head at Tana.

Unobtrusively she tagged along behind him through to the changing room. Nobody followed; but she double-checked.

As he divested himself of his clothes and showered, his face flushed with the excitement and adrenalin, they talked about inconsequential things, for the sake of security, though just below the surface of their conversation she could detect a tension that was almost palpable. And, she realised, it had nothing to do with affection, sexual attraction or hormones.

Once dried and changed, Laco briefly said a few goodbyes to fellow performers and then they left. He got behind the wheel of Janek's car and drove off.

As Tana told him what had happened during her meeting with Demek, he grew stern. At certain times he still tended to show more anger than was good for him, she thought. But the throbbing temple-vein indicated how strongly he was attempting to hold his temper in check.

He didn't say 'I told you so' as he was a realist and knew that she had good reason for going to the Alcron and showing bravado. At least she'd been able to identify Grishin and now knew that Major Kasayiev was implicated in some way with the mole.

Further on, the country road was blocked off with a diversion sign: '*Objzdka*'.

Laco ignored it and turned onto a farm track. The car ground to a halt by a country gate with a dilapidated shed nearby. Through some sparse bushes and tall junipers she spotted a van parked on a side road.

Laco led her to the shed, along a rutted track. 'Janek feels safer in the van we acquired for him!' Laco chuckled, pointing at the vehicle. 'He'll keep lookout.'

Inside, the light from a candle on a small table revealed two people, one standing, the other in a wheelchair. As she approached she noticed how pale and grim their faces were.

Also on the table was a bottle of absinthe, four glass tumblers, a jug of water and a bowl with sugar cubes. She wondered if this was the old traditional version of the liquor that was banned many years ago because it was hallucinogenic. Doubtful.

'This is Kramaric,' said the one standing. 'One of Ruzyne's ex-inmates.'

Now, her eyes accustomed to the poor light, she saw Kramaric clearly. He was bent forward, weak brown eyes almost lifeless. Nerves irregularly twitched his facial muscles and his left hand. The rest of him seemed preternaturally still, as if paralysed. But, like his fellow Czechs, he seemed determined despite being broken.

'The treatment they dished out aged Kramaric prematurely.' The speaker was middle-aged and quite stout, seeming obese alongside the gaunt Kramaric. 'But,' he added, his tone full of irony, 'of course this was after Comrade Husak decreed there'd be no more torture in Czech prisons!' Tana understood the reference: in 1951, during the Stalinist period, the Secretary General of the Party had been arrested and condemned to life imprisonment; hence his 'decree' on later attaining power. Lip service.

'Zdenek, this is Tana,' said Laco levelly.

'You are welcome,' said Zdenek, pouring a measure of absinthe into the four glasses. He dropped a sugar cube in each then pulled out a lighter and set the absinthe-soaked cubes alight. He offered Tana one of the glasses.

'Thank you,' she said, taking it, adding, 'only a little water.' Zdenek poured a few drops of water in her glass and she swirled the contents to mix them.

All four clinked glasses. '*Na zdravi*,' said Kramaric bravely. Your health.

It didn't seem appropriate but she returned the salutation, anyway, '*Na zdravi*.' She swallowed in one gulp and it burned only a little on the way down.

Laco sipped at his drink and turned to Kramaric. 'Can you give us a plan of Ruzyne's layout since the rebuilding?'

Mouth creasing in a gap-toothed smile, Zdenek thrust a crumpled sheet of coarse brown paper into Tana's hand. 'Here's a complete map. Kramaric got together with some comrades. He worked a good four hours on it.'

As she glanced at the sheet Tana couldn't help but picture the shambling wreck of a man shakily scrawling the lines with his palsied hand, producing the spidery-lined map to the best of his ability and friends' memories. Each drawn line doubtless re-igniting past horrors best forgotten.

She knelt by Kramaric's side, closed her hand over his, which felt cold. The shaking didn't lessen. 'Thank you,' she whispered inadequately, and her lips pecked his quivering cheek. He flushed.

A sharp blast on the van's horn alerted them.

'Someone's coming!' Zdenek said.

Tana stuffed the map into the top of her boot.

'It's all right,' Laco whispered, peering through a small circle that he'd made in the grime-covered window. 'At last. The cells have finally arrived.'

The shed door noisily swung wide. A half-dozen thickset men entered, their boots clattering on the wood. Broad grins met Laco; beards bristled good-humouredly. Suddenly the newcomers fanned to either side and the unmistakeable Demek strode through, face impassive but eyes aflame. He stopped in front of Tana, stared fixedly.

Her eyes held his. 'You managed to get away, I see.'

He nodded. 'Thanks to you, yes.' A lengthy pause followed while he eyed her steadily, approvingly. God, these conspirators were sticklers for pregnant pauses! Finally, he said, 'You have my cell's support, Tana. And that of the others.'

Unrestrained grins broke out. Zdenek proposed that this was a good reason to have another absinthe but both Tana and Laco suggested that one was enough. Then they began running through Tana's proposals for the break-in.

The plotters broke up and Janek returned home in the van whilst Tana drove the Fiat with Laco onto the E-12, the Pilsen road.

Turning left at the sign for Karlstejn, Tana continued until she came in sight of the fourteenth century castle's cluster of turrets, high crenellated walls and looming towers that emerged from the pine-covered hill. She pulled into the side of the road and opened her window.

Not long after, an Auto Moto yellow cab drew up beside their Fiat. The uniformed patrolman stepped out and advanced, boots crunching on the road. He leant through Tana's window. 'Hi, Umbra. I managed to blackmail Anna into getting the Top Secret file that you want. Tonight, she says.'

Laco listened attentively, all but ignored by the 'yellow angel'. He'd never seen the man before but was aware that Tana was using a code name so he had no intention of letting her name drop. He did wonder if she really was called Tana, though.

Tana leaned back and told Laco, 'This is Jiri - a cousin I met in Prague earlier today.' Cousin - spy-talk for CIA. They shook hands warily. 'He's made contact with a secretary in Number 33 - and if she manages to photograph the Tana Standish dossier, we just might learn who - if anyone - is the traitor.'

'But,' Laco asked, 'won't they be using code names?'

'Probably. But the depth of information will finger who is betraying us. At Interprises we always ensure that associates only learn things on a "need to know" basis.'

Both Laco and Jiri exchanged amused glances; their limited introductions had been on that same understanding. Jiri, too, was a code name.

'It is the best way,' she said.

'Let's hope so,' Jiri said. 'I'll be in touch.'

'Take care, Jiri,' Laco called as the freelance swung into his Auto Moto cab and drove off.

Sitting in the car by the roadside, watching the cab's blue exhaust fumes dissipate, Laco shook his head. 'You never cease to amaze me, Tana.'

'Life's more interesting that way, isn't it?'

Laco laughed - such a zestful expression of humour. She wondered if he laughed much these days.

Leaving Karlstejn perched on its crag overlooking the Berounka River, she drove west along the watercourse and through a rocky valley. A couple of times they were stopped as geese blocked the road.

The Gothic Cathedral of Pilsen soon became visible, even from a distance, as it towered over the town centre.

Plane trees shimmered, bordering the road. With hearty appeals to national pride, a village tannoy urged the workers to increase their daily workload. Laco lazily waved to a chubby smiling milkmaid among her herd: 'She likes her *knedléky* too much!' he chuckled.

'Her and a few thousand others, I think,' Tana added, her

stomach rumbling.

Entering Pilsen proper, Tana parked behind the towering Cathedral of St Bartholemew, the landmark seen earlier. That particular saint seemed to get around in this country, she thought. Saint Ubiquitous.

Dusk was slanting shadows across the Town Square; a bird flew out of the sharply-defined darkness beneath the gabled attic of the square's Renaissance town hall. The rest of the square was lined with bourgeois houses, some neo-Gothic. So many town squares in this land, she mused, yet every one different, each spread of cobbles doubtless providing a different story. In fact, she reminded herself, Pilsen has less baroque façades than many Bohemian towns.

To the south-west stretched the Czechoslovakian-Bavarian border, with its Bohemian Forest. And the Sumava Mountains that formed a kind of screen on the horizon.

'Wait a moment,' Tana said as they stood outside a traditional pub, a *hospoda*. She concentrated on the township, their immediate environment, blanking out all the faint yet familiar everyday sounds, slipping into a surface-level trance, listening, sending psychic feelers, attempting to sense any threatening thoughts, any tension.

It only lasted about half a minute, but the time was sufficient for her to be reasonably sure. 'It's all clear,' she said and they entered the building.

Kazakhstan
As Karel Yakunin entered Raisa he abruptly stopped thrusting as his mind was suddenly filled with aerial images of old grey buildings, an ancient cityscape, strong sealed doors and shuttered windows. Perhaps it was Prague, he thought. She's still in Czechoslovakia. What is she doing there?

'What's wrong?' Raisa whispered breathlessly against his ear. 'Is it Bublyk?'

'I think so,' he lied.

'Then let's give him a thrill as the creep spies on us!' she urged, thighs squeezing against him.

Her pelvic muscles moved and he was again aroused. He felt guilty as he made love, unwilling to mention that the English woman had been fleetingly inside his head at such an intimate moment.

CHAPTER SEVEN: Dobranice

Czechoslovakia

Two men glanced up briefly at the moment that Tana and Laco entered the pub and then resumed their serious drinking, their moustaches foam-soaked.

'My psychic surveillance check usually takes only a moment and it isn't foolproof,' Tana said to Laco, 'but James Fisk and I are working on a few mental protocols that might improve matters. We're very close to mastering remote viewing too.'

Laco shook his head and ordered two glasses of Urquell lager. 'I don't even pretend to understand what you're saying or how you do what you do. But if the gift keeps you alive, then I'm all for it.'

She smiled grimly. 'But I don't know how it works either.'

They took a table and ordered from the 'with your beer' menu: Laco chose *klobásy*, spicy pork sausages served with mustard on rye bread and Tana opted for *bramborák*, a pasty made from strips of raw potato and garlic. 'In defence against vampires,' she remarked.

'If only it worked against the Soviets, we'd all reek of the stuff - and gladly!'

'Do I reek then?'

'Mostly tantalising pheromones, I think,' he said, grinning.

The food was delicious. Laco, like so many Czechs, ate too fast, wolfing his food down. She'd noticed it about him before; food wasn't ever going to be the prelude to a night of seduction for him.

For well over an hour Tana and Laco sat at the table nursing their beers. It was companionable time and their reminiscences were tinged with some regret.

Finally, the contact arrived, his shoulders stooped, eyes furtive.

Although he had obviously washed, coal dust still clung to the pores around his soft-looking bulbous nose; his brows were bushy and unkempt, the rims of his eyes red. He sat down and Laco ordered another round.

After being served, the shabby individual sank half his glass, wiped his mouth on a sleeve. Neither knew his name; only his worn grey suit with a dried-up yellow flower in the buttonhole identified him as their contact.

'What do you do at the mine?' Tana asked conversationally.

'Why are you asking me questions?' he demanded, eyes narrowing.

'A friend.'

'I thought you were this fellow's cover.'

'You have nothing to fear from me.'

'Fear? Hah, you don't know the meaning of fear unless you've been a guest of Comrade Husak!' He appraised her upright posture. 'And I can see you haven't.'

'Just answer the lady's question,' Laco urged sternly, leaning across the table. 'Then we can get down to business, eh?'

'Ah, business, yes.' The miner cocked his head and shoved a finger in his ear, twirled it round, extracted it and wiped the grey wax on his fingertip against his sleeve. 'You have the money?'

Laco nodded.

'Well then, to answer your question,' he said, eyeing Tana, 'I'm a power loader. I work at the coalface.' His bloodshot eyes glanced about, at the other two drinkers.

'They're harmless,' Tana assured him.

'Nobody is harmless, lady.' He shook his head. 'I shouldn't be seeing you here in full view like this.'

'Have another drink. Relax,' Laco said easily, though his eyes tended to bore into the little man, almost ordering him to get to the point.

The drink came and when the barman had left, the miner swallowed the rest of the first glass and loosened up a little, his eyes ruminating on the froth at the top of his fresh glass.

'What's all this about a new secret weapon?' Laco demanded.

Chin drooling, the man looked up and stammered, 'I - I can't be sure; we only go so far into the mine. But I've seen things. The gear that's in that place - it has nothing to do with mining. And the guards.'

'Guards?' Tana echoed, arching an eyebrow. She leaned forward. Perhaps she would have something for Mikhail, after all.

The miner abruptly faced her and looked enquiringly at Laco.

'We've been over this already,' Laco said. 'She's my boss.'

The miner's eyes lifted to heaven, showing their dull whites, as if he couldn't understand the ways of the modern world where there were women bosses. 'Yes,' he said, still speaking to Laco. 'We're checked in and out - more like a diamond mine than damned anthracite!' He gulped the pale golden liquid, licked his lips. 'Anyway, as I've said, I've kept my ears and eyes open. As soon as I saw the Red sentries being posted on the perimeter fence, I knew something was happening. I nearly panicked and ran off, I can tell you! My parents died in a concentration camp, you know. I was lucky.'

'The weapon, man!' Laco snapped.

The miner blinked. 'Oh, well, I don't know what it is really. But I've heard noises.'

'What kind of noises?' Tana asked.

He squinted at her as if she was mad. 'You know, humming, drilling. Noises. Construction sounds. But nothing like the machinery you normally hear down a mine. And our coalface has to stop short of the real payload!'

'You think there's something behind the payload - other tunnels?' Tana suggested.

He nodded and pursed his lips, impressed. 'That's it.'

'Where'd they come up?'

He mined his ear again, wiped the waxy deposit on his sleeve and shook his head, eyes clouding. 'I wouldn't like to say - maybe that new building beside the washery. All those damned radio aerials sticking out of it - gives me the jitters!' He looked from one to the other. 'What do you think? It must be a new secret weapon, eh? All those guards.'

'Is that everything?'

He swallowed thickly. 'Yes. Can you do anything about it?'

Tana bit her lip. 'Your observations will be of immense value to us.' She smiled reassuringly. 'Perhaps one day soon you'll read in the *Rude Pravo* about the Soviets' embarrassing exposure!'

'Somehow I don't think so. But if you can cause those Red bastards a bit of embarrassment, that will be fine by me!'

As Tana rose to leave, money changed hands under the table.

They left the contact drinking more beer and stepped out into night. The street lights were not very bright; shadows abounded.

Their footsteps echoed along the cobbled passageways. Tana said, 'Do you believe him?'

'Could be a trap.'

'Then let's recce tonight - now.' She caught the glint of his grin under a pale street lamp.

'Why not,' he said.

There was a large coalfield near Pilsen and the Dobranice mine complex was to the south of this, on the lower slopes of the Sumava Mountains.

Leaving the car behind a gorse bush that was well off the roadside, they scrambled up the beech and spruce filled slopes with a pair of 10x50 binoculars that had been concealed in a specially designed secret seat compartment.

The moon was unmasked by clouds. Stars glimmered.

The first thing she noticed was the unusually strict security complex surrounding the mine. Their contact's comparison with a concentration camp wasn't that far-fetched.

Trees had been cleared for about a hundred metres all around the complex. Dotted at regular intervals along the perimeter fence were watchtowers. Sensing devices in the no-man's-land area? An electric fence? Seismic sensors? Highly likely. The length of fence was in constantly roving beams of light from these towers. No movement registered in the towers themselves but they appeared to bristle with weapons. Automatic defences? Probably.

In the northern sector were half a dozen slag heaps. And in front of these were the wheels and headgear and the winding engine house. To the east of this was the fan house, while to the west was the washery.

Roughly in a direct west-east line from the pithead was the new radio building, sprouting radar masts and antennae.

Rail tracks snaked all around, through the pitheads to the slag heaps and railway sidings.

A couple of lorries and a halftrack stood empty and unlit. Quite a few soldiers were coming and going; three emerged from the radio building.

But as far as she could see there was no clue to any tunnelling other than for coal mining.

Yet the unusual amount of security belied the appearance of a simple coal mine.

Tana signalled Laco to return to the car and she stealthily followed. They had not spoken a word; it was possible there were microphones concealed in the woods - or even directional mikes scanning the area.

Once back in the car, they headed for the outskirts of Pilsen where they abandoned the vehicle to the river: Janek had expressed a wish not to see its ignominious end and she could understand that, particularly as it was his ersatz apartment. Sacrifices made in the name of freedom, without recompense, without compensation. Already in Britain she had seen a growing culture of seeking redress - compensation - which disavowed common sense and accident. She could see this new blame culture permeating all levels of society. But definitely not this side of the Iron Curtain.

They walked into Pilsen and caught a bus. Some way off from the dacha they left the bus and trudged the rest of their way through autumn leaves.

Tana took the opportunity to outline her plan.

'It might work,' Laco agreed.

'There's another reason for rescuing Marta and Antonin. We'll create our own diversion. While they're running in circles trying to find them, we'll get into the Dobranice complex.'

'Just like that? Didn't you notice all that security?'

She grinned. 'Oh yes. There are ways. But the easiest method depends on your cell's thoroughness.'

Laco stopped walking, intrigued. Arms akimbo, he said, 'How?'

'You know the Prague Institute for Research?'

'Yes.'

'Have you anyone in there we could use?'

'Yes, as it happens, we have. Naturally we like to keep a check on what they're up to.'

'One of the things they're working on is some incapacitating bacteria, if you must know.' She paused, allowing her information to sink in. 'A sort of dysentery. Not fatal but very efficient and highly effective. I'd like to get hold of some of that bacteria.'

Laco whistled. 'As the Americans say, shit happens, I guess.'

Tana grimaced. 'Lavatorial humour doesn't suit you, Laco. Besides, that wasn't in the least funny. And I'll need forged papers. I'll give you the details I want on them when we get back.'

'Well, that depends on what you want. But we have a couple of experts and a nice little library of documentation they can copy. Shouldn't be too difficult.'

'Plus, if possible, latex facial moulds.'

Laco shook his head. 'Anything else?'

'No. But I'd like all this tomorrow. We're hitting Ruzyne then.'

'Christ almighty! Forgeries take time, Tana, as you well know.

I'm not sure that they'll manage it by tomorrow night.'

'They can work round the clock, without sleep, as long as they do it.'

Thick pillows flounced on either side of him, Kasayiev sat up in bed and jabbed at the dozen or so pickles surrounding the Russian crabmeat and mayonnaise. 'Damned pickles with everything!' He swore, eyes red with lack of sleep.

Though he was still verging on irritability, the breakfast went down well, washed all the way with jet-black Turkish coffee. His discoloured teeth crunched the tiny cool pickles. He ate them only because the doctor said they helped break down body fats. He preferred Spanish onions, though. He belched and realised that he'd come a long way since those far-off days in Spain.

He remembered the day well: 16th September, 1936. As a recruit of six months' experience, he had arrived in Spain at the age of sixteen together with fifty other pilots. To fight for the Republicans.

A lump still rose in his throat as he recalled first seeing his own I-15 Ilyushin standing on the airfield: the Spanish dubbed the I-15s *Chato*, snub-nose - yet he had thought it the most beautiful creation on earth - and all his!

His fellow pilots had difficulty curbing his youthful exuberance. He dearly wanted to slaughter the Nationalists, to blast their Fiats, Heinkels and Junkers.

But training classes demanded his time and attention. Recognition classes; strategy; and, laughably, he was expected to teach Spaniards to fly as well. Him, with only a hundred hours under his belt.

Then came his first kill. His heartbeat quickened at the memory. He had been dawdling negligently when he spotted a squadron of nine Fiats above him, appearing from behind a bank of cloud. The dryness of mouth and rapid pulse rate came back to him as if the events had only happened yesterday. He had slammed the throttle wide open and climbed to meet the enemy, the exhilaration of surprise attack quashing any fears he harboured. He didn't have time to be afraid.

Yanking the stick hard over, he kicked on the rudder-bar and was abruptly swinging in behind the formation as it slid past. A Fiat drifted into his sights and he fired, wide eyes peering with a mesmerised glaze through his goggles as the bullets flashed and sparkled on the enemy's wings. Then tracer lanced past his cockpit and he knew fear; pure survival instinct hauled back on the stick, and the craft frantically bounced higher. He glanced back. The Fiat was nosing earthwards, blazing furiously, and his heart soared. He never did recall landing.

That kill had been his introduction to the slaughter of battle. It seemed so clinical, far removed from the hand-to-hand fighting on the ground.

By the time the Italians attacked Madrid in March 1937 he was a hardened veteran of the skies. Together with his compatriots, he systematically cut the Italians to ribbons, strafing endlessly as the poorly led rabble became bogged down in the mud left by recent rain. It was sickening to begin with, but after the ninth or tenth run in, it became automatic, merely capricious target practice. The Barcelona highway was littered with burning transport and hundreds of corpses, creating their own bottleneck, enabling the Chatos to deliver their death blows at will. Carnage was too mild a description of their efforts.

Bloodlust figured in Kasayiev's life from that moment. He revelled in inflicting pain on his women in Madrid and particularly relished the death of an enemy especially if he could see the poor pilot futilely beating off the flames as his plane plummeted.

Much of the credit for the Italians' rout was attributed to Commander Berzin, head of the Intelligence Directorate of the Soviet General Staff and codenamed 'Goriev' whilst in Spain. Berzin became Kasayiev's hero.

So late in 1937 he was shattered when he learned that Berzin had been recalled to Moscow under a cloud. Berzin faced charges of being a Trotskyite; the tribunal found him guilty and he was shot, as were so many high-ranking officers in Stalin's senseless purges.

With the memory of Berzin's execution constantly in his mind, Kasayiev determined to keep his nose clean and actually distinguished himself. Throughout the years of 1937-38 the great purges kept most officers in thrall; many were grossly unhappy at the prospect when the Soviet hierarchy decided to recall them on realising that the Republicans' cause was lost.

But Kasayiev was not among those singled out for purging. Instead he found himself halfway around the world at Langchow, embroiled in the Soviet-Japanese conflict, flying his I-15 amidst the twisting mêlée of a hundred aircraft. He acquitted himself in countless sporadic duels with the Mitsubishi ASMs. But he soon discovered that his beloved I-15 was quite inferior to the Japs' Nakajima Ki27s: he was shot down but survived with only minor wounds.

It was while recuperating that he allied himself with a sallow character in the Intelligence Section, Lieutenant-Colonel Lobanov.

He then remembered his hero, Berzin, and guessed correctly where the real power lay. Not in a soldier's hands, nor an airman's, nor a sailor's. But in the Secret Service.

On his return to active duty he repeatedly requested a transfer to Intelligence and finally, in 1942, he was successful and joined the NKVD in time to fight the Nazi menace.

He had committed some vile things in his time, mainly to satisfy his gross appetite for blood. But nothing he had perpetrated could match the vileness of those Nazi pigs.

Kasayiev's fingers trembled at the memory of the concentration camps he had personally seen. And he lit a hashish cigarette to calm himself.

As the hemp coursed through him and did its work he cursed his susceptibility.

Every time he reminisced on his career he came round to his numerous encounters with the Gestapo. He should know better by now.

Whenever he came across an ex-SS man – usually working in another Security Department, such as the First Chief Directorate or Department V – he couldn't refrain from revealing his naked hatred.

And, oddly, he should be feeling quite elated right now, he thought, throwing back the bedclothes.

He dressed slowly and methodically, savouring the early hours of this morning.

The phone's insistent buzzing had cut into his sleep but his annoyance vanished when he learned the reason.

Anna, one of the building's clerks, had been caught photocopying the Standish dossier.

Shrugging on a housecoat, he had gone downstairs to confront her.

She had been scared stiff. In a hell of a state. It was obvious the arresting soldiers had gang-raped her: her hair was dishevelled, her clothing torn and she was bruised and trembling with shock.

'Never rape one of my prisoners again,' he reprimanded them. 'At least not until I've finished with them!'

In truth, he wished he'd been there.

As Anna's story came out - after unusually little persuasion from him - he was slightly amused. She'd been ensnared by one of their own methods - blackmailing the lovesick bitch with compromising photos which would kill her mother and father if they knew.

Stupid bitch!

Though all too brief, he had enjoyed the interrogation. Of course, filled with a misplaced sense of love and loyalty, she'd been reluctant to divulge any addresses - until pressed.

And he enjoyed pressing. Afterwards, he allowed the two guards to take turns, while he watched, though he was surprised to find he was no longer aroused.

Eventually, they dragged her away and he had retired to his dreams in which he was once again a young virile man in war-torn Spain.

Now, on being awoken with breakfast, he was informed that the agent who Anna had finally identified was under arrest and awaiting him.

Defiantly, Jiri glared at his captors. His lower lip trickled a little blood and his left eye was discoloured and already swelling, half-closed. Otherwise, he appeared unmarked. The guards stood impassively at his side.

At least they'd taken my earlier warning to heart, Kasayiev thought, and hadn't raped the poor bastard. He knew full well that a couple of the guards enjoyed the power trip, no matter what the sex of the victim.

Sweat beaded Jiri's stern face. His eyes were steady, almost apathetic.

A perverse feeling of compassion swept over Kasayiev. The stupid fool had attempted bluffing, knowing the detailed search of his apartment revealed nothing incriminating. Even the salacious photos of Anna were still missing - well hidden elsewhere.

'It's only her word against mine!' Jiri snapped, struggling with the ropes that tied him to a ladder-backed wooden chair.

So he guessed that it was Anna who had talked. Kasayiev smiled.

The fool's resistance appeared quite good: probably a product of the CIA. But too stroppy and overconfident.

Kasayiev leaned forward and squeezed Jiri's throat just hard enough to send the blood flushing into his face. 'The CIA may teach you resistance to interrogation at "The Farm",' he said, 'but no matter how much they put you through the mill, I can promise that you *will* crack with me.'

Of course, they'd have fed him different levels of knowledge, each cover story an untruth which needed to be peeled back like a Spanish onion's skin until the real truth was laid bare. The secret was knowing when you'd hit the genuine truth level - otherwise you could keep digging and destroy the subject before he talked.

Jiri's eyes held his, unflinching, though it was evident he was in increasing pain as his air passage was stifled.

Kasayiev let go, leaving white finger impressions.

Coughing and trying to suck in air, Jiri jerked ineffectually in his chair.

'Sleep-deprivation, physical torture, intense pain. We're masters in all those techniques,' Kasayiev said.

Jiri eyed him balefully. If looks could kill.

'But no matter how much they prepared you,' Kasayiev went on, 'you must realise that the real thing would one day be *much* worse. Of course, some things the interrogation sessions couldn't prepare you for - *if you were to remain a man.*'

And he had great satisfaction in seeing the unsaid threat nibbling at his captive's thoughts.

Of course, every field agent knows the very real threat of genital and anal torture but puts it to the back of the mind, something not to dwell on. Now, though, the terrifying ordeal was foremost in Jiri's thoughts.

Psychologically breached, Jiri visibly crumbled before Kasayiev's eyes while the two uniformed guards cut away the agent's trousers and undershorts, carelessly slashing the skin on his thighs with the scissors.

'You have some pluck, fool - but not enough to see you through this.' Kasayiev uncovered the squeaking trolley to reveal a bizarre assortment of rusty bloodstained surgeon's knives, dials, wires and electrodes.

Jiri's eyes widened, whites showing all round the irises.

Kasayiev sighed and shook his head. 'Yes, there's a real risk of blood poisoning with these tools.' He felt a tremor of anticipation squirm through his stomach. 'Please don't talk too soon, will you?' he whispered, licking his scarred lip.

After a little while, Jiri talked. But he didn't mention Umbra or her meeting with Mikhailevich; his training had buried that deep.

'Thank you, Jiri,' Kasayiev said. 'You have been most helpful.'

Jiri started, surprised that his interrogator knew his code name.

'Let me repay you,' his torturer said.

Then Kasayiev leaned closer and spoke softly: 'You wanted to know the traitor's real name, didn't you?' He chuckled and whispered Trumpet's name hoarsely into Jiri's ear - and the agent's eyes started in anger and comprehension.

The poisoned needle penetrated his spinal chord just beneath the occiput and Jiri's eyes continued to stare, lifeless.

I'm going soft, Kasayiev thought, ending it too quickly for the fool. Then he turned to the onlooking guards and said, 'Dispose of him - and the woman Anna.'

So Tana Standish wanted to know the details in her dossier, eh? Not surprising, really. There were a few large gaps, but it still made interesting reading. She moved around a lot, too.

She first came to Moscow's notice ten years ago in Singapore, then Odessa three years later, followed by Prague. Here she'd teamed up with Laco Valchik who seemed to be as elusive as that damned fictional Pimpernel!

There wasn't any definitive proof, but two operations were compromised in Elba and Mombasa which pointed to her involvement. The woman never seemed to rest, he thought.

He was annoyed with himself. He shouldn't have told Grishin to apprehend her - he'd tipped his hand too soon, he felt sure. Scared her off. Damn Grishin for his incompetence!

But he was confident that the net was closing on Standish. As long as she stayed in the country, she'd slip up and they'd trap her. Just a matter of time.

His current strategy gave him moments of worry, true. He knew she was a gift from Trumpet, the traitor.

I could have been waiting for her at the airport, he thought. By now all her secret knowledge could be spewing out of her and I would get some of the glory.

But he so wanted to ruin the Czech underground as well. And Standish was the key to him achieving that. Yes, just a matter of time.

CHAPTER EIGHT: Ruzyne

Tana and Laco lay back against the bed's headboard and silently sipped the thick sweet Turkish coffee, the aroma of ground mocha beans dispelling the sleep-cobwebs.

Her torso clammy with sweat, she had awoken from a disturbing dream which could be nothing at all. Yet sometimes her dreams had the knack of foreshadowing something to come. It had involved Jiri. There was nothing she could do, though it was possible that Ilyichev might come in handy more than once.

Laco grinned, looking a bit more awake now that he had his Czech breakfast inside him. 'We've a few hours to kill and I feel a new man already after that coffee!'

'I can feel the new man as well!' Laughing at his renewed vigour, she broke free of his embrace and rolled out of bed, landing on her feet. 'First, I want to go over the Ruzyne plans again. And don't forget, we have a prisoner to feed.'

'Damn, I'd completely forgotten about the swine!'

'We must have him looking fit and well-fed if he's to help us,' she added, padding to the bathroom.

Ilyichev's stomach rumbled loudly. The ropes securing his hands behind the chair back had effectively restricted his blood's circulation to a mere trickle and his fingers were numb. Apart from these discomforts he was suffering a savagely wounded pride: the bile of anger hovered sickeningly in his throat.

It was pitch-dark. The dust in the air clogged his nostrils. He was surprised to be alive; if he had been in Standish's shoes, he wouldn't have hesitated to kill.

The key turned in the lock above and a shaft of light disclosed the flight of wooden stairs. He registered the shapely silhouette of Tana within seconds then swiftly scanned the rest of the cellar.

Facing the stairs, his wooden chair was in the centre of a stone-flagged floor. To his right was a boarded-up window, set high up. If a board could be prised off, a nail might become a means to cut the ropes or even a weapon. Cobwebs draped from the rafters. A number of tea chests were stacked to his left, the topmost few open and spewing wood-wool. Just within range of vision beyond the chests lay the rusting frame of a bicycle, without handlebars and chain.

'I've brought you breakfast,' Tana said.

His first instinct was to release that bile and spit in her face and refuse to eat. But that wouldn't be of much good to him either. Instead of making a childish and worthless gesture he must eat to keep up his strength.

She freed only one hand and stepped back smartly before his blood started flowing properly into his fingers again.

The pins and needles were excruciating and made eating a discomforting and laborious business but he persevered, continually eyeing Tana and her levelled automatic. He would do as she bid - at least until a chance for freedom presented itself.

Kazakhstan

Professor Bublyk chewed on a German sausage sandwich and studied young Antonin Borodin who sat next to Yakunin.

Leaning over his desk, brow creased, concentration deep, Borodin let his trembling hands hover over the map in front of him. He specialised in scanning China - a massive task. Such a vast country, so many minds!

Bublyk already knew that psychic power didn't just manifest itself in the minds of the intelligentsia - it could just as easily flourish in a farm labourer living along the Yangtze.

Borodin was good - almost a match for Yakunin and Savitsky - but Bublyk feared that he seemed to be trying too hard. Yet he got quite impressive results. He had even managed to identify two Chinese secret agents, Wang Wu, an assassin and a woman, Ah Lam Chou, an experienced industrial spy. It was easy enough to discover their names; they're so damned formal all the time, often referring to each other by name.

But Borodin was too intense and wanted to be the best in The Group. Unfortunately, he wasn't. So he tried harder. A vicious circle that could lead to mental breakdown.

In a way, Bublyk blamed himself. He'd been too engrossed in Yakunin's discovery. Up to now, the woman in Czechoslovakia seemed to be more powerful than the German, French and Italian psychic spies the others had detected.

As the Americans would say, he thought, I haven't kept my eye on the ball. I've been neglecting the others in The Group.

Now he studied Borodin. The stress signs were plain. If he wasn't careful, the man was going to burn himself out. And that wouldn't be good for the upcoming inspection. Particularly as there were still questions being asked about the two adepts, Horwitz and Kosloff, who died last year.

I must stop being obsessed with Yakunin, Bublyk thought. Each one of my psychics is precious. Must get the balance right and not push them *too* hard.

Then it came to him, the ideal compromise. Of course, it's so simple! I'll use Raisa to spy on Yakunin. It won't take much to control her and make her do my bidding.

He glanced at the clock. Midday already.

They had all been working solidly for five hours, since breakfast.

'Time for a break,' he announced on the tannoy. 'Psychics disconnect.' He felt a little like a mother hen, he thought, and chuckled at the absurd thought. 'Disconnect.'

Nonchalantly, he strolled over to Raisa and whispered, 'You've done well, lately, my dear.'

She hooked her headset to the side of her desk and smiled up at him. 'Thank you, professor.' Such a trusting girl.

As she stood and pulled her chair back to leave, he added, 'Stay behind for a few minutes, will you?'

Raisa looked at the other psychics as they left the room. None of them, not even Karel, noticed she wasn't joining them. 'Of course, sir.'

'I have a little training protocol which should benefit your performance.'

'I'm honoured, comrade professor.'

Czechoslovakia

It was only a few minutes after midday when their Tatra limousine pulled up outside the three-storey Ruzyne prison.

One of the two sentries ran down the wide entrance steps as Laco got out, machine carbine carelessly slung over his shoulder.

Ilyichev played his part well, answering the sentry's shower of questions with a silent glare and his green KGB identity booklet. The sentry closed up like a clam, saluted and hastily joined his comrade at the studded double doors. He pointed down at their group, whispered to his comrade-in-arms.

Tana and Ilyichev ascended the steps and faced the pair.

The older guard was cautiously eyeing Ilyichev but he didn't give Laco and Janek more than a cursory glance. They were disguised as special MVD troopers and their forged papers would pass muster as originals. But the guard was intrigued by the presence of Tana: his black eyebrows raised. 'Who is this, Comrade?' he demanded of Ilyichev, nodding his helmeted head at Tana.

The temptation to reveal all must have been great; but Tana knew he was no hero or martyr. Her threat earlier today in the cellar doubtless remained with him, showing its presence in every ounce of sweat that clung to his short-cropped neck. 'Don't try betraying us,' she'd told him. 'We'll still accomplish the breakout, only you won't be alive to see it.'

'Th - this is the English woman Major Kasayiev's been after. I've brought her in connection with the student arrests.'

'You wish to see the Commander?'

'Of course!' Ilyichev scowled so intensely that the guard took a step back. 'Now let us in!'

Blanching, the older guard turned and hammered on the thick wooden door with his carbine butt. The blows resounded, seeming to last for ages. Then the Judas door slid back and a pimpled face appeared.

'KGB with escort and prisoner to see the Commander!' barked the shaken guard.

'Well, it isn't in my schedule, but if you say so,' grumbled the pimply soldier, 'I suppose it's all right.'

The heavy bolts crashed and the door creaked open. The group entered, boots echoing on the tiled floor. They were swamped in the light reflected from drab green walls and ceiling, lending a sickly hue to their faces.

Two yards ahead of them was a ceiling-high wall of bars with one central door. Beyond this, two separate tubular steel desks. The pimply soldier led them to the bars and unlocked the gate. Seated at the desks were two more soldiers wearing Administration arm-badges. Name plaques declared their respective names. Filing cabinets lined the wall behind them; there was a door on each side. A white line had been painted on the floor in front of the desks.

'Don't cross that line!' bawled Musgorsky on the left.

Musgorsky's tunic was unbuttoned at the neck and foodstains blemished its green-serge colour. He was in need of a shave - and a lesson in manners. He leaned forward, hand outstretched to Ilyichev. 'Now, where are your committal papers?' he snapped.

Musgorsky's companion, Petrov, amusedly watched from his own desk, his feet up, boots in need of repair and a polish. Tana sensed his eyes undressing her but remained with head slightly bowed. But she was taking in every word and every inflection of speech - and Ilyichev knew it.

'No time to go through all that red tape,' Ilyichev explained. 'My prisoner has some vital information on those two students.'

He sounds convincing enough, Tana thought.

Pausing for a moment, Musgorsky toyed with some blank forms. 'Very well, we'll take her to the Commander now. He'll get it out of her soon enough.' He sneered. 'She doesn't look much.' He shuffled the forms. 'Name?' he demanded, pen poised.

Tana didn't answer.

Musgorsky looked up. 'You can go now, Comrade,' he said to Ilyichev, and waved his hand in dismissal. 'And take those crease-proud dolts with you!'

Ilyichev cast a livid glance at Tana. Her eyes held no compassion. He swallowed. 'No, she's *my* prisoner. I want to see the Commander with her. Is that clear?' He thumped his fist on the desk, scattered the papers to the floor.

Petrov jerked to his feet, undecided how to deal with the situation.

'Now, take me to him at once!' Ilyichev seemed to be enjoying bullying the bureaucrats; give them a desk and a pen and they think they run the bloody country.

Musgorsky returned Ilyichev's icy look unflinchingly.

Laco and Tana exchanged a worried glance.

Petrov's hand hovered near his holstered pistol - a nervous reaction which didn't go unnoticed by Tana.

'Well, man, where's the Commander?' Ilyichev growled.

Eyes momentarily evading Ilyichev's, Musgorsky went pale, his bristled upper lip quivering.

The browbeating had come off, Tana thought, but she didn't relax.

Musgorsky shrugged his shoulders exaggeratedly. 'Be it on your own head, Comrade. The Commander's in the Interrogation Room.' He turned his back on Ilyichev. 'I'll show you the way.'

Ilyichev followed Musgorsky through the left-hand door; Tana, Laco and Janek immediately on their heels.

They passed through a short corridor and the ferrous smell of cabbage wafted from an air-vent on their left.

Another door, which worked by remote control.

Everywhere they went Tana noticed surveillance CCTV cameras. At the end of the corridor they came out onto a large floor space. To right and left warders sat at utilitarian desks and in both corners were metal spiral staircases. In front of them, more bars. The rows of stone cells beyond the bars were partitioned off by a wall down the centre.

The silence of the place struck her. Most cells were windowless and all were bound to be soundproofed. Wouldn't do to wake the neighbours.

Along the wall were three vacant patient trolleys.

Musgorsky conferred with the warder on the left. A service lift stood open beside the warder. 'Second floor,' Musgorsky told Ilyichev. 'Warder Iranov will escort you.'

Once they were inside, the lift rose.

Warder Iranov had phoned up and they were expected.

On the second floor the layout was much the same. The door in the bars opened hydraulically on well-greased runners. Iranov led them along another corridor, the cells branching to their left in blocks of twelve. 'This is the men's side,' Iranov said conversationally. 'The women's section on the other side of this wall is exactly the same.' He chuckled. 'No discrimination here!'

Pungent disinfectant smell hit them. 'Latrines are along there,' he said unnecessarily, pointing to the left as they came upon a great length of black wall with only one door, also black. He chuckled again. 'This is the only place where we permit the men and women to get together - the Interrogation Room!'

He inserted a plastic card and the door slid open.

Inside, everything was painted black, illuminated by sickly green lighting. There were no desks or guards, only an empty room with one wooden bench running along the left-hand wall and above it a solitary barred window. Rather like a dentist's waiting room - though without the magazines. On the right was a door with a red light flashing above it.

Iranov indicated the light. 'The Commander's still busy on the stubborn bastards!' He stepped over to an intercom by the door. 'I'll buzz him. Wait here.'

As if they had anywhere else they wanted to go to. They waited.

Tana glanced out the small window. They were two storeys up, immediately above an empty courtyard measuring about sixteen feet by four. Exercise yard? Possibly. A watchtower emplacement overlooked the courtyard from the corner of the prison wall.

'We can go in now,' Iranov said. 'The Commander's intrigued by this woman here.' The door opened.

A smell of singed hair wafted out and a sudden high-pitched scream greeted them; it could have been from either sex.

Tana was suddenly in motion. She barged past Iranov, ramming his head against the metal door.

The Commander appeared to enjoy his own dirty work. He was accompanied by two assistants.

Both Marta and Antonin were strapped into metal chairs without benefit of seats so their naked buttocks hung painfully through.

An old bucket was held over Antonin's head by one assistant. The mallet in a stocky henchman's hand had just hammered the metal bucket and its ringing noise was only now dying. The waves of pain that hit Tana's mind showed how profoundly the resounding noise had eaten into Antonin already. His hands were tethered to wooden props at either side. The Commander stood poised with a jug of steaming hot liquid in one hand and another jug issuing fronds of cold air in the other. Antonin's hands were alternately blue and red, veins distended and his pigeon chest heaved spasmodically. Tana knew from reading MI6 archives that similar torture was used in Hungary in the 1950s. Why change something that worked?

Marta sat to one side visibly trembling, scald marks on her breasts and abdomen. Her lovely wide eyes just stared blankly. It seemed as if she wasn't aware of anything or anyone in the room.

Tana took in this sight and her forward dash faltered for about a second.

The Commander and his two assistants noticed her at the very moment her feet left the echoing tiled floor.

The tremendous leap punched her feet into the stocky henchman's chest and she heard some bones distinctly cracking. He rocked back into a bench of implements and the intercom.

Flustered, the Commander dropped the two jugs and yelped, wincing as the scalding water doused his leg. Snarling in pain, he fumbled at his leather holster and withdrew the revolver as Tana landed cat-like on all fours; but he never got to use it.

Laco's knife flew over Antonin's bowed head and sank deep into the Commander's throat. With a horrible gurgling sound, the torturer crashed into a pile of stretchers.

Tana was intent on Ilyichev now and he knew it and didn't move a muscle.

The second assistant backed into Marta, pushed himself off in revulsion, his face deathly pale.

'Keep him alive!' Tana exclaimed as Janek grappled with him and swung the snivelling man's arm up his back.

Once they had released Antonin and Marta and eased them out of the chairs, they found their problems had only begun.

'We can't take them out like this!' shouted Janek feelingly, virtually in tears at the sight of his younger sister.

'Marta's made of sterner stuff than you!' scolded Tana.

Her tone brought Janek out of it. The effort at self-control took its toll on him but he finally straightened, wiped his cheeks and nodded.

Both Marta and Antonin had withstood a great deal of pain, bodies mottled with various forms of scalding and burns. Their faces contorted as the recycling blood sent fresh agonies through them. Marta's sprained ankle was hugely swollen and obviously hadn't been treated, the discolouration now up to her kneecap.

Tana knelt, tore strips off the Commander's jacket. She turned to Laco. 'Is this their new soft approach to questioning?' She was annoyed at being unable to control the sudden outburst. She was trembling almost as much as Janek. Of course - his reactions were being funnelled into her! She set up psychic blocks and was immediately calm and professional again.

Laco didn't answer; he was too busy getting the two students into their torn clothes.

Iranov lay still by the door, his neck broken. Damn, she thought. Sometimes I don't know my own strength.

Tana crossed the room and checked the assistant she'd felled: a couple of cracked ribs. He'd live as he wasn't vomiting any blood. 'You'd better pull yourself together,' she growled at him, strapping up his ribcage with the strips of uniform. 'You can help with a stretcher - or suffer more broken ribs.' It didn't seem possible, but he paled even more.

'Laco - you can partner him. Carry Marta, she's the lightest. Janek and your snivelling little captive can take Antonin.'

They nodded agreement.

From the moment that they had entered the Interrogation Room only three minutes had elapsed. Ilyichev stood stunned by the speed of events. No sooner had he realised he'd been left alone than Tana was there, barring his escape, ordering her men about.

'Ilyichev will escort me at the rear,' she said to the Russian. 'Won't you?'

He nodded, eyes damning her.

'I'll tell you what to say,' she said.

Laco and the wounded assistant lifted Marta. Though the stretcher was light, the man was streaming in sweat with the nagging insistent pain. They went first, followed by Antonin on his stretcher, then Tana and Ilyichev side by side.

At the lift the warder from the right-hand desk came over. He opened up and let them out. 'Where's Iranov?' he enquired. 'Loafing again?'

'No. He's helping the Commander,' Janek explained levelly.

'Gregore!' the warder exclaimed, staring at the wounded assistant at the front of the stretcher. 'What's the matter with you? You don't look too well.'

The pain-racked Gregore forced a brave grin, sweat beading his forehead.

'A fever, I think,' Ilyichev hastily interceded. 'We're dropping him off at the sick quarters on the way out.'

The warder pulled a face. 'Be careful, Gregore - you're my relief next weekend!'

'Right, I'll be here!' Gregore wheezed.

Throughout this exchange Tana kept an eye on Ilyichev. He didn't look comfortable at all. And as he saw his chances of escape dwindling he might be tempted to run a few unhealthy risks.

On the ground floor they transferred the stretchers to two trolleys parked by the lift doors. None of the warders had questioned their right to bring Marta and Antonin out. If they had, then the shooting would have begun.

As they emerged into the reception room again, the Admin Officer, Musgorsky, exclaimed, 'What's this? Where's the Commander?'

This would probably be Ilyichev's biggest hurdle. She stood very close to him, tensed and watchful like a bird of prey.

'The Commander's on the phone to my headquarters right now. It seems these three are willing to direct us to a secret arms cache.'

Musgorsky was bright. And suspicious. It was obvious he didn't particularly like the KGB either. 'Why do you need three of them for one cache of guns, eh, Comrade?'

A thinker! Using logic. Definitely wasted on this duty, Tana thought.

Ilyichev expelled air through his nostrils. 'I thought it might've occurred to you, since you're so clever. Each one only knows a part of the route. Blindfolds, there and back.'

Good thinking, Ilyichev.

'Oh. But why can't the Commander get them to talk? He's usually pretty good at that.'

'He could - in time. But they've got more than just guns. There are two nuclear warheads with them. *Now* do you see?'

Musgorsky nodded vigorously, his eyes filled with a new respect for the KGB. He saluted. 'Sorry to doubt you, Comrade, but I have a job to do.'

'All right, man, all right - just let us get on with ours, eh?'

Musgorsky personally saw them off the premises. They left the trolleys at the top of the steps.

Two Tatras drew up alongside the kerb and the captives and escapees bundled in.

'You did very well, Ilyichev,' Tana said. 'Indeed, I think you missed your vocation as an actor.'

'I might have been a dancer, if you hadn't crippled me.'

She studied him, narrowing her eyes. 'I can't see you in a tutu.'

'You know damned well that tutus are for women. I would have worn tights.'

She shook her head. 'The Bolshoi doesn't know what it missed, does it?'

'It hasn't been fun, you know, being a cripple!' he snapped, suddenly exasperated, 'Thanks to you!'

'Actually, I saved your life. As far as you're concerned, the SAS had shoot-to-kill orders but I got to you first.'

Ilyichev was suddenly very thoughtful and quiet.

On the outskirts of Prague they pulled in at the roadside and stripped the two assistants.

'What about me?' Ilyichev asked as they drove off, abandoning the naked shivering men.

'Sorry, but we can't risk losing you. You've been to our hideout. In fact, now you're something of a liability.'

Ilyichev kept quiet, trying to block out the thought that Standish or her criminal friends might dispose of him with a bullet in the back of his head.

Even though she was awake, Tana sometimes dreamed. This time the images and sensory impressions that assaulted her were fleeting and over before she could analyse them. But they had been very powerful. She sat in the Tatra beside the slumped shivering form of Marta and sweat poured out of her. She pressed her hands on her thighs and still couldn't stop her legs from trembling.

The waking dream had been vivid. She had been in a hot country, trapped inside an ill-lit sandstone funnel of masonry. Cool air was blowing upwards, death waiting below. Her heart was pounding as she lowered herself.

Over in a second, the stark episode had to be showing her something yet to come. When and where remained a complete mystery to her. Maybe she'd know if she experienced a *déjà vu* sensation.

God, she thought, wiping her brow with a sleeve, I hate it when that happens!

Kazakhstan

Professor Bublyk was worried about his psychic star, Yakunin. These days he walked around with mental blocks set up. Bublyk tried probing, but to no avail. The young man was good, but didn't seem to comprehend that he was putting his future in jeopardy. Indeed, all their futures could be at risk. He felt sure it had something to do with his link to the British female psychic in Czechoslovakia.

Haven't heard anything from Raisa yet, either, he thought. It's probably too soon. She isn't as effective as Yakunin. Perhaps I should talk to him, warn him. Tell him straight that any upset could close down the research funding.

Karel Yakunin was aware of Bublyk's concern though he was not powerful enough to actually read the professor's mind.

Irrationally he could not resist being attracted to the British woman. For a very brief moment he felt agitated and worried and knew that the sensation was channelled from her, highlighted by the name *Janek* which of course meant nothing to him. Then just as abruptly the feeling vanished, clamped on by the dark cool presence of an iron will.

He admired her willpower. During those few instances of contact he detected shadings of grief, pain and sorrow and he deduced she had undergone more in her lifetime than he could ever hope to imagine.

He thought of Raisa and realised his feelings for her had changed. Yet she didn't appear to notice. In fact, if anything, she seemed more sensual than ever, almost clinging in her behaviour. He must continue the pretence of romance, though, if only to divert Bublyk.

And Yakunin was suddenly afraid of himself, of what he was becoming.

CHAPTER NINE: Janek

Czechoslovakia

Demek's men left to dump the vehicles, leaving him behind with Laco, Janek, Tana and the two students.

Tana came out of the bedroom.

'How are they?' Demek asked, his face pinched with concern.

'In shock and I suspect that no amount of painkillers will help them,' she said bitterly. 'But they should live - though I wouldn't guarantee they'll have a restful night's sleep ever again.' The way she said it, it was as though she was no stranger to sleepless nights.

Janek nodded, his face ashen but rigid, fighting back the threatening onset of tears. 'I've arranged the escape route for this evening. Should I delay the plans?'

Tana eyed him. 'No. We all feel they must be taken away from here as soon as possible. Chances of recovery will be better in a safe country.' Unsaid but acknowledged was the fact that their own country was not safe - for anybody.

'Very well then,' Janek said firmly. 'But I must ask that they be got ready. In their present state, I think we must set out with them now if we're to maintain our schedule.'

'How do we go?' Laco enquired.

Demek grinned. 'You've done your part, friend. It's up to my people now.'

Tana closed her eyes for a moment. Listening to him, it was as if a much older man were talking. Certainly older than the man she had met yesterday. The world was getting old before its time.

Demek leaned over a map. 'My men will be waiting for us here. At the crossroads. '

The crossroads meant something to Ilyichev as he had studied the map of the area while tracking Tana to this dacha.

Nursing a bruised forehead, he crouched at the top of the stairs, a glass cupped to his ear.

The group had been more concerned for Marta and Antonin to bother with him. They simply threw him into the cellar head first. He had landed badly and his lame leg had started acting up again. But his anger let him ignore that and he soon pulled himself together and rummaged in one of the crates and fished out a glass tumbler.

Whether he would be able to make use of what he was overhearing was another matter.

At least he doubted that they were going to kill him. If they had intended to do that, he'd be dead already.

His apparent betrayal of his country troubled him. The staff of Ruzyne knew him from his ID and he would have a lot of explaining to do as it was, should he get free. But if he could glean enough information as a bargaining chip, then he might not only survive the humiliation of the Ruzyne breakout, he might even get rewarded. That possibility goaded him on; otherwise he might as well defect right now, which was totally unpalatable to him.

Listening intently, Ilyichev committed to memory every detail and every name.

'They will have tracked down your car by now,' Tana told Janek. 'Won't you reconsider going with Antonin and Marta?'

Janek shook his head. 'No, I've spoken with Janna and she agrees. Next time. Besides, Demek here has only arranged for two.'

'Four, actually,' Demek corrected, looking askance at Tana. 'The

English woman, she thinks of everything!'

They all broke into grins.

'No, I'll stay - but thanks anyway.'

Demek chewed on his lip, his face grave. 'We'd best be leaving. Can they walk, do you think?'

Tana nodded. 'It's not far - they'll make it. Laco and I will tag along to help. At least, up to the crossroads.' She turned to Janek. 'Since you want to stay, would you watch the dacha?'

'Of course.' He glanced towards the bedroom.

'You can say *au revoir* to your sister now,' she offered, 'and tell her it won't be long before you're reunited.'

Janek went inside and was left alone with Marta for a brief chat. When he came out he was a little happier. 'She's able to walk. Even with her bad ankle.' He smiled, tears in the corners of his eyes. 'She's going to be all right, she says. Typical, really, but she's more worried about me!'

Demek shrugged into his jacket and said gruffly, 'Time to go.'

They waved to Janek and were swiftly swallowed up by the forest.

Laco was able to give Marta a piggyback for quite long stretches. Antonin hobbled along, supported by Tana and Demek.

As he stood watching them vanish into the forest, Janek was torn in two. He ached to go with them and take Marta all the way to safety. He wanted to escape with her so he could look after her throughout her lengthy recovery. But he must also think of Janna. She was so close to her parents, she wouldn't want to jeopardise their lives by running off. So he had lied: he would not go out the next time; in fact, never as long as Janna's ailing parents lived, never as long as the possibilities of reprisals existed. They all remembered the massacre at Lidice too well.

In May 1942 Hitler's butcher, Reinhard Heydrich, was assassinated by the Czech patriots Jan Kubis and Josef Gabchik near Prague. In what seemed like a random reprisal, the village of

Lidice, some eighteen kilometres northwest of Prague, was chosen and, on a day in June, all its men were shot, all the women and older children shipped to the Ravensbrück concentration camp, while the younger children were farmed out to German foster homes. The village was burned and bulldozed so that no trace remained. The arrogant SS filmed all of it.

Janek's rage turned in on itself. He had to direct it at something, someone. Then he recalled Ilyichev. Why hadn't Tana killed him once his usefulness was finished? He checked his machine carbine and deliberately strode over to the cellar door.

He stood there, his legs unsteady, as if he was on the edge of a precipice. An inner part of his mind warned him. Killing in cold blood was not their way. They weren't butchers like Heydrich; they must fight repression with non-violence. They must create confusion and strife amongst the Soviet occupying forces. In the true Svejkian manner!

The Czech writer Jaroslav Hasek's character, *The Good Soldier Svejk* had been adopted during the war - and again at the time of the Soviet invasion. Svejk, the little fellow, fighting authority, by following orders verbatim, reducing bureaucrats and politicians to absurdity. '*Svejkovina*,' Janek whispered to himself: the way Svejk does it.

But another part of him wanted blood - repayment; revenge even. They had tortured Marta and must pay in kind. Then it came to him in a flash - he would shoot the swine's foot off! Tana and the others would be angry - but once it was done, they could not undo it. If he needs the doctor, he thought, I will foot the bill! He chuckled at his little joke. But his eyes were filled with moisture.

His heart seemed to beat louder and faster as he unlocked the door and opened it. He pointed the gun in front of him and peered into the musty darkness, eyes not quite adjusted to the change in visibility.

'Ilyichev, you bastard!' he shouted with all the pent-up anger in him.

There was no answer. The swine was probably cowering in a corner, fearing the worst.

Janek descended the stairs slowly, a step at a time.

As the boarded-up window came into view he felt his mouth go dry. 'Ilyichev, you coward, show yourself and face me!' Now he could make out the angular silhouettes of crates. The swine was probably hiding behind them. They're all the same, cowards hiding under the protection of the powerful state apparatus.

There was a blur - some kind of shadow - in front of him. His hate evaporated in the wake of sudden raw fear as he sensed more than saw the blow coming. Before he could exert any tension on his trigger finger, the gun was knocked out of his hand.

A bicycle frame swung down out of the semi-darkness, pedals smashing into Janek's face, shattering his spectacles.

'Hey!' Janek barked, instantly worried about how he could afford a new pair.

But the attack didn't stop and he lost his footing as the shooting pain swamped his brain. He fell back onto the stairs, hardly feeling the hard tread digging into his back and neck. Blood - his blood - blinded him. Weakly now, he tried warding off Ilyichev's successive blows, his anger forgotten, only the pain, the pain. Pain swamped him.

Slightly buckled now and bloody, the frame of the bicycle was flung across the cellar. Hardly giving his actions a thought, Ilyichev stepped over the limp body of Janek and climbed the stairs, his feet leaving bloodstains as he went.

The light in the living room glared. The air - and revenge - tasted sweet.

Must get in touch with Kasayiev, he thought, stepping outside.

His future didn't seem too bright since he'd failed to inform his superiors when first spotting Tana, nor after locating her here at the dacha. He'd let himself get caught and, worse still, he helped the Ruzyne breakout. The CCTV cameras would identify him, he knew.

No, this information on their escape route would barely compensate and hardly redeem me, he thought ruefully.

But he had few options open, short of fleeing the country as a suspected defector, to be hunted by KGB assassins just like him.

Ilyichev hurried towards the nearest road and, eventually, he managed to thumb a lift into Prague.

Father Alois Neruda had been ordained for five years and though Rome never recognised ministers like him in the *skryta cirkev*, he regularly and bravely performed his religious rites behind closed doors to avoid persecution. Just like today.

There was a young woman and two families kneeling at the table which served as a makeshift altar and he gave the children a blessing and their parents the wafer and wine.

When he came to Elena Sevelova, he tried not to look into her large grey-green eyes. She kept her blonde hair covered with a headscarf because she was respectful, as she had been brought up to be. She proffered her open mouth and delicately he placed the wafer on her small pointed tantalising tongue. God forgive him, but he felt that she seemed to eat the Host sensuously, her eyes never leaving his.

He returned with the cup and she sipped more wine than most people.

As he concluded the service, he offered a blessing on all of them and their families and friends, whether they believed or not. It was no secret that most of the country was atheist. Perhaps it was their live-and-let-live attitude that had permitted the Soviets to trample all over them?

But it wasn't his place to get involved in the politics of his country. Though the agents of his country's politics hounded him and his congregation, harassing believers.

God tries us hard, he thought. And he remembered the lingering handshake of Elena. She was infatuated with him, that much was obvious. And, God help him, he didn't seem mature enough to handle it.

This was the hard part about being a priest. Denial. She was the attractive daughter of a highly respected doctor and he had no business even contemplating lewd things concerning her.

An hour later the StB battered down his door because someone had informed on him. His robes were stripped from him and his religious possessions destroyed and burned. He was taken away in handcuffs.

Within the hour he suffered a severe beating that left the vision in one eye permanently impaired, then he was put on a train for a gulag in cold inhospitable northern Russia.

Yet throughout what seemed like eternal damnation he prayed to God and asked that Elena would come to no harm.

Tana and Laco handed over responsibility for the students to the remainder of Demek's men at the crossroads. They left the small group in a clearing a few yards to the south of the junction.

'Let's get back,' Laco said.

The prospect of the return trek wasn't appealing, even after all Laco's ecstatic erotic promises. 'You'll be too tired to lift a finger,' she chided, 'let alone anything else.'

'Your comment deflates me!' he countered.

'I have another penetration in mind, Laco. Remember?' Tana was troubled. Perhaps that bullet graze had wearied her, or maybe she had expended too much nervous energy during the breakout? She was surprised to find that the idea of penetrating the Dobranice mining complex tonight was daunting.

About forty minutes later they arrived back at the dacha and the unwelcome but familiar dark foreboding hit her before she stepped onto the loggia.

Laco sensed her unease at once. 'What is it?' he whispered. He withdrew his CZ52 automatic.

She shook her head and gestured at the door. 'Nobody there,' she said, her voice cracking.

Laco barged in and she was fast on his heels and scanned the room. Nothing seemed to be amiss.

'The cellar,' she whispered, already fearing - no, knowing - the worst.

The cellar door was open. Laco paused a moment at the threshold then ducked through and slowly descended. 'Ilyichev!' he snarled.

She found Laco bending over Janek, one hand cradling the man's head, the other a fist clenching in anger. 'Janek's dead,' he said coldly.

The after-image of Janek, smiling after speaking with Marta, merged with the thought-picture of Marta bidding her goodbye and thank you at the crossroads. It was like a cold shower as Tana realised the truth. 'Demek's route,' she said. 'I think Ilyichev overheard the plans.'

Laco swore and glared moist-eyed at her. 'For God's sake, why did you insist we keep Ilyichev alive?'

Tana marvelled at her self-control. Seeing Janek there was like losing a part of herself. In the brief moments of psychic contact when she had snatched Janek's thoughts, she had grown very close to him. Now he was dead. 'I wanted him as a swap - for Jiri,' she explained, knowing that Laco would not understand. 'Last night I dreamed they'd taken Jiri. And since he hasn't made contact I must assume my dream was accurate.'

Laco looked capable of exploding. 'For a - a *dream*?'

'Yes, Laco, for a dream. I'm sorry Janek's dead - more than you can ever know. But right now we have more urgent problems. Is there some way we can warn Demek? And you'd best tell this friend of yours that his dacha's no longer safe.'

Laco's eyes searched hers. 'I don't really know you at all. I thought I did - the times we've...' He stopped, tenor changing: his calculating mind was one of his attractions. 'But you're right, of course. As for Demek...' He shrugged. 'We must trust that Ilyichev couldn't organise anything in time.'

Tana heard the sound of a car approaching and turned towards the doorway. Her face clouded and sadness swelled in her breast and her throat was dry as she said, 'We'd be wrong in that assumption.'

Demek's man - she didn't know his name, but he'd driven one of the Tatras earlier - stumbled in off the loggia.

'Ask him,' she said heavily.

He was white and trembling. 'I drove straight here - I don't know what to do. Demek, the others - they're all dead.' There was the background sound of his car motor still idling outside but nobody seemed to notice.

Laco moved forward and held the man's shoulders. 'What the hell happened?'

The worst had happened, Tana knew, yet we still must know all the gory tragic details.

'I - I had a puncture, couldn't help being late at the rendezvous point,' he whined. 'But before I got to the shack I heard shooting.' His eyes stared horror-struck, reliving the scene. Tana held the man's arm but couldn't detect any thought-pictures; that wasn't unusual, since the 'gift' was erratic and couldn't always be voluntarily applied.

'Someone betrayed us!' he wailed, now shaking Laco.

Laco slapped his face.

He broke down and sobbed. Then he choked back his tears and the rest came out in a rush. 'Demek stood his ground, sent the boy and girl to me. He just stood there shouting abuse at the bastards. Shooting his machine gun. And they blasted him to hell. The girl was limping badly; they both stumbled a couple of times. Kamil and Frantisek ran up behind, helped them along. I - I couldn't stay there - bullets whining all round - there were shots hitting the ground at their feet,' he wailed, eyes wide and moist. 'I - I backed out, drove off. Came straight here. Nowhere else to go, I had to come here. Demek's hideout's too far away.'

Face suffused with revulsion, Laco let go of the shaking man and sank onto a dining chair.

Tana had never seen him look so devastated, so defeated. Laco seemed to shrink visibly before her eyes.

'Did you see what happened to the students?' Laco asked hoarsely, an elbow on the chair arm and covering his eyes with long fingers.

The man nodded repeatedly. 'Yes, yes, they wouldn't have got anywhere near my car. Their legs were shot from under them before I'd finished my turn. I - I couldn't save them - if there'd been a chance. Honest to God, I - I would've tried.'

Tana held Laco's shoulder. 'Don't blame him too much. When fear singles us out, we behave irrationally.' She thought that the man could have reversed towards Antonin and Marta - and the enemy; but even then their chances would have been very slim.

Laco turned, stared at the man. 'But if they only shot them in the legs - they'll take them back to Ruzyne!'

'No,' cut in Tana. 'Both Marta and Antonin swore they wouldn't be captured again.' She said to Demek's man, 'Did the students carry guns?'

Dumbly, he nodded and looked away, his eyes seeing things he would not be able to expunge for the rest of his life.

Laco sighed, understanding. 'Those poor kids.'

And he was only twenty-five! Tana thought.

She glanced up as Jan Smidke entered. 'I've just heard,' he said. 'On the Gazik's radio on the way here.'

'Did you manage to get the latex moulds?' Tana asked.

Laco's mouth dropped open, as though unable to credit that she could still consider going into Dobranice after the number of deaths already reported.

'We planned the breakout as a cover, Laco. Now, Kasayiev and his men will be crowing victory and celebrating. We cannot let all those deaths pass for nothing.'

'I see that - but...'

'There will be time enough for mourning,' she said.

'She's right,' added Smidke.

'And the water supply?' she asked Smidke.

He nodded, his voice edged with tension. 'Treated. A couple of hours back, as instructed. The complex should be suffering acute dysentery by now.'

At any other time that piece of news would have brought out a grin at their enemy's discomfiture. Now it was received solemnly.

'Good,' was all that she said. 'Papers?'

Smidke handed her a brown waxed-paper parcel. 'All there. They should pass muster but you'll appreciate it was a rushed job?'

'Yes, Jan.' She unwrapped the parcel and studied the contents. 'They did well.'

He hesitated a moment then added, 'Can I go with you?'

Tana had foreseen Smidke's request and paused before replying, counting the dead so far. She shook her head and looked into his eyes. 'No, Jan. Sorry.'

It was an awkward moment. She had left the obvious unsaid, but she could see in their eyes that they both understood. Should anything go amiss, Smidke was designated as Laco's successor for the area.

'Perhaps you're right,' Smidke said grudgingly.

'Look after this fellow, will you?' She thumbed at the trembling Demek man. 'We'll have to leave now.' She grimaced and laughed without humour. 'They're probably on their way here already! Oh, and don't forget to warn off your propaganda artist friend, he can't come back to his dacha now.'

'He won't be too pleased.'

'His sacrifice is nothing compared to the others, is it?' she replied acidly.

'Sacrifice...' Laco looked at the cellar door.

'And, Jan,' Tana added, her tone lighter than she felt, 'please tell Janek's wife - Janna - that her husband died well.' Lies, all lies. Why do we still persist in sugaring the bitter pill? Nobody dies well.

Smidke nodded, his face like stone. 'Is that all?'

'Yes, I think so.' She took his hand but his grip was feeble, as if he had already decided that life on this planet was no longer desirable. 'Thanks, Jan,' she added, giving him a brief hug and kiss on the cheek. 'Keep fighting.'

From that brief contact Jan Smidke seemed to find an inner strength and hugged her back. 'I will, Tana.' At least the despairing look had gone from his eyes. 'Hard though it is.'

Tana stepped off the loggia and joined Laco in the Gazik that Smidke had brought. Two of his men sat in the back and nodded abrupt greetings. They were carrying bulky parcels of clothes. The engine was purring.

She waved. 'Good luck, Jan!'

'Take care!' Smidke shouted after them as they headed for the main road and the mysterious Dobranice complex.

CHAPTER TEN: Laco

The white searchlight picked out the Soviet red star on the bonnet as the Gazik bounced along the dirt track, leaving a wake of dun-coloured dust. A sentry called down to them from the watchtower over the Dobranice gate. Light glinted off the barbed wire. The other gun-emplacements continued undisturbed, automatically scanning the no-man's-land of truncated trees around the perimeter fence.

'Doctor Perouschka from the Institute in answer to your Commandant's signal message!' called the Red Army lieutenant in the front passenger seat. Shoulders hunched, two people sat in the rear wearing white coats; one appeared to be female.

The gate opened but the barrier stayed down. A guard stepped out of a small guardroom by the side of the road. 'Documentation.'

Blithely handing over their ID Cards, the lieutenant said, 'Don't take all night, soldier. The signal said it was urgent.'

Looking paler than he should in this light, the sentry forced a smile. 'I won't be keeping you long, sir!' He then fleetingly checked over the two passengers in the back, returned the IDs then saluted. 'Well, I hope you can put us all right, Doctor!' He winced. 'Excuse me - !' And he ran knock-kneed into the guardroom. The toilet door slammed shut.

Abandoned to his own devices, the lieutenant shrugged. 'Might as well go in, I suppose,' he said loudly to the driver. He stepped down and raised the barrier. The Gazik was driven through then braked, waiting. The lieutenant jumped aboard and they headed into the shadows of the slag heaps.

The mining machinery itself was unlit. The headlamps cut swathes of muddy grey light through the deep-rutted road and beside a railway track that skirted the tall overshadowing screens. With the headgear on their left, they passed the funnel of the washery which was bathed in a ghostly glow from the perimeter fence lights. There didn't seem to be much activity. Soldiers were quite scarce.

Laco, feeling constrained in his Red Army lieutenant's uniform, whispered in English, 'What if the traitor's with us now - in the Gazik?'

Tana's prominent latex brow furrowed uncomfortably. 'I think not, Laco. Just a feeling and I tend to trust my feelings. Jiri was on to something - and I suspect the traitor has more privileged information than any of your cell could muster.'

She scratched her false nose and recalled the three lectures at the Fort given by Mike Clayton on surveillance and disguise. It was only much later that she had learned he was MI6's 'Master of Disguise'.

'Subtle is best,' Mike had emphasised in his growling tone, his fathomless brown eyes glinting. 'There are two basic methods. The immediate quick change and the deliberate disguise.'

During assignments she had adopted both methods. She had adjusted her stature by stooping or limping and changed her body size with padding. As the situation demanded, she'd changed from Miss Average into Miss Nondescript. Yet at other times, it was useful to stand out, as long as she looked different. And women found it so much easier to change their appearance than men.

Once, she put a small stone in her shoe to create a realistic limp. Far better than just pretending. A moment's forgetfulness and you didn't limp - dead giveaway.

She'd used the Perouschka disguise before so it was a simple matter to give Jan her prosthetic measurements. Coloured contact lenses would have been useful, but there'd been no time to get prescription ones made up. Eyes - windows of the soul? Maybe. Must talk to James Fisk about that, she thought.

Windowless, the new white prefabricated building loomed out of the night, its radio antennae and radar dishes dominating the night skyline.

The Gazik grated to a halt at the foot of the entrance steps. The driver stayed with the vehicle while the other three strode inside the automatically opening doorway and up to the Red Army clerk at the reception desk.

Tana flashed her documents, forged to testify that she was a Doctor Perouschka qualified in treating tropical diseases and in particular dysentery.

'That was quick, Doctor,' the Red Army clerk remarked, relief on his face. 'We haven't had a reply to our signal yet!'

She smiled at him. A reply would not be forthcoming as the resistance movement had set in train their sophisticated jamming apparatus, installed courtesy of Uncle Sam.

'They did say it was urgent, soldier,' Tana said.

'Yes, Doctor. Glad you got our signal before all this interference.'

'It sounds like a strong strain - to have acted so quickly,' she observed.

'Yes, it happened so fast!' The clerk gave their papers a cursory check then directed them to the lift. 'You'll want the fourteenth level.'

Deep, thought Tana, estimating the height of this room, multiplying by fourteen. She entered the cubicle with the other two and pressed the 14 button.

Lifts always made her feel insecure. It was not so much a feeling of being confined, as she'd overcome that fear a long time ago in the Warsaw sewers. But if her identity were known, it was an easy matter to trap her there. True, they could break out through the trapdoor above and climb the cables; but no amount of logic could dismiss her irrational unease as they descended.

At the fourteenth level they were met by another soldier. The place was impressive, with its fluorescent lighting, tiled walls and the muted hum of air-conditioning. A short corridor, then, turning right, they faced an airlock. This was opened and, once through, shut after them.

Her ears popped. The opposite lock was opened and they entered yet another corridor, where the air was noticeably fresher.

Closed-circuit television camera eyes peered down from corners at regular intervals. The complex reminded her of the Kimball missile silo she had visited, deep under Nebraska; even in the Land of the Free they didn't entirely trust their own soldiers.

Fifteen yards along, they came to a bulky door on the left. It rumbled open. They were led along a corridor with branch-passages at regular intervals on the right. The walls were matt-grey stressed concrete and looked blastproof.

She had tried keeping her bearings in relation to the pithead and it looked as though their miner contact at Pilsen was right. This complex was just beyond the mine tunnels. There was definitely a connection with the mineshafts, she knew. On emerging from the lift, immediately ahead had been a gate. The light had not pierced far beyond the gate's bars but she had made out machinery and what looked like a conveyor belt. Then they had turned and entered the airlock before she could see more. There had been a sentry on duty at the gate though.

Now, third block along, they stopped at a door labelled in Cyrillic stencil: *Commandant*, she translated.

Barked commands cut into the night. Branches and twigs cracked and leaves rustled. Bathed in the headlights of armoured carriers, the dacha appeared quite eerie.

Looking like a great bear in his astrakhan coat, Major Kasayiev crouched behind the mudguard of one of the carriers. Ilyichev was by his side and not looking too pleased.

The tear gas swirled in great fronds out of the windows and

doorway. Troops in gas masks charged, weapons at hip level.

Three tense minutes later, they emerged empty-handed. Nobody there.

Kasayiev glared at Ilyichev.

The Russian agent quaked where he crouched. 'That damned driver - in the car that got away - he must've warned them!'

'That's blatantly obvious!' Kasayiev turned to watch a body being carried out. 'Who's that? No, don't tell me; it's the one called Janek, isn't it?'

'Yes.'

'*Your* brilliant work again! It might have been nice to question him first, you know?'

Ilyichev felt cold. His head throbbed where it had been hit on his fall into the cellar. He was tired with nervous exhaustion. And he was afraid for his career and his life. His damned leg ached insistently, adding more fuel to his impotent anger. He rubbed his eyes, asked tentatively, 'What do you plan on doing now, sir?'

Kasayiev shrugged expansively. 'I should hang you from the nearest tree and leave you for the damned birds! As it is, I'm getting soft in my old age. You can help ferret out all known subversives!'

'But - we don't know the main ones. That's why you had Grishin tailing Standish, wasn't it? To lead you to them?'

'Indeed! A pity you didn't inform HQ of this place and her whereabouts earlier!'

Ilyichev bit back on a retort.

'Root out all known resistance movements!' Kasayiev demanded. 'Make arrests. Get me information on this woman's whereabouts.'

'But the Party Secretary doesn't want to use the hard line,' Ilyichev said cautiously. 'He doesn't want a repetition of the Stalinist trials.'

Kasayiev stared. 'Who said anything about trials? Just arrest them and get me answers!'

'Where can I locate you - if I have good news?'

'*If?* There better be good news, damn you, Ilyichev! I'll be at Dobranice. Grishin's there now, investigating a curious outbreak of dysentery.'

'But that's not the KGB's province, is it?'

'True. Though we tend to get all the shitty jobs, no?' Kasayiev grinned at his joke then linked Ilyichev's arm in a comradely fashion which made the agent's skin crawl. 'But what would you say if I told you a nearby Czech institute has cultured some bacteria specifically for that purpose?'

Tana was shown in. The smell of disinfectant mixed with faeces was stronger in this enclosed area. Draped in field-grey serge blankets, the Commandant lay on his bed, drawn and pale. 'Quick, doctor,' he pleaded, 'give me something to stop...'

He was sincere and in great pain. But she had detected another mind, hostile, calculating. Familiar, too.

She swerved round, face to face with Grishin who slammed the door shut with only her and Laco inside. Recognition was dawning in Grishin's eyes and it wasn't a pretty sight.

Smidke's man hammered on the door.

Her disguise had only been superficial, to avoid any obvious similarities with her description which was bound to have been broadcast after the breakout. But the eyes were always a giveaway unless disguised with coloured contact lenses. And when you've fought eyeball to eyeball with an enemy, the enemy doesn't forget the eyes.

Grishin's recognition was quite fast but his actions were too slow.

Tana's foot shot out and broke Grishin's kneecap and Laco instinctively followed her lead with a blow to the man's chin with his gun butt.

Grishin slumped to the tiled floor as the Commandant sat up in bed. He was about to yell when Laco clubbed him senseless too.

'I'd dearly love to shoot them, but we need to be quiet,' Laco explained.

Tana nodded and they turned and swung the door open. Smidke's man seemed distressed. He looked worse, his mouth wide, when he saw the two unconscious men: 'What do we do?' he demanded.

'We lock them in here and go searching this complex for-' She never finished.

Grishin was in great pain, but his hate was greater. He withdrew his automatic and fired at their group standing in the doorway.

Smidke's man thudded into the doorjamb to the echoes of the gun's blast.

Laco replied immediately and his shot sent Grishin skidding across the floor.

A strident klaxon abruptly sounded.

'Run for it!' shrieked Smidke's man, his white lab-coat reddening as he lay there.

An officer rounded the bend, took in the scene at a glance and went for his holstered gun and fired hurriedly. He hit Smidke's man twice and Laco returned fire and killed him with a single shot.

'Hell!' Laco breathed. 'Now we'll have the whole place down on top of us!'

Tana cast a glance back as Laco's gun stopped barking. Grishin's body had left a gruesome trail and was slumped against the skirting. The Commandant was leaning out of bed, speaking into a phone. Further retribution wouldn't help - Grishin's shot had set the alarm off and he'd paid. She checked the throat-pulse of Smidke's man: he was dead.

'We'll have to fight our way out,' she said, shrugging off her coat to reveal figure-hugging black trousers, black bridle leather assault belt, sweater and boots.

They left the Commandant's office and ran down the corridor.

'The cameras!' Laco swore as they reached the end of the corridor and the doorway they'd last entered. He shot the camera to pieces as the door opened.

An armed trooper jumped through, collided with Tana. They fell to the tiled floor and his gun skittered. She met his chin with a resounding kick. He didn't get up.

Retrieving the soldier's gun, she stepped through the doorway with the weapon in the crook of her arm.

A single shot sounded behind. The agony of it hitting home made her wince and her steps faltered. But she hadn't been hit. Then she realised that it was Laco.

Leg pumping blood spasmodically, he collapsed. Oh, God, the bullet had hit an artery.

'Go on!' he called, pulling himself round to face three troopers who were closing in. 'I'll hold them off!'

The Commandant was groggily supporting himself against his office door, one hand on his bleeding forehead. '*Keep her alive*!' he barked at his men. The troopers didn't fire again.

Tana hesitated, undecided, old images returning, of her brother Ishmael being gunned down on that steamer so long ago.

Laco kept on firing at the advancing troopers, moving towards them on his elbows, dragging his legs behind, leaving a red trail on the floor tiles. But she could see that the pain from the wound was affecting his aim. He peered back at Tana, eyes starting. '*Go!*'

One of the Russians fell but the other two didn't slow; nor did they shoot. Brave men or foolhardy. Then Laco's gun must have overheated and jammed as he changed the magazine. Tana watched horrified as the two soldiers pounced. Though he struggled, they began dragging him away, down the corridor, all the while the Commandant grinning stupidly.

So they'd wanted Laco alive as well and hastily set up a snatch-squad. He knew much, a great deal of value; about her and about London. As well as Jan Smidke and many others.

Tears streamed as she backed into the doorway, the Soviet machine gun raised. '*Sorry, Laco!*' she cried inwardly, hoping the rapport they shared would help him pick up her distressed thoughts. She shot the two Russian soldiers in the back and they fell like stringless puppets. In that brief second she glimpsed Laco holding two thumbs up. He knew, she thought. Her single shot hit Laco at the base of his skull. No mistake. She didn't stop to watch him hit the tiles but dived through the doorway.

Her heart empty, she wiped her eyes and sought her bearings.

She turned right then stopped dead. Half a dozen troopers were piling out of the lift. She fired a short dissuading burst over their heads and chunks of concrete flew dangerously in every direction, making them duck. She swerved left instead.

Running alongside the blastproof wall, she noticed some construction work ahead. So, whatever they were up to, it wasn't finished.

Fifteen yards on was a corridor on the right but she ignored it, drawn by the international symbols on a door another ten yards ahead on the left.

RADIOACTIVE.

Tana tried the door. It was locked so she rammed the butt of the machine gun down on the handle, the action bruising the palm of her hand, but the door burst open and she stumbled through, slamming it shut after her. She leaned her back against the door.

Breathless, she found herself on a concrete balcony, which appeared to be some kind of viewing platform.

And there before her was the reason for this huge subterranean complex.

Pounding footsteps on the other side of the door sounded very close. They would have seen her enter. Way below the balcony a few figures in white overalls pointed up at her. She was trapped – and they knew it.

The continuous blare of the klaxon thrummed hypnotically.

Still leaning against the closed door, she allowed a twist of irony to crease her mouth. She had found their secret weapons, but nobody in London would know. So damned near.

Tana let the machine gun fall from her grasp. It would be so easy to hold the hot smoking muzzle up to her throat and pull the trigger, save that she was out of ammo. But the thought alone assaulted her imagination - and her dormant religion - anyway.

She had hoped they would shoot to kill. Even that had been taken away from her. And bullets wouldn't penetrate this door. No, they would capture her then torture her with great delight, insinuating themselves into her mind and they would do unspeakable things, wresting all her secrets from her - in photographic detail.

With the tip of her tongue she sought the right molar in her upper jaw.

Outside, the footfalls stopped.

'Come out, you murdering bitch!' A gun butt boomed on the door and she felt it vibrate against her shoulder blades.

She would not be taken alive, she thought, her mouth suddenly very dry. Her tongue worried at then dislodged the death pill that Geraghty had embedded within the molar cavity. *Damn them all*!

'God forgive me,' Tana said and, offering up a prayer, she thought of Ishmael and bit into the pill.

CHAPTER ELEVEN: Message

The pill didn't work!

And before she could throw herself from the balcony to a crashing death below, the door fell in, rammed into her back and sent her stumbling forward, full into the safety rail. Winded, she sank to her knees. Two troopers laid hands on her, twisted her arms up her back and snapped on handcuffs. Someone slapped her about the head several times and she felt the nostril of her false nose tear away slightly.

Her head swam as she sucked in air and her diaphragm was suddenly very painful.

They led her unresisting towards the Commandant's office. On the way, they passed the bodies of guards, and after passing, each one her captors thumped her shoulders with their gun butts.

Skirting Laco, they kicked his corpse and she wanted to hit out at them for showing disrespect for a brave young man. At that instant she dimly realised she was losing her logic faculties for personal rage. Laco was dead and wouldn't mind. He lived on in her memory. Memory. They'd want hers.

They pushed her through the Commandant's doorway and she was forced painfully to her knees. She felt the wet stickiness through the material of her trousers and realised that she was kneeling in a pool of Grishin's blood.

The Commandant hobbled forward, his face sickly green. His shaking hand reached out, clawed at her face and callously tore off some of the latex mould – the pain was similar to waxing and tears pricked her eyes.

'So you're the woman Comrade Kasayiev is after?' His whole face was contorted with abdominal pain, his eyes red-rimmed and bleary, dried blood trailing down the side of his face from the blow to his head.

She kept quiet, trying to organise herself mentally, to dismiss the throbbing waves of pain emanating from her back and torso. She couldn't hope to overcome continuous mind-bending but she might be able to resist for a while until help could be found or she could contrive to kill herself.

Tana stared ahead emptily whilst, within, her whole being was sucking up reserves of energy for the ordeal to come. She closed her senses save, for the moment, hearing and touch. Transcendental meditation was not possible under these conditions - and she had no wish to go into a trance yet: things were not irrevocable. When the torture was inevitable she would go under - but not until. In the meantime, she would store her energies for possible escape and evasion.

'So you choose not to talk?' the Commandant snarled, slapping her face. 'Well, I've already contacted Kasayiev and he's sending a specialist to interrogate you. Doctor Schneider. Yes, soon you'll be only too happy to talk.'

She had numbed her nerves and lessened blood flow to her torso, which actually reduced the pain. Adrenalin was still pumping – far too much for the inactivity at present.

'Take her to the Interrogation Room!' the Commandant ordered.

Whatever new facility they build, she thought sanguinely, the bastards never forget to install an interrogation room. It was as essential as hot and cold running water and a toilet.

She was under no illusions. During her counter-interrogation course she'd watched the film *I Can't Answer That Question* that MI6 made at the Fort. Subjects were hooded, physically exhausted, beaten up, lied to, kept cold and verbally abused. White noise and sensory deprivation were employed. The rather ominous voice-over ended by warning that only those who could anchor their reason firmly in the world they remembered would be able to resist.

Vaguely she was aware of being roughly hauled to her feet and shoved forward. Normal motor muscles did the work; she went where they pushed. Closed in on three sides, arms handcuffed behind her back, she had no hope of escape from her guards, and any failed attempt wouldn't result in death, only a beating which would weaken her body and mental resolve.

Kazakhstan

'She's being beaten, they're hurting her!' Yakunin exclaimed before he could stop himself. He glanced up from his desk, his face beaded in sweat.

Everyone in the room was watching him, their eyes cold and without feeling. Even without resorting to psychic voyeurism, he knew that they were worried he was putting their jobs in jeopardy. He appeared to be too closely involved in his subject, an enemy agent. Emotionally attached. And, although none of them knew, it seemed he was somehow physically connected, too.

Yakunin's side and back ached from blows he had not received.

He had no option but to call Bublyk over and explain what he had detected.

But for now he would hide his concern for her – and his strangely induced bruises. That was private and none of Bublyk's business.

Private? Was there such a thing as privacy here under Bublyk's psychic gaze? He hoped so. Time would tell, Yakunin supposed.

Czechoslovakia

Time lost all meaning for Tana as she sat in the centre of the small Interrogation Room. She couldn't see now. Oblivious of her surroundings. She slid into a trance, her heartbeat shallow.

She was no longer a body.

Only a mind.

Mind.

Demand for oxygen diminished to a negligible amount. No conscious thoughts occurred. Outside stimuli couldn't impinge.

She was mind only.

Before entering her trance she had formulated the message. She could have relayed the information she'd discovered here. But that wouldn't stop the Soviets brainwashing her and obtaining details from her photographic memory. If she could, she would have wiped her memory clean, but that wasn't possible. Nothing short of brain damage could do that.

So, Tana decided on a lengthy and explicit message in Interprises' latest code. There were three methods she could employ: she tried them alternately.

Send the thought-message to the nearest receptive mind, use that mind and the person's inner psychic reserves to boost the message to yet another mind; then another; leapfrogging until, finally, the message would reach London. As the message was subliminal, the unwitting couriers were ignorant of their part in the process. And they couldn't subconsciously divulge the information because it was in code.

After the first stab at the second method she was saturated in sweat but then it became progressively easier. Electrical thought-impulses left her and the room by utilising the electric circuitry. The maze of cross-currents, the plethora of counter-messages made her first attempts garbled; but, by perseverance and practice, she was able to use the antennae, riding the radio waves they emitted. The encrypted message could go out on the ether - but she couldn't dictate how or where it would be received.

Lastly, she attempted direct-link, picturing Keith Tyson, the closest person to her in Interprises - *sorry, Alan*. Besides having been lovers a few years ago, they were still good friends and had a strong rapport. Subconsciously, it might be enough - he'd proven receptive before.

She'd accomplished distanced thought-picture transference in excess of seven hundred miles on two separate occasions roughly three months ago: though being so far below ground might create corrupting disturbances or even total washout.

Of all three methods, she had the greatest faith in the last.

Tana to London. Imprisoned Czech complex Dobranice. Vital discovery. Cannot resist interrogation indefinitely. Directions for penetration via mine tunnels. Depth 200ft. Head east-west till contact guarded gate then through airlock along corridor.

She tried to be explicit with her directions and completed the message.

Then they started in earnest and she closed down every conceivable reserve to combat their onslaught.

Doctor Schneider flashed his ophthalmic light into Tana's unresponsive eyes, scrutinised her for a moment and then straightened up. 'She's in a trance of some sort.' He turned to the watching Commandant in his blood- and sweat-stained uniform: 'You haven't drugged her?'

'No, of course not, I wouldn't dream of it!' the Commandant was quick to reply.

'Dreams, yes. An interesting subject, this one,' Schneider remarked, polishing his glasses. 'Do you dream, Commandant?'

The Commandant looked askance. 'Of course, Doctor. We all do, don't we? Why do you ask?'

Schneider tapped Tana's head as if conducting a tutorial. 'The brain is a computer. Better than we can ever produce – and I'm not being unpatriotic by saying that. It's just a fact. Well, when you're awake the brain is online, like any computer. But when you're asleep, the brain doesn't rest but switches to offline, when it sorts out programs, discards others, revises and updates the data received whilst online. Dreams are an interruption of this offline process, jumbling the events and data and the dormant conscious tries to make sense of it, but only succeeds in grasping a kind of Alice in Wonderland meaning.'

'I'm afraid I am not at all technical, Doctor.'

Schneider glanced at the trolley of metal tools and elecrtrical shock equipment. 'No, I can see that, Commandant.' Peeling back Tana's collar, he held up a hypodermic and gave its contents a little squirt into the air. 'Hallucinogens like this here kick the dream mechanism into action whilst the brain-computer's still online, contrary to the fundamental rules of cerebral mechanics.' He inserted the needle and drained the phial.

'What happens – what will happen to her now?'

Schneider's balding head shone under the huge operating lamps. 'There'll be a steady deterioration in her ability to distinguish between inner and outer reality. In a word, she'll become schizoid. The online dreaming will make her hyper-programmable. Any stimuli or data fed in will be incorporated in a major program: trivial events will assume massive significance, and vice versa.'

'But that sounds like brainwashing, Doctor,' the Commandant said in a worried tone. 'Major Kasayiev doesn't want her brainwashed, he wants the information in her head.'

'It's not washing in the normal sense, Commandant,' Schneider sneered. 'She'll be pliable, unable to appreciate what's important and what isn't. She'll be quite capable of giving us anything and indeed everything in her head. We simply ask.'

The Commandant shook his head, his eyes darting, worried. 'I still don't know if I should've let you go ahead before Comrade Kasayiev gets here.'

'Don't fret yourself, Comrade Commandant, I can handle Kasayiev!'

The d-Lysergic acid diethylamide would cause changes in Tana's perception, creating a weird distortion of time perspectives, colours, movement and sound. But Tana's perceptions were no longer on the plane of time; the external stimuli such as colour, movement and sound had no meaning in her trance-like framework. The boundaries between the senses would fade, except that she was not using her senses. Sounds would normally give rise to visual sensations, but not for Tana as no sound registered through her psychic defences.

But other chemical changes would be assaulting her brain, juggling with the chemical honeycomb of memory cells. Cracks in her defences did inevitably occur. She was unable to combat a sudden regression of jumbled experiences from her past: reliving sad and happy moments; tears welled but she didn't feel them. Painful assignments flashed into raw focus: intense beauty, of countless sunsets in numerous foreign lands; intense horror of near-death in a blazing ship, sulphurous fumes suffocating; all mingling, verging on the unbearable.

Seeing again all those people whom she had loved and lost. Each with smiling eyes; memories to hearten at a re-telling. Lost! And her enemies were resurrected, now superior, invulnerable, violent - again and again they appeared, threatening, hurting repeatedly, bathing in the gory splendour of letting blood - her blood.

Her heartbeat quickened. Shocks to her system gnawed at her trance.

With the utmost inner concentration, her mind hovering as if over a mountain range, and though violently shaken as if by powerful thermals, she conquered the assaulting images, beat them back, and lapsed into an all-pervading deep tranquillity. The occasional shocking chemical bursts were now alien and hindsight and revelation no longer produced profound, damaging emotional reactions.

But her psychic energies were gutted.

Kazakhstan

Head swimming, Yakunin wrenched off his headset. Jumbled in with disturbing psychedelic images and shimmering shapes of an old street with its ancient doors throbbing and wavering under some invisible onslaught, his mind was bombarded with a single name - *Keith* - and strings of letters - obviously code - repeated over and over again.

His mind reeled at the sheer strength of the message, deafening on a psychic level.

He had no option but to write down the code and hand it to Bublyk who was watching him closely now.

Yakunin felt he was betraying her.

Oxfordshire, England

Keith Tyson's finger trembled but he was unaware of it. Some scientists believed the Ouija glass is affected by the subconscious exerting subtle pressure on the sitter's motor muscles without that person knowing. He didn't know what to think. Tana reckoned he had psychic leanings, if only he let them out, but he wasn't convinced.

'Bloody hell, it's working!' young Wilf Ashley exclaimed, freckled face gaping.

'You're not moving it, are you, laddie?' Jock McTaggart asked Tyson.

Keith Tyson shook his head. 'No.'

'It's uncanny,' said Alan Swann, the session's fourth member.

Zigzagging, the glass seemed to be spelling out answers to their questions while Tyson faithfully jotted down the letters selected by the glass.

Then everything changed. The letters were gibberish and the glass didn't answer any more of their questions.

Yet it was familiar. Tyson had come across that grouping recently.

'Well, that's our lot for tonight, I reckon,' Alan remarked and took his hand away.

'No, wait!' Tyson snapped. Q-13-ZTL: Tana's message-coded name. My God, it's all in code! His black eyebrows arched rakishly as the incredible truth dawned. 'Keep at it, for God's sake!'

Though Tyson was senior to Alan both in age and rank in K-Section, he rarely bothered with such things. The urgency of his voice alone instilled immediate obedience.

Alan replaced his finger on the tumbler.

Again the glass sped over the table.

Tyson could hardly keep track of the letters so mysteriously indicated by the glass.

The tension mounted palpably.

Eventually, the glass slowed.

Finally, it stopped.

Releasing a long sigh, Tyson took his finger away and leaned back on the swivel chair. He threw down the pad. The wrist of his writing hand ached. He rubbed his brow wearily, leaden eyes levelling on his three associates. 'I think we've just received a message in our latest code.'

Wilf jumped up from his seat. 'You can't be serious!' Agitatedly, the twenty-four-year-old technician ran a hand through his red hair. 'It's just a lark, a game, isn't it?' Nobody answered him.

Calmly, his cold blue eyes quite steady, Alan asked in his mellifluous voice, 'Are you sure?'

'I'll just check the ciphers.' Tyson crossed the room, opened the safe and pulled out a thick book. Scanning the plastic pages, Tyson began decoding the Ouija message.

He worked in total silence.

The telex clattered once then was still; nobody moved to consult it.

Their normally tedious weekend duty stint in the Fenner House Communications Centre had suddenly taken on a very weird aspect.

Alan Swann was twenty-nine last month and had been a Royal Navy rating and then a field agent for Interprises almost from the beginning and thought he'd seen it all.

As a young communications rating, Swann was as reckless as any other able seaman. However, he quickly learned he had a facility for foreign languages. He picked up Malaysian and Indonesian while stationed in HMS *Terror* in the Far East.

Then the sheer chance of sharing a Mercedes taxi with Keith Tyson, all the way back from a Sembawang village brothel, changed his life. He got chatting with Tyson and they found they both had a strong interest in languages.

Tyson took Swann under his wing and they spent several evenings out on the town, down Bugis street, tasting the exotic foods on the street stalls and frequenting the girlie bars while avoiding the attentions of the convincing catamites and transvestites. A place with a heady atmosphere, spicy aromas and Tiger beer.

Although Keith never mentioned the SAS, it was obvious to Swann that his new friend was secretly fighting in the Borneo conflict and had just managed to swing a brief ten days' leave in Singapore.

As far as he could see, Swann could never hope to transfer to the SAS as they recruited from Army regiments. There was of course the SBS, but he didn't particularly like going to sea, and travelling in Gemini landing craft didn't appeal. He supposed that fact would have excluded him from the SAS selection anyway.

Still, spurred on by Tyson's example, Swann wanted to get involved in clandestine work of some description. So he studied German, Russian and French, hankering after promotion to Radio Supervisor (Special), whose tasks involved listening in to foreign radio broadcasts and messages.

He continued to excel at sport, was keen on climbing, and completed a survival course on the moors when seconded to the RAF and on his return was immediately debriefed by Admiral Sands who worked for the Director of Naval Security (DNSy). It was at the time of an RN officer defecting – Swann's previous Divisional Officer, in fact - and the ramifications went deep. He was interviewed with zeal; his responses and observations actually impressed the Admiral a great deal. And one of the referees he tendered happened to be Keith Tyson.

Swann didn't re-engage beyond his initial engagement, mainly because he was headhunted by Sir Gerald Hazzard, a friend of Admiral Sands.

Obviously, there were still surprises to be had, Swann thought as he scoured the Comcen room's shadows. At the opposite end stood the formidable network console, its various indicator lights flashing routinely, keeping track of their agents throughout the globe. He forced an amused ironic grin.

When Keith invited them in to relieve the boredom, he'd been struck by the absurdity of holding a Ouija session right here in the heart of the Interprises Comcen.

To start with, they'd self-consciously asked questions. What was his grandfather's middle name? Where were Jock's brother and sister born? That sort of thing. And, alarmingly, the glass had spelled out some answers correctly. Then the gibberish started.

But, in the final analysis, it didn't seem to be gibberish.

CHAPTER TWELVE: Dossier

By the time Keith Tyson deciphered the first paragraph, he felt sick inside. It was about eight years since they'd been lovers, but they were still close, passion replaced by respect, comradeship and something indefinable. He wondered if that quality had anything to do with his receiving the message.

He wasn't sure how Alan would handle the news either. Only a few in the Section had noticed that Alan Swann was hopelessly in love with Tana and had been since their assignment in Elba. Hopelessly, because she didn't want that kind of commitment. Keith understood that, but Alan wouldn't or couldn't.

Unsmiling narrow mouth beneath a salt-and-pepper moustache, Jock stubbed out half-smoked cigarettes repeatedly. He was a bag of nerves since his last mission. It was plain on his face that he knew this astral message was very bad.

At last Tyson put down the pencil and raised his grey eyes. His expression was solemn. 'It's from Tana,' he said. 'They've got her.'

Alan Swann's face lost most of its colour as he leaned forward. He queried softly, 'Where?'

'Czechoslovakia.'

Following the first mind-numbing shock, Tyson contacted Sir Gerald Hazzard and the Ops Officer, Merrick.

'Jock, nip down to C-Section. Everything we've got on her.'

'Och, I'm away already,' the Scotsman said and left.

Alan flashed a large-scale map of Czechoslovakia onto the

conference room wall screen.

'Home in on the Bohemian Forest region - south of the E-26 road,' Tyson said, consulting the notes he hastily typed with an electric typewriter.

The projectionist complied and the image blurred as the detail zoomed in.

Wilf said, 'Sorry to bother you, sir, but - I still can't credit it. I mean, how many miles?'

'Tana's an incredible woman,' Tyson replied, leaning back in his chair. 'But there are plenty of recorded cases of long-distance telepathy. One of the favourite incidents Tana likes to relate involved a Russian woman. She was seven hundred miles away when she suddenly realised her husband was in danger from a fire. She concentrated on the room she knew he'd be in. He woke up feeling someone was calling his name and smelled the burning. He saved himself just in time. And you'll realise by now that Czechoslovakia is only just over six hundred miles from here - as the crow flies.'

'Do the Russians take it seriously, sir?'

'Yes. And so do we - and the Americans.'

'Can she really read minds?'

Tyson chuckled. 'No. But she can pick up *some* thoughts and emotions. You'd have to talk to Dr Fisk to get the full story, though I suspect he wouldn't tell you.'

'No,' Wilf nodded, 'probably not.'

Moving over to a bank of desks, Tyson inserted his report into the photocopier and it churned out sufficient individual copies for the Extraordinary Meeting.

Turning from the Xerox, he nodded in greeting to Sir Gerald and the doctors as they entered the room, inevitable black leather briefcases gripped possessively. Jock came in just behind them and handed Tyson the bulging red file.

It had taken a while to accept what amounted to a walking skeleton as his boss. Six feet tall, limbs merely skin-covered bone, cranium devoid of hair save for a sparse pate above his ears, facial skin stretched and lined over his skull, Sir Gerald was an unprepossessing sight. Yet his brain was as agile as a young man's.

Sir Gerald seated himself at the head of the table, immediately opposite the map of the Bohmer Wald and the East German-Czechoslovakian border.

Alan Swann sat on Sir Gerald's left and his face still looked pale, worry lines appearing on his brow. His black hair looked unkempt and his tie was loose, top shirt button undone. He's taking this damned hard, Tyson thought.

Black pebble-like eyes in deep recessed sockets, shining intelligently, Sir Gerald nodded at the assembled men and said, 'This is grave news, gentlemen. She's one of our best.' His high-pitched piping voice grated when Tyson first met the head of Interprises. The voice sounded girlish; but he soon became attuned and now he didn't even notice it.

Tyson stood beside the map-screen console at the other end of the table. 'She's the best we've got, sir.' He walked down the side of the room. 'Her dossier, here, testifies to that.'

He handed Sir Gerald the thick red folder, stamped with security classifications and STAFF-IN-CONFIDENCE.

Sir Gerald didn't need to read it but made a brief show of scanning a few pages. Indeed, the dossier revealed only a little about Tana's past. A Jewish orphan escapee from the terror of the Warsaw uprising, she had stowed away on a freighter that had been torpedoed by the British submarine *Umbra*. The Commanding Officer, Lieutenant Hugh Standish, picked up what survivors there were, and Tana was among them. Later, Standish and his wife Vera adopted her.

Apart from her traumatic origins and education, the dossier had nothing to say about Tana's childhood and did not mention her unusual gifts. Not so much an oversight by the Positive Vetting officer, simply a called-in favour for an old friend, Hazzard.

Hazzard knew her history, even if it was absent from the dossier. While it was soon realised that Tana possessed a photographic memory, it wasn't until she was seven that her first paranormal experience occurred. She awoke one wintry night and thought she saw a figure standing at the foot of her bed, sobbing, rounded shoulders racked with tears. It looked like her adoptive mother. Tana sat up and was alarmed to find that there was nobody else in the room. The incident chilled her so much that for a very long time she kept it to herself.

The following week, Hugh Standish was killed in a car crash and, as Tana attempted consoling her bereaved mother, she poignantly recalled the earlier vision.

These moments of precognition were rare and she had no control over them. For many years they were random and apparently meaningless.

Many a child of her tender years would have been incapable of coping with these extra-sensory manifestations. Yet it seemed that Tana's early upheaval from her home in Poland and the horrors she had witnessed while still an impressionable youngster had provided her with an iron willpower capable of accepting paranormal phenomena.

Then in 1951 her change - as she called it - happened. The advent of her menstrual cycle was the catalyst. At first she showed typical signs of acute hysteria in a broad spectrum of behaviour: vomiting, dyspepsia, convulsions, and severe over-sensitiveness.

Then disaster struck. Tana went blind.

Their doctor declared it was psychosomatic, which was little help. For months Vera Standish worried about Tana's future; indeed, if she would have any. Then in the spring of 1952 she met an old acquaintance, Sir Gerald Hazzard, and explained all about Tana's problem over afternoon tea.

'Interesting subject, psychic research, my dear Vera,' Sir Gerald had remarked. 'Allow me to make an appointment for Tana with an enlightened doctor.' His death's-head smile was surprisingly reassuring. 'I'm sure he'll be able to put your mind at rest.'

Doctor Marchelewicz, the psychiatric consultant, was a short man with unruly grey hair, a high forehead, prominent ears and pince-nez glasses. The texture of his skin suggested that he had suffered a serious illness at puberty. When he welcomed Mrs Standish and Tana he was most solicitious and offered her a lovely gentle smile. Fortunately, he quickly discovered that Tana was still able to perceive mental images of her environment. 'I cannot explain it, Mrs Standish, but I do not think we should worry unduly.' Vera Standish's eyes widened and she was about to object but the doctor raised a hand and added, 'Let me finish, Mrs Standish.' He smiled benignly and she nodded. 'Thank you. I believe that Tana's condition, although quite alarming to you and me, is only temporary - very much like hormonal changes at puberty.'

Temporary. It gave Vera Standish something to cling on to. Temporary meant that Tana would get better and become normal again. Thanks to Sir Gerald, she was able to afford to keep Tana under Doctor Marchelewicz's observation on a regular basis. Tana's schooling didn't seem to suffer; she soon absorbed all the lessons she missed while undergoing tests with the psychiatric consultant.

After about four months, during which Tana seemed to turn the known human physical laws on their heads, Doctor Marchelewicz concluded, 'We're in the Dark Ages of psychic science, Mrs Standish, so you must appreciate that there are many unknowns involved here.'

'Yes, doctor, but will Tana recover? I do recall you said all this would be temporary.'

He nodded. 'I have no doubt of it. Only this morning Tana's eyes could detect glimmers of light. She's coming out of the tunnel, I feel.'

'Oh, thank God!'

Gently taking Vera Standish's hand, the doctor added, 'You must be strong for your daughter. Untrammelled psychic forces are still at work within her, as if extending her senses, trying her out for possession.'

'Possession?' Alarmed, she withdrew her hand. 'Oh, my God.'

He smiled and added softly, 'No, please accept my apologies, I am phrasing it badly, I fear. I do not mean... No, it is not demonic possession. It is like learning a new skill; you possess new knowledge and abilities. Something akin to that, I think.'

'I see. I will try to be strong for her, of course.'

Without the doctor's guidance and understanding - and that of her mother - she could well have been certified during these periods of psychic change.

On fully recovering, Tana returned to school and soon caught up with her contemporaries, moving on to the University of Edinburgh where she read Psychology, gaining her BA Honours in 1958. She found it strange that there were so many of her fellow students in support of nuclear disarmament, following the calls of the MP Michael Foot, the philosopher Bertrand Russell and even the writer J B Priestley. The month after Kruschev's toppling of Bulganin, the marchers paraded round Aldermaston.

When emotions within her were running wild, or when someone nearby was hyped-up with strong feelings, she often heard them say something, but on questioning, they hadn't said anything aloud at all. Yet the voice, the intonation had been crystal clear and identifiable. Unwillingly, she had to conclude that she'd momentarily 'heard' their thoughts. At that time the unwanted phenomenon was limited and could not be called upon at will.

With her eidetic imagery she could call up detailed and vivid pictures from the past, projecting them mentally on a wall or flat surface, and study them. Needless to say, nobody else could perceive these pictures; it was just a means for her to stabilise the images.

Her academic success was simply attributed to her remarkably accurate photographic memory and no mention was made of her fledgling psychic abilities. She had little inclination to advertise her quite unreliable talent. However, on leaving university, she volunteered to assist at the Parapsychological Research Unit in an old mansion house in the Northamptonshire countryside.

One day, Tana's examiner was busy arranging another, more complicated test. Before it was set up, Tana told her the solution. The examiner was stunned. Tana explained: she had pictured the solution - in the examiner's mind. She was taken to see the Director of the Unit and the man looked as though he was a cat who had slurped all the cream. She emphasised that her abilities could not be called upon at will. 'No matter, my dear,' he said. 'In time, you - or we - should be able to train you to control this remarkable gift you possess. For now, I think we should change your syllabus.'

She nodded. 'Anything, so long as it helps me to understand what I can - and cannot - do.'

'I suspect that in time there will be no limitations on what you can do, my dear.'

That sounded rather ominous, she thought, but shrugged it off.

Tana was given leave every other weekend, if she wished. Every amenity was available to her, such as stables, a racetrack and a swimming pool; virtually anything she could possibly want: so her weekends away from the research unit were quite rare.

To remain fit, Tana took up athletics and learned how to use her body properly, by employing willpower and a yoga-like intensity of concentration.

The Unit's physical training instructors shook their heads in disbelief when observing her outstrip many of their best female athletes. Her build couldn't account for it; stamina wasn't enough without muscle-power and intensive training to back it: she was performing on willpower of unguessed at strength - and simply for relaxation.

After several months, she found that thought-transference was only possible under great stress; her stress or the thought provoker's.

There were many frustrating times, though. No matter how the parapsychologists persevered, she couldn't read thoughts at will. Occasionally, she managed to communicate with other subjects similar to herself at the Unit. But really she was far in advance of them; it was like a seven-year-old talking to an infant.

None of her old student friends seemed to wonder why hundreds of refugees poured into West Berlin every day - and the number rose into the thousands when Kruschev forced on them the collectivisation of small farms. Of course, they hadn't lived under the jackboot of an oppressor nor feared for their own and their family's lives.

Despite the much-lauded Macmillan arms talks with Kruschev, Tana didn't trust the Soviets. Kruschev went on about 'peaceful co-existence' yet he flooded England with his spies. Whenever she could, she took an interest in what was happening. The final straw was in August 1961 when the Berlin Wall went up. How any ruler could treat his people so badly was beyond her. Families split, livelihoods abruptly cut, property bricked up or even demolished, garish flags awarded for shooting escapees.

The apologists for communism never adequately explained why people fled towards the West but never to the East - save for the spies, such as Abel and Lonsdale, who were swapped for the likes of Powers and Wynne. Even drab Moscow was preferable to a prison cell.

For about three months each year, Tana travelled around the world and gave lectures on eidetic imagery and memory techniques, the fees helping to support her. She was also given a retainer by the research unit.

Over the next few years she travelled to the United States several times, even taking part in tests at Duke University. And on one occasion she visited Moscow at a symposium on psychic research. The Soviets were unaware she was psychic, only believing she had a remarkable memory. This was in fact the first time that she came to the notice of the intelligence community. She was able to pass on useful 'insights' - as she called the occasional plucked thoughts of Soviet agents she encountered - to the British Embassy agent-in-place. Up to that point in her life, in 1962, she perceived that the darkest time was definitely when Kruschev and Kennedy went head-to-head over the Cuban missile crisis. When Kruschev backed down, she felt that the West had not actually won, because she knew that the Soviet Premier's days in power were numbered from that time and his successors were unknown quantities.

However, she had to admit that there were two bright spots in those years: the test ban treaty meant no nuclear tests in the atmosphere, in outer space or underwater; and the hotline was opened between Washington and Moscow. Despite their posturing, neither side wanted a nuclear conflict. It was a last resort. Both sides relied upon propaganda and subversion; the West was good at the former and the Soviets were superior at the latter.

There was a dark cloud though, and that was Kennedy's assassination; at least that appeared to have nothing to do with Soviet intervention, though the Communist links to Oswald were quite chilling.

Duke University's Parapsychology Unit, the bastion of psychic research in North Carolina, was shut down in 1965, ostensibly because modern scientists were no longer impressed, when in fact the Defence Agencies had taken over the bulk of research under the aegis of national security.

Apart from the publicised card-memory-tests with astronauts and men on Polaris submarine patrols, telepathy was also being studied by the British SIS and this research went on at the secret Psychic Phenomena Institute at Fenner House, a mansion near Abingdon purchased by Sir Gerald when he set up International

Enterprises as an adjunct to MI6.

Tana's dossier stated that Sir Gerald Hazzard heard about her while visiting one of his operatives convalescing in a country sanatorium near her research unit. No mention was made of his links with her family going back to the 1950s.

One day in early 1965 Sir Gerald turned up at the research unit and asked to have a talk with Tana. They'd kept in touch by letter and occasionally met when she visited her mother.

There was no hint of any sexual relationship between her mother and the peer; they just seemed good friends. Indeed, over the years he had maintained a discreet interest in Tana's psychic career.

The funeral of Sir Winston Churchill had just gripped the nation. What kind of world would it have been if Churchill had gone to war - as had been expected - against Russia immediately after Germany surrendered?

Sir Gerald recalled the Joint Intelligence Committee's chilling post-war assessment: 'Communism is the most important external political menace confronting the British Commonwealth and is likely to remain so in the foreseeable future.'

They predicted that Russian policy would be aggressive by all measures short of war and, judging by the arrests of Abel, Lonsdale, the Krogers, Gee, Houghton and Blake over the years, they had no intention of letting up. How many more were buried deep as sleepers? Was there a fourth man? A fifth? He was still uncomfortable with the spy-swaps; on humanitarian grounds, they made sense, but the West never seemed to get the best deal. Powers for Abel, Wynne for Lonsdale, for God's sake. Nobody yet for Blake, though - why was that?

Sir Gerald's gaunt frame was standing among the flowering red geraniums at the huge picture window of the warm conservatory that overlooked the grounds.

Tana entered. 'Sir Gerald, it's good to see you. How is Mum?'

He turned slowly and the skeleton smiled though it was more

like a grimace. 'She's fine. I saw her only last week. She does say you don't visit as often as you used to. I imagine that you're busy, working here?'

She didn't answer at once but sat on a white wooden bench. He joined her.

'Time has a knack of flying by,' she said, finally. 'I seem to be at the end of any meaningful research actually,' she confessed.

'Really? Why is that?'

'We're just repeating the same old experiments. Can't devise any new ways to activate my... gifts.'

'So what will you do now?'

She shrugged. 'I haven't given it much thought. I'll probably visit Mum and talk it over with her.'

'She would appreciate that, I'm sure.'

'Getting a proper job, as Mum calls it, is going to be difficult. My CV is going to look, well, odd, to say the least.'

Sir Gerald stood and smiled down at her. 'Tana,' he said, 'I think it's time you worked for me and your country.'

She had smiled then. It was as if she had been waiting for this moment, preparing to join the fight against an insidious menace - only last year, a state of emergency was declared in Malaya against communist incursions.

That was ten years ago.

Closing the dossier, Sir Gerald pursed bloodless lips and lowered his eyelids briefly, as if wiping away those memories with a nictitating membrane. Of course, he remembered, it was the year after he recruited Tana - George Blake was sprung from Wormwood Scrubs, so they hadn't needed a swap deal for him.

He eyed the room and said, 'I don't understand how they could capture Tana.' He looked pointedly at Merrick. 'She was issued with the usual suicide pill, wasn't she, Ops?'

Merrick cleared his throat. 'Yes, sir. As it happens, I was at the dentist at the same time, so I know she kept the appointment.'

'Surely you're not inferring she wouldn't accept the implant?' Tyson growled defensively.

'No, no, of course not,' Merrick hastily replied. 'I'm simply vouching for her presence there.'

The thought made Sir Gerald quite weak, but it needed to be voiced, so he went on, 'If they caught her, then why didn't she just bite the pill? Her mind and its knowledge wouldn't now be at jeopardy.'

'We don't know the circumstances, sir,' said Dr James Fisk. 'There may have been a possibility of escape with vital information. Indeed, on the face of it, her message implies she has found something of great importance.'

Tyson said, 'We can't leave her, sir.'

'Too bloody right we can't!' Swann exclaimed.

Sir Gerald nodded. 'I agree. And I also accept what James says. But that photographic memory of hers would do untold damage.' He studied Merrick. 'Ops, I can't see how we came to risk her over there in the first place. Refresh my memory, will you?'

'Something's nagging the old man,' Tyson whispered to Alan. 'There's nothing wrong with his memory.'

Merrick's podgy fingers agitatedly collated his sheaf of papers. 'You authorised the mission, sir,' he responded petulantly.

'I know that, man, but what were the facts again?'

Merrick's normally pale anaemic complexion reddened. His paunchy build hunched over the dossier in front of him as he withdrew a typed document and scanned it, lips moving slightly. He glanced up, cleared his throat. 'A routine mission of recruitment and information-exchange was bungled by Torrence. Two arrests were made. The whole underground closed down. Running scared. We needed someone very experienced to get in there and reorganise fast. I chose Tana Standish as she was familiar with the territory - and one of their leaders.' He closed the dossier, firmly pressed a hand on it.

'Yes. And I endorsed it.' Sir Gerald's thin bony fingers drummed on the shiny table. He looked round the room, then eyed Merrick piercingly, parchment skin stretched tightly over his skull. 'I could have sworn you emphasised there was minimal risk.'

Staring unwaveringly, Merrick replied, 'My assessment was that the risk was minimal to an agent of Standish's calibre, sir.'

Tyson glowered at Merrick then glanced anxiously at his wristwatch. Time! He nodded at Doctor Fisk. 'James, how long has she got - before she cracks?'

With steady, ice-blue clinical eyes, James Fisk rose and addressed the room in general. 'Even after all our tests, it must still be a hypothetical question. However, I have her medical record here, complete with tolerances documented.' He leafed through. 'Torture level is ten hours - at the most. That's on the estimate that they'll want her coherent and alive for a long time after she cracks. She has a great deal to divulge, I believe.' He eyed Tyson who nodded.

'It isn't such a tall order for their experts, you know,' Fisk said. 'All they must do is break through her resistance and obtain one tiny secret. After that, she'll *snap* wide open.'

Swann jerked in his seat as Fisk emphasised the word.

'The rest will follow in time.' Fisk hesitated then consulted his file again.

Tyson paled and felt the muscles in his jaw knotting. He remembered only too well his long-ago introduction to the interrogation part of his SAS selection course, following immediately on from the escape and evasion techniques. At the time he had told himself it was only twenty-four hours, he'd only give them the Big Four, all that was required: number, rank, date of birth and name.

'They won't actually beat you,' he was reassured by an instructor. 'It's an exercise in disorientation and stamina actually.'

The instructor lied in part. Stripped naked, Tyson was left in a room with a hood over his head and his hands tied behind his back. He had to stand in one position all the time so when he tired and relaxed or slouched, he was reminded with harsh blows from rubber truncheons on the backs of his thighs.

Time lost all meaning but he never divulged anything other than the required Big Four.

When they took off his hood and told him the ordeal was over and asked him how he felt, he again replied with the Big Four. They told him what the time was, that the twenty-four hours were up. But how could he trust them? He'd long since lost track of time. It could be a tactic to confuse him into saying something, anything.

Dazed and tired, he was led away and he feared that he had failed. But in fact he had passed the test.

And Tana would be undergoing far worse, he thought, glancing around the table.

Alan looked terrible, his eyes staring into nothing. Don't go there, Tyson told himself, reluctant to let even a smidgeon of jealousy to surface. He waited for Fisk to continue.

Idly brushing back unruly greying hair, Fisk said, 'However, with pentothal or lysergic acid, I should think that the ten hours I stipulated could be halved. I don't think they'd use the LSD, *if* they realise who she is. There could be brain damage, or even a burnout of psychic reserves.' He studied everyone at the table and sombrely scrutinised his fob watch. 'I'm afraid that doesn't give us much time.'

It was 22.00, an hour since her message stopped.

'It has to be a snatch, sir,' Tyson said.

Sir Gerald steepled his fingers and nodded. 'I tend to agree with you.'

Round face and prominent cheekbones glowing hotly, Merrick leapt up. 'Sir - operationally, I'm against it. We can't risk another operative.'

'Our operatives do seem to be falling like flies, don't they?' Sir Gerald remarked icily. 'Cornelius, Segal, Toker. And now

Standish. It is *very* worrying.'

Merrick added, plaintively, persistently ignoring the subject of the missing agents, 'The chances of getting her out...'

'I know what the chances are, man! And I'll see to it that whoever volunteers is aware of them. You're overruled on this, Ops. She *has* to be brought out.' His eyes lowered and a nerve twitched once in his forehead. 'Or silenced.'

'It might be possible,' Tyson said, hastily dismissing the thought of Tana being 'silenced'. 'She gave suggestions - at least up to a point. We must assume they started on her in earnest then.' He sought the psychiatrist, Dr Andrews, for corroboration. 'I'm guessing she shut down mentally to combat their treatment.'

Andrews nodded. 'She wouldn't be able to send this message and resist torture or drugs at the same time. Women are more adept than men at multitasking, but that would be asking just too much, even of Miss Standish.'

Swann ran his hands down over his gaunt face and stood up. 'I'm fluent in Russian and conversant with their communications systems.'

Tyson cleared his throat and shifted in his seat. 'You are, Alan, but I'm the most fluent here. And I have a little more experience.'

Swann eyed Tyson dully.

Alan knew about some of Tana's past, obviously, Tyson thought. Would she have told Alan about me? Probably, as she had nothing to hide regarding her relationships. As far as Tyson was concerned, it was ancient history, anyway. Alan and Tana had been hot and cold for about four years now, mainly because Alan couldn't let go and move on. Tyson had moved on. Yet he still fondly remembered dropping by to have tea with her mother, a lovely old lady. Mrs Standish was all for making wedding arrangements - until Tana put her straight.

'Are you both volunteering?' Sir Gerald asked.

'I should go, sir,' said Swann.

'This is a one-man insertion mission,' Tyson explained and

glanced at Swann. 'I've done this kind of thing before.'

Raising a bony hand, Sir Gerald said, 'Sit down, Alan.' Swann sat. 'I appreciate your reasons for going too.'

So, the Old Man knows, Tyson thought.

'However,' Sir Gerald added, 'I fear your emotional attachment could prove counterproductive.'

'Emotional attachment?' queried Merrick. 'I don't understand.'

'We won't go into that here and now, Ops.' Sir Gerald turned to Tyson. 'It's your mission, Keith.'

'Thanks, sir.' Tyson depressed a button on the remote control console by his chair and the map of the Bohemian Forest further enlarged. Bold black print, sans serif: **DOBRANICE**. Nearby was a symbol for a coal mine. 'She's there, though God knows why!'

'How soon can you leave?' Sir Gerald asked.

'I'd like to be on my way by the end of the hour. If you could arrange a Phantom overfly, it would help. And transport. I'll contact the armoury and uniform sections now.'

Within minutes, the conference room and Comcen were quiet, emptied of everyone save young Wilf Ashley, who had dazedly relieved Tyson.

The electric clock moved relentlessly: 22.15.

CHAPTER THIRTEEN: Overflight

Czechoslovakia, August 19, 1968

The American Military Intelligence Service request for an overflight was authorised by the CIS Defence Department. A Lockheed SR-71 aircraft of SAC's 420th Strategic Reconnaissance Wing was sent from a secret airfield in West Germany and the USAF high-level reconnaissance along the East German and Czechoslovakian frontier went ahead.

With a maximum speed of over Mach 3, the SR-71 was at the time regarded as the U2's successor, capable of operating at an altitude of between 70,000 and 90,000 feet.

At a height of 80,000 feet the SR-71's horizon stretched away for three hundred miles.

Its advanced electronic reconnaissance equipment located radar signals originating deep in Poland and Czechoslovakia and obtained high-resolution photographic coverage of large areas of East Germany and the western part of Czechoslovakia.

The pilot, Lou Makepeace, confirmed the West German BND's intelligence reports of Warsaw Pact troops preparing for an assault.

This information was filed and ignored.

The invasion's H-Hour was 23.00, 20th August. Two hundred thousand Soviet and Warsaw Pact troops entered Czechoslovakia from thirteen bases.

RAF Dahlen, West Germany, 1975

Now, just over seven years later and seemingly many more years wiser, Lou Makepeace was busy delivering a briefing to an RAF Phantom crew.

'I've flown this airspace before - and it's hell on the nerves. You guys're probably better equipped with these here FGR2s. Your advantage is supersonic hedge-hopping, dodging the radar.'

'What kind of competition are we likely to meet along the border, sir?' asked the Phantom pilot, Richard Freemantle.

'I was just coming to that, Dick. You'd think I'd've been pretty safe at eighty-thou - but the latest MiG-25s - Foxbats - can easily attain ninety-eight thou at Mach 3 in a straight-line dash. They're developed as all-weather interceptors - so you've got your work cut out.

'I hit snags with these Fox - sorry, MiGs - over Baluchistan three years back. Flying a beaut of an A-11 supersonic cruiser. Damned lucky to get out alive.

'So - those NATO instructions on MiG outmanoeuvring - read 'em well. The Israelis learned hellish fast. Their SAM-avoidance is still the best. At one time our guys were aces at dealing with MiGs; but since the shutdown of Vietnam, we've gotten awful rusty.

'My briefing was to inform you on avoidance techniques with emphasis on the peculiarities of the Reds hereabouts. Never try combat, I'm supposed to tell you. Now,' he sneered, mouth twisting wryly, 'that's a tall order to give any guy, 'specially with a MiG on your tail, sweating on an Ash-2 missile burning your ass off at any minute! My unofficial advice is, if you can't throw the MiG, shove a Sparrow round at him pronto. Microseconds count, obviously. You're better off facing a court martial for disobedience - even if you do cause a diplomatic incident! Better that than being dead!'

'How important are these pictures, sir?'

Lou Makepeace whistled. 'I sure as hell don't know, Dick. From what I've been told, I'd say a very important mission mightn't get off the ground at all - and that could end up in our side getting egg on its face pretty bad. I can't say more'n - keep your eyes skinned and...' he jabbed a baton at the blown-up map of the target area, '...report everything of note along this A3 - A7 stretch.'

The Phantom specially attached to RAF Dahlen was equipped for the type of surveillance required. The two-seat fighter-bomber had arrived minutes after the way had been cleared by a FLASH signal through Comcen Rhine. And Richard Freemantle and Desmond McGrath were its crew. Dressed in full flying rig, they had descended the steel ladder to be briskly met by the Station's Group Captain. Freemantle was used to the reverence of senior officers; having flown the 'slow-boats' of last war and piloted various makes of desk since, they invariably marvelled at the supersonic speed at which the new breed of pilots worked.

'I take it you don't know why you've been sent out here so suddenly?' Group Captain Brooke-Clifton asked.

Freemantle had elected himself spokesman. As the navigator, McGrath was quite content to take the back seat. 'Right, sir,' Freemantle replied. 'It certainly was at damned short notice! We'd just returned from...' he paused, reflective, '...from another mission. Our Phanta was herded off, gone over before she had a chance to calm her nerves. We didn't even have time for a half-hour's doze! The films were replaced and she was refuelled in no time. I've never seen erks move so fast!'

Group Captain Brooke-Clifton shook his head. 'I don't know what's going on either - I only learned of this op twenty minutes ago!'

'But why us?' Freemantle asked. 'A close-look satellite would've produced the goods, surely?'

'My thought too. But if the satellite pictures were all that super, you chaps would have been out of a job long ago! No, I think it's a case of there being no appropriate satellite over the area at the right time. It would take too long, collecting the film with a scoop-plane and so on. And the timing is of the essence - hence your fast redirection out here.'

'We were told something about being briefed.'

'Yes, an American. He landed about ten minutes ago. Name of Makepeace, would you know.' In response to Freemantle's raised eyebrow, he added, 'Makepeace has flown quite a few recces over Czechoslovakia before.'

'That border?'

'Yes, didn't you know?'

'No, just a hostile border. To suit Phanta and her tree-skimming speciality.'

With a low-altitude speed in excess of 900mph at ground level, the Phantom was too fast for ground fire or fighter defences: the craft could easily fly below the limits of radar cover and reach the objective before the defences were alerted.

'Well, he's going to give you a few tips on evasive action.'

Czechoslovak airspace

And they certainly needed evasive action.

They had foreseen the problem from the outset. The stretch of border the Ministry's directive wanted surveying was on the other side, the northern slope of the Sumava Mountains. And tree-hopping only kept them out of radar-sight until they topped the peaks.

At more than twelve miles a minute, they followed every curve and dip in the land's contours. On their right-hand side moonrise was splashing the night sky, silvery-white, merging into a deep blue. The many instruments took on a ghostly hue.

There was little margin for error at these speeds, even with their sophisticated aids. The special radar display sensed the shape of the ground ahead, projected an image of it into Freemantle's line of sight: he flew accordingly, living his life instants in the future.

For McGrath, as navigator, the countryside was continually foreshortened and distorted at this low altitude. Landmarks, remembered from pre-flight immersion-study, appeared and vanished in fleeting glimpses. He was constantly checking on their position.

But things altered on topping the Sumava Mountains, which attained heights of between 2,250 and 3,300 feet. Inevitably, when they appeared over the top, they came full into radar-view. It would take about one minute to cover the objective and get out. It should be enough. However, if there were any MiGs airborne in the area - or SAMs conveniently trained - those sixty seconds would be far too long. And such was the case.

Sighting of the border, and the Dobranice complex abutting onto it, took fully twenty-seven seconds. Most surveillance crews jokingly referred to their personal back-up system, Eyeball Mark One Intelligence: a visual report on the sighting. Amazingly, when living life in seconds you tend to absorb more. After very little practice, many remarkably clear details stick and are reported on back at base.

They also had highly specialised instruments and they used them.

The Vinten F95 was installed in fans of five in the reconnaissance pod slung beneath the fuselage, to give the low-level photography wide coverage. With its wide aperture lenses and 70mm film, the Vinten F95 clicked off a dozen frames a second, shutter speeds down to one three-thousandth of a second.

As an additional back-up they employed another camera, more suitable to poor lighting. The aircraft's own computer triggered the compensation for image-improvement and automatic exposure control, while a photo-flash set off the shutter automatically through a photo-electric cell.

The third camera was loaded with infra-red false-colour film, able to show healthy green foliage in varying shades of red, water as deep blue, and dead foliage and most painted surfaces as matt black. Camouflage-painted vehicles, weapons and installations - including camouflage nets woven with dead or imitation foliage - stood out black against the pinks and reds of their surroundings.

Lastly, an infrared linescan picked up heat-emission from the ground beneath the aircraft through a fast-moving mirror system which focussed the infrared rays on to a special detector: this scanned a film to build up a heat picture of the ground. Able to operate at night without obvious aids like flashes or flares, it could pick up the exhausts of jet engines being ignited. Tonight, it showed a helicopter parking spot on a stretch of open ground - slightly cooler than the surrounding concrete because the parked aircraft tended to shade it. The detector also indicated which parts of the radio building were working and which were shut down; it showed whether fuel tanks in the foreground of the railway yards were full or empty.

The intruder appeared at two o'clock red about four seconds after the overflight was completed. 'Dick, we've got company,' McGrath said matter-of-factly.

'Can we lose him?'

'Possibly.'

'But - ?'

'I compute he's going to out-think us, shoot over the mountains from high altitude. He's climbing.'

Phanta was flying at 900mph now, gaining height and speed for a loop over the mountains. But the MiG would already be at high-altitude flight-speed, in excess of Mach 3. At over 2,300mph he'd be on them in seconds, Ash-2 missiles cutting them down.

The beginnings of air turbulence hit them, bucking the craft. Freemantle unlocked the Sparrow missiles. McGrath threw the ECM switch. Their earphones crackled with interference, electronic countermeasures beaming all around them.

Clouds obscured the moon. The night was too starless and black for a visual sighting so the MiG would have to rely on his radar; they'd be in the midst of snow on the MiG's radar screen now. The MiG would probably continue on course anyway, though the snow would confuse; but he would also hedge his bets by loosing a couple of Ash missiles, hoping their heat-sniffing apparatus would nose in on the Phantom's jets.

'Cut ECM!'

McGrath obeyed.

After-image snow lasted fractions of seconds. Then Freemantle glimpsed the dot of the MiG - much closer. Plus a smaller pod, breaking away. Only one. 'Fired one only, Des. Fox him!'

Curving up the mountain range, still skimming the conifers, 2,500 feet and climbing, the Phantom rocked in the turbulence. Sweat soaked Freemantle as he gripped the stick.

In seconds, they were over the top. McGrath slammed his countermeasures button and a solitary missile sped from under their port wing.

'Christ, they'd better be Ash-2s!' McGrath prayed aloud, fervently.

Fox, the decoy, shot ahead and looped over them, dropped behind and followed their tail. It would stay there until the attacking Ash missile was within predesignated range then plummet. The boffins said it worked and had shown innumerable films to prove it. Yet, for those vital endless milliseconds when the Fox dropped and the crew waited to see if the Ash took the hotter bait, it was agony on the nerves.

Fingers poised over the ejector seats' buttons, they climbed into black night sky and -

It worked!

The Fox sped for the forest far below and the Ash caught its tail. The explosion fleetingly lit the sky and was as quickly a distant memory as they left the mountain range behind, still climbing, ECM again sending snow in all directions. The MiG would be radioing for reinforcements. By rights, they should be safe, back over home ground. Still, it depended on the MiG.

'Switch off and let's see where the bastard is.'

Snow stopped. The MiG was closer.

'Hang on, we're going down!'

G-forces drove them into their seats.

McGrath now used the counter-countermeasures, for it was highly likely the MiG would learn from his previous mistake and send two missiles out next time, one after the other; when the first one was Foxed, the second would home in on Phanta, the real target. And such reckoning would be correct for they could only afford to carry two Foxes; the rest of their armament was Sparrow missiles and cannon.

But the CCM allowed for this type of countermeasure. The second Fox was a little bigger than its brother, more sophisticated.

As Freemantle set his plane in a deep dive, the Fox continued on their previous course, appearing on the MiG radar screen as large as the Phantom would. And, to compound the deception, snow emanated from the Fox while none came from the descending Phantom.

Even so, the MiG pilot was careful, releasing two Ashes after the Fox and, after a time delay, one more to follow the dropping Phantom.

In their sudden descent, they had closed down radar, radio, every apparatus detectable; the jets had dimmed to quarter-thrust to simulate a decoy.

Night saved them - they were all flying blind, reliant upon instrumentation. For the two crewmen, however, the blind fall at over 1,000mph was extremely nerve-racking.

Instruments on again, they detected shadows of fast-approaching ground.

'Full thrust!'

Freemantle yanked on the stick, the whole craft juddered as they hauled her up in a tight curve. Freemantle had left it just late enough: with barely milliseconds to spare and the Ash about to make contact, he'd pulled the plane sharply up off-course.

For the Ash, one instant it had a hot tail to chase, the next – nothing. The manoeuvre had been perfected by the Israelis on SAMs. Now, the Ash continued on course, lost, and hit the earth explosively. The blast shook their Phantom as it rose away from the area of destruction.

Levelling off, Freemantle brought the Phantom down, at low-altitude again. The blip of the MiG was getting further away. Too late, the Russian would realise his mistake. Anyway, he'd used his full load of missiles. His report would make interesting reading.

They'd been lucky.

Dahlen was ready to receive them, a Harrier VSTOL warmed up, set to transport the films and tapes at Mach 2 plus.

Ordinarily, the removal and processing of the films, providing them ready for viewing, took thirteen minutes from touchdown. Freemantle and McGrath transferred to the Harrier.

Time: 23.07.

Oxfordshire, England

While their sortie's quarter-mile of film was fed on to high-speed processing equipment, capable of turning out one hundred and twenty feet of finished film a minute, Freemantle and McGrath sat before Sir Gerald Hazzard and Keith Tyson and tried in vain to relax.

The debriefing began.

'First, the Dobranice complex is a lot closer to the accredited border than your maps say. Some of the buildings are well up the Sumava slopes.' Freemantle looked at his navigator.

'I counted a dozen half-tracks,' McGrath added. 'And a hell of a lot of high-gain radio antennae.'

'The perimeter?' Tyson asked.

'Apart from the border fence, watchtowers; and the complex fence; gates. No soldiers or movement that we could see.'

The pictures then arrived from the interpreters, the military detectives. High-magnification and crystal-clear definition had helped them ferret out the information. Each blown-up photo was accompanied by a sheet of double-spaced typed explanation.

Sir Gerald rose after viewing the accompanying film of three hundred and twenty-four frames. The slight forward movement of the aircraft between the taking of consecutive shots had produced a stereoscopic 3-D effect; he blinked.

'You've done well,' he told the two airmen. Then he faced Tyson.

'Have you sufficient data to work on?'

Tyson nodded slowly. 'I'd still like some special equipment, sir.' He handed over a list.

Sir Gerald read it. 'You can leave immediately you get these items?'

'Yes.'

CHAPTER FOURTEEN: Mikhail

Czechoslovakia

Two soldiers stripped Tana and sat her on a metal chair in the middle of the room then left. They had put Tana's trousers, shirt, bra, briefs, assault belt and boots on a metal table to her right. The Commandant puzzled over the black slim leather pouch which was about eighteen centimetres long; he opened it and several very fine metal needles spilled onto the table top. He swore and shoved them back. He was familiar with the cartridge case, the sheathed knife and the compass and left them to turn his attention to the prisoner.

Dissociated, mind hovering, Tana looked down on them and objectively surveyed Schneider fondling her passive, naked shell. He pummelled her bandaged ribcage and ripped off the tapes but she felt nothing.

Looking uncomfortable, the Commandant stood beside her belongings.

Schneider's twitching fingers tapped her head. 'I don't know if you can hear me, Juden cow, but I'll have great pleasure handing you over to our surgeons in Novogorosk - after you talk, of course. They'll perform such a little operation, and remove the temporal lobes of your brain - here,' and he finger-jabbed just beside her ears. 'Permanently degrading your memory... so you'll become an imbecile. You won't even remember how to walk and talk!'

Deep within her mind, she employed a common memory technique, mentally walking along the Karmelicka Street of her childhood, placing items in various doorways. If she required these remembered items, she mentally strolled along the same street, stopped at the appropriate doorway and extracted the item. As a defence against standard brainwashing methods, she could lock all the doors in the street. But, like any real door, they'd give under continuous, ruthless battering.

Tana Standish had been under the drug for over an hour, Schneider realised, and he'd learned nothing. He regarded her unusually successful resistance as an insult to his ability.

Pursing his lips, Schneider swung his hand, resoundingly slapping the side of her face and cutting her lip: his knuckles reddened and he licked her blood off a finger.

'Bitch!' His eyes glazed. '*Talk!*'

The Commandant held out a restraining hand. 'Major Kasayiev also wants her to talk, doctor, so go easy on her mouth.'

Teeth clenched, Schneider swung on him. 'Don't you dare touch me, you stinking Cossack! In my day, you'd be cleaning out the gas chambers! Don't you realise we must rid the world of these filthy money-grabbing swine?' He hit her again, solidly. Her cut lip split bloodily and she sprawled to the floor like a rag doll. He kicked her where she lay. 'See? They're all the same! Spineless! Brainless lumps of flesh and bones - animals!'

He stooped, grabbed Tana by the hair, thrust her back into the chair.

The Commandant gasped as the door opened.

Schneider swerved round. 'I told you not to dist...'

'*Leave her!*' Kasayiev snarled.

'But...'

The KGB major felt a perverse tremor through his loins and stomach at sight of Tana Standish. Seeing her blood and her defenceless shapely body, his pulse had quickened. But he'd entered at the instant Schneider lifted the woman up like a sack of potatoes, and the sight had sickened him; he'd reddened with anger and shame. He felt no hate towards Tana; she was a professional and had very probably given Ilyichev everything that he deserved. The poor wretch deserved better than this, he thought, surprised at himself.

'Quiet, Schneider!' Kasayiev growled. 'Or I'll see to it your private experiments cease forthwith.'

The doctor's mouth dropped open. 'But I - I couldn't live without...'

'That could be remedied as well.' Kasayiev's threat struck home and the doctor's lips clamped tightly shut.

The Commandant stood immobile, holding his breath, complexion bloodless.

'Just be careful, Schneider. Less of the Nazi brutality.' Kasayiev sneered, 'We're civilised now.'

He turned to the trembling Commandant. 'I'll want a complete report on everything that transpired in here since Dr Schneider began his interrogation. Understand, Comrade Commandant?'

'Yes, Comrade Major,' the Commandant said.

Kasayiev gave the place a swift appraisal. 'No complex would be complete without an interrogation room - and I see this one's well equipped,' he observed sanguinely, nodding at the electrical apparatus, encephalograph and tape recorder on the bench behind Tana.

He walked round Tana. 'I've seen trances like hers at the Troitskoye Asylum - a deep-level trance. They used electric shock with notable success there.'

Tana was slumped in the chair, knock-kneed, lifeless, her chest apparently without motion, her body glistening with sweat and blemished with unsightly contusions.

Kasayiev said, 'I think we should try in her case, doctor.'

'Electric shock...' the Commandant whispered. 'Won't that affect her? You mightn't get anything at all then.'

'No, no,' Schneider said impatiently. 'The major's quite correct. I must congratulate him.' He bowed his head just a little. 'You see,

Commandant, the brain can be abused with electric shock or even quite heavy doses of chemicals. Yes, without fear of obliterating, disorganising or degrading the memory. If you'll recall my analogy to the computer - now, if you tried abusing the computer...' He sniggered knowingly. 'Chaos!'

'Enough chatter!' Kasayiev snapped. 'Tie her down while I get the electrodes.' Why wouldn't she just talk? So much easier and not as messy! He shook himself, fingering the shining electrodes. At one time he had savoured interrogations like this. Even that stupid secretary - Anna or whatever her name was - he'd enjoyed making her talk. Why the repugnance all of a sudden? Was he perhaps seeing himself, as a professional? Do unto others? Most likely he was just feeling his age.

Now strapped to the chair, Tana sat unmoved as Kasayiev placed the electrodes over the electro-jelly patches on her skull. He hadn't the stomach to attach the remaining contacts to the other parts of her body. He stepped back and felt sick again as he watched Schneider take great delight in completing that task.

They connected the encephalograph. At present it registered a steady, remarkably subdued flow-pattern. But, he thought, in a few moments the graph would alter dramatically.

Kazakhstan

Yakunin paced his bedroom. It was night. Dark. And cold. The damned heating had packed in again. He was naked, yet oblivious of the drop in temperature. Raisa lay fast asleep under the blankets.

He rubbed his hands down over his face, eyes closed, but the flashing images persisted in his mind. She was out-of-body, he felt sure, looking down at herself. He found no emotion, only a cold subjectivity that appalled him. Stark very brief images flashed into his head, assaulted his mind.

Flash: She was naked, strapped to a chair, electrodes fastened to her. He sensed no fear, no concern, no anger, nothing, and he broke out into a cold sweat and his breath gusted in a thin miasma in the cold air.

Flash: Two men stood watching. The one in the white coat pressed a button. He flinched on seeing them, eyes staring at snow outside this building in Kazakhstan, but seeing only the subject of their interrogation: a beautiful and vulnerable woman.

Flash: She twitched and jerked and her back arched. Blackness.

Yet even when there was blackness, he sensed the coded message trickling out, slower now, more disjointed, but still in sequence.

Earlier today Professor Bublyk had been very pleased. He had rushed off to the Cryptographic Section with the woman's coded message. Later, he returned with a downcast face because the code seemed unbreakable.

Yakunin knew instinctively the code was a cry for help.

At this realisation he stopped pacing and sat on the bed and shook Raisa awake.

Czechoslovakia

Like so many times before, Smidke and his two teenage sons sat down to supper beneath their fine Breughel print. His wife's arm brushed the tall potted plant to his right as she dished out the chicken in paprika goulash. The children smacked their lips in anticipation, anxious to taste the scrumptious Slovak-style gnocchi. 'You've done us proud again, Mother,' Smidke complimented her.

Then a hard, imperative knock on the door sounded.

'I wonder who that can be?' his wife said. All their friends knew they ate at this time and wouldn't think of disturbing the *vecere*.

With the first sharp taste of paprika on his lips, Smidke rose to answer the door. His heart had already sunk by the time he saw them. The red ID cards were but a formality. Someone had talked. Again!

His wife came forward and protested as they shouldered in. She was roughly pushed aside. Blood drained from her face.

'Tell your wife to be quiet, Smidke,' one of them said.

The children watched, silent, hateful, eyes wide, registering everything.

Instead of being systematic, they covered each other's tracks in their vain search. The ugly-looking wooden cupboards and bureau were ransacked, drawers tipped on the floor, bottoms ripped out. The ponderous beds were slit open. One of the secret policemen started sneezing, the feathers affecting his asthma. They raked out the porcelain stove and clumsily cracked the blue flower pattern.

'What have you come for?' Smidke and his wife repeatedly asked.

'You know,' came the ominous reply.

Finally, Smidke was led away, the meal cold, greasy and dry. But they had all lost their appetites anyway.

Smidke knew the charge he would face. There were plenty of 'dissidents' in jail now. 'Did... stir distrust... act hostile... towards the State and its society.'

Ilyichev was pleased with Smidke's capture. The Demek man had been recognised by one of the police snipers and they had easily traced him. He had talked almost at once. Thus the threads interweave. But Kasayiev would want more than a few important prisoners.

They'd raided the Underground Press first. The bag had been a small one, of mixed nationality. There were no foreign repercussions; the foreign helpers were questioned and released and informed to keep their noses clean in future. What about their friends? That is of no concern to you, foreigner. They will be charged, tried and dealt with appropriately.

Gestetner machines were pushed to the floor, their silk skins slashed, inks sprayed all over the young printers' faces. Ilyichev had to exert some power of command before the arresting officers lost control. As it was, there were a few too many cracked skulls.

What really irked Ilyichev was the way they didn't resist arrest.

Yet it was obvious that the arrests and the usual accompanying trials were severe blows to their organisations. They all believed that the publicity would prove that people did exist who didn't accept defeat or the present oppressive regime. For the world's press had an uncanny knack of ascertaining most of the facts virtually at once. Not that any of this worried the Government here or the Kremlin, Ilyichev thought. World condemnation was infantile; where had it led with Ulster, the Arab guerrillas, or even the invasion here? A bad press, the cold shoulder for a time. Just an incident in the past, the rebels and martyrs fading from the fickle public's mind.

This night there would be no T54s and T55s, no deafening rumble of steel juggernauts and the stench of their powerful diesel engines. The raids would be concerted and swift.

The Czech resistance movement could resort to their transistors for moral support and advice from the underground pirate radio stations - as in '68. But this would be one 'silent fight' they would lose. In '68 the one-hour general strike of 22nd August had gained total support. He remembered the ghostly sight of the wide deserted streets at midday. But then they'd had a leader, a cause, a belief in themselves that had since eroded with time and compromise.

But tonight the swoop was already nearing completion.

Earlier on in the evening, prior to the capture of Smidke, Ilyichev had witnessed a dramatic chase through Prague's suburbs.

A youngster had been stopped for careless driving, having mounted the pavement with his Simca. The patrolman had sniffed alcohol, which is strictly forbidden when driving. The lad had panicked and slammed the door in the officer's face. He'd motored away, barely missing a lamp post, and slewed to the right just in time to avoid Ilyichev's chauffeur-driven car.

Ilyichev ordered his driver to give chase over the jarring cobbles, past the decaying villas of the bourgeois Thirties, with their grandiose porches and heavy steps.

The youngster must have felt very conspicuous driving through the gaslit streets, for there was no traffic about; only the grinding noise of the evening trams carried up the twisting steep hills.

Finally, in his mad haste, the boy drove up a blind alley. Brakes screeched. He crashed into an assortment of bins and crates.

He had run for good reason. Ilyichev recognised him as one of Smidke's right-hand men. He shook his head: only a boy! Not more than nineteen; and now dead, his head through the shattered windscreen, carotid bubbling its last of lifeblood.

In the boot were roneo pamphlets, proclaiming a 'quiet revolution' with the words *mir* and *svoboda* scattered throughout. Peace! Freedom!

Hah, that'll be the day! Ilyichev mused.

Now he remembered what Smidke had said when put in his cell. 'Freedom's a much-abused word, comrade. Used by guerrillas and murderers. But we Czechoslovaks are a civilised people.'

The words grated, especially as he recalled hitting Smidke immediately afterwards. Why did these people behave so differently?

It wasn't because they were weak or cowardly. He had been in Prague during the Invasion of '68. He saw students leaping onto the Russian tanks, trying to discuss matters with the soldiers. Where else would a show of arms have produced such a reaction? 'Why did you come? We didn't call you,' they'd said. 'You were our friends,' they kept saying to the soldiers. Some simply spat on the tanks. 'Why did you turn into our enemies?' others cried. 'We're communists too!'

Some hotheads responded as the High Command had hoped, and had been met with instant, bloody death.

But the Russian war machine had been made to look foolish, even after the remarkably swift invasion had surprised the Western observers.

Dr Sebelova's daughter, Elena, had bad news for Dagmar and

Rudolf. 'They've taken my father,' she said simply.

Both young men bit back words of tenderness; they didn't express astonishment or shock. The arrest had to happen some time. Rudolf, a twenty-six-year-old technical assistant at Skoda, and Dagmar, a twenty-four-year-old sales clerk, had been recruited by Elena in the selfsame restaurant in which they were now sitting. Two tables away sat a Czech talking with the Russian First Secretary of the Stavropol district, though nobody recognised him.

'Did they get any proof?' Dagmar asked after a while.

Elena shook her head of blonde hair. 'Father's too careful. But they don't need proof, Dagmar!'

'What happens to your father's group now?' Rudolf asked.

'I've tried warning most of them. A couple are hoping to get east on their passports then use English ones - get into the West through Hungary and Yugoslavia.'

'But you don't hold out much hope?'

She lowered her eyes. 'I'll take over from Father. But I could do with some help.' She paused. 'Can I count on you both?'

Both of them had been in love with her since they were children. 'Why not?' Rudolf smiled. 'We're in deep enough anyway!'

'If you want to back out, you can. I think they'll release most of the others within a few weeks. They're after the few armed resistance people, not our sort. They'll keep them just long enough to frighten them. Word will get around; recruits will be hard to come by for a long time.'

'I - I'll help, too, Elena,' Dagmar said, finally. And with that, he flung himself from the table, yelling, 'Run for it!'

Both Rudolf and Elena sprang to their feet at once. They took in the arrival of Ilyichev and his men. Dagmar sprang from the mezzanine floor, full into Ilyichev. As the bodies sprawled, Elena and Rudolf melted into the kitchen, amidst the crashing of pots and pans.

As she ran, one thought impinged insistently. 'Did they make

Daddy talk?' In which case, she might as well go into mourning - he'd had a weak heart. But, as he'd said often enough: 'I'd rather put what little heart I've got into fighting these apparatchiks than pamper myself, darling. I've had a good life; I want you and your future family to have an even better one! One day, Elena, we will all be free!' So he had probably given his life for his simple hope.

Her cheeks felt wet as she ran. She didn't dry them.

The First Secretary of Stavropol was going prematurely bald and his Czech companion, Zdenek Mlynár, joked about it. 'Mikhailevich, you are a marked man now; you're losing your hair over the talk about you and Andropov, no?'

Mikhail Sergeyevich shrugged. 'No, he's just been a good friend, that's all.'

'Even though he's head of the Committee for State Security?'

Mikhail laughed. 'Precisely because of that, Zdeny!'

At that moment Ilyichev and his men had barged into the restaurant and Mikhail's heart sank. It was finished before it had begun, after all! He'd been a fool to trust the British woman and that Jiri fellow. Not even Andropov would understand or approve.

But no, they were after other fish, it seemed. Smaller fish. Inwardly, he breathed a sigh of relief and remembered the meeting in the Jewish cemetery, when Tana Standish had turned at hearing the rustle of an overcoat against marble headstone.

'Umbra?' queried the gentle, cultivated voice in Russian.

'Yes,' she said.

'Jiri said we could meet here.'

'Yes, it's safe. What do you want to talk about, First Secretary?'

'Do you know who I am?'

'Yes, Mikhail Sergeyevich.'

'Enough. Good. My friend Zdenek has discovered unsavoury whispers about the place called Dobranice. Have you heard of it?'

'Yes. The mining complex.'

'If you were to find out something about it, would you tell me?'

'Why don't you ask your much-vaunted KGB - especially as you're a protégé of its head?'

'Because there are many people in the KGB who would wish me ill.'

'You're definitely in Andropov's camp. What's in it for me - or for us - the British?'

He grinned, eyes glinting, his magnetic charm affecting her despite herself. 'I think it was Lord Palmerston who said, "Britain has no eternal enemies or eternal friends, only eternal interests." I firmly believe we can do business, not only you and I, but your country and mine.'

'But it isn't your country - it belongs to Brezhnev and his cronies.'

'For now, Umbra. But Yuri is ideally placed to become his successor, and with his help and that of others of like mind it's only a matter of time before I go to Moscow, I think.' There was an engaging stubbornness in his tone, his choice of words. She believed him implicitly. 'I feel it is foolish to keep the country completely isolated from the rest of the world. Change is essential to our survival - my country's and the world's.'

'You think Yuri Andropov will go along with that idea?'

'Certainly. Like me, he is bitterly opposed to the corruption and extravagance of other Party officials. He has no liking for the sputnik rhetoric of our present administration.'

She smiled. 'That's a new one on me. Sputnik rhetoric?'

He hunched his shoulders and moved his arms expansively. 'Flying very high but burning into ashes when it approaches the earth.'

'Oh, I see. Their ideas don't stand up when they come down to earth?'

He grinned, nodding vigorously. 'I'm sorry we have to be enemies, Tana Standish.'

'You know my name?'

'Jiri knows you as Umbra. But once I saw you, I recognised you from Yuri's file.'

'Should I be flattered?'

'I do not think you flatter easily. The photograph was taken two years ago in Mombasa. Some may say it is my duty to have you arrested as we can only ever be enemies.'

'We don't have to be, Mikhail Sergeyevich. This is a very brave thing you're doing right now. I appreciate it. If you and your friends can relieve the darkness clouding your great country, then perhaps a new openness can result in a better world. My father taught me that everything's possible, if you believe hard enough.'

He sighed. '*An angel can illumine the thought and mind of man by strengthening the power of vision, and by bringing within his reach some truth which the angel herself contemplates*. I've paraphrased St Thomas Aquinas's words, Tana Standish, but perhaps the vision you've just presented is not too far-fetched. Will you be able to help us? Yuri and me?'

She held out her hand. 'I promise.'

His handshake was firm, as was hers. 'Yes,' he said, 'I think we can do business.'

Now, in the restaurant, Mikhail used the napkin to wipe his sweating brow. He hoped the girl would get away from her pursuers and then absently wondered if his hair would continue to recede so that his livid birthmark - not seen for forty-four years since he was a baby - would become so distinctive it would brand him a pariah or a saviour.

CHAPTER FIFTEEN: Ransacked

'It's the night of the swoop!' old men in inns whispered, each secretly thankful they had wisely steered clear of controversial activities. The young would never learn. Soldier Svejk was the only answer, not armed resistance movements. But they then remembered the resistance during the war, the fighting in the Bohemian Forest, the mountains. They had been young then.

A few talked about Hrabel's little book - *Closely Watched Trains* - too, finding parallels with their lives under the Soviet heel and the book's Czech partisans in the Second World War. It was a short narrative, encapsulating courageous deeds of heroism and small acts of defiance, while surviving under the yoke of oppression.

Whispers went around, like the days of the invasion. Some of the jokes were old: The optimists thought that the Russians would transport at least four million of them to the uranium mines of Jachymov. The pessimists believed that they would have to walk. The joke was as old as the war. And as long as brave hearts beat beneath oppression, the jokes wouldn't be stifled.

The swoops, though wide-ranging and surprisingly well coordinated, were selective and only amounted to just over ninety individuals.

A good third of these would be released within a week or so, Ilyichev knew. But he had done what Kasayiev ordered: disrupted the movements. And created future distrust, because some of those released would be under suspicion of having been 'turned'.

And they had also picked up useful information. Yet again, they uncovered some CIA-supplied jamming equipment. This little lot was discovered on an abandoned railway siding, disconnected and now useless. But it seemed likely that the same equipment had been used earlier in the evening to jam many of the frequencies.

'We're a people of fourteen million Dubceks!' shrieked one woman who still remembered the First Secretary. 'Do you want to murder all of us?' And she spat in her guard's face. Ilyichev turned away as the prisoner with her started to harangue her for spitting.

These people! Ilyichev mused, sitting at his desk.

Lighting a cigarette, Ilyichev was reminded of Jan Palach. He was not alone in his recollection. The student had originally been the first of four human torches to protest against the invasion and the Soviet political reprisals. But the others hadn't gone through with it. Ilyichev had heard through TASS of similar incidents around the world, especially women and priests in Vietnam, using napalm of all things! He shivered now, gripping the telephone as he asked for Major Kasayiev.

He couldn't understand how the authorities allowed the hundreds of people to visit Palach's grave every day, laying garlands of flowers - a sort of pilgrimage. Just removing the nameplate from the grave didn't deter them at all. But when he discovered that Palach's body was finally taken away from Olsany cemetery, reportedly at the request of his parents, and then cremated, Ilyichev wondered at the lunacy of the instigators. They'd acted three years too late!

As the echoes of footsteps resounded in the earpiece of the phone, Ilyichev shook his head in dismay. You cannot bury the memory of brave men by digging up their bodies. The martyr is his own memorial; his gravestone is in people's hearts, their minds: unbreakable.

'Major Kasayiev is busy at the moment,' said a tremulous voice. 'Can I help? I'm the Commandant.'

'Is Grishin there?'

'Oh - Comrade Grishin has been... He's dead.'

At the same instant that his gammy leg played up again, things fell into place. The SECRET grading of the Dobranice complex and manpower; the sudden outbreak of dysentery there; Kasayiev's remarks on the coincidence; Kasayiev joining Grishin at Dobranice; the jammed signal traffic. The Ruzyne breakout could have been a diversion - a costly one. What seemed to clinch it was that Tana Standish was in the area.

Threads wound together. 'Is the Standish woman there, Commandant?' He barely managed to control his voice as he asked.

The hesitation told him anyway. 'I - well, yes - but... everything's under control. Major Kasayiev's with her now, interrogating her. I'm sorry, I have said too much already.'

Ilyichev gritted his teeth. He'd wanted the exquisite pleasure of tearing her apart, piece by bloody piece! 'Tell the major I'll deliver my report in person.'

Not waiting for a response, he hung up.

'Get my driver!' he called out into the corridor.

With a sandwich between stained teeth, the driver ran up, buttoning his tunic. 'Sir?' he mumbled.

'Take me to Dobranice.'

The encephalograph recorded a dormant pattern. But the continuous though low-key charges through the skull electrodes were having a noticeable effect.

Gradually, Tana's awareness could be seen as more and more of her brain mustered its energies to tackle the pain.

Schneider hummed happily, observing the progress.

Kasayiev was only intent on noting her gradual mental decline, in order that he might step in as soon as she was amenable to talk - thereby curbing Schneider's sadistic pleasure.

Awareness came. Excruciatingly. Now she knew. The stark image she'd snatched on arrival at Ruzyne airport - the screaming woman - was her.

Tana screamed as additional body electrodes were switched on.

She could no longer withdraw her mental faculties. She needed them all for combating the unremitting pain.

Still no idea of time passing - it could be minutes or hours.

Then, fleetingly, a thought - an emotion - hit her: remorse. In Russian, coloured like Kasayiev.

Inwardly, she thanked him for that.

When her defences were down, they would resort to more LSD or pentothal derivatives and weasel the truth out of her. She didn't think she had much time left before she was breached. Not much longer.

Covered in sweat, she writhed and moaned, as the mounting pain ransacked her reason, toppled her barriers.

Eyes tight-squeezed, she ran down the mental image of old Karmelicka Street, checking the doorways, the locks.

Intact. But buckling.

Tana screamed again as her body betrayed her, voided its waste, cloyed her nostrils with the faecal and tart stench.

The poor bitch! she heard Kasayiev think.

Kazakhstan

'Raisa, you're on the British desk. Have you detected anything at all - any psychic messages?'

Raisa sat up in the bed, hugging the blanket round her. She shook her head. 'No, I'm not as powerful as you yet. I need more training.'

'You feel nothing now?'

Her brow furrowed. 'Now? What do you mean? You are not linked to the apparatus. You can't feel anything without the energy boost.' Her eyes widened as realisation dawned. 'Oh, Karel. You can sense that psychic woman, can't you?'

He nodded, turned away. Until now, only the professor even guessed at the full extent of his talent.

Raisa backed up against the headboard, her face drained of blood. She now feared Karel Yakunin and his ability.

Czechoslovakia

Increasing agony, her mind torn apart, colours flesh-pink around the edges, reddening, distorted. Warmth. Metallic taste. Of blood. Her tongue. Bitten.

As though outside, she heard herself gasping, straining for air, the repeated shocks taking their toll.

Her heart was pumping maddeningly, being arrested fractionally.

And her head just wanted to explode.

Although deep inside she knew the technique required only controlled surges of electric shock, it felt as though the jolts were continuous, unbroken, sending her whole body jerking drunkenly, spasmodically.

She gagged again and again.

But her stomach was the least of her troubles.

Her senses were no longer cut off: the vile stench of her own burning flesh made her retch. Salt of sweat, body odour, vomit, the exuding fear: smells she'd never be rid of ever again. To haunt her, if she lived. But she wouldn't live; they wouldn't let her. She didn't want to live.

Outside, klaxons sounded.

Kasayiev's voice penetrated: 'See what's going on, Commandant!'

Tana writhed and screamed and wanted to be dead. Either that or cut out her tongue - because she knew it wouldn't be long before her broken sentences betrayed every detail of secret knowledge that she possessed.

CHAPTER SIXTEEN: Tyson

Kazakhstan

'Are you sure you haven't detected this woman again?' Bublyk wanted to know, leaning menacingly over Yakunin's desk.

So far Raisa had only reported to him secretly twice. On both occasions, Yakunin's contact with the woman had been brief, nothing of any great importance. But what was significant was that Yakunin was capable of making the psychic link without any mind-boosting apparatus, and he hadn't disclosed the fact.

'No, professor,' Yakunin said in reply and eyed Raisa on the adjacent desk. She looked away guiltily. 'As you probably already know, I lost the woman last night. Just blackness.' He tried to keep the despair he felt out of his voice, out of his mind. 'Now, I can find no one.'

Bublyk studied him, eyes narrowing suspiciously. 'You're holding something back about her, I feel sure.' Raisa had implied as much; there was a hint of jealousy in her tone when she last reported.

Shaking his head, Yakunin said, 'No, professor, I'm just tired. I didn't sleep well last night.' Which was true enough. How to explain the shock of sharing another person's mind, however fleetingly, and to share in her pain and desolation, unable to help, then to lose her. 'I'll be all right.'

'I don't believe you!' Bublyk snapped, irritated beyond belief by the mental brick wall Yakunin had successfully erected. 'Guards!' he shouted, harshly removing the headset from Yakunin. 'Arrest this man!'

Dismayed, Yakunin was forced from his chair by two sentries. As they scuffled, he cast a fearful look in Raisa's direction. She opened her mouth to say something but didn't speak, looking away instead.

Yakunin was marched out of the room and the rest of The Group stared, worry in their eyes.

'Come on, now, back to work!' Bublyk said, clapping his hands. 'We have an inspection in two weeks!' And that thought alone sent Bublyk into a cold sweat.

England

Sweating already at the tight timescale he'd been set, Tyson boarded the Harrier.

2358. Nearly three hours since Tana's message had stopped. The deadline, on Dr Fisk's estimation, was 0300. He had to get her out by then. Of course, Fisk could be terribly wrong. She could crack before his deadline - or last a lot longer. There was no way of knowing.

If she had talked, he'd still try bringing her out of there so they could learn what she'd told them. With any luck, perhaps he could eliminate her interrogators there and then, effectively blocking the leakage.

'Time-check,' he said to the jump-jet's pilot.

'2359 Zulu, sir.'

Since *Operation Ouija* had been given life at Interprises, they'd used GMT times on all signal traffic relating to it. The Zulu time zone was the Service equivalent of GMT. He'd keep his watch on Zulu time, although Czechoslovakia was one hour ahead. He would have no need to refer to Czech clocks anyway.

Having already inspected the equipment he specially requested, he stowed the haversack behind his seat and proceeded to marvel at the Ferranti black box by the pilot's knee. They had been airborne about ten minutes when he asked about it.

'Uses a combination of gyros and accelerometer coupled with a computer, recording every movement of the aircraft, sideways, up and down,' the pilot informed pedantically. 'Depicts this moving map. If I press this button I'll also get a corrected reading of the direction to and distance from the target - to an accuracy of about 600 yards after a 200 mile flight.'

The device could also be used for automatic delivery of cannon, rockets and bombs.

Tyson was fascinated by technology and always had been. As a young man he enjoyed an active, outdoor life; a sort of contradiction, being a studious type as well. After obtaining his Spanish degree at King's College, Durham, he drifted for a couple of months then on impulse joined the Royal Engineers. As the advertisements of the time stated, the Army made a man of him. He thrived on the kind of activity they dished up; a fit body and an alert mind, plenty of action, good money and good food. He cut out drinking, save for special occasions, and then always in moderation. He had never smoked as he couldn't see anything sensible about ingesting smoke into his lungs.

In his spare time he took a seamanship course and soon obtained a Coxswain's certificate. His eyes were good and after hours of practice he attained marksman standard with a Browning pistol: heavy but damned accurate - unlike some toy-like automatics he'd tried.

Two years later he joined the SAS, successfully passing their rigorous courses, proud to be given his wings and the sand-coloured beret.

In Borneo he spent about ten months in a four-man team, training Border Scouts, the local tribesmen, who became the Army's eyes and ears to defend the Malaysian border with the Kalimantan region of Indonesia. They were good liaison officers with the locals and also acted as additional infantry and guides.

While his fighting impulse was more than satisfied, he wasn't being academically challenged until his patrol met up with the

Kalabit, a headhunting tribe who didn't particularly like the Chinese communists. The Kalabit taught Tyson their customs and, more interestingly, basic Malay, which was far better than the short course he'd undertaken before being shipped out.

Unfortunately, in September of that year the Long Jawi Scout Post was massacred by a group of Indonesians. Tyson had known and trained many of the dead and openly grieved for them with other Scouts. Thereafter, the Scouts were solely used as intelligence gatherers and acquitted themselves well for another three years. But Tyson didn't share in their successes as he'd moved on to Aden in April 1964 shortly after two SAS soldiers' heads had been displayed impaled on stakes in the main square of Taiz, across the Yemen border.

Tyson and his new team – Dave, Benny and Mark - were ordered to bring back some enemy heads and they did so. It was grisly work and Benny Bateman suffered severe leg wounds that meant he'd never walk again. But they got him out - and brought back six FLOSY heads.

On his return from that mission he was recruited into the Counter Revolutionary Warfare unit to cope with the insurgents in the port of Aden itself. Here, he learned counter-insurgency skills which later would be honed against terrorists.

But he didn't have much opportunity to use these new abilities as he was asked to attend an urgent hush-hush meeting in a shed at Khormaksar airport. Here he was introduced to Admiral Sands, a short man who seemed uncomfortable in civilian clothes.

They shook hands and it was all very informal. 'I'm authorised by your CO to put to you an unusual request, Sergeant,' Sands had said, his sharp features lightening with a slight smile. 'We're talking wheels within wheels here, you realise?'

'Sorry, sir, but you've lost me already.'

'That's my fault. I've been with the cloak-and-dagger crowd for four years now and you tend to go all cryptic. Let me explain.'

Admiral Sands was there on behalf of a certain Sir Gerald

Hazzard from a covert company called International Enterprises. 'An autonomous bit of MI6, actually,' Sands said.

Tyson's life was about to change dramatically. It began with the unorthodox assignment Sands had been sent to set up. Tyson with three other members of the SAS were parachuted into Brazil under the directive of the Defence Minister; top-secret diplomatic clearances had been arranged, complete with sweeteners in the form of generous trade agreements. Two Interprises agents, Mason and Cally, had kidnapped a high-ranking KGB Director of Peru. But their plane crashed in the Brazilian jungle. Interprises had no available operatives up to the rigours of jungle tracking; so the SAS had been brought in.

Tyson and his two comrades rescued the Russian and the Interprises agents, taking them to a secret rendezvous with the country's first nuclear-powered submarine, HMS *Dreadnought*.

Landing at Rosyth, the two Interprises agents spirited the Soviet spy away. Tyson left his three comrades to some well-earned leave in Edinburgh while he caught the train down to one of Sir Gerald's country homes just outside Morpeth, as instructed.

'I've already had a report from Mason and Cally,' Sir Gerald said. 'They were greatly impressed and again send their thanks.'

'I was just doing my job, sir,' Tyson replied, sipping Vichy water. 'They held up pretty well in that jungle, all things considered.'

'Yes.' Sir Gerald grinned and Tyson thought that his features slightly resembled a death mask from Borneo. 'Think about what I'm going to offer you. No guarantees, mind. We don't work that way.' He gave Tyson a card. 'Should you want to get in touch.'

There was something about the man that inspired trust. You really wanted to follow him. Tyson wondered what Sir Gerald had done in *his* war.

For days afterwards he couldn't settle. That indefinable 'something' that he'd been chasing all his adult life, it seemed to be on offer from this mysterious organisation called Interprises. Certainly, it was linked in some way to MI6. Yet it had autonomy, which he liked. And it was run by a man he could believe in.

On the fourth day he fished out Sir Gerald's card and telephoned the man.

Although he was in the middle of a meeting, Sir Gerald made time for him. 'I'd like to join your team, sir. There's just the one problem – I'm signed up for –'

'Your release can be taken care of, no problem,' Sir Gerald interrupted.

'Then I'm your man.'

'You're happy about doing more training?'

'No problem, sir.'

'And although we're keen on team players, you'll often be quite alone in hostile territory. You're used to working in a four-man team. Being alone won't bother you?'

'No, sir. I'm comfortable with my own company.'

'I thought so. Welcome to our little organisation then, Mr Tyson.'

It felt strange, being called that. Mister. He quite liked the sound of it.

Within the month, his resignation was sanctioned and he received instructions about training at the Fort, where, of course, he'd met Tana Standish.

After completing their training, they split up to go on separate assignments - she to Singapore, he to North Yemen. When they met up again while relaxing at Fenner House, he was drawn to her by her selfless businesslike approach to work, a kindred spirit.

As they got to know each other he found himself sharing thoughts with her. Literally. It was uncanny.

'But I'm not psychic,' he said.

She shook her head and smiled. 'Everyone is, to some degree, Keith. It just needs nurturing, bringing out.'

'I'll refrain from making any double entendre there,' he said.

'Oh, Keith, I'd already seen that thought coming!'

Only then did he begin to understand how she excelled in almost every endeavour.

'It seems like cheating, doesn't it?' she said once.

'No.' He was quite adamant. 'It's a talent, a gift. And if you have such a gift, then you should use it.'

Perhaps it had been inevitable that they would become lovers. It began in Naples on their second assignment, in 1966. They'd managed to keep it quiet but after the Izmir episode the following year, their relationship became an open secret.

But they were adult about it, understanding there could be no commitment. 'We live for the moment, Keith,' she'd said one evening, early on, sitting on a balcony with a clear view of the bay and the dominating volcano, Vesuvius. Often the summit was shrouded in cloud, as had been their assignment until they had discovered the truth behind their contact Aldo Ferrara.

And though he would have liked their relationship to be more than that, Tyson had agreed.

So when Tana took him home to meet her mother, the only one with any hopes of marriage was Mrs Standish, hopes they gently dashed.

'Oh, this is all so terribly modern,' Vera Standish remarked when they both explained their 'arrangement'.

Then, in a quiet moment, while Tana made a fresh pot of tea, Mrs Standish gently tapped his knee and whispered, 'Do look after her, won't you? She's all I've got.'

He remembered placing his big hand over her small-boned wrist and gently squeezing. 'She's a strong woman, Vera. She can cope with almost anything, I'm sure.' He took both her hands in his and looked into her eyes. 'I promise, if I'm able, I will look after her.' He grinned and let go. 'But, for God's sake, don't tell her I said that!'

'Dear boy, Mum's the word,' she said, tapping her nose with a finger, and giggled.

At that moment Tana came in. 'Mother, what *are* you giggling about? You haven't been at the sherry yet, have you?' she joked.

'No, dear. I much prefer a draught Guinness these days. Once we've had this super tea you've made, what about popping down to *The Wyvern* for a drink?'

That had been quite a visit; he'd seen Tana in an unexpected light, homely and comfortable.

He'd driven Tana back to her flat in Alton, where they'd made long languorous love until three in the morning.

Sadly, Tana never took him to see her mother again, which was a pity as he really liked the old lady. It had nothing to do with the fact that their 'relationship' cooled. That had been as inevitable as it beginning in the first place. But they stayed friends. Tana probably didn't want her work to get too close to her mother to affect her.

Tana never seemed to relax until she came back from that Karachi assignment. Something happened there - probably to do with Clayton, the old goat! Her psychic ability seemed heightened, her determination to be the best even stronger. She confided in him less, but he was there if she wanted a friend and every few months they went out to a restaurant to unwind and savour the good life.

As much as he was able in their closed society, he followed her assignments and attended two of her debriefings. They remained close, even after Swann fell for her in a big way in Venice.

Christ, she was better than any man at compartmentalising her emotions, her work and her love life. Fortunately, Tyson wasn't the jealous type. He had his memories and they were good.

And he always remembered his promise to her mother, impossible though it might be to keep.

A bit old-fashioned, he knew, but he liked to keep his promises. Sometimes, it might take a while - even years - but he tried never to forget a promise.

And now, after so many years, it seemed this was to be his greatest test, he realised as the jump-jet neared the Sumava Mountains twenty-one minutes after take-off.

The pilot slowed just before the crest and hovered on vertical jets.

CHAPTER SEVENTEEN: Sumava

West Germany

A couple of miles outside the small Bavarian town of Landshut stood the Rhine Army's 149 Signal Squadron camp; on the northern banks of River Isar. With Whitehall's most recent manpower cuts, the base had become a backwater; a token presence. Only inspections and occasional 'paper exercises' disturbed the boredom.

Yet at the instant that Tyson boarded the Harrier at 2358Z, Major Lambert Galbraith was shakily gripping MoD UKLF's MOST SECRET signal, now in clear.

In four weeks he was due for relief, all set for UK and a Golden Bowler in ten months' time. Ever since his posting here he had eyed the close proximity of the Eastern Bloc's border with suspicion and fear. Politicians and spies - what did they care? They would ride roughshod over anyone or anything in their private cold war of brinkmanship. All of a sudden, he felt an innocent pawn, to be moved at whim, sacrificed if need be.

This - this Directive - he stared at it mistily - was deadly serious.

Didn't they realise what they were asking?

He was ashamed of his doubt and disloyalty. Still, he'd better set things in motion fairly fast.

Fingers trembling, he dialled.

Christ, he was too old for this sort of thing.

Army pilot Robbie Iorns and his navigator Mal Short clambered into their helicopter with similar misgivings.

They strapped in and ran through the sequential checks.

'Bloody Top Brass!' intoned Iorns. 'They want a good...' The whirring rotors smothered his purple prose.

Czechoslovak border
At first, Tyson had envisaged parachuting from the Harrier. Then he learned they were equipped with ejection seats; even if he'd managed to find room for his own 'chute and had clambered onto the wing during hover and jumped forward, he'd have been sucked into the jet intake. If he'd jumped back he'd have risked either incineration from the reheat - afterburn - or pummelling from the very powerful eflux - exhaust.

Time of course was of the essence and the Harrier was the fastest available aircraft. Parachuting to the Dobranice mine complex would have been the quickest method of insertion, but he'd had to find a different approach.

Within seconds of the Harrier touching down in a barely adequate clearing, Tyson climbed out, waved to the pilot and leapt to the forest floor.

The Army chopper was two hundred yards away, rotors chomping on air, a torchlight flashing, signalling.

Navigator Short helped him in. 'Hang on, sir - the ride's going to be rough!' All lights were shut down as the craft lifted off.

Here, on the Sumava slopes, there was no border guard - the fence and natural barriers were considered sufficient deterrent.

Czechoslovakia
It could have been only minutes later when Iorns hovered over the dark shapes of the northern side's trees while Tyson struggled down the bucking rope ladder.

No sooner had his feet hit the dried leaves and sod than the chopper - barely glimpsed in the starlight - was rising, the ladder being hauled in rapidly.

Concealing himself behind an ivy bush, he removed his boots and slipped on leather moccasins from his haversack. He tensed for a moment as some leaves rustled. Just a marmot or a mink, he guessed. An owl screeched some distance away.

As he clambered through the stunted bramble, holly bushes and between tall conifers, he welcomed the cool night wind brushing down the slopes. The lower he got the stronger the smell of sap, mushrooms and mould.

Reaching a small clearing that commanded a perfect view of the lower slopes and Dobranice, Tyson unfastened the nightglasses from his haversack. Covering a small area at a time, he mentally tallied each building with the information gleaned from the Phantom overflight.

The Dobranice mine complex was a hotchpotch of buildings and superstructure, like any other mine - except for the perimeter fence and the tall watchtowers. Huge wheels and rusting girders soared in the background. They were still. No nightshift.

A half-track sluggishly patrolled around the railway sidings, flashing a small spotlight on the idle coal trucks that rested on their rails. Beyond the complex the slag heaps made their brooding presence felt, casting a dark shade across the whole area. The land on the outside of the perimeter fence had been razed, now dotted with numerous tree stumps and scorched grass.

Slowly and almost soundlessly, he negotiated the rest of the way down.

At the forest's edge, he again ran his binoculars over the structure.

Straddling the fence, the watchtowers were a good hundred feet tall. At regular intervals along the fifteen-feet high fence were concrete posts and fastened to these were self-firing weapons at varying heights. All he need do was touch the thin metal wires running along the fine mesh and the radio-controlled guns would be triggered, discharging a rain of steel bullets from both sides into his body. Four years ago, details about the automated firing device were brought to the West by a defecting Border Command soldier. The devices were installed along the German border, for escaping East Germans, poor sods.

These top-security precautions were ample testimony that Tana had stumbled onto something big. The overflight had also reported an unusual concentration of radioactivity. Could be an underground reactor.

Time: 0033. Bloody tight!

No-man's-land was constantly in the glare from watchtower lights - yet he could see no guards in the towers, save for someone above the entrance gateway. The Phantom pilot had suggested that the fence might be under television surveillance.

Unwittingly, the Soviets had helped him by scorching the grass: he could crawl practically unnoticed wearing his black coverall. He snaked over the hard, stubbly surface, keeping to the darkest patches.

Face down, weaving slowly, he finally reached the fence. But he didn't congratulate himself. He knew that an alarm might have been set off without him knowing – heat- or vibration-sensors, perhaps.

He had chosen fairly well. From this point of the fence he could see the pithead baths and canteen directly ahead, some ten yards away. To the left of these was a squat winding engine house, its generator humming. And to the left of this, the fan house, with air-shimmer above the square roof; a large duct curved from the fan house into the surrounding concrete; this duct would slope underground, meet up with the upcast shaft, and afford ventilation.

Beyond these buildings were the two houses for the headgear and airshafts, connected by a twenty-foot overhead enclosed gangway. Far to the right, the screens, washery and railway sidings.

Unlike many collieries, this one obviously washed the coal, before it was transported anywhere, and dumped the waste from the process in ugly piles - yet another example of the Soviet unconcern for pollution. They built factories and processing plants wherever they liked, not caring if their industry blighted the land. Acid rain from Poland was already stripping the leaves from trees in North Bohemia. Ecology protesters wouldn't stand a chance on this side of the Iron Curtain though.

The inspection half-track was parked outside the radio building near the washery, its engine still running. Headlamps spilled a dull yellow glow around it.

Concrete posts supporting the fence and weapons were about fifteen yards away each side. A watchtower straddled the fence some hundred yards off.

Wriggling out of his haversack, he clipped the rubber-covered torch onto his belt and removed some gear. He retained the two hundred foot coil of dark nylon rope across his back and secured a pair of calf-length boots to his belt. Thanks to the overflight he had come prepared.

Sweat poured, which wasn't surprising, as he was fully clothed beneath the coveralls.

Now he placed a small box, like a doctor's beeper, on the earth by the fence and switched it on. If it did its job properly, the radio signals would divert the radio-controlled rifles.

Slipping his hands into a pair of rubber gloves, he then clipped bypass wires simultaneously to the wire fence on his left and right and then to all the fence wires in front of him so he could snip a hole with impunity.

He cut the wire.

And all hell broke loose!

Alarms blared.

Hurriedly, he finished clipping an adequate hole and pushed the haversack through.

A searchlight probed.

Lying spreadeagled, half through the fence gap, open haversack in front of him, he was fully visible in the blinding beam.

The electronic box-beeper had thrown the rifles to begin with but now, out of the corner of his eye, he could see them training on him. They were using nightsight TV, overriding the automatic sequence, aiming at him. He'd be caught in a crossfire.

CHAPTER EIGHTEEN: Infiltration

Another alarm clanged somewhere, awakening soldiers in the barracks behind the radio building.

Tyson speedily removed from the haversack his mini-mortar, some eighteen inches of rifled tube and expertly assembled it. He slammed home a couple of three-inch cartridges, ignoring the pain as his thumb caught on the loading mechanism. He fired them off staccato-fashion.

Not waiting for results, he pulled himself through the gap instants ahead of a salvo of lead. Puffs of dust and spurts of mud sprayed his back as he rolled through puddle-filled ruts and over clumps of coarse grass, seeking deeper shadows.

Moments before, gouts of electrically charged tinfoil had mushroomed from the burst cartridges, sending the radio-controlled guns haywire. The infrared television cameras were next to useless as well, buzzing with snowy interference. Wherever the monitoring screens were, the sentries would be cursing. Rather than give up altogether, they were directing the guns anywhere, in the hope of a chance hit.

Tyson lobbed a couple of anti-riot grenades in front of a group of soldiers running from the radio building. The grenades burst into red clouds, providing a smokescreen; the irritants in the smoke would also stop the troops' advance.

Crouched low, he was more concerned with the whereabouts of the half-track and mounted machine gun.

Discarding his haversack, he took to his heels.

Bullets zipped overhead, some echoing against corrugated sheds.

Prudently, he had retained the clippers; they thumped heavily against his thigh as he made a mad dash for the black bulk of the washhouse and canteen.

Blinding white lights were flashing on, yet the mining buildings still remained blacked out, his only real haven.

Breathless, his shoulder rammed hard up against the brick wall of the canteen.

The commotion he'd left behind was unbelievable.

Their automatic rifles had gone berserk; the running troops were pinned down, firing spasmodically at the fence guns.

Clinging to the shadows, Tyson threw another smoke-grenade into the back of the half-track as it roared past the winding machine house on his right. As the smoke erupted in a bright red pillar, the vehicle suddenly veered, ran over two soldiers and ploughed on towards the fence, bullets whining off the armour plating.

Darting from shadow to shadow, he crossed over to the winding engine house, whose taut cables climbed steeply to the wheels above the airshaft buildings. He could attempt getting down the shaft by shinning up the wire then lowering himself through the roof. But the idea of silhouetting himself on a wire didn't particularly appeal.

The shimmer of warm air climbing out of the fan house caught his eye.

He had no warning. Out of the shadows leapt an enormous dog. Its approach had been completely silent but now it flew through the air with a low guttural snarl.

Instinctively, Tyson warded off the jaws with a karate block. The beast yelped and was down only for an instant. It shook its head, then, its length reaching almost to his chest, it leapt again.

He was ready for it: grabbing both forepaws, he held on tight and opened his arms wide as the impetus of the dog's weight pushed him onto his back. The dog's legs parted with a brutal snapping sound from their breastbone, as simply as a chicken's.

He kicked the poor animal's thick silky underbelly over his head, its brindled markings flashing by. As the carcass hit the earth softly, he thought that the firing seemed more sporadic now.

Surprisingly, he had still gone undetected.

Ears tuned, he skirted the fan house, filtering out the distant sounds of soldiers, of their guns, of the monotonous knocking of a padlock against a door somewhere near. He was intent only on the immediate vicinity. Nobody was in the fan house: he rubbed a patch of dirty window to confirm. Empty. One of the windows was broken; he squeezed a hand through, unfastened the catch. Lifting the window up, he heaved himself in and shut the window after him.

Moccasin soles padding soundlessly, he flashed his torch for a few seconds, hoping that if anyone noticed they'd mistake it for a reflection from the blazing half-track at the fence.

He located the airduct's inspection panel. The duct had to be large enough for a man to clamber through for maintenance purposes. If his lightning study of mines with an ex-NCB representative were correct, the duct should join onto the upcast airshaft some fifteen feet below the surface.

Wire mesh covered the inspection panel. He fished out the clippers and resoundingly snapped the grille. A fetid breeze redolent of coal dust and damp earth wafted up to him.

He lowered himself through the aperture and snaked along the circular metal duct.

Obviously, maintenance men didn't come in his size; his shoulders painfully hit the roof time and again. He was lathered now but couldn't afford to take off his coveralls just yet.

Suddenly, he brought himself to a stop, felt the smooth metal floor ahead looping away beneath him.

He flashed on the torch: yes, the duct was curving; he remembered the piece outside the fan house, how it arched into the surrounding concrete. It would be a vertical drop then a gradual slope to the airshaft.

At the point where the metal duct met the earth, it became a round red-brick funnel. Tyson braced his back and feet against this funnel and slowly descended, salty sweat stinging his eyes. Each movement strained his stomach, shoulder and thigh muscles and his tendons soon began to ache with the exertion.

At last the brick duct levelled off.

He relaxed a bit and shrugged his shoulders to ease the ache. He wanted to cough on the choking air but feared he'd be unable to stop so he tried steadying his breathing, taking small comfort from the updraught.

From this point on he could crawl in a stooped posture. He kept the torch on.

A black circle appeared up ahead and gradually lightened as he moved towards it.

His heart sank: it looked as though the duct had been bricked up!

But that didn't make sense; it wouldn't account for the continuous, choking updraught. Then, as he approached, he realised the bricks ahead were part of the adjoining airshaft itself.

As he crawled towards the edge, he squeezed his head and shoulder out of the coil of rope. The torch pierced quite a way down the shaft.

Two cables hung about two feet away from his nose. One skip was stationary above, its connecting brother doubtless at the bottom of the shaft on their shared wire. Roughly three feet below the brick level of the shaft and airduct, the shaft was walled with wooden crossbeams, like catwalks on end.

Turning around, he lowered himself over backwards, his feet feeling in the dark for the topmost beam of wood.

Time: 0130.

He found a foothold and lowered himself further. His feet located the next lower beam and, using the greasy winch-cable as support, he was eventually low enough to wrap his hands around the topmost beam. He wouldn't like to rely on the cable for an upward climb as it was far too slippery.

Gritting his teeth, he held onto the beam with one hand and shone the torch. The rock above the beam was firm - but...there! Soft shale, a small deposit, just above the beam. He tucked the torch in his belt and scraped the shale away with the clippers until he had made a hollow above and behind the beam, sufficient to thread the rope through and secure it with a figure-of-eight knot.

Fingers on his right hand throbbing with the effort, he dropped the rope down the shaft. He hoped the two hundred foot length was enough.

The strength had temporarily deserted his right arm with the concentrated strain on his fingers and wrist.

Using his feet to take his weight and act as an anchor on the rope, he slowly descended, hand over hand.

A sucking sound disturbed him for a moment; like a dockside donkey-boiler; probably the pumping engine at the shaft's bottom, removing the excess water.

He continued to descend.

Eventually, after what seemed an age, he came to the first level's tunnel entrance, with its wooden duckboards right up to the edge and caked in mud.

He swung in and lowered his head to avoid the top wooden beam of the entrance. He landed firmly though a little loudly then hauled the rope in; there was about ten feet of it left: so this was the two hundred foot level Tana's message had mentioned.

Tyson left the rope dangling and consulted his wrist-compass and recalled Tana's directions, '...Head east-west.' This tunnel went southwest. He trusted her implicitly: he would follow it as it currently headed in a westerly direction.

After a few yards he approached an airlock. It was relatively new and well-greased, the metal reflecting his torchlight. He twirled the pins and entered. There was a rush of air and his ears popped.

A wooden beam overhead groaned and dripped water into puddles, the sound echoing like some cracked bell in the blackness.

The miners' train cart was well-greased and now idle, very likely left over from the dayshift.

For a good ten yards he walked through the puddles and over slippery and creaking duckboards.

Finally, he came to a junction, his tunnel carrying straight on in a south-westerly direction.

The intersecting tunnel was at right angles and ran northwest.

Stepping over deflated hoses, cables and pump tubes, Tyson chose the northwest route.

Pit props continued to groan overhead, the dripping blackness hardly relieved by his torch.

Tyson came to a T-junction at the end of the tunnel. This fresh tunnel passed at right angles, going west-south-west. He turned left and walked alongside a wide conveyor belt with pieces of coal on its worn surface. At some places the tunnel was quite narrow, pit props taking up most of the room where presumably a weak point in the roof had been identified.

Running the length of the conveyor was a metal rail along which the power-cutter would move with the aid of a pulley-chain; he almost tripped over this more than once.

A whirring noise startled him at the same instant as he spotted a light at the conveyor's end-block further down the tunnel.

He clicked off the torch.

Tana's last words had been: '...till contact guarded gate. Through airlock along corridor.' From the direction he was moving in, it looked as though this was it.

Stealthily, he sidled along the tunnel until he was at the corner.

Light from an entrance on the right filled this part of the mine.

A small rail-line with empty coaltrucks stood immobile in the tunnel on his left. To the truck's right was the coalface.

Glistening steel bars blocked the entrance.

A Soviet army sentry sat with his back to him, dozing in the refreshing breeze from a rotating Hitachi fan.

The airlock must be beyond this gate, Tyson realised.

Unfastening the quiet nylon zip of his coveralls, he stepped out of them. He checked his Soviet Colonel's uniform for any telltale rents or dirt. Apart from sweat patches under his arms and at the base of his spine, it seemed all right. Careful not to make a sound, he squeezed into his black boots. He removed the Tokarev pistol from its holster and checked the magazine: eight rounds, fully loaded. He used the coveralls to wrap up the moccasins and torch and left them wedged behind a pit prop.

Sweat gathered in his palms and his mouth went dry as he stepped into the glow cast by the striplights at the entrance.

The guard, totally unaware, continued to bask in the fan's breeze.

'Sentry!' Tyson growled in a thick Georgian accent.

Upsetting his chair, the guard whirled round, his mouth open in shock. Surprised though he was, he still brought round his Kalashnikov rifle and aimed it at Tyson's belly.

'You're supposed to guard, not daydream!' Tyson berated.

The soldier's porcine features squinted as if in physical pain.

Tyson snarled, 'Now, open up!'

'But...'

'Don't *but* me, man! I've spent the last hour checking on security in these damned accursed mineshafts and I'm in no mood for incompetence!'

Guilt-ridden visions of Siberia in his weak Mongolian eyes, the guard shouldered his rifle, fumbled with the coded console button keys and unlocked the gates. 'I - I've just come on duty, sir - my comrade didn't tell me about...'

'Excuses!' Tyson laughed, bending his tall frame to enter through the gate. 'That's enough, soldier. I won't report you this time.'

'Thank you, sir.'

As the gate clanged shut, Tyson said, 'Take a break' and pivoted round, thrusting the heel of his hand into the guard's vulnerable chin. Neck broken, the soldier crumpled to the blue-tiled floor, body clumping, the rifle clattering.

Quickly retrieving the fallen Kalashnikov, Tyson covered the four yards to an airlock on his left. There was a lift door straight ahead.

He sped along the corridor, illuminated by fluorescent lighting, only slowing his pace when he came into range of a rotating camera-eye. The first camera he came across was on a corner, fifteen yards along the corridor, just by a green-painted door marked NO ADMITTANCE in Cyrillic.

It was already 0203 and time was running out and he had no idea where Tana was being held.

He was tempted to try the green door but then he decided to scout further up the corridor first and come back this way later.

Ten yards on there was a corridor on the right, corners bristling with more camera-eyes. A couple of lenses were shattered and there was evidence of recent bullet-scores in the walls. He didn't have to be psychic to know that Tana had been here.

A sentry stood outside a door on the far corner of this adjoining corridor.

Tyson was about to turn and accost him when he noted a radioactive symbol and warning skull and crossbones on a door about twelve yards further ahead. At the extreme end of the corridor, some construction work was still going on, welding sparks flashing.

The door with the radiation sign wasn't locked and opened easily. Tyson stepped onto a concrete platform and looked down upon an intriguing subterranean complex.

He had stumbled upon the secret that Tana had discovered.

The platform was a good eighteen inches thick and apparently served only as a viewing balcony as it was fenced off and led nowhere.

He was about one hundred and fifty feet above the floor of the complex. Directly in front of him were three nuclear reactors enclosed in distinctive concrete shields, control rods pointing to the roof. Secondary circulation pumps led to the condenser pipelines from the massive generators and turbines. Beneath the shields were the reactor cores that contained uranium rods.

Having once been called in to the UK Atomic Energy Authority's establishment at Windscale when sabotage was suspected, he was familiar with the reactors' configuration.

Gigantic concrete extensions of the shields branched off towards five shining steel silos still under construction. He was just able to see other concrete buildings at the far end, the last two complete with narrow view-slits.

He mentally checked the direction he had travelled since entering the mine, the estimated distance covered, and his reckoning seemed to tally.

The Soviet missile silos were actually over the border, in the heart of the Sumava Mountains, but deep below West German soil.

Judging by the size of the two completed silos nearest to him, he reckoned they'd accommodate the new 30-megaton SS11 nuclear-powered missiles, capable of blinding anti-attack radar and knocking out all the US Minutemen missiles. The crafty bastards! Fully aware of the satellite surveillance, they'd built silos in a place where the Western agencies wouldn't think to look - on their own side of the Iron Curtain.

The way the Russian war machine worked, producing a nuclear submarine every month, while strike-torn Britain strained to get one out every eighteen months, he wouldn't be surprised to learn that the silos would be at a perpetual state of readiness within a few more weeks.

He allowed himself to smile. If this were some spy-melodrama from Hollywood, he'd perform countless brave feats and blow the lot sky-high. But there'd be no cinematic heroics here. Nuclear weapons certainly aren't that easy to destroy; besides, the explosion, if he could have managed it, would probably precipitate escalation.

His only hope was to report this information back at Interprises. The knowledge of the silos' whereabouts would considerably reduce their strategic value.

Time: 0214.

And he still hadn't found Tana. He decided to have a look at the guarded room he'd been tempted to try earlier then hesitated as footsteps approached the door.

Brow beaded with sweat beneath his peaked cap, Tyson propped the Kalashnikov against the balcony and stepped out. No self-respecting officer would carry a rifle, after all.

An unarmed soldier was passing. Tyson caught sight of the identity disc: 'Federov!' he snapped.

Federov crunched to a halt and saluted. 'Comrade Colonel!'

Tyson said crisply, 'I'm just in from Moscow, Federov. The woman spy - Standish. I've a new method of–'

'Oh, I'm sorry, Colonel, but I fear that you're probably too late.'

Tyson's heart sank. His pearl-grey eyes lanced. 'What?'

'She'll be singing to Major Kasayiev by now, sir. Such a pretty creature, too.' He shook his curly blond head. 'The guardroom's looking forward to having her afterwards.' Grinning, he made a lewd gesture.

At least she was still alive! Appalled at what the man was implying, Tyson barked, 'Where are they?'

Stepping back, Federov paled at Tyson's tone and menacing glare. He shakily pointed ahead. 'First left, fourth door on the left, Colonel...' He glanced at Tyson, seeking a name and, at the precise instant that Federov eyed his tunic, Tyson realised the Interprises costumiers had slipped up.

'Your identification disc, sir - it's missing.'

Feigning surprise, Tyson looked down at his chest. Also absent was a small oblong quartz-fibre dosimeter for registering radioactivity levels. He frowned. 'Must have lost it. I'd better report it right away. Thanks for noticing, Federov.'

Federov saluted and walked back the way he had come. But his eyes had given him away. Tyson continued to watch as Federov reached for a wall-phone at the corner on the left.

He had no choice, nor any compunction - especially as he recalled the man's prurient observations about what they'd do to Tana after the interrogation. Unholstering his pistol, Tyson fired once, killing Federov instantly. The soldier's body thudded into the wall then, his death grip ripping the phone from the wall, he crashed to the floor tiles.

Tyson ducked through the doorway and collected the Kalashnikov.

Klaxons sounded. Deafeningly.

He shot out the camera-eye on the corner and as the guard at the fourth door on the left unslung his automatic rifle Tyson cut him down.

It took him only seconds to reach the door. Stepping over the soldier, he kicked the metal door by the handle. It gave resoundingly, slamming against the inside wall.

Kalashnikov switched to automatic fire, Tyson rushed inside and his stomach lurched violently.

The time was 0218. Tana had lasted nearly five and a half hours. But, seeing her now, he wondered at what cost.

There were two men in the room with her. The one in civilian clothes was short and stocky and looked quite haggard, sleep-deprived and old. And he seemed to age visibly on seeing Tyson's Kalashnikov pointing his way. Tyson placed him now - Major Kasayiev. The other man was wearing a stained long white coat; he was bald, tall and rather gangling, and he'd been so intent on the shock-machine connected to Tana that he hadn't even noticed Tyson's entrance.

Bile in Tyson's stomach threatened to erupt as he heard the bald interrogator cackling, calling Tana vile names.

Tyson had always maintained iron control in any stressful situation; but now he nearly went completely over the edge.

He didn't know how she could possibly have managed, but Tana opened her tearfilled eyes, red-rimmed and awash with horrific pain, and there was an almost immediate light of recognition there.

His heart overturned as he heard her mind cry inside his head, '*Kill me, Keith!*'

'Doctor Schneider...' croaked Kasayiev, his eyes wide in alarm, hand gesturing vaguely.

For the first time, the bald inquisitor realised someone else was in the room; Schneider turned and suddenly paled, thyroidal eyes on Tyson's automatic weapon.

'For God's sake,' Tana said hoarsely, 'now, before they get...'

Tyson steeled himself and fired.

CHAPTER NINETEEN: Needles

He had switched the gun back to single-fire and aimed carefully, shattering both of Doctor Schneider's kneecaps.

Screaming in a high-pitched girlish voice, Schneider stumbled backwards and rammed into the electrode-charge machine. His hip hit it badly and he slipped on his own blood. A sudden powerful charge threw him across the floor and the left side of his face was now an ugly red weal. Mumbling incomprehensibly, Schneider lay there, his whole body twitching spasmodically.

Kasayiev's right hand trembled a little, as if he wanted to reach out and comfort the racking shape of Tana. But Tyson misunderstood the gesture and fired. Three of Kasayiev's fingers were brutally amputated by a 7.62mm bullet and they hit Tana, splattering her with blood, then dropped to the stained and soiled floor. Tyson was surprised that the Russian stood his ground after the first traumatic shock. But Kasayiev was finished: defeated but unable to lie down.

With an effort Tyson controlled his rage, closed his ears to the insane whimpering of Schneider and shut his thoughts to the stoic Kasayiev. Deep inside he wanted to hurt them as they'd hurt Tana. He wanted to shove the electrodes into Schneider's gibbering mouth and turn up the current. But he calmed down.

He slung the Kalashnikov over his shoulder and ran over to Tana.

She had slumped since his dramatic entrance, head lolling on her lathered chest. Leather straps had dug deeply into her wrists, ankles and throat. The smell of excreta and burnt flesh made his stomach overturn.

Annoyingly, his fingers trembled and he seemed to take ages to unstrap her.

Finally, she was free of the restraints and he gently lifted her to her feet and hugged her, held her steady in his arms. God, she was soaking wet and her flesh was terribly cold.

'I've come to get you away, Tana,' he said into her ear. 'Don't give up on me now, love.' He kept whispering soothing words of encouragement while keeping a wary eye on the door.

Glassily, Tana's once lovely topaz eyes recognised him again. 'Keith.'

As if in a dream, her body shaking in irregular spasms, she steadied herself against him. Summoning up hidden resources, she nodded at a table behind them. 'My clothes.'

While he supported her, she shakily and awkwardly stepped into her trousers and donned her shirt. He could tell that wherever he touched her, she ached painfully, yet she stoically ignored the hurt.

With a palsied hand she brushed aside matted wet hair from her forehead and her lips trembled. 'My spying days are over, Keith, but I'll take these...' She coughed hoarsely and winced as she buckled on her assault leather belt.

She was suffering from reaction. She was terribly weak and couldn't stop shaking. He knew that if he let go of her, she'd just collapse.

'Here, you'll need this.' He tucked his pistol in her belt.

Tana grimaced and the old light in her eyes almost extinguished. 'Can barely walk.' Her mouth narrowed stubbornly and a glimmer of defiance shone briefly. 'But I'll try - if you want to take me.'

'I came for you and I'm not going without you,' he told her in a croaky whisper.

All the while she had known what his orders would be: if he couldn't get her out, he must kill her. And she'd accepted it; part of the rules of a very dirty business.

'Whatever you say, dear Keith,' she murmured.

Tyson nodded, mouth suddenly dry again.

He spotted the tape recorder, ejected the cassette and pocketed it. 'At least we'll damn well try.'

'Wh - what about him?' She looked at Kasayiev and there was no malevolence in her eyes.

'We'll use him!'

Shouts came from the corridor outside, getting nearer.

Leaving Tana shakily supporting herself with a hand on the back of the chair in which she had been tortured, Tyson ran to the doorway and peered out.

A couple of soldiers and a workman were turning the far corner. The workman stayed at the junction, professionally studying the shattered camera-eyes.

Tyson crossed over to the prostrate Schneider, ripped off strips of material from his coat and wrapped Kasayiev's bloody hand with it. 'No tricks,' he warned the Russian.

Kasayiev only nodded, docile, eyes slightly glazed. He looked a bit dreamy, nerves twitching. Pale-faced, he whispered, 'Want another hashish cigarette.' His sleepy nerves were torn apart, screaming now as they came awake.

Tyson ignored the Russian as Tana stumbled forward and managed to stand independently. She offered a brave smile.

But she looked so lost and pathetic. Tyson pulled a plastic container from his tunic and broke out a hypodermic. 'Stimulant.'

She nodded and he quickly injected the drug into her left arm.

He checked the door once more. The two soldiers were slowing down as they approached the door and their dead comrade. Tyson ducked out again and in a short burst from the Kalashnikov he shot their legs from under them. The workman at the end raised his hands and stood transfixed to the spot.

Tyson turned and grabbed at Kasayiev and shoved him towards the door. 'When I say, you move to the right!' he snarled.

Feverishly, Kasayiev nodded.

Tyson then helped Tana to the door. 'Are you up to walking?' She didn't want to be a burden, he could tell; it was in her eyes. But her body was too abused to respond, even to her strong will. He feared that try as she might, she could not walk on willpower alone.

Kasayiev stopped in the doorway and looked at them enquiringly.

Tyson shrugged. 'Fireman's lift it is, then.'

Obediently, Tana slumped herself over his shoulder. He took her weight and for the first time realised how much energy he had expended since crossing the border. His knees wobbled a little. He could do with a bloody stimulant as well! For a fleeting treacherous moment he feared they might not get out, then dashed such defeatist thoughts aside.

'All right, go on,' he told Kasayiev.

Kasayiev stumbled out, clutching the improvised bandage round his damaged hand. He moved to the right, as told. Tyson followed seconds later and they headed towards the workman at the end. The man was frozen with fear, a small puddle round his feet, his eyes staring at the blood dripping from Kasayiev's arm. He didn't move as Kasayiev walked past without looking at him. Not until Tyson and Tana had passed did he move, rubbery legs propelling him along the corridor, away from the carnage.

'See the silos?' she rasped.

'Yes - anything else?'

'Multi-warheads,' she croaked businesslike. 'SS11 using ECM.'

As he'd guessed. He never ceased to marvel at her stamina; the stimulant was doubtless helping by now.

Kasayiev finally spoke: 'Look! You - you can't get away... the complex - it's full - full...'

Both the Russian and Tyson spotted the Commandant with two infantrymen unwittingly barring their path. Rifles resting, they talked heatedly by the airlock near the gate-entrance into the mine tunnels. Then they saw Tyson, Kasayiev and Tana and their reactions were four seconds too late.

'Brace yourself!' Tyson warned Tana and traversed the weapon.

Bullets whined deafeningly against concrete and metal and abruptly silenced the cries of the Russians. The stench of cordite was overpowering.

During the murderous onslaught, Kasayiev pressed himself against the wall. Staring wide-eyed, he trembled violently.

Tyson snarled, 'Get a move on - keep going!'

Kasayiev did as he was bid, though shakily, each shuffling step smaller than the last.

At the gates, Tyson stooped and lowered Tana against the wall. He sucked in fetid air and was glad of the respite from the burden of her weight. He replaced his rifle with another, complete with a fresh clip of ammunition.

As he stepped into the claustrophobic mine tunnel, gently guiding Tana, he ordered Kasayiev to stand still. The Russian nodded; he wasn't going anywhere as he seemed to be slipping into shock.

Tyson fumbled around in the dark, on the left. His torch was still there. He switched it on, lanced the beam down the tunnel immediately in front of the gates.

On the left was the tunnel he originally came along. He walked back to Kasayiev and shoved him ahead of him. 'Now, Comrade, move - down there.' He indicated the tunnel in front.

Kasayiev stumbled into a disconnected compressor and sucked in air with fresh pain. On their left a conveyor belt ran the length of the tunnel, leaving about two feet width to walk along.

Bracing himself, Tyson again shouldered Tana's weight.

The constant dripping moisture and thick dusty air was increasingly irritating to their lungs. As they penetrated deeper, the insistent blare of klaxons diminished.

After a while, Tyson called to Kasayiev to halt and they stopped. 'Tana, I'm going to put you down again for a minute, get my breath back.' He was aching all over. Breathing was difficult in this closed atmosphere. God knows how miners could stand it, day in, day out.

'Right,' she whispered. 'I've got Kasayiev covered.'

He lowered her and she sat on the conveyor, which gave slightly under her weight.

Kasayiev eyed them both, swaying dreamily. 'Cigarette - have you got one?' he pleaded, steadying himself against a pit prop.

'Smells of hashish,' Tana said. 'He didn't want me to suffer, Keith.'

Tyson stared down at her, then at the shambling wreck of a man, a man once to be feared, a member of the dreaded KGB. Her torturer. And she said he hadn't meant her to suffer! 'But...' He was left speechless, unable to put into words what he felt at seeing her strapped naked in that stinking interrogation room, covered in her outpourings of fear and pain and trampled pride.

He stared as she fumbled in the thin leather pouch on her belt and extracted two long thin metal needles and carefully stuck one in the fleshy piece of skin between her thumb and first finger and the other in the upper part of her ear lobe. The relief was almost instantaneous and her lips curved in a small smile.

'That's a little better,' she said as the needles adjusted her body's *chi* flow along meridian pathways: the hand point was called "large intestine 4" and would deactivate pain sensors while the ear needle pierced the lung point to help her breathing.

'What the hell? Acupuncture?'

She nodded. 'They deaden the pain but leave the mind clear.'

Kasayiev stared at her and blinked.

'Bring him to me, will you?' There was a hint of the old steel in her voice now.

'Is that a good idea?' Tyson said. 'He might make a play for your weapon.'

'I don't think so. Bring him over.'

Tyson nodded and walked up to the Russian.

Kasayiev cringed, the crooked fingers of his free hand digging into the coalface. He was sweating, the pores of his nose large and grotesque. Dirt stuck to the sweat. His collar was frayed and he looked a pitiful sight. It was plain that he feared that he was going to be killed at any moment when it suited them.

Roughly grabbing Kasayiev's lapels, Tyson dragged the man over the rough-hewn ground and stood him in front of Tana.

The sound of Kasayiev's scuffling brought her out of a shallow recuperative meditation. She blinked and realised where she was and what she needed to do. She concentrated very hard and aimed the pistol at Kasayiev. 'Kneel,' she told him in Russian. He understood English, but she wanted him thinking in his accursed mother tongue.

Quivering, eyes screwed up tight, Kasayiev knelt in front of her. At least he didn't plead, she found herself thinking.

Still holding onto the pistol, she reached forward and gripped Kasayiev's head between her hands, the trigger-guard pressing into his scalp. She had expected him to flinch at her touch but he didn't seem to notice. Before the interrogation, she'd have been strong enough to crush his skull between her hands.

Now, she felt herself trembling, tremors assailing her.

It was this man's fear, transmitting itself into her fingers and hands. And she was physically weak, couldn't counteract the effects, even with the aid of the acupuncture needles and the stimulant.

But she needed to know.

'Tana?' whispered Tyson in concern but she hardly heard, she was already shutting off external stimuli and delving.

'You captured Jiri, didn't you?' she said, her voice a monotone.

He nodded slightly under her hands but said nothing. His thoughts were a mess, images flitting past, of Jiri tied to a chair, of Jiri's fearful eyes as understanding dawned.

At that moment she wanted to blow this bastard's brains out. One shot was all it would take. He didn't deserve to live.

'He's dead, isn't he?' she coaxed.

'Yes.' The needle's image was clear. A blessedly quick death.

Every part of her ached. She wanted to curl up into a little ball and hide from the world, from everything. The needle seemed like a good solution right now.

Forcing those traitorous thoughts aside, she focussed on this excuse for a man kneeling in front of her.

The secret wasn't too deep, after all. At first she detected the image of an orchestra, then a solo performer, a trumpeter. The name didn't take long in coming.

Tana gasped and suddenly let go of Kasayiev's head, thrusting the man back on his haunches.

He stared, eyes wide-open, whites all round them.

She gasped. The sensation as she broke contact wasn't unlike the electric shock treatment from Schneider. She gulped in air. She'd suspected, but now she knew.

Kasayiev half-knelt, half-lay on the ground, shaking his head. Perhaps he finally comprehended the great prize that had been handed to him but now eluded him. The gift from Trumpet that he had squandered.

She focussed on him and shook her head, lowering the pistol, its weight almost too much for her. 'He's of no use to us now, Keith.'

Tyson stepped forward, reluctantly helped Kasayiev to his feet. 'What did you do, just now?'

'It doesn't matter. We might as well let him go.'

'What, after what he's done?'

'Keith, a hostage won't help us. He'll just slow you down.'

Dismayed, Tyson stared at Kasayiev. 'Did you hear what she said?'

Never moving his eyes from Tyson's, Kasayiev slowly nodded. His lips soundlessly formed the word, 'Yes.'

Revenge, the will to kill and maim, to slaughter indiscriminately, had never affected Tyson before this mission. But on seeing Tana suffering at the hands of these people, it was as though he'd had a brainstorm, swathing bullets at every person that dared to oppose them. Now he felt completely drained, the desire for revenge replaced by a sickly taste in his dry mouth.

'Get the hell out of here!' Tyson snapped, lips curling in disgust.

Kasayiev looked blankly at him, as if incapable of believing he was being released, that he was free to leave. He wasn't going to be killed.

To emphasis his command, Tyson pushed Kasayiev back along the tunnel. 'Go on, go back!'

Kasayiev banged into the conveyor, upsetting scraps of coal. Righting himself, he stumbled almost blindly towards the distant lights of the barred entrance, his bloody rag-covered hand dangling horribly.

Kazakhstan

Yakunin's eyes opened but he didn't move. For a fraction of a second he wondered where he was - as though he was in a tunnel, a dark strange place that swayed and shimmered. Disorienting.

Then he realised he was lying in a dark and cold place. His cell. The room was chilly. Moonlight reflected off the ice on the window outside.

He pulled the thin cotton sheet over his naked bruised body but it didn't help much. The guards had given him a beating when they threw him in here, venting their jealousy on one of the privileged from The Group. At least the cold deadened that ache.

He shivered and recalled his room where last night he'd been snuggled close with Raisa under fur blankets, fitting his groin against her warm bare buttocks, the touch of her soft flesh arousing him.

The memory now aroused him, despite the cold and the beating. Shivering, he smiled in the moonlight.

It had been the fleetest of connections, only a glimmer, a faint image of an orchestra, a trumpeter, of all things, but it was enough. The woman was suffering from pain and dizziness and his all-too-brief link with her had brought him out in a sweat that seemed to freeze on his flesh. He needed to take his mind off her and since Raisa wasn't there he caressed himself.

After a moment, Yakunin turned over and closed his eyes. He must set up blocks while he slept. Must be careful not to dwell on what he knew, in case Bublyk probed.

But now he was content enough and could sleep, knowing that the English woman was alive.

Czechoslovakia

Ilyichev arrived an hour after Dobranice was put on Red Alert with a suspected intruder. He was eager to come face to face with Tana Standish again, to mete out his own revenge, instead of which he found himself virtually a prisoner, unable to move from the radio building's lobby. 'What's happening now?' he demanded irritably.

The sentry assigned to him shrugged. 'The saboteur's dead, but he blew up one of our half-tracks - it's gone out of control, barged into the perimeter fence.'

'Which has set off all the accursed alarms and automatic weapons firing at thin air!'

Hesitation. 'Yes.'

He'd had enough! 'I'm going down to see the Commandant,' he declared and brooked no intervention. Purposefully, he strode toward the lifts. He stabbed the button and it lit up: the lift was coming.

The doors slid wide to reveal the mortally wounded Commandant lying in the corner of the cubicle. 'M - more re-in - reinforce...' the dying officer stammered, blood spilling from his mouth.

Ilyichev pivoted and called the guards. As they ran over, he knelt beside the wounded man. 'We've sent for a doctor,' Ilyichev lied; that always made them less worried, more talkative. 'What's going on down there?' he asked softly, careful not to stain his clothes.

He had to lean close to catch the Commandant's words. 'The

woman's escaped... had help. It's all a... mess. She has photo-photographic mem'ry. Inval-valuable. Idiotic Schneider's ruined her brain, st-stupid idiot. I w-w-was... questioning guards at lift. She with... the other one, they fired on us... escaped to... to mine tunnels...'

The guards clattered to a halt by his side as Ilyichev peered up. 'Get this man out of here!' he ordered and they grudgingly obeyed.

Treading carefully, Ilyichev entered the lift and jabbed the 14 button.

So Kasayiev had bungled it as well! And he'd had the nerve to threaten me, Ilyichev thought.

Now, if I could either capture or kill Standish, I'd surely be exonerated in the eyes of any tribunal. And, more attractively, it would likewise damn Kasayiev. If only I could get hold of that bitch!

The lift reached the fourteenth floor and the doors slid open on two dead soldiers in the passage. Ilyichev immediately took in the absence of anyone about and reached for the airlock to the right and slammed it shut, locking the pins. He smiled grimly to himself and picked up a fallen Kalashnikov.

According to the Commandant, Tana and her rescuer were now in the mine tunnels.

Ilyichev limped through the barred gate, into the tunnel. Light from the entranceway helped in the immediate vicinity of the entrance, but beyond it was black - save for a tiny glow directly ahead.

And then a shuffling, stumbling sound sent his pulse racing. Sweat beaded his brow. He peered up at the tunnel roof, but could see no movement, no risk of collapse. Nervously, he gripped the rifle and waited. Maybe they'd hit a dead end and were coming back?

He couldn't believe his luck as Kasayiev staggered into view.

Kasayiev hadn't seen him and was bleeding in many places, his hair bedraggled and his clothes torn.

Then Ilyichev noticed the bloodied bandage round Kasayiev's hand. 'Comrade... are you all right?' Ilyichev enquired loudly, voice rebounding from the walls.

Startled, Kasayiev looked up. He smiled recognition and quickened his laboured pace fully into the ring of light. 'Ilyichev, you came... to rescue... me!'

'No, Comrade Major! Look at you; you're a disgrace to your uniform and to our motherland!'

'But Ilyichev... I was taken... captive...' He glanced around, unsure of his surroundings, the pain, shock and hashish jumbling up reality. 'I... I think I escaped...'

'So, you'd have me strung up from the nearest tree, would you?' Ilyichev sneered, forcefully bringing the gun butt down on Kasayiev's shoulder.

Kasayiev shrieked in fresh agony as his collarbone snapped. The arm with the bandaged hand fell across his chest and he unavoidably sank to his knees. 'Ilyichev... this isn't right... you shouldn't address me so...'

Hashish dregs fogged Kasayiev's mind; that and delayed shock and the pain. Strangely, he remembered the Spanish girl he'd tortured all those years ago. One of the first. He took pleasure in inflicting pain, gloating over it, just as Ilyichev was doing now. All the people who had suffered at his hands seemed to parade past his blurred eyes, shaking their heads, their eyes sad, none of them gloating.

'That English woman has plenty to pay for, Comrade! The bitch, beating you like this!' Ilyichev snarled and hit him again.

'She spared me. For pity's sake, Ilyichev, man, do the same!'

'You're too old, that's why she beat you.' Ilyichev's arm seemed to be tiring after delivering so many blows.

Now Kasayiev was incapable of talking, almost insensible. The Spanish girl was crying, tears mixing with the blood. What the hell, what was she doing now? Was she holding out her arms to him? Offering something? Offering what? Forgiveness?

'That's why she shot you like a dog!' Ilyichev might as well have been speaking to himself.

Kasayiev didn't hear the words and couldn't see anything except the parade of victims in his mind's eye.

Ilyichev shot the KGB major twice, cold-bloodedly, professionally, as he'd been trained. The shots echoed throughout the tunnels.

Feeling strangely elated, he leaned back against the wall and calmed down. His hands still shook, his frenzy had been so intense. He stared at the bloodied shape. If only this had been the Standish woman!

Ilyichev glanced down the tunnel and his heart overturned. Panic unsettled him as he realised that the pinpoint of light that had been ahead was no longer there - it had vanished!

Calm down, he told himself. They can't have gone far. Must have turned a corner.

Leaving the hunched bundle of Kasayiev, Ilyichev limped blindly through the black tunnel, stooping low to avoid the majority of pit props and overhead rocks jutting out. He stumbled on, using the Kalashnikov as a blind man would use a white stick, swinging it in front of him to detect obstacles. But he still ended up tripping many times, continually falling into puddles and barking his shins on the conveyor or a pump or stacked pit props.

Puffing and panting, he stopped repeatedly, listening, trying to detect the fleeing spies' whereabouts.

At last he skidded to a halt as he could see a small light down a tunnel on his left.

Ilyichev was lathered in sweat as well as the blood of Kasayiev. His pulse raced in anticipation. All the glory would now be his! What matter the bitch's brain and photographic memory? All he wanted was to kill her.

The silhouettes of two figures appeared ahead. He couldn't slow his telltale breathing. His leg ached in reaction to the uneven running. In the darkness, he counted the bullets he had left. Five. Enough. More than enough.

CHAPTER TWENTY: Shaft

Tyson relieved the weight from his shoulders for quite a distance by using the mine carts lined up along the tunnel that led to the upcast shaft. Now, he lifted Tana out of the cart and slung her over his shoulders. 'You seem to get heavier each time I carry you,' he said.

'Schneider's Diet Plan doesn't work, I guess,' she croaked.

'Or maybe I'm not as fit as I was.'

'Not for me to say, Keith. Just don't jostle me so much, will you, I'm in a lot of pain here.'

'Sorry.'

'I'll let it go this time. You just can't get a decent fireman lifter when you need one.'

'Keep the light steady, Tana.'

'Right. Sorry, I'm gabbling. You should've told me to shut up.' She steadied her outstretched arm and shone the torch ahead.

'Talk if it keeps you awake,' he urged while he carried her the rest of the way to the shaft.

'I hope you have a plan, Keith,' she said.

He didn't answer.

And a little later, she added, 'I'll be seriously pissed off if your plan doesn't come together.'

As he arrived at the airlock a distinct scrabbling sound reached them.

'What was that?' she asked.

'Somebody's following us.' It couldn't be Kasayiev, he wasn't up to it. But he'd probably sent his men after us, Tyson thought angrily. The echoing shots they'd heard a while back had him puzzled too.

Tana closed her eyes and strongly resisted the sinuous insidious sleep that hovered behind her eyelids. If it hadn't been for the acupuncture needles, she'd have lost it by now. 'I can hear heavy breathing. And we don't have a phone.'

Heavy strained breathing, like someone who has been running. She recognised the sound; she'd heard it at the dacha, so long ago. 'It's Ilyichev,' Tana whispered and extinguished the torch, thrusting them into darkness. 'He's alone.'

But this time the darkness wasn't her ally. She was helpless slung over Keith's shoulder.

Tyson gently lowered Tana through the airlock. 'Stay here,' he whispered. 'I'm going a little way back - we can't risk having anyone behind us when we climb up.'

Feeling in the dark, Tyson stumbled along until he found a pit prop to wedge himself behind. He held the rifle ready and waited.

It could only have been for a few seconds but it seemed much longer.

In the rarefied air down here, Ilyichev was having difficulty getting his breath.

Although it was black as pitch and his eyes strained in vain, Tyson still sensed a figure pass by in front of him, a slight disturbance or movement of the air current. Tana was right, it seemed; it sounded as though there was only one person.

Tyson committed himself and swung the rifle round and down.

The weapon broke with the jarring impact and Ilyichev fell forward, yelling in pain as he headbutted the hard uneven tunnel wall. Loose earth fell away.

Ilyichev fired off a shot and it lit up the tunnel for a fraction of a second, too fast to provide any visual information. The bullet ricocheted harmlessly, echoing down the tunnels.

With his rifle broken, Tyson ran forward over the uneven ground, estimating where the Russian was by the flash of the gun-muzzle.

They were both breathless, but Tyson was in worse shape, having carried Tana for almost half a mile. He had also been on full adrenalin-release for virtually three hours. The constant exertion was telling, the strength seeping from his arms, his thoughts scattering, reflexes slowing down.

Tyson barged into Ilyichev's stomach. The Russian dropped his rifle and they both tumbled over the hard metal lip of the airlock.

In the mad scramble of arms and legs and fists, Tyson sensed Tana's presence.

'Tana, the torch!' he called, dislodging Ilyichev's hands from his throat. 'Here!'

She shone the torch and both men were pinned in its weak beam, grappling on the muddy boards, about two feet away from the edge of the tunnel. Beyond was the black well of the shaft.

Ilyichev was getting the better of him, Tyson realised. He was hard-pressed to ward off most blows now.

He managed to deflect the karate jabs and punches aimed at his face, but those to his ribs and kidneys he could do nothing about.

He was already too weak to retaliate, could only defend.

Suddenly they stopped rolling on the boards and Ilyichev knelt, pinning Tyson's arms under his legs.

In the glare of Tana's torch, Tyson looked angrily through bruised eyes at Ilyichev's exultant face. Tyson felt helpless. His head was reeling and he could feel no surface or support under his head. Christ, I'm on the very edge of the shaft!

The Russian had Tyson by the scruff of the neck, pulling his head back over the shaft rim, offering up Tyson's exposed throat. Ilyichev raised his free hand into a fist, shoulder height.

With his arms pinned, Tyson's windpipe would be crushed with a single strike.

In that very instant the Russian must have felt Tana's presence, though too late: he looked round before he delivered the blow and her revolver cracked against the side of Ilyichev's head and his fist plunged harmlessly into the air by Tyson's ear.

Instinctively, Tyson heaved his torso up with all his might and Ilyichev unbalanced and shrieked something unintelligible as he pitched forward into the shaft. His body bashed and rebounded off the shaft walls. The crash and splash of his landing a hundred feet below reached them seconds later.

In the torchlight he saw Tana leaning against the shaft's upright post. She stared down the black shaft. 'That's for Janek,' she croaked.

Every muscle in his forearms and upper body ached as Tyson used the nearest wooden post for purchase in his struggle to get into a sitting position. Wearily, he checked his watch. 'Deadline's at 0400,' he told her, trying to get some circulation back into arms that stung unremittingly and were limp and useless. He didn't mention that the time was already 0330.

'What's the time now?' she asked.

'Close. But we can make it.' Slumped against the wall, he steadied his breathing, closed his eyes and attempted gathering what little strength remained. Who was he kidding?

'You won't make it, Keith,' she whispered, 'unless you send the skip down for me. Or leave me here - with this pistol.'

His mind rebelled at the idea of deserting her, especially after all they had been through. He shook his head slowly, adamant, and felt his neck muscles beginning to knot. He could delay no longer. 'All right. I'll send the skip down.'

He caught the nylon rope at the third attempt, and sighed, for a brief moment discouraged by the prospect of a climb of over one hundred and eighty feet. 'I won't be long,' he said and almost laughed at such quixotic optimism.

He grunted at first as his muscles rebelled then, ignoring the dull pain and labouring over each pull, he heaved himself up. Dust dropped into his eyes and mouth.

Below him, Tana held the torch, directing its beam up the shaft for him.

After each energy-sapping heave, he rested for a second or two, gripping the rope between his feet, one on top of the other.

By the time he'd climbed thirty feet, the weak torch-beam was ineffective and beginning to go dim. Another piece of faulty equipment? His stomach lurched at the consequences if those cartridges of tinfoil had been duff. Christ, I'd have been cut to ribbons! Tana would... Don't think about it! Move, damn you!

He shinned up again. Mustn't stop for so long, he berated himself. Each time he started to climb again, it got harder.

The ascent was all the more mind-destroying for he had no way of knowing how far he had left to go. With no target in view, his spirits and strength couldn't rise at the prospect of an end in sight.

As his knuckles grazed wood, his watch read 0340. Not much further! Not so frequent rests now. Keep going!

About a minute later he reached the top of the wooden beams and the end of the rope. Now he had to get into the air-duct.

The topmost beam was only three feet below the brick of the air-duct, so if he kept his balance and pulled himself waist-height to the beam, he should be able to reach the lip of the duct.

Retaining any kind of balance was doubly difficult in complete darkness. He gently leaned forward until his forehead pressed against the rock then slowly raised first one foot then the other, pressing all the time against the rock with forehead and hands, tentatively seeking footholds on the beams until his hips brushed the topmost beam.

Now, arms and back aching, he stretched up and his hands curled around the brick lip. Collecting himself for the effort, he pulled himself up and through the hole.

No longer mindful of his grazed knees and torn hands, he hurriedly crawled along the brick air-duct till it curved upward.

The last hurdle! He paused only for sufficient time to regain his breath - again. His arms felt weak, trembling, the strength drained. He hadn't felt this knackered at any time in the SAS course. He'd been a lot younger then, though. And he had trained constantly, every day. Worse, his brain was tired, thanks to the foul air in this godforsaken place. He wasn't getting enough oxygen into his lungs.

Oh, God, he thought, I don't think we can make it.

CHAPTER TWENTY-ONE: Winch

At the vertical section he braced himself then pressed his aching back and feet against the brick and started to shin up the funnel, his shoulder and thigh muscles straining to breaking point.

But he was nearly out. That thought kept him going.

The contrast with before was startling. As he had descended - so long ago - he had been accompanied by the yells, shots and deafening explosions caused by his break-in. Now, silence reigned - save for the occasional banging of old machinery in the wind and the faint purring of a vehicle's engine.

One fear was uppermost: would they have located the sheared ventilation grille on the duct's inspection panel? If so, they could be waiting to pounce - or to cut him down as he made his exit.

Just below the inspection panel, he stopped, listening intently.

Not a sound from the fan house. He waited for a full precious sixty seconds, in which time he thought he had regained a little strength.

Then he squeezed out. The fan house was as he'd left it - how long ago? The time was 0344. He had been underground roughly two and a half hours - and it seemed so much longer.

Peering out of the broken window, he had a good view of the damaged perimeter fence, the half-track still smouldering. The searchlights continued to illuminate the fence, sweeping mechanically, highlighting the bodies hanging from the gutted vehicle. Across to the left was the winding machine house.

The commotion had died down out here, though he wondered

for how long as he gulped in fresh air. No time to savour that welcome draught, though, he decided and leapt from the fan house window. He started to sprint but ended up just loping towards the winding machine house. His chest ached and his muscles ached. His body was one big ache. Above the sound of his own heavy breathing he heard a monotonous hum coming from the large generator behind.

The doors were padlocked but a window covered only with wire mesh offered access. His elbow shattered the pane, buckled the mesh. Gingerly reaching inside, he unlatched the window.

Within seconds he was in, poised and watchful on the balls of his feet, scouring the dark grease-smelling room. Because of the positioning of the windows, unlike the fan house, quite a bit of light came through. A kind of twilight revealed the cogs and wheels of the machinery, the massive barrels for the winching cables.

He found a long thick metal lever that he surmised acted as the brake and shoved it forward. A tremendous creaking noise shattered his high-pitched nerves as well as the silence. Christ! He'd awaken the dead, let along the bloody sentries! He was committed now, though.

Tyson stabbed at a bulky console of buttons.

The machinery whirred into clamorous life.

Cogs meshed, wheels turned, and the winch-cables juddered, tautened and moved round the reels. The wheels above the shafts clanked into life too. He'd set the whole system in motion, or so it seemed. He felt very vulnerable here without benefit of any weapon, and decided to get out, before he was trapped.

Leaving the machinery running, he clambered out the way he came in and pulled the window shut.

Quietly, he slunk into the shadows. The deadline was hellish close. Too close. We're not going to make it. It was already 0347.

A couple of Russians shouted from the direction of the gates. A lorry revved up.

He clung to the dark, edged along beneath the overhead cables that glinted greasily in the reflected glow from the fence. He must get to the entrance of the upcast airshaft. He hoped Tana had been able to get onto the rising skip and stay there. If she hadn't - or had passed out - she'd be finished.

The vehicle's engine sounded louder, the area to the front of the two shaft-houses lightened and then the blinding glare of headlights illuminated the entire stretch of ground between the buildings. At the first sound of the approaching vehicle, Tyson dropped to the muddy ground, face down near a puddle of water.

'Look! Over there!' called one of the Russians in the truck.

He'd been spotted.

Leaving the truck idling, two of them ran up to him, leant down and turned him over. 'What happened, Colonel?' a young Lieutenant asked solicitously, wiping wet mud from Tyson's eyes and mouth.

Tyson grimaced and it wasn't all play-acting. 'They've escaped from the mine tunnels - came out of the fan house. I tried stopping them... overcome.' He wheezed, let himself go limp.

'Why do you think they started up the machinery?' the private asked his Lieutenant.

'I don't know, comrade - but once we've got the Colonel here inside the truck, we'll go and investigate!' They lifted Tyson between them. 'Make sure your carbine's loaded!'

Time! The minutes were rushing by. As they struggled to bundle the limp form of Tyson onto the tailgate of the truck, he jerked into startlingly active life, catching both completely by surprise. The base of his palm connected with the Lieutenant's nose, forcing the head back until the neck snapped. As the private tried bringing his rifle round, Tyson swung off the boards and kicked at the soldier's kneecap, breaking it. The man crumpled in pain and Tyson finished him off with a swift karate chop behind the ear.

He stood for perhaps five seconds, gulping in air and collecting himself. Then he picked up the fallen rifle and half-walked, half-ran round to the driver's cabin. It was empty, the engine still running.

Tyson swung the metal door wide on squeaking hinges and hauled himself behind the wheel. Slamming the door shut, he disengaged the clumsy handbrake at the second attempt and shoved the truck into gear. The vehicle shot forward, splashing mud onto the two bodies.

He steered round to the front of the shaft-house buildings, mounted the railway tracks that ran under the padlocked double doors of the right-hand shaft-house and held his foot full down on the pedal.

The doors gave on impact. He was thrust forward with the jarring thud but saved from going through the windscreen by the large steering wheel. Splinters of wood shattered the windscreen and flew into the cabin.

The vehicle bucked as he drove over the fallen doors. He dipped the headlights.

On either side was a conglomeration of machinery, piping, pumps and compressors, and spare railway carts. The rail-lines ran straight ahead into the middle, where a derrick-like structure tapered up through the roof. The winch cables descended from the wheels over the roof, entered a large square hole in the ground - the shaft! - that was surrounded by wooden boards and metal mesh gates.

In the pale yellow headlights he could see Tana slumped against the mesh, the two acupuncture needles glinting. She'd made it!

He left the engine idling and leapt down and hurried over to the metal gates. He located a piece of heavy piping and rammed the padlock. It gave at his second attempt.

She fell into his arms. 'Come on, love,' he urged, 'we've nearly done it!'

His mental clock ticked off the minutes.

Cutting it damned fine.

They stumbled together across the rail sleepers. He roughly piled her into the truck's cabin and slid behind the wheel and slammed the doors. He yanked the gears into reverse. They grated, vibrated and slipped out. Impatiently, he firmly slammed them home and thrust his foot down hard again.

Bucking and rattling, the truck backed over the battered doors, out into the starlit night.

He ran hand over hand on the wheel - it had a damned large lock - and pulled the truck in a tight curve.

Some shots sounded but too far off to worry about. He revved for the open space about two hundred yards ahead - the helicopter pad the overflight had disclosed. There wasn't a chopper in sight, though.

He could only get 60kph out of the old truck. The fuel-gauge bobbed between empty and quarter-full. Enough to serve as a bomb, if needed - or blow us both to kingdom come!

Shots rebounded off the bonnet, leaving shining metal furrows. Some bullets penetrated the metal and clanged against the engine casing. He dropped behind the wheel and peered through its spokes, but kept his foot down.

The watchtowers would have a perfect view.

'Hang on, Tana!' he cried. 'I'm braking hard!'

Tyres screamed and burned on the quadrangle of tarmac. The truck swerved and skidded, the rubber on its wheels probably bald. After a long moment it came to a rattling stop and almost toppled on one side but then it righted itself with a final shudder.

Before he hid behind the dashboard he had one last glance out through the shattered windscreen. Tana had seen them as well.

A circle of troops moved out from the radio building and the men's quarters beyond. They were advancing slowly, deliberately, weapons at the ready.

The impression he had was eerie, almost ghostlike, with swathes of smoke momentarily obscuring the figures in greatcoats.

His watch said: 0400.

'Deadline,' he whispered and held Tana firmly as the first LSD kickback traces played havoc with her senses.

CHAPTER TWENTY-TWO: Deadline

Tana was trembling in his arms and seemed as white as Siberian snow. Her eyes were clamped tight-shut, as though she was trying to erase the hideous visions that undoubtedly flitted across her mind.

Tyson held her and felt completely helpless and wondered what damage they'd done to her mind. It might be academic in a few minutes. He checked the pistol he'd taken off Tana: enough bullets for her and me, he thought.

The pinging of bullets stopped abruptly.

In the sudden lull he risked a peep out of the quarter light window.

The time was a few seconds after 0400. And his hopes suddenly rose as a white streamer trailed down at supersonic speed from the pre-dawn sky above the Sumava Mountains.

It was a Harrier. He couldn't tell if it was the same one he'd hitched a lift on only hours before.

The Soviet troopers had seen it as well and were now spreading out in panic, dispersing to cover - the fan house, the winching houses, the canteen, anywhere but the exposed helipad.

Now he could hear and see the Army helicopter, emerging from the darkness of the forest, leaping the fence through a smokescreen. A half-dozen anti-riot missiles shot out from its underbelly pods. Yellow smoke lightened the drab scene as the whining banshee wail of the rotor blades came nearer and nearer.

Like some great ugly mottled beetle, the chopper lurched then briefly bounced pneumatically and came to rest on the pad.

The Harrier screamed down again, rotated its jets and hovered over the soldiers, the downblast blowing them off their feet, by which time Tyson had already pulled Tana out of the scarred cabin and hefted her over his shoulder. One last effort, he promised his groaning body.

Side in stitches, breath burning his lungs, he somehow made the dozen yards through the downdraught.

Halfway up the helicopter's small metal ladder with Tana on his shoulder, Tyson's legs almost buckled but then navigator Short grabbed hold and hauled her the rest of the way inside.

Growing bolder now, the surprised soldiers were reassembling, some taking potshots at the aircraft. Fortunately, they were just over three hundred yards off, out of range.

Tyson slipped on a rung, righted himself and fell against the fuselage-hatch. 'Have you room?' he gasped, chest on fire.

Grim-faced, looking like some visiting spaceman with his anti-glare visor and oxygen mask dangling loose, Short said, 'We'll *make* room!'

They huddled in behind the pilot as the rotors lifted them. Bullets screamed across the craft's bulbous nose and whined harmlessly away into the night.

From the moment Tyson drove Tana out of the shaft-house, three and a half minutes had passed.

Guns cracked futilely as the aircraft lifted higher and higher.

'Hang on, folks!' Short called out. 'Next stop Landshut - then home!'

But even in his exhausted state Tyson could tell that Short's joviality was forced. He had seen the look on the airman's face as he lifted Tana up. And she was no better now.

Liberally smudged with coaldust, her flesh had taken on a goose-bumped alabaster hue, fingers and lips dry and cracked. Her countless bruises looked dull, yellowish blue; and her eyes were sightless, staring into a deep fathomless void, some place where no human ought to go.

And all he could do was wrap her in the blankets that he had unloaded from a survival pack. He couldn't risk administering anything from the first-aid kit: her pulse rate and heartbeat were so shallow, he had to really strain to detect either.

He kept the spare oxygen mask on her. It was so little though. He felt so bloody useless!

'How is she?' the pilot asked on the intercom.

She had been beautiful, lively. He shook himself and swore. Stop being so bloody morbid. He was tired, so bloody tired. Every bone and muscle in his body ached. And he had a splitting headache. 'She's alive - just.'

'How are you? There's medicinal brandy in the first aid.'

'No, thanks all the same. I want to keep awake.' He looked down at Tana cradled in his arms. He slowly rocked her. 'I think you understand.'

There was a pause and some crackling. 'Yes. I hope she pulls through.'

CHAPTER TWENTY-THREE: Visitors

Kazakhstan

Karel Yakunin underwent intensive questioning and suffered several beatings, all to no avail, as he had nothing to divulge.

Even though Professor Bublyk knew he was holding something back, he was unable to invade Yakunin's mind to find out. That act of defiance alone warranted exile or execution, Bublyk thought acidly.

But what mattered now had nothing to do with Yakunin's obsession with a Western psychic woman. What mattered was the appropriations. He needed his star psychic to show off to the visiting top brass who held the purse strings. Borodin was good and so was Savitsky. But he needed Yakunin, damn him.

So one night he visited Yakunin in his cell and said, 'We believe you. She must have died on a mission. There's no other explanation.'

Nursing a bruised cheek, Yakunin sat up against the brick wall. 'I've heard and felt nothing since that blackness,' he lied. 'She was good, professor. Such a waste!'

Bublyk bit his lip but refrained from responding. Instead, he helped the young man up. 'The Group has missed you, Karel. You must put this episode behind you and return to your work for the motherland. It is too important.'

Nodding, Yakunin, supported by his mentor, walked out of the cell.

Inwardly, deeply submerged, he smiled, because at that very moment when he crossed the threshold he again sensed something, a vague yet identifiable presence.

Yakunin knew now with certainty that she wasn't dead, only very badly hurt.

He must go back to work in the hope of detecting her again.

One day, he felt sure, he would find out her name and meet her.

London, England

Tyson felt marginally better after a hot shower and an hour-long steep in a Radox bath. But no amount of washing could cleanse him of the dead he'd left behind. Mostly innocent soldiers, doing a stint of guard duty, unaware of the complexities of international politics and espionage. He'd seen peasant stock in the eyes of many he'd gunned down. Bullets probably ripping into family photographs as well as flesh and blood.

He didn't think about the killing much. The first time had been the worst, naturally. Morality didn't enter into it. Usually, it was kill or be killed. Brutal and basic.

Now, though, he was just killing time until he could visit her.

Once he'd had a shave and cleaned up, he'd get back to the hospital.

Tana was in a private ward and restricted to only one visitor at a time. There were two vases on the bedside table near the window – one with carnations and the other holding daffodils. For the last ten hours she'd floated in and out of consciousness and the consensus was that she was suffering from memory loss. They'd done scans and all manner of tests but hadn't announced any conclusions yet.

She remembered talking briefly to James Fisk and Sir Gerald. Her mother knew she was in hospital but though she was reassured she was advised not to visit just yet.

Merrick, the Ops Officer, had called by, as had Alan Swann and Keith. Dear Keith. And she had a vague recollection of someone called Karel, whoever he was. Sounded foreign. Can't have been a visitor, though, as she felt sure that he'd been in the corner of the room, on the ceiling. Most odd. Probably LSD traces, a hallucination.

Names and faces came and went. Faces and places. All jumbled up.

The French spy Sophie Dubois: she hadn't been in Naples with Keith, she'd been in Singapore, surely? That Dutch bastard, Klaas Dykstra: he'd almost killed Keith in Izmir – or was that the Odessa mission? No, it couldn't have been, Keith wasn't there with me. No, Yakov Minsky was Odessa. Did he get away? Can't remember - except for his leering sneering face.

Handsome and charming Aldo Ferrara: how did I ever trust him? See Naples and die? Keith almost did. If I hadn't got there in time, God knows what would have happened.

Karachi and dear lovely Mike Clayton, and Iran with the wonderful psychic healer and human rights campaigner Savak Hoveyda and troubled scientist Shabour Daneshian, overjoyed with his one-year-old son and troubled by his mind control research. HMS Jufair, with its cheeky sailors, where some good times turned really bad.

And Ilyichev's face appeared, together with the murderer Fergus Magilly, in bandit country on the border of Ireland. Go to hell, Ilyichev! He must be there now.

Alan who won't let go; he fought off that German spy twice his size – Jorg Knef ended up in the Grand Canal and we laughed, if only briefly, before the terrors began.

Wonderful philosophical Nadim Igbal in Mombasa, who saved my life.

Diminutive gorgeous Mei Soo, she was betrayed and murdered by Wang Wu in Hong Kong not so long ago... on my last mission - before Prague.

And Laco, young and patriotic when we first met; still too young to die.

Memories of places and faces and names. Haunting me always.

All manner of strange dreams never seemed to stop, even in her waking moments, and they were terrible and heart-rending.

She caught glimpses of a room with submarine lighting, men and women crouched at plotting tables, wearing headsets. Very much like the operations room of a warship, but this was on land - hostile territory, the signs on the doors and walls in Cyrillic.

Her mind was being invaded, she was convinced. Or was she damaged - unhinged? Going insane? All those electric shocks, like sledgehammers against a computer's motherboard.

James Fisk couldn't suggest any answers. His steady ice-blue clinical eyes always calmed her. When they first met, she had asked him if he hypnotised her and he answered, 'No, I only enchanted one person, and that was my late wife, Charlotte.'

James's thin lips broke into a gentle smile. 'You've taken quite a battering up there, Tana,' he said, tapping his own skull. 'To put it mildly, they weren't particularly gentle.' He ran a hand over his perpetual five o'clock shadow, the sound rasping. By now she was used to this mannerism. 'Not too removed from electro-convulsive therapy, if you ask me.'

'I don't think Kasayiev really understood who he had in the interrogation room,' she said. 'At least, not until I probed him in the tunnel.'

'The combination of electrical stimulation of the brain and drugs can work, Tana. It just depends how carefully it's done. In your case, I think that the way they went about it, they ran the real risk of causing brain damage.'

Tana shuddered, realising he was talking quite coldly about her brain. 'But the scans say I'm all right, don't they?'

James nodded and Tana felt sure she could sense her heartbeat decelerate and return to something like normal.

'You're whole and sane, my dear,' James said. 'As for this Schneider chap, he sounds like a rather nasty reject from the SS camps, he really does!'

'I think he probably was involved with them, you know. He was old enough.'

'You don't mind talking about it?'

'Mind, James?' She grinned, adding, 'You do choose the most apt words sometimes!'

'Well, yes, quite,' he mumbled, scratching the side of his unruly greying hair. 'As I was saying, you shouldn't be surprised if you suffer a little temporary intellectual impairment after Schneider's shock treatment.'

'Is that double-speak for memory loss?'

'Yes. Diffuse amnesia. Some ECT patients have suffered a general weakening of the ego. Our American brethren even considered using ECT for brainwashing at one time.'

'Nasty.'

'Quite. Anyway, the bottom line is that it might take a while to sort out, you know.'

Tentatively, she made herself walk Karmelicka Street. Nearly all the doors were buckled and seriously fractured. Doors can be fixed. The information behind them was intact. But the street's cobbled main road and pavement were littered with chunks of coal, shell casings, parts of weapons, scraps of paper marked TOP SECRET and scattered among all this were severed limbs and heads, with blood everywhere. And her hands, when she looked down at them, were covered in blood too. Warm, wet and sticky, it dribbled through her fingers, an ocean of blood.

She awoke each time covered in sweat, her heart hammering. And her pillow and cheeks were damp. Sweat and tears, though. No blood, thank God. She sat up against the bedhead, knees up to her chin, tightly clutching the sheets to her, rocking backwards and forwards.

Tana wrapped her arms round her knees, hugged herself and cried.

Kazakhstan

Hugging Raisa beneath the warm furs, Yakunin whispered, 'Was that good this time?'

She nodded her head against his chest. 'Best yet, Karel,' she purred.

He breathed in the warm musky scent of her and smiled. He had been foolish to think that he would ever come to know the English woman. This is what he knew. Here, this privileged life in The Group, with Raisa.

He stroked her warm flesh and felt aroused again.

'So soon?' she whispered.

'That's the effect you have on me, dear Raisa. You're not complaining, I hope?'

'No, I'm not.' Raisa was very happy now because it seemed as if Karel had put the English psychic woman out of his mind. She had mastered insinuating into his mind's foremost thoughts at the instant when he ejaculated and she detected nothing save waves of pleasure which only served to heighten her own orgasm.

'Bublyk can watch us if he wants,' Yakunin murmured. 'I have nothing to hide.'

London, England

Deep down. Tana was submerged. It was like those days as a child in her father's submarine, HMS *Umbra*. A constant background of engine noise. People going about their busy daily duties. She lying there, recovering from her ordeal in the Baltic. Recovering. Deep down.

The private ward was comfortingly cool and dark, just a faint glimmer of light coming through the Venetian blinds which were almost fully closed.

Out of the corner of her left eye she glimpsed for a brief moment a tiny cluster of spots. 'Floaters,' the doctor had explained. 'Probably nothing to worry about. Quite normal. If they persist, though, it might be a warning of a detached retina. But I think the eye will settle down, given time.' Now, it was just annoying. But it might be dangerous if she persisted in discounting the appearance of the floaters; her reactions relied on good and reliable peripheral vision. She closed her eyes, willing her body to heal.

'We know you have a quite remarkable ability to recover,' James had said earlier. Today or yesterday? Does it matter? 'But I'd strongly advise against you trying to test your psychic abilities for a week or two. Once they let you out of here, fine. We'll do some minor tests at Fenner House. All right?'

'Whatever you say, James.'

Now, the ward was cool and dark.

Comforting.

In deep. Deep down.

She lay quietly in her pale blue pyjamas on top of the bed, breathing steadily, as the visitor entered the room. He stealthily walked to the foot of the bed and lifted up the clipboard and read the name: Tana Standish.

She had heard him come in but kept her eyes closed, senses highly attuned, despite her state.

Something was wrong. A threat. Somebody was watching, hanging on the ceiling in the far corner of the room, as if guarding her. Was that the mysterious Karel? She too was watching from this aerial perspective, as if through Karel's eyes.

The visitor wore a white doctor's coat and slowly he began to withdraw an automatic pistol. It had a silencer attached, which made it difficult to extract from the deep pocket in one swift motion. He carried himself like a professional yet foolishly for some reason he said, 'Sleep tight, Tana Standish!' as he aimed the weapon.

In that same instant as the assassin spoke, she snatched a warning in Russian: *Stand and fight!*

Tana opened her eyes and launched herself sideways, out of bed on the side opposite from the door - about a half-second before three silenced bullets hit into the pillow where her head had been resting.

Weak though she was, she could still move fast.

'Christ, he said you're good! Didn't see that coming!' The visitor calmly leaned on the bed with his free hand and aimed the automatic in her direction. She flung the vase of carnations at him.

He sprang back from the bed and with his free hand he swatted it away and the glass shattered on the floor. A bullet hit the ceiling and his white coat got soaked.

Those few seconds of distraction were all she needed.

Deep reserves of energy put spring in her moves as she vaulted the bed, both feet kicking out at his gun hand as it moved downwards again. The man's wrist broke on contact and the weapon fell to the bed. Tana grabbed it and, as he swivelled round to reach for the door handle, she shot him behind the knee. He buckled in mid-run and tumbled sideways into the guest armchair. She slowly levered herself off the bed, keeping the weapon levelled on him.

The fact that he wanted to kill her and she had never seen him before did not matter, she realised, reaching for the bedside telephone. Somebody wanted her dead and this man was the chosen instrument. An assassin. Very much like her.

The switchboard girl asked what number she wanted. 'Can you get me Keith Tyson, please? You have his number, I believe.'

'Righto, ma'am.'

Tana glanced up at the bullet hole in the ceiling. Then she checked the far corner but, naturally, there was nothing - or nobody - there. She shuddered, goose-bumps running up the back of her neck. That experience had been very similar to some she'd had while testing out remote viewing with James Fisk. Most odd.

CHAPTER TWENTY-FOUR: Debriefing

Kazakhstan

Yakunin sat up in bed, surprised at how carefully he moved. He had no wish to disturb Raisa who was fast asleep, her eyes flickering rapidly under the lids. She turned in her sleep, away from him.

It was difficult to contain the exultation that coursed through his veins. Even while making love to Raisa, he was able to link up with the English woman. And now he had a name. Tana Standish, the threatening yet doomed voice had said. Yakunin realised that he would have to be careful.

Guiltily, he glanced at Raisa. He was truly fond of her.

But perhaps his earlier decision had been too rash. There was a meaningful connection between Tana Standish and me, he argued, and it must have a reason. I might be mistaken, but I feel sure I've just saved her life.

Because his thoughts were elsewhere, Yakunin was totally unaware that Raisa was feigning sleep. Facing away from Yakunin, she felt salty tears trickling down her cheeks. Karel had been so intent on the Standish woman - she had captured the name from his thoughts - he hadn't noticed Raisa's mental presence.

Raisa felt betrayed. But she decided that she wasn't going to tell Professor Bublyk any of this yet.

Bide my time, she thought. He must pay for this insult. I shan't rest easy until Karel Yakunin pays.

London, England

Tyson sat in an easy chair across the table from the Ops Officer, Merrick, and resisted the impulse to use his superior strength to give voice to his feelings.

Throughout the silent reading of Tyson's report, Merrick had nodded intermittently. 'It seems in order,' observed the Ops Officer curtly.

Always the same. No thank you or well done, old chap. No wonder Merrick wasn't liked.

Prominent cheekbones slightly flushed, Merrick sighed, eyes lowering to his hands flat on Tyson's report. 'Alas, I'm afraid your reference to Torrence is of little relevance. You see, this morning he was found hanging halfway down a Cornish cliff. Most curious, really.'

Tyson had had enough. Without warning, he rose from his comfortable seat, though not without reluctance; his entire body protested. He grabbed hold of Merrick's shirt and yanked the officer out of his chair and onto the shining table. The report sheets scattered to the floor.

'Tyson!'

Tyson slapped his superior hard. Twice. 'Be quiet and listen!' In disgust, he let go, thrust the quivering man away. He remembered Kasayiev.

Merrick fell back, upset his chair and landed clumsily on the carpet. 'I'll have you...'

'Quiet, Merrick,' Tyson snarled between gritted teeth. So much menace hovered behind his words that the Ops Officer did as he was told and kept quiet.

Merrick shakily righted the chair and sat on it like a chastised schoolboy. His sallow complexion had become completely drained. His furtive eyes kept flashing, at Tyson, then at the door.

'If you move I'll break your scrawny little neck. And enjoy it!'

Merrick noticeably sat very still and seemed to believe him. Just as well, because he meant every word.

'I don't know why you're a traitor, Merrick, and I'm not particularly interested - we have enough "experts" prepared to find out.'

Merrick tried to stammer a denial but his coordination was shot to hell.

'I've seen your sort before. You can merrily send countless poor sods to their deaths without a thought. But confront you with your own shortcomings and you're a snivelling–'

'Please! I...'

Tyson's steely glare silenced him. 'Are you going to admit it then? You sent Tana into Prague on Soviet orders, didn't you? You could've sent me - or even Jock and Wilf. The mission was botched by Torrence because you made sure he'd panic. The mission required a simple rebuild and recruit job after that fiasco. But you wanted your twisted masters in the Kremlin to have a special gift - Tana with her photographic memory!'

Merrick was trembling violently, unable to stand or sit still. He was going to pieces. But Tyson didn't care. His head pounded; the paracetamol hadn't been a good idea on an empty stomach. He felt sick, drowsy. He shook himself, leaned forward, pounded the table and made Merrick jump.

'You switched the death pill when you visited our dentist while she was getting the molar fitted - Dr Geraghty distinctly remembers your visit.' He put a hand to his throbbing temple. 'Do you know what they did to her?' he shouted, picturing again the sight. He feared it would live with him forever, every time he saw her. 'Your masters wanted her alive, to brainwash, didn't they?'

Merrick was nodding now, repeatedly, holding hands to his ears, murmuring under his breath, 'Please, yes, please stop. Stop, please...'

'How many other agents have you sent out with dud pills? You were clever, mind - never too many. What happened to Cornelius and Segal? Toker in Istanbul, now that was a bloody mystery. You sold them all down the river. Didn't you?'

No answer.

'Christ, you must have trouble sleeping nights!'

'I - *me*?' Amazingly, Merrick found his voice. 'What about you bastards? Trained to kill at a b-blinking of an eye! She only got what she deserved! The SAS that spawned you is worse still: brainwashed killers!'

Tyson hadn't meant to lose his temper. The blow sent Merrick reeling off his chair into the wall. Blood dribbled from the traitor's mouth. 'Don't get self-righteous with me!'

With Tana's knowledge, Interprises operations would have been critically jeopardised. She had stored in her photographic memory information Merrick was not privy to; so Merrick had ensured she would have little chance of escape.

'Now I know why you were against my rescue mission,' Tyson said levelly, calming down. 'What was it you said? Why risk another operative on a suicide mission? You only agreed when overrode - and then reluctantly.'

Merrick wiped his cut lip. 'You'll pay for this...'

'I don't think so. I'm surprised you didn't warn your friends I was coming! Of course, you wouldn't want to endanger your position here - the notice so short. Besides, who'd have thought Tana would hold out so long? And, anyway, what were the odds against me getting to her, let alone us escaping together?'

An ugly scowl. 'You were lucky, that's all.'

'Aren't you going to give Tana any credit, Merrick? Do you know what Fisk told me? If I'd given her as much as even one more dose of stimulant, she'd have been dead! Have you seen her? No, of course not! She's a physical wreck, held together by willpower.'

'I've had enough of this.' Merrick swore colourfully and groggily struggled to his feet. 'I'm leaving!'

Tyson didn't make a move to stop him. He slowly opened a drawer, revealed a tape recorder. 'You're on tape for posterity, Merrick, and there'll be no wiping these! You can go.'

The Ops Officer paused at the door and assumed a posture of

superiority. 'You can't blackmail me. Tapes aren't evidence.'

'Sir Gerald will believe them,' said Tana, entering the side door.

'Tana,' Merrick said silkily. 'I'm glad to see you're well enough to leave the hospital.'

She looked anything but well. Tyson knew she was in no shape to be up and about. Fisk would have a blue fit. She'd stubbornly left the hospital against the doctor's orders.

When she rang him from the hospital and explained about the attempt on her life, Tyson had rushed round at once.

Tana was no longer the ramrod-straight feline creature he knew, but bent, vaguely resembling a battle-scarred cat after a recent torrential storm. Her cheeks were badly bruised and her lips mere slits.

The hired assassin hadn't talked. Then Tana dropped her bombshell: 'You were hired by Merrick, weren't you?' He may have been professional, but that was with firearms; he was hopeless at poker and his eyes gave him away.

'I thought so,' she said.

Tyson made a phone call and a short while later the assassin was taken away, to be questioned elsewhere.

'Merrick?' Keith said when the two of them were alone in the ward. 'Our Merrick wants you dead?'

'Yes.'

'But why, for God's sake?'

'I'll explain,' she had said.

Tyson had asked her not to come; he had wanted a showdown with Merrick himself. But all hate and anger evaporated virtually as soon as Merrick began whining.

Bruising shone under Tana's eyes. Yet her eyes were aflame, smouldering with some terrible intensity.

'I've lost a lot of friends because of you, Merrick,' she whispered hoarsely, gripping onto a chair for support. Even though she looked so helpless and broken, she radiated elegance under stress, dressed in a simple black turtleneck sweater and trousers.

Moving away from the door, Merrick grinned without humour. 'You don't want to believe what Tyson says - he's keen for promotion.' He laughed over loudly. 'Probably after my job!'

Tears sprang into Tana's eyes. 'Good friends.'

He wasn't listening!

'They were Czechs, Tana! Not worth it! Full of brooding melancholy, the lot of them! They *like* being dominated.'

For all her injuries and the obvious pain she was still suffering, for all the drugs and lack of energy, Tana moved astonishingly fast.

She swung the chair she'd been leaning on straight into Merrick's shins.

The chair stayed in one piece but Merrick's shins didn't. He fell back to the floor, yelping. 'Shit!' he hissed, trying to ward off the pain. 'Shitshitshit.'

'They're freedom-loving, Merrick,' she cried. 'When the Soviet soldiers came, they wanted to fight! A great friend - a true friend - said that's the terrible unanswered question all the Czechs will keep asking themselves. Whether they should have fought and died.'

'You're insane!' Merrick screeched, holding his broken shins.

'I had to kill a friend in cold blood.'

She looked as though she was going to succumb, to break down, but she didn't. She glared at Merrick. 'Kasayiev betrayed you to me while we were down the mines. Moscow Centre gave you the code name *Trumpet*. He gloated about it while he killed my contact Jiri.'

Tyson took a step towards her. 'So that's what you did,' he whispered, understanding at last why she needed to touch Kasayiev's head in the tunnel. She never ceased to amaze him.

But he was really concerned for her now. Coming here from the hospital, facing Merrick, it must have taken a lot out of her.

He'd never seen her like this.

And her distress was also tearing him apart. Theirs was a precarious way of love. Attachments were not recommended in Interprises. 'Passing ships in the night' was the best you could usually manage. But with Tana it had been different. She belonged to no man, yet for those few she cared about she had a deep reservoir of affection.

Tyson took her in his arms and stroked her dry matted hair and felt moisture prick the corners of his own eyes. He looked up mistily and gritted his teeth.

Merrick was painstakingly crawling towards the door, his face contorted grotesquely.

'Get the hell out of here!' Tyson growled with all the venom he could muster.

The door slammed shut.

Merrick was finished: two Special Security men were waiting outside for him. He'd be driven down to Berkshire for intensive questioning. But, damn him, he was alive. Tyson had intended shoving him out of the window - appropriate since defenestration originated in Czechoslovakia. There'd have been little left after a fall of eight storeys.

He held her as Tana sobbed and sobbed, tears wetting his shirt front. And the reaction of the mission soaked through his frame too and he had difficulty standing, needed her for support.

James Fisk had warned him that kickback traces of the drugs would ravage her many times more over the coming weeks. 'But she's bloody tough. She'll pull through,' James had said.

Now Tyson whispered to her and promised he would stay to comfort and to tend her. And he remembered his promise to her mother all those years ago.

'It's all right, Tana, you're safe now. You can relax.' Did she really know how? Her damned psychic gift couldn't let her relax, could it? 'We got out in one piece. It's all right,' he whispered gently.

'But at what price, Keith?' she murmured. 'Was the cost too high?'

'God knows, Tana. Only time will tell.'

He hugged Tana Standish, his friend, and let her cry.

AFTERWORD: Dismantled

IN THE EARLY HOURS OF YESTERDAY AN RAF TRAINING FLIGHT HARRIER OVERSHOT THE CZECHOSLOVAK-WEST GERMAN BORDER. A MINISTRY OF DEFENCE SPOKESMAN SAID THAT PROBLEMS WITH THE INERTIAL NAVIGATION SYSTEM WERE TO BLAME. THE SOVIET AMBASSADOR WAS NOT AVAILABLE FOR COMMENT. (REUTERS).

THE TIMES, TUESDAY, 28 OCTOBER 1975

The new openness heralded by Mikhail Sergeyevich Gorbachev enabled me and other journalists to look over KGB records as well as Moscow's secret Ramenki underground city. And of course since then the head of Russian intelligence has even offered to withdraw his spies from countries that agree to stop spying on Moscow. As a result of differing attitudes. And for financial reasons. The system could no longer support such a massive intelligence organisation - though the present incumbent Putin seems now to be hankering after the old Cold War days. Tana's mission promise to Gorbachev was fulfilled.

Through carefully constructed channels she alerted Gorbachev about the secret Soviet missile silos under West German soil, ostensibly engineered by a breakaway cadre of the Russian military and KGB. He was able to convince Andropov of the truth of the situation.

Andropov was wily enough to know that it was probably no 'breakaway group' at all - that had been a 'face-saver' thought up by Tana - so the head of the KGB confronted Brezhnev with the facts and the old bear tried blustering that it didn't matter. But Andropov suggested a possible nightmare scenario - again hinted at by Gorbachev at Tana's instigation: the hawks in the military were willing to aim the missiles at Russian cities so they would appear to come from the West, thus justifying in the eyes of the world a massive retaliation. Brezhnev paled at the suggestion, it appears. Clearly, he did not want a nuclear exchange either. Andropov emphasised that not only was any surprise about the missiles now lost - the break-in at the complex had ensured that - but also the credibility of the various attempts at détente would be flushed down the pan - or words to that effect, so my sources tell me.

Within six weeks, the reactors and silos were dismantled. The originators of the scheme were dismissed and ended up in Siberia. If you look on any modern map, you won't find Dobranice. Sometimes the Russians proved to be exceptionally good at removing all traces.

For fourteen years the priest Alois Neruda suffered terrible hardships in the gulags and every day he prayed for forgiveness for having impure thoughts. And when he was released after the fall of communism he found that he and all the other secretly ordained priests were not recognised by Rome, even though there was a world shortage. Having no choice but to renounce the church he suffered for, Alois actually found Elena and they married and now have two sons and a daughter.

Zdenek Mlynár was a university friend of Gorbachev, then later a leader of the Czech Communist Party during the Prague Spring, though after the Russian intervention he was expelled from the Party and eventually went into exile in the West. The KGB learned of at least one meeting between Gorbachev and Zdenek. However, Yuri Andropov protected Gorbachev. It seems that Andropov was impressed by Gorbachev's restrained lifestyle, as the head of the KGB was bitterly opposed to the corruption that was rife in the Party.

Gorbachev was made First Secretary of Stavropol in 1971. Among his favourite books are those by Aquinas, Rousseau, and Hobbes, which probably explains the quotation he used when meeting with Tana.

For at least seven years, Andropov had been preparing the way to become Leonid Brezhnev's successor. Brezhnev died on 10 November, 1982. Yuri Andropov took office as General Secretary two days later and died on 9 February, 1984 to be succeeded by Chernenko who died after only fourteen months in office.

Gorbachev was elected Party leader by the Politburo on 10 March, 1985, almost ten years after first meeting Tana Standish.

Alexander Dubcek, at the age of seventy - long outliving Brezhnev and his cronies - died from injuries suffered in a car crash in 1992. Apparently, there were no suspicious circumstances. Shortly afterwards, his posthumous memoirs were published in *The Sunday Times*.

The Berlin Wall fell in 1989 and in January 1993 Czechoslovakia split into two independent states.

These events put Tana's adventure in the context of recent history.

Tana took about four months to recover physically from the trauma of the Dobranice interrogation. Between subsequent assignments in Peking, Bulawayo, Mogadishu and Cairo, she studied remote viewing with James Fisk. Then she was sent on a mission to Iran in April 1978.

POSTSCRIPT

The next manuscript – *The Tehran Transmission* – covers Tana's first return to Iran since 1970 and her involvement with SAVAK in the months leading up to the Islamic revolution.

In subsequent books, she links up with Mike Clayton in Afghanistan at the time of the Soviet invasion – *The Khyber Chronicle* – and then goes on to Argentina and is embroiled in the Falklands conflict, which will be revealed in *The Caldera Caveat*.

Nik Morton
Portsmouth/Alicante - August 2007

GLOSSARY

AK	Avtomat Kalashnikova
CND	Campaign for Nuclear Disarmament
cukrarny	sweetshop
erk	RAF slang: aircraftman
dramma giocoso	funny drama
FLOSY	Front for the Liberation of Occupied South Yemen
Gazik	four-wheel drive Soviet Jeep
Gehenom	The next world, a kind of hell (Jewish)
horky parky	Czech hot-dog
hospoda	pub that serves basic meals
Hradcanske Namesti	Hradcany Square
Karluv Most	Charles Bridge
KGB	Komitet Gosudarstvennoi Bezopastnosti (Committee of State Security)
knedliky	dumplings
Mach	speed of sound (762mph @ sea-level)
Most 1 Maje	First of May Bridge
MVD	Ministerstvo vnutrennykh del (Ministry of Internal Affairs)
Narodni Trida	National Avenue
Namesti	Square
Namesti Sovetskych Tankistu	The Square of the Soviet Tanks
obed	dinner
objzdka	diversion

Olam Haba	Heaven (Jewish)
ouija	Yes, yes: French-oui/German-ja
pivnice	pub without food
skryta cirkev	concealed church
slivovice	national plum brandy
Staromestske Namesti	Old Town Square
Státní Bezpecnost (StB)	Czech political security police
28 Rijna	28 October, Czech Independence Street
Tuzex	state-owned store
Ulice	Street
Vaclav	Wenceslas
vecere	supper
'yellow angel'	Czech slang for Auto Moto Klub patrolman

DON'T MISS THE NEXT TANA CHRONICLE
THE TEHRAN TRANSMISSION

THE TEHRAN TRANSMISSION
(Tana Standish in Iran, 1978-1979)

FOREWORD: Manuscript

Portsmouth, Hampshire, England

We were in our usual booth, where we couldn't be overheard. 'We can't keep on meeting like this,' I said.

'Very droll, Mr Morton.' Alan Swann didn't seem amused, I could tell. He idly nursed a whisky and dry ginger. His eyes were still the same cold blue, one of them glass.

He was tall, dark and sanguine and at our first meeting I had thought he was in his early fifties but subsequent researches suggest he was fifty-nine when we met. All things considered, he was wearing well. His black hair sported a white streak on the left; a livid thick scar continued from the white streak all the way down that side of his face. The bottle-green worsted suit was bespoke, the shoes patent leather. His gloves and dark grey trilby lay on the seat beside him, spots of autumn rain still peppering dark blobs on his shoulders and hat. The slight limp was the same, so whatever caused it was probably permanent.

Swann was a secret agent working for International Enterprises, a cover firm for an adjunct to MI6, though I hadn't known all this at our first meeting in this Portsmouth hotel bar.

Despite the very visible scar, it was obvious he had undergone some plastic surgery: the aging skin round eyes and cheek contrasted starkly with the pristine sheen of his square jaw. Not for the first time, I wondered when he had received such devastating injuries; as far as the last manuscript went, he was completely fit and in one piece in 1975.

I recognised the briefcase he lifted onto his lap: it was the same one he brought to our previous clandestine meeting. With difficulty I refrained from salivating at the prospect of relieving him of more Interprises secrets.

He had implied he was still in the field, but I reckoned he was a desk man now, relegated to the strange-looking headquarters building on the Thames because of his physical appearance. Let's be honest, he wasn't going to melt into any background. Besides, nowadays he was the wrong ethnic type for infiltration; now they were gunning for terrorists, not greedy or maladjusted ideologists.

He clicked open the metal clasp on the briefcase and fished out a ream of paper and I felt my heartbeat rising in expectation.

'We all read *The Prague Manuscript* with interest, you know.'

'Glad you liked it.'

'I didn't say I actually liked it.' He glanced away then fixed me with his one good eye. 'Well, not all of it.'

'Can't please all of the people, et cetera.' I didn't feel as flippant as I sounded. We writers like praise, not brickbats.

He added, 'I thought *The Standish Code* would have been a better title, actually.'

I ignored that comment; I'd thought of that title as well as *The Prague Portent* and *The Dobranice Manuscript* but felt that the first was too portentous and the second was probably going to be misspelled and mispronounced. 'I didn't take *too* many liberties, surely?'

He shook his head and it was obvious to me that I had conjured up some painful memory because now his eyes wouldn't meet mine. I'm no detective or psychologist but I could tell he was thinking about the sections where I had mentioned him and his strong affection for Tana.

He sipped his drink and then said, 'This is the next instalment.'

'Sounds a bit like a hire purchase agreement,' I remarked as he handed me a typescript secured by a thick elastic band. The corners were turned and the sheets had lost their whiteness.

The corners of his mouth turned too but he chose to ignore my remark. 'Another disclosure - and Top Secret - so of course that's why we want you to write it as fiction.'

I took a good gulp of my cool *San Miguel*, just to remind me of sunnier climes. The summer had melted away in a five-day heatwave and now it was raining again. Let's hope the Indian Summer isn't the monsoon variety.

I nodded at the bundle of paper. 'And this one is about where, exactly?'

'Iran just before the revolution in 1978.'

'That's three years after Dobranice.' I'm pretty good at maths.

'Yes,' he agreed. 'It seems appropriate to consider this period now.'

'Because it's still very much in the news almost thirty years later.'

'Just so,' he said. 'Though the seeds of the situation there go back *much* further.'

'I'm sure they do. The past has an uncanny knack of catching up with us, doesn't it?'

He shrugged. 'That's quite prophetic of you, Mr Morton, if I may say so. You'll understand why I say that when you read the manuscript.'

This one took a little longer than the first Tana chronicle, mainly because I had the opportunity of interviewing a number of survivors from that period.

Here, then, is *The Tehran Transmission,* which is again about the psychic spy Tana Standish.

ONE: Heart

Friday, September 8
Iran

Dressed in his sinister black SAVAK uniform, Captain Hassan Mokhtarian looked every inch the evil man he was. A man who deserved to die.

Tana Standish could see him quite clearly through the telescopic sight, even making allowances for the poor light as dusk descended over Tehran and the city's surrounding mountains, turning the overshadowing snow-capped cone of Mount Damavand a delicate shade of mauve. At least today the city smog didn't obscure the peak of the volcano which still belched out sulphurous fumes from time to time and killed the odd stray sheep.

Hassan exuded an air of danger with his pitted complexion and deep-set ebony eyes under a prominent forehead ridge. While SAVAK was a civilian organisation, many of its officers were military men and they relished wearing a uniform which instilled fear in the population.

Standing in the open doorway of his villa, he exhaled smoke through his nostrils and dropped the Marlboro cigarette to the lightly coloured marble-tiled step, grinding it under the toe of his boot. His eyes glinted, as if he took pleasure in the destruction of even small things.

'Don't wait up, Rosa, my dear!' Hassan called over his shoulder.

'I'm going to be rather busy this evening. A particularly difficult client!'

'Yes, dear,' a woman's gentle voice replied. 'Take care.'

One of his female servants - he never bothered finding out their names as the headservant Roxana hired and fired - slunk out and swiftly scooped the demolished cigarette butt into a plastic dust pan and hastily backed into the shadowy vestibule.

Hassan smiled as he closed the door behind him and stepped down to the waiting limousine with its bulletproof smoked-glass windows. It was not a pleasant smile, the pallid protruding lips curving like a grimace so that his barbula - the small black tuft of hair under his bottom lip - jutted out. He rarely smiled - except when doing his work.

Takhti, the government driver, opened the door for him.

Going to fat, his open-necked black silk shirt taut against his stomach and a waist that bulged over his weapons belt, Hassan paused, one shining boot in the vehicle, and glanced back at the window to the right of the entrance.

Dutifully wearing bright red lipstick, kohl eyeliner and a revealing Western dress, his wife Rosa waved as he left his home.

He had excelled himself with the *Koofteh Berenji*. The balls of meat - each the size of an orange - had been filled with barberries, walnuts and fried onions. They were delicious, as he knew they would be. Normally, Rosa arranged for Roxana to buy their meat for the chef, but on this occasion he'd insisted they take from the freezer the most recent gift from headquarters.

Rosa allowed his odd whim - it was about once a month, he supposed, that he dictated what they ate and actually cooked it himself. It just depended on the quality of the source - and the sauce too! He joked that it made him stronger, more capable of doing the Shah's work, and of course the chef got a day off into the bargain.

Now he grinned broadly at the memory, licking those pallid lips, and he experienced a thrilling shiver down his spine as he noticed

Takhti shudder in fear: it was said that Hassan Mokhtarian hardly ever grinned and if you caught him doing so, beware...

Hassan wondered what Rosa would say if she realised the ground meat they'd eaten was the heart of Savak Hoveyda, a particularly recalcitrant activist for "people's rights".

He used his big hairy nicotine-stained fingers to brush back the oiled hair from his forehead, gave Rosa a cursory wave and, abruptly, his heart lurched and his normally emotionless features contorted in distress, deep furrows appearing in his prominent forehead, and his eyes screwed tight as sudden intense pain assailed his hands. It was as if his fingernails were being pulled out by the same pincers his men had used on Hoveyda, the same he had planned to use tonight on the anonymous Mojahedin woman.

Shaking violently, Hassan staggered back and fortunately Takhti caught him before he could fall on the hard marble steps.

Tears streamed down Tana's face and dampened the black cotton material of her chador as she watched Hassan Mokhtarian stumble backwards into his driver's arms. The optical telescopic sight - the Mauser SP66 had no obscuring iron sights - provided her with a very detailed picture of her target's sudden facial transformation.

It wasn't enough though. It never would be, she thought, the familiar taste of iron in her dry mouth.

Thought-transference was something quite alien to the self-satisfied torturer of the Shah's Security and Intelligence Service, SAVAK. It pained her as much this time as it had when she'd received the psychic echoes from her friend Savak Hoveyda - so ironically did they give their security and intelligence service the acronym which was a common Persian name!

At the time of Savak's death - barely three weeks ago - she had been working undercover in Abadan, the British-built refinery town. She was closely aligned with the People's Mojahedin Organisation of Iran. PMOI comprised Shi'ite extremists and

Iranian women activists carrying on the protest of martyred Fatemeh Amini.

A graduate of the University of Mashhad, Fatemeh was an attractive teacher with dark hair and eyes. She had joined the Mojahedin eight years ago and built up extensive contacts with the network of Mojahedin families and knew many of the sympathisers. Then, inevitably, she was arrested at a meeting place - the secret police had ears and eyes everywhere, so exposure or arrest was always a risk - and she was tortured by SAVAK officers to extract a confession that she was a communist.

For over five months Fatemeh Amini endured torture and didn't betray anyone, even though she was repeatedly whipped with electric cables and burned. She was so seriously maltreated that she became paralysed and, finally, she died at the hands of a torturer closely resembling the description of Hassan Mokhtarian.

Tana had arrived in Iran's Mehrabad airport on April 24 and then secretly left Tehran so that she could check out the MI6 Listening Post north-east of Taybad. She'd been chosen since she was the only one available with impeccable Farsi, Dari and Russian.

It was thanks to her photographic memory that she was able to learn so many languages and speak them fluently. That and a good ear for sounds and intonations, of course. Unfortunately, those very skills also made her a valuable target for abduction by the opposition.

On the very day of her arrival in Iran she had experienced a bloody precognition of events over the border. She was familiar with Kabul, so there was no mistaking the place; but there was no telling *when* the events would happen.

Soviet-built MiGs of the Afghan Air Force were making precision bombing runs against the Radio Afghanistan station.

Cries of distress and shrieks of the wounded filled her head in that fleeting instant. This was no minor rebellion or a skirmish but something orchestrated, with the backing of the country's troops.

More planes strafed and bombed the Royal Palace.

She captured images of President Mohammed Daoud Khan, his bloodshot eyes staring disbelievingly as he was injured. Then seconds later he was buried alive under tons of rubble.

Tana asked Interprises to inform the Director of SIS - 'C' - and especially the Yanks since their embassy was next door to the radio station.

Sir Gerald Hazzard dutifully forwarded the message to 'C' and also Langley's DCI but the Central Intelligence Agency dismissed the report, stating their man on the ground had detected nothing untoward. Thomas Ahern was the CIA station chief in Tehran and his deputy was Miles Olsen; they had nobody in Afghanistan, though they'd never say so. At least they responded; 'C' – Sir Arthur Franks - never did.

Three days later, it was announced that the entire Afghan leadership in Kabul had been wiped out.

Irony piled upon irony: five years earlier Daoud deposed the king of Afghanistan, Zahir Shah, when he was out of the country in Rome, by staging a *coup d'état* and now, aided by Pakistan's President Zia, Muslim extremists stormed Daoud's palace and massacred him and most of his family. *What goes around, comes around*, Sir Gerald said in one of his wordier signals.

The new régime, led by Taraki and Amin, embraced the Communizing of Afghanistan. *Moscow likes the sound of that, damn their eyes*, observed Sir Gerald on getting the report.

Feeling vindicated though annoyed with the US Administration and the Foreign Office, Tana made her way back to Tehran and linked up with her new friend Marzieh Goudarzi and fellow activists Behjat and Zarah. In the PMOI Tana wore a chador and was known as Ashraf Nikpay, an activist from Birjand.

The women of Iran were regarded the most free of all the Middle Eastern countries; thousands had adopted the Western dress style and wore make-up; unfortunately, from time to time a religious bigot seemed to take offence and threw acid at a woman who dared to bare her face. Some women believed the chador signified backwardness and subjugation, while others saw it as protection from strange men's eyes.

As Ashraf, Tana could have adopted Western dress, but she didn't want to invite too much attention and, besides, she was dealing with a group who harboured more than their fair share of extremists, not least the misogynistic unbending fundamentalist, Karim Akbar.

One fateful day the women sealed their friendship by pandering to young Zarah's whim. She wanted a photograph of all of them – 'Sisters of Solidarity', she called them. Tana was reluctant but couldn't make a big deal of it as Ashraf so she went along with it: Mansur Khan, a sympathetic Shi'ite who often acted as go-between for these women and conservative activists, obligingly took four Polaroid photographs of them all huddled together: Behjat, Zarah, Marzieh and Ashraf. It was one of those defining moments Tana would cherish; she felt she belonged with these courageous women yet was saddened that she was spying on them as well as their implacable foes.

She had no specific mission objective now, having confirmed that Seabright at the Taybad Listening Post was quite safe from extremists who seemed in the main anti-American. So she was free to roam wherever she wanted to glean information.

For agents in place this was often the norm, lying low and reporting back the mood of influential groups, the perceived loyalty of the troops and so on. Some agents stayed as sleepers - there were supposed to be some in Afghanistan and Iraq, though for obvious reasons she wasn't privy to their names or whereabouts - except for dear old Mike Clayton, gentle lover and master of disguise, who was undercover in Herat the last she knew.

Sir Gerald was quite happy for her to stay in place, especially as she'd mentioned several premonitions of unrest in the country, all eclipsing anything that had gone before. *Keep your ear to the ground,* he advised in a signal.

There was a considerable British presence in Iran and if it was necessary to get them out fast, they needed all the warnings they could get. And Sir Gerald didn't trust the Foreign Office to get it right. He also added, *And don't get captured again.* He left unsaid that her photographic memory was too valuable to fall into any foreign hands. She was pleased with the old man investing his faith and trust in her. She'd been assured that the suicide pill definitely would work this time. That's comforting, she thought.

When she could get away from the PMOI organisation and the bargain basement Hotel Mashad on Amir Kabir Street, she secretly entered the Interprises safe house on Mozaffari Street, three blocks from the embassy. Here she dressed in Western clothes, glad to be free of the chador's constraints. Here, too, she was able to use a rare modern WC rather than having to squat like an animal, using a bucket of water to wash afterwards. No wonder there were no left-handed people in Islam. Then she was Tana Standish again, representative of International Enterprises and working with the British Embassy to further trade between Iran and Great Britain - in effect, on the cocktail circuit.

She actually saw Hassan Mokhtarian for the first time at an embassy party, which had been arranged - spending British taxpayers' money - to feather the nests of some businessmen from the so-called deprived north-west of England.

At these occasions the elite Iranians eschewed *ta'arouf*, the ubiquitous formal politeness; it was assumed that all present were on equal terms at such gatherings; otherwise the evening would have been interminable.

'Charmed to meet you, my dear,' Hassan said in a hoarse smoker's voice, bowing slightly, his shoulders hunched. He clung to her hand and kissed the knuckles with quite unpleasant dry protruding lips. His nicotine-stained fingers held onto her longer than was necessary and his thumb massaged the back of her hand.

'The pleasure's entirely mine, Captain Mokhtarian,' she lied in Farsi, feeling gooseflesh riding up her arms. She claimed her hand back. 'It's not every day I meet someone who has the ear of

General Nematollah Nassiri *and* the Shah.' Nassiri was the head of SAVAK – not an appealing man - with a fat round pockmarked face, cold yellowish eyes and lips as thin as knives.

Mokhtarian made a limp attempt at modesty, averting his eyes - thank God! - then he twisted his mouth in search of a smile, which came out like a grimace. 'How pleasant to find a British woman who can pronounce my name correctly.'

His clothes smelled strongly of cigarette smoke, his deep-set ebony eyes now piercing hers, as if he would rather interrogate her than bother with idle cocktail party chit-chat.

Then she was relieved to see a big-boned square-shouldered tall man striding up to them, his small round greyish-brown eyes flicking bird-like behind gold wire spectacles. 'Ah, Miss Standish, could I borrow you for a moment?' interrupted Malcolm Coppersmith in his deep cultured voice, bowing slightly to her and the Captain. 'Sorry, sir, but this lady's work is never done.' His big hands, more like hams, started gently guiding her away. 'You know how it is?'

'Of course.' Captain Mokhtarian managed somehow to grab her hand again. She refrained from punching him and smiled sweetly as he planted a wet kiss on her knuckles.

'Thanks for the rescue, Coppersmith,' she said as they walked off. 'He's a particularly unpleasant man.'

'Indeed he is.' Coppersmith was her Foreign Office contact with links to MI6 and now whisked her away. 'I want you to meet someone,' he said, steering her past a blustering corpulent industrialist from Manchester. 'It's someone I've been cultivating - a rather influential Iranian minister, Gorban Bakravan and his Scottish wife.'

Tana wondered about Coppersmith's choice of words. The minister's wife was middle-aged and very attractive.

That gathering was some weeks before she saw Hassan Mokhtarian again - through her doomed friend Savak's eyes.

By the second week of May, Tana was on the point of returning to England for further psychic training at Fenner House. It was during one of these psychic sessions - in the middle of her convalescence after Dobranice, in 1976 - when she had first intercepted a mind watching her. Before that, she'd had an inkling, when some strange astral presence saved her from an assassin's bullet while she was recovering in hospital.

Whether between assignments or on active duty, the presence made himself felt. She was sure it was a man - and a Russian. On each mission, whether Bulawayo, Mogadishu, Cairo or Beijing - he was there with her, as if watching over her shoulder. It should have been an uncomfortable feeling, but it wasn't.

The psychic voyeur seemed benign, though at the edges there was some unidentifiable threat, she felt sure. She would like to intensify her training and try to draw out the mysterious presence.

But she had to postpone the flight out when the Shah cancelled his visit to Hungary and Bulgaria with his third wife, the tirelessly charitable Empress Farah.

'Sorry, love,' said Coppersmith, handing her the MOST SECRET signal from Sir Gerald. 'The Shah's got a cold. Won't be going anywhere. And neither will you, I suspect.'

He was right. In fact, there were thousands of demonstrators marching through Tehran shouting 'Down with the Shah' and other inflammatory slogans and the government seriously feared for the lives of the occupants of the Peacock Throne. Posters and graffiti were blatant, proclaiming, 'Death to the Shah.' Illicit posters of Khomeini started appearing. In dire tones the government warned that they would not tolerate unrest by a 'few thousand opponents' and threatened to crack down on any rioters.

Interprises urgently wanted Tana to discover the degree of threat the unrest posed to the Iranian government and the country's oil production. They felt that the messages coming out from the Americans were too rosy. Sir Gerald knew that she was well placed to supply such information and sanctioned additional funding for her extended stay.

It had been obvious for over two years that many Iranian men were becoming bolder in their denunciation of the Americans and, by association, the British. Graffiti announced that 'Bleached jeans are a sign of American cultural corruption!' Western women had been spat upon, cursed and even suffered the ignominy of being flashed at. It wasn't only western women who were targets, either. Small gangs of Iranian women delighted in scratching the faces of pretty girls who didn't wear Islamic clothing. Some of the annoyances were petty, others malicious. Tana was surprised that nobody in authority seemed to acknowledge the groundswell of dire critical opinion.

One of her PMOI associates, Mansur Khan, had been particularly helpful to her in arranging for Mojahedin to infiltrate government organisations so in her guise of Ashraf she linked up with him. The trouble was, infiltration and the passing of information took time.

The civil unrest continued unabated as the months passed and Tana dutifully reported everything she learned. The unpleasant atmosphere persisted against foreigners, particularly women. Iranian people vanished from the face of the earth. SAVAK - and Captain Mokhtarian - were kept very busy.

Coded signal traffic to the embassy grew more frequent and most concerned yet, seemingly immune to the impending implosion, the US elite flaunted their superiority in their tailfin Buicks.

And then in July Tana experienced two strong bloody precognitive images:

Iran's president Amir Abbas Hoveyda was tied to a metal ladder. He had been badly beaten. Then he was summarily shot by robed mullahs.

More gruesome still, she recognised SAVAK's General Nematollah Nassiri on the roof of the Komiteh Building. Then he was shot to death and gleefully hacked to pieces.

She passed on her misgivings and received a conciliatory coded signal from Sir Gerald: *I believe you, Tana. Unfortunately, some power-players at the* CIA *are still living in 1953.*

She knew what he meant; she'd seen evidence of the Americans' sense of self-importance and invulnerability often during the last few months.

Stay put, keep an eye out, Sir Gerald advised in his latest signal.

Tana maintained her two identities without discovery over these months. Her hotel - Mashad - was in a noisy grubby area which was full of car workshops and spare-part emporia, businesses that would never be out of work in this country of fanatical drivers. She'd rather it had been the upmarket Mashhad, diagonally opposite the US embassy; that was expensive and you didn't have to share a bathroom with backpackers and Iranians who considered any woman on her own as fair game.

Whenever she needed extra money, she left a message for Coppersmith at one of three dead-drops and he brought the rials to a secret meeting place and she signed a chit for them.

Every day she was mindful of detection but carried on obtaining information and writing and encrypting reports for Interprises to analyse and pass on to MI6.

It was comforting to sense the psychic watcher too, though she wondered about him. He seemed different. It wasn't possible there was someone else, surely? The watcher was only detectable at times when she used her psychic talents. She yearned for this mission to end so she could get back to Fenner House and construct a controlled experiment with James Fisk, the Interprises psychologist that might even ensnare the watcher.

Hardly a day went by when she didn't hear about another disappearance or SAVAK atrocity. It was likely some were rumours, possibly spread by Iraqi fifth columnists or communists in the outlawed Tudeh organisation.

Action which seemed to be having some effect at least. In the first week in August the Shah promised free parliamentary elections next year. He was getting worried by the unrest, but she feared he was offering too little too late.

And now, earlier today, martial law was imposed on Tehran and eleven other cities.

The bolt-action Mauser wasn't her chosen weapon for sniping, but it was the best that Coppersmith could come up with in the timescale she had given him. While there were plenty of new weapons courtesy of the United States being manhandled by the Shah's secret police and army, neither she nor Coppersmith had direct access to their armouries.

This rifle barrel was a mite too heavy for her taste, but it did have the 'short throw' Mauser bolt which reduced the amount of movement she'd need. It was only two years off the production line, so she wasn't too confident only one shot would do, but practice seemed to indicate it was reliable enough, and the 'lock time' between pulling the trigger and the bullet leaving the muzzle was extremely short.

The magazine held three rounds, but one should be sufficient.

While she checked over the specifications of her sniper's rifle, she continued sending painfully dredged up images from her mind, images unwittingly sent to her by the receptive mind of her friend Savak.

Hassan Mokhtarian had broken into a sweat. His wife rushed out and mopped his brow with a lace handkerchief but he brushed her aside abruptly. 'Leave me alone,' he snarled in his usual disdainful hoarse voice, 'you stupid woman!'

She backed off and suddenly he convulsed. His genitals felt as if they were on fire.

Hassan screamed.

Though, thought Tana sanguinely, Hoveyda hadn't cried out the first time they'd applied the electrodes. Her mouth was very dry, a normal physiological response to intense psychic activity, as was the now familiar dull ache at the back of her neck.

Now Hassan was really confused. At first he thought he saw - through the blur of tears - his brother Ahmad leaning towards him, the same pallid protruding lips taunting him - his own brother, in Allah's name! - but he quickly realised it wasn't Ahmad, as his tormentor's chin had his own trademark barbula. No, Hassan saw *himself*, leering, explaining that he didn't need to get any information. Indeed, he enjoyed torturing for the sheer fun of it. 'And I promise you, Hoveyda, I shall eat your heart!'

He retched now, disgorging the pieces of his victim's heart that he had eaten earlier.

Hassan couldn't understand any of this. What was happening to him? How could he see and feel what it seemed that bastard Hoveyda saw and felt? He wasn't in the least superstitious but could it have something to do with eating the man's heart?

His ebony eyes started from his deepset sockets as he gripped his temple on both sides and shook his large square head vigorously.

'Go away! Go away!' he shouted hoarsely and his driver and wife stepped back, assuming he was talking to them.

When the .300 Winchester Magnum bullet entered Hassan's chest, he jerked against the steps. Then he peered down, surprised at the growing dark stain that felt sticky to his touch.

He grinned because the terrible pain in his hands and groin - and those nightmarish visions - had stopped. They had gone away, leaving only a dull ache in his chest.

As if listening through cotton wool, he heard Rosa's voice pleading to the driver: 'Help him, please help him!'

What was she going on about now? Help who?

Absently, he felt Takhti ease him into a sitting position. There was an iron taste of blood in his mouth and his vision was blurred. Dimly he heard a dog howling. Was that Mithra, his wolfhound? Howling enough to raise the dead.

Go to Hell, Hassan Mokhtarian! said a voice in his head, echoing. A woman's voice.

He tried to press against Takhti for support to stand up and confront this woman, wherever she was, but his legs seemed like jelly. Too weak to move.

Must chastise Roxana, this awful mess on the entrance steps just won't do. The mess seems to be getting worse, too. Strange, but it reminded him of many cell floors in the prison.

Hassan's lifeblood was pouring onto the villa's marble steps.

That woman's voice. The timbre was slightly different, but he'd heard it before, pronouncing his name. But where?

Incredibly, his memory dredged up something, a place and a name, which he whispered into his driver's ear.

Then everything went black. Black like his heart. His dead heart.

Printed in the United Kingdom
by Lightning Source UK Ltd.
133001UK00001B/116/P